CONCLUDED

A BUREAU STORY

KIM FIELDING

The Second Coming (first stanza)
William Butler Yeats (1919)

Turning and turning in the widening gyre
The falcon cannot hear the falconer;
Things fall apart; the centre cannot hold;
Mere anarchy is loosed upon the world,
The blood-dimmed tide is loosed, and everywhere
The ceremony of innocence is drowned;
The best lack all conviction, while the worst
Are full of passionate intensity.

Song of the Open Road
Walt Whitman (1856)

5

From this hour I ordain myself loos'd of limits and imaginary
lines,
Going where I list, my own master total and absolute,
Listening to others, considering well what they say,
Pausing, searching, receiving, contemplating,
Gently, but with undeniable will, divesting myself of the holds that
would hold me.
I inhale great draughts of space,

The east and the west are mine, and the north and the south are mine.

I am larger, better than I thought,
    I did not know I held so much goodness.

All seems beautiful to me,
    I can repeat over to men and women You have done such good to me I would do the same to you,
    I will recruit for myself and you as I go,
    I will scatter myself among men and women as I go,
    I will toss a new gladness and roughness among them,
    Whoever denies me it shall not trouble me,
    Whoever accepts me he or she shall be blessed and shall bless me.

*

14

    Allons! through struggles and wars!
    The goal that was named cannot be countermanded.

Have the past struggles succeeded?
    What has succeeded? yourself? your nation? Nature?
    Now understand me well—it is provided in the essence of things that from any fruition of success, no matter what, shall come forth something to make a greater struggle necessary.

My call is the call of battle, I nourish active rebellion,
    He going with me must go well arm'd,
    He going with me goes often with spare diet, poverty, angry enemies, desertions.

CHAPTER 1

*L*os Angeles
January 2025

"AGENT SPANOS, you need to get back in that bed and—"

Ignoring the nurse, Achilles Spanos continued looking around the little room for his clothing. He knew his wallet, phone, badge, and gun were in a little cabinet near the sink, but there were no signs of his other belongings. "Where's my pants?" he demanded. "And my shoes?"

The nurse, a formidable-looking man named Kyle, shook his head. "Everything you were wearing was destroyed. We threw it all away."

Although Achilles hadn't felt any particular attachment to that suit, he frowned. "Fine. Get me new ones." And then, because Kyle had taken good care of him, he added, "Please."

Kyle didn't budge, however. "You don't need them. You're still recovering. The doc says—"

"*Another couple of days.* I know. I don't care. I want my own bed in my own apartment. And I want to get out of this goddamn building."

Since Kyle didn't seem willing to give in, Achilles grabbed the sheet off the bed and wrapped it toga-style. Together with the hospital's johnny and bright-blue socks with grippy treads, it would have to do. He gathered his belongings from the drawer and, well aware that he was not following protocol regarding weapon handling, marched to the door. He was afraid that Kyle would try to stop him—they were a good match in size—but in Achilles' current condition, he knew he wouldn't win. Fortunately, Kyle simply sighed, muttered something under his breath, and let him go.

The little hospital occupied its own wing of the West Coast Bureau HQ, which meant Achilles had a long walk down the hall to the main lobby. His wounds *hurt*, especially the long slash across his abdomen, but hell if he'd turn back. He simply gritted his teeth. When he reached the expanse of the white-marble lobby, he ignored the agent gaping at him from the reception desk and continued to the bank of elevators, letting out a sigh of relief when the nearest doors immediately slid open. As he rode to the top floor, he resisted the urge to lean against the wall. Someone was bound to be watching on the security cameras.

There was another long trek after he exited the elevator, and midway he had to stop and catch his breath. Normally he could run for miles without being winded; he wondered if he would manage to achieve that level of fitness again. Maybe he'd always ache when he moved.

Finally, he flung open the door to the reception area of the chief's suite. Probably with a little more drama than necessary, which caused him to pull his stitches and hiss with pain. He hurried inside... and faced a demon.

"Where's Holmes?" Achilles demanded. Victor Holmes had occupied the chief's outer office for as long as Achilles could remember. Not that Achilles particularly missed the guy—he was terrifying—but the absence threw him.

The demon Tenrael sat on the desk, black wings neatly folded. He would have looked almost demure if he weren't naked. But at least that meant Achilles wasn't the least professionally dressed person in the room.

"Agent Holmes is on assignment." Tenrael's face didn't betray any emotion.

"But… he's in a wheelchair." And had been for years, ever since he'd been injured on assignment. Very much like Achilles, except Achilles could still walk.

"Agent Holmes is a valuable Bureau employee."

"Of course he is. But whatever. I need to see the chief."

Tenrael's red eyes didn't blink. "My master is busy."

"I'm sure. This'll be quick."

After a moment, Tenrael shrugged and gestured to the closed inner door. "He is not in a good mood."

"Is he ever?"

Without waiting for a response, Achilles limped to the door, knocked once, and entered.

When the previous chief had been in residence, the office had always smelled strongly of cigarettes and whiskey. Those scents had disappeared with the new tenant, who brought instead a medley of sweet aromas. Today the office smelled like a donut shop. The chief sat behind his battered wooden desk, gaze fixed on the open pages of a thick book. "What?" he barked without glancing up.

Achilles set his badge and gun on the desk. "I quit."

Now Chief Grimes did look at him. His eyes were an odd green color that always unsettled Achilles for some reason. "You're too young for retirement," he said.

"Not retiring. Quitting."

"The doctor told me you'll be fit for duty in a week or so. I'll give you some less active assignments for a while."

Achilles started to cross his arms but had to stop and readjust the makeshift toga. All of which spiked a sharp pain through his chest. "I *quit*. I wish to no longer be employed by the Bureau."

"Because you were hurt? You've been hurt before."

"Exactly!" With effort, Achilles moderated his voice. "I get banged up pretty often. I've been clawed, bitten, punched, stomped, burned…. We all have. And what about Santiago? He was *killed* this time." The bear shifter had ripped Santiago to shreds while Achilles lay on the ground, too badly injured to help but still plenty capable of hearing Santiago's anguished screams.

"I'm well aware of Agent Bautista's death," Chief Grimes said gravely. "It's a serious loss to the Bureau. Are you quitting because you're afraid to die?" He cocked his head as if fear of death was something odd.

"I'm not— Well, yeah, I'd like to remain alive. But that's not my reason. It's just… what's the *point*? We go out to deal with monsters, maybe we get our asses kicked or we end up in a coffin. And still the world is full of monsters. We're using an eyedropper to bail out a sinking ship."

Chief Grimes leaned back in his chair, looking weary. Rumor had it that he was over a hundred years old, and while most of the time he looked close to Achilles' age—early forties—right now there was something ancient about him.

"How many lives have you saved, Spanos?"

"No idea. But it doesn't matter because—"

"It *does* matter." Grimes leaned forward, brow furrowed. "Every damn life *matters*. Every human and NHS, staying safe in their homes, loving their families and friends, sharing a meme or running through the forest or dancing among the waves. And not only that. Every act of kindness matters. Every exercise of justice, of empathy, of shared joy. Every. Fucking. One."

Achilles, who had never heard the chief give a speech, had to think how to respond. Finally, all he could say was, "I don't have it in me. Not anymore."

"I don't believe that."

"There are lots of other agents. Even with Santiago gone. Lots of them are better agents than I am."

A soft sound came from behind Achilles. "But what if you are the one?"

Twisting around, Achilles saw that Tenrael had entered the room. He was always an imposing figure, but now his wings were spread, the glossy black feathers glistening in the overhead lights.

"What 'one'?" Achilles asked.

"All living things—and some things which are no longer living—are connected. We are all part of a puzzle that has existed for millions of years and constantly reshapes itself. A single piece, even a tiny one, affects the whole. You may be the piece that shifts the balance in what is to come."

Achilles had never been a spotlight sort of person. As a student, he'd always sat in the middle of the classroom, earning good grades but never exceptional. As an agent, he'd been content to follow his superiors' orders and operate as part of a team, not as a lone hero.

"I'm not that piece. I'm not important." And dammit, if he stood here any longer he was going to collapse, which he didn't want to do in front of Grimes and Tenrael. Somebody would certainly drag him back to that hospital bed.

"I quit," he said again. Firmly.

Nobody stopped him when he walked past Tenrael and out the door.

He made it all the way down to the lobby before remembering that his car wasn't here. And even if it had been, he was in no shape to drive. At least he'd been able to keep his phone charged while he recovered. He ordered a Lyft.

A young woman in a Toyota pulled up to the main entrance a few minutes later. She goggled at Achilles—likely due to both his attire and his obviously rough condition—but didn't comment as he collapsed into the back seat. A few minutes later, however, she couldn't help herself. "Are you okay?"

"Don't worry. I won't get any bodily fluids on your upholstery." Achilles closed his eyes and gritted his teeth against the stabs of pain caused by the car's jostling.

"Well, I appreciate that. But do you need medical help or something?"

"I've had more than enough of that. I just need to get home."

"Well… okay." She sounded skeptical but fell silent and continued driving.

Luckily, traffic was light and his condo was only a few miles from HQ, on a tree-lined street just off Ventura Boulevard. She pulled up in front of the building, and he mumbled his thanks before shuffling toward the door. Most of the neighbors were likely at work, and he didn't care if those who remained might be staring.

His code let him into the building, and he again had a moment of gratitude for elevators as he rose to the third floor. Normally he loved his home, which he'd chosen and furnished with care. But today it smelled stale and slightly fusty, probably because he'd been gone long enough for food in the fridge to go bad. The fact that his loft bedroom was accessed by stairs was a nice architectural feature, but today he just couldn't face the ordeal. Instead he collapsed onto the couch and more or less passed out.

ortland, Oregon

"I CAN'T DO IT." Dee had to speak loudly to be heard over the whir of the nearby espresso machine and the lively chatter of other customers.

The man gave Dee a petulant glare. "My cousin said you sold one to her friend."

"Then one of them is lying. I don't sell love charms." Dee leaned back in his chair. Rent was due soon, and his wallet was thin. "I've got one to improve your luck and one to boost your confidence. Those might help you win someone over."

But the man remained perched on the edge of his seat, arms crossed. "That's not the same thing."

In the past, Dee would have pasted on a sincere-looking smile and amped up his charisma. He would have made himself—and by extension, his wares—seem so appealing that the man would have practically begged for the chance to buy whatever Dee was willing to sell. Now, though, despite the looming rent, Dee couldn't muster the energy for it. He spoke plainly instead, barely bothering to hide his disdain.

"Look, let's ignore the fact that love charms are morally repugnant, what with the consent issue and everything. I'm guessing you don't care about that. But also, they never work out well long-term. Sure, the object of your affection may fall for you, but it's… artificial. Like fake flavoring. Doesn't feel quite right. And in the end it usually turns bitter and even nasty."

The barista called out for a customer named Pearl, a toddler screeched something unintelligible at its parents, and a bus on the street outside engaged its air brakes with an ear-splitting squeal. Dee thought about the packet of gummies he'd finished off the previous night and wished he'd saved one for today.

The man glowered. "I want a love charm."

"I don't have one to sell you."

"My cousin *said*."

Dee shrugged.

After a long pause, the man got to his feet. "You're a fraud."

"If I was, I'd sell you a useless trinket and tell you it was a love charm. I'm telling you the truth."

"Loser." The man stomped off, abandoning the latte he'd barely touched.

"Well, fuck," Dee muttered. That's what he got for being honest.

Anger simmered inside him—at the would-be customer who'd just left, yes, but even more at himself. He should've just sold the bastard a love charm. He had done it before, and he'd probably need to do it again very soon if he didn't drum up some cash. Morals were all well and good, but they didn't pay the rent. He'd rather be a devil with a full belly and a warm bed than an angel out on the streets.

He finished his Americano because he'd already paid for the damn thing, then he grabbed his well-worn messenger bag and ventured out into the midafternoon gloom.

Contrary to popular belief, it wasn't always rainy during Portland winters. In fact, the previous week had seen a run of chilly but clear-skied days. But now the clouds and mist were back. Dee's mood had been foul even when the sun shone, and now his outlook was worse. He felt grimy from the inside out, his withered soul an unreasonably heavy burden. Even though his apartment was only a few blocks away, the trek felt miles long.

He was almost home when he realized that someone was following him.

There were no other pedestrians visible, and all of the cars were quickly passing by, but Dee had been tailed before and the sensation was unmistakable, an unreachable itch between his shoulder blades. Well, he had nothing much worth stealing, and if push came to shove —literally—he could put up a decent fight. Hell, in his current state he might welcome a skirmish, and he probably wouldn't even care if he got the worst of it. A blade or a bullet didn't seem as terrible as they once had.

In any case, nobody accosted him before he reached his place. His apartment was in the center of a C-shaped brick building constructed a century earlier. The central courtyard, filled with blooming roses in the summer, was gray and deserted now, with moss growing on the paving stones. As always, he had to jiggle the lock to get it to function and then push hard on the perpetually stuck door. He tossed the messenger bag onto the couch and then stood in the middle of the living room, unsure what he wanted to do next.

It wasn't a bad apartment. Small, yes, with a cramped bedroom and a kitchen barely big enough to turn around in. It didn't get much natural light even on sunny days. But the wood floors and trim were original, as were the glass doorknobs and leaded glass windows, all giving the apartment a sense of permanency. It was quiet too, with walls so well insulated that he rarely heard his neighbors. There were shops and restaurants within walking distance, and the rent was reasonable by local standards—although that didn't matter when you were broke.

Finally he collapsed onto the couch and stared at nothing, wishing he still smoked. He'd take it up again, except he couldn't afford cigarettes. Or more gummies.

Gods, how had he ended up mired down like this? Was it even worth trying to fight his way free?

He'd nearly sunk into a nap when a heavy knock sounded on the front door, launching Dee to his feet. It was a cop's knock.

"Fuck me sideways," Dee muttered wearily as he went to answer.

Instead of a uniform, the guy at the door wore dark slacks, a white dress shirt, a long wool overcoat, and an old-fashioned hat. He looked more like a character from a noir movie than a cop. Also, he seemed a little too old for law enforcement. Early sixties, maybe, and still handsome, with a full head of white hair. He was on the short side, and he was grinning widely as if something about Dee amused him.

"Dee Martell?"

"Who wants to know?"

The smile didn't fade. "I do. And if you'll let me in out of the rain, I'll explain why." The man had the kind of old-fashioned New York accent you didn't hear all that often anymore. He sounded as if he should be standing on the Lower East Side in a vintage movie, not in Portland in the twenty-first century.

"I don't want to buy anything, and I'm not converting."

That brought a chuckle. "My people don't believe in evangelizing. And even if we did, I don't think I'd be anyone's first choice to do it. C'mon, kid. Let me in and I'll tell you everything."

Although Dee was tempted to slam the door in his face, he was also curious. And fuck it—he didn't have anything better to do with his afternoon. Maybe this guy would buy a charm from him.

As soon as Dee stepped aside, the man came in. He hung his coat and hat on the rack near the door, revealing a body that was surprisingly good for someone his age. His compact muscles and trim waist reminded Dee of a gymnast.

The visitor glanced around and nodded, as if the apartment pleased him. "Nice place. Those modern houses, I guess they're practical, but they lack soul. They lack *spirit*." He laughed, although Dee didn't understand the joke. Then he stuck out his hand and they shook. "Abe Ferencz."

"What can I do for you, Mr. Ferencz?"

"Call me Abe." For the first time, Abe looked entirely serious. "And you can do a great deal. Maybe."

"Can you just—"

"I'm here on behalf of the Bureau of Trans-Species Affairs. You heard of 'em?"

Dee slowly shook his head. They didn't sound friendly. "Look, if you're here 'cause I skipped probation, that was a long time ago. I don't think apprehending me is a real priority for the great state of Wisconsin." Or New Jersey or Tennessee, but those had been in the more distant past and so he didn't mention them.

"The Bureau doesn't care about whatever you did to offend Wisconsin."

That was a small relief. Dee squinted at him. "Aren't you kinda past retirement age?"

Clearly not offended, Abe's hearty laugh echoed. "You have no idea, boychik. I retired from the Bureau years ago. But I get a little bored sometimes, since my partner died. I do some contract work for them now and then. Right now, the chief is tied up in some kind of *mishegas* and his agents are spread thin, so he hired me to come visit with you."

"About what?"

Instead of answering, Abe strode to the couch and sat down as if he owned the place. There was something odd about him, although Dee couldn't put his finger on it. Maybe it was his eyes—warm and brown, but brighter than they ought to be. "You don't happen to have any whiskey, do you?" Abe asked. "Or any other liquor will do."

"Your boss know you drink on the job?"

"My last boss drank more than I do, and that's saying something. The new one doesn't drink at all."

Dee folded his arms. "Well, neither do I." Alcohol didn't agree with him. It made him unpleasantly dizzy without truly getting him high. Screwed-up brain chemistry, probably. According to his father, Dee's mother had been the same way. Drugs worked just fine, though.

Abe sighed. "Shoulda brought my own. Okay, I'll make this quick.

I'm here because of your charms. And I don't mean that handsome face of yours."

Shit. Not again. Dee threw himself heavily onto the other end of the couch. "They're just rocks and stuff, okay? I don't give my clients any substances that might harm them, I don't encourage my clients to do anything illegal. Yeah, they might be a little poorer when they leave me, but I'm not charging that much. And people spend money on useless shit all the time."

"Oh, *sheifale*, we don't care about your charms that don't work." Abe stared at him for a moment through eyes that seemed ancient. "We care about the ones that do."

Although Dee's gut clenched, he tried to keep an even tone. "I don't know what you mean."

"Fake charms are a good schtick. Tell a schmuck that the tchotchke you sold him will give him good luck, and every time something positive happens to him, he'll give the charm credit. If he stops believing in it, he's not going to run to the cops. He didn't lose enough for it to be worth the hassle, and besides, he's a little embarrassed about being taken in." Abe shrugged. "Not much harm done. Back in the day, I used to… well, let's just say it's a con I know well." He winked.

"Then why are you here?" Dee was thoroughly confused by this encounter. He hated not having his feet firmly beneath him.

"Because from what we hear, with you it's not always a con. Sometimes you sell a schmuck a good-luck charm and he wins the lottery five days in a row. A woman comes to you because she wants a baby and all the doctors have given up on her. You sell her a charm and nine months later, she's a mother. Or someone—"

"I don't know what you're talking about," Dee lied. He was caught. If he kept denying what he could do, then he was committing fraud and would get hauled back to jail. If he admitted it, then he was… something else.

"Don't look so frightened," Abe said gently. "I'm not here to get you in trouble. Remember what I said before: I'm here because maybe you can help me out. Help us *all* out."

"You want to buy a charm?" Dee asked doubtfully.

Abe shook his head. Gently, he asked, "How do you make them work, Dee?"

"I don't know what you're talking about."

Dee was a big man, a good six inches taller than Abe and heavier, not to mention twenty years or so younger. Logic said that Dee would have no trouble taking him in a fight. But Abe showed no sense of fear no matter how heavily Dee glowered, no matter if Dee's hands were drawn into tight fists. If anything, he looked slightly disappointed, like a teacher who'd expected more from a student.

After a moment, Abe stood, but he didn't collect his hat and coat. He crossed to the dining area, where a window looked out at the puddle-filled parking lot. It wasn't a particularly nice view, yet Abe stared for a long time. When he turned back, his expression was solemn. "My old boss liked to give cryptic lectures. Rarely to me or Thomas because we were the ones who made him what he was—and nearly the only ones who knew what he truly was. But he lectured everyone else. I think he avoided me and Thomas when he could. And now, the new chief isn't much of a talker at all. Which means I have only a sketchy idea of what's going on. And to be honest, I know more than I want to."

Dee had been uneasy since Abe appeared, but now his fingers tingled and his lungs didn't want to work right. He was scared shitless and had no clue why, especially since he didn't understand what the hell this guy was talking about. "What are you—"

"You can feel it, can't you? The world trembling on the edge. We've been here before. Even though I was in San Francisco in the thirties, I could sense this… this tipping. This sliding. Back near my homeland and creeping ever outward. Couldn't do much about it, but I *knew*—"

"You're not old enough to have been alive in the thirties."

Abe gave a humorless grin. "And you can't make real magic charms. The *point*, boychik, is that we're tipping again. Most of the time, we hold a delicate, precarious balance. We're losing that balance now. And I'm here because we need all the help we can get to stop the tipping, and the chief thinks you can contribute." He held his hands palms up, as if he'd explained everything.

He'd explained nothing. Except… Dee knew exactly what Abe was talking about. And it was the reason why he assiduously avoided listening to or reading the news. Why he felt so bleak even though he'd been broker than this in the past. Why on some days, getting out of bed didn't seem worth the effort. Why he startled awake in the middle of the night, heart pounding and sweat dampening his sheets, quickly repressing memories of dreams about falling.

"A good luck charm isn't going to bring about world peace," Dee said.

"No. But this isn't a game of big plays. Remember what I said: *delicate* balance. One or two small things can tip it either way."

"I'm not the kind of guy who can save anything."

"Then are you the kind of guy who can cause us to lose it all?"

Of course Dee should deny that. He should insist that although he cared more about himself than he did anyone else in the world—and he didn't care much about himself—he was nothing worse than a selfish asshole. He wasn't a real threat. But looking into his own dark heart, he wasn't sure that was true. Sometimes indifference had worse consequences than hate.

"I don't know how I make the charms work. Sometimes they just do." That, at least, was the truth.

After staring for a long moment, Abe sighed. "Maybe this is something you need time to think about. So okay, I can give you some of that. But not much, sheifale. Once we tip too far, there's no going back. And we're almost there." Then he brightened a little. "But we've got some strong people on our side, and we still have hope. Hope turns tides. And I hope you'll come around."

He slowly put on his coat and buttoned it up, then settled the hat on his head at an angle he must have known made him look dashing. He pulled a card from his coat pocket and set it on the little table that generally collected keys, mail, and sales circulars. "Call that number if you do come around."

Dee didn't answer.

Abe paused with one hand on the doorknob, then turned to look at Dee. "Your name. Is that your legal name? A nickname?"

"What difference does it make?"

"Just curious."

"It's an initial. My birth certificate says Damnation Martell."

Abe snorted a laugh. "There's a story there, I bet. And I'm going to give you some homework. Read the poem 'The Second Coming' by Yeats. See how that hits you."

Without another word, Abe left, shutting the door firmly behind him.

Dee remained slumped on the couch, stomach still roiling. Outside, the rain intensified, pounding a beat against the windows. He did not pick up his phone to look up that poem.

But he knew he would, eventually.

CHAPTER 3

Four days after returning home, Achilles was still convalescing. He'd managed to clean out the fridge, but doing almost anything else was slow. He spent the bulk of the day dozing on the couch and staring blearily at the TV. Most of his meals had to be ordered in. His body still ached, although at least he could make it up the stairs to his bedroom, and he'd even managed a shower or two. Wow.

Nobody visited or called or even texted. His parents had died years ago, he'd lost touch with his sister, and his job with the Bureau precluded most friendships and romantic relationships. A lot of the agents socialized with one another, some even ending up with another agent as a spouse or partner. But although Achilles got along with his colleagues just fine, he'd never really clicked with anyone. A lot of the time he didn't mind. Some of the time he did.

He was supposed to be figuring out what to do with the rest of his life. At forty-one, he could have several decades still ahead of him. Slumped on the couch and watching *Titanic*, that notion was more daunting than getting sliced and diced by a bear shifter.

"Wallow," he said out loud. He'd been talking to himself quite a lot lately. "That's what I'll do—I'll be a professional wallower. I'll make self-pity an art form."

The Bureau paid well, and Achilles had made some good investments. He could live off his savings for a year or two, probably. Maybe by then he'd have his head together. Hell, the way things were going, maybe by then the world would implode and he wouldn't have to worry about his future.

"That's gold-medal wallowing right there," he muttered.

Maybe he should just take up drinking.

As he considered whether to take a nap or send for a bucket of pho, his phone buzzed. He didn't recognize the number, which had a 209 area code.

Hey Spanos let me into your bldg.

Huh. That had to be a new form of spam texting. He ignored it, but then another message came through a minute later. *Let me in or Im gonna crash thru that big bedroom window and thats gonna cost you a fortune to fix.*

Crash through his window? What the hell? *Who is this?* he demanded, wishing there was some way to display anger and righteous indignation without resorting to emojis.

Your friendly neighborhood dragon.

"Shit." Although Achilles frowned, there was a part of his psyche that cheered up like a neglected dog given a friendly pat. He didn't know why Ralph Crespo was here. For all Achilles knew, Crespo was here to barbecue him as punishment for not sticking with the Bureau. But at least it meant that Achilles wasn't being ignored. Or forgotten.

He opened the security app and pressed the button to buzz Crespo in. Then he took his time hauling himself off the couch and to his front door, which he opened. A few moments later the elevator doors parted, and a man in jeans and a red flannel shirt walked toward him.

"You look like shit," said Crespo by way of greeting.

"And you look like a low-rent Paul Bunyan."

Crespo laughed. "Let me in. We gotta talk."

Decades ago—long before Achilles was born, in fact—Crespo had been a Bureau agent. According to gossip, he'd been around almost since the agency started. But eventually he'd quit and moved to the Sierra foothills, where he occasionally did some contract gigs for the Bureau. Now and then, a dragon came in handy. Achilles had worked with him briefly three or four times and had respected—as well as been slightly envious of—his abilities.

"Nice place," said Ralph once he entered. "We've had our couch since 1973 and Anton refuses to get rid of the thing, but maybe he'd consider trading it for one like yours. Hang on." He used his phone to snap a few pictures of the piece in question before sprawling on one end of it. He was a tall man with salt-and-pepper hair and eyes that shifted colors as if lit by a disco ball.

Achilles gingerly sat down in his armchair. Movements like that still hurt. "Did you fly here?" He didn't mean via airplane.

"Drove. Gets me a lot less attention and it's a lot easier to bring a suitcase. I'm working on a job for Charles, but he asked me to drop in on you while I was in the neighborhood."

The puppy inside Achilles wagged its tail, although Achilles was cautious. "What does the chief want?"

Crespo screwed up his face and rubbed the back of his head. "It's a mess, isn't it? I mean, I've seen bad before—hell, I served in the Marines back in the forties, and that was…. But this feels like it could be worse."

"*What* does?" Although Achilles had been avoiding the news, he had some sense of what was going on in the world. He didn't know whether Crespo's looming apocalypse was related to those current events or something else.

"Just the vibe. Last year there was some hinky shit in Wyoming, and Charles is spooked. I think *Tenrael's* spooked, and that's not good, my friend. Not good at all." Crespo looked at his hands as if the answer might be there, then shrugged. "So I'm doing what I can."

Achilles didn't know if that was meant to be a jibe at him, since he was doing nothing at all. "What does the chief want?" he repeated.

"Just a little mission. You can do it on a contract basis if you want, but Charles hasn't processed your resignation yet, so you can just keep pulling regular pay."

"I *quit*. Turned in my badge and gun."

"Nevertheless. Look, all he wants you to do is make a little trip to Portland. There's a guy up there who's important somehow. Charles hasn't shared the details with me, and honestly, I don't really care. I trust him. He wants you to talk the guy into meeting with him, I think so Charles can recruit him."

A startled laugh escaped Achilles' throat. "Is someone who just resigned because he couldn't deal with it anymore really the best recruiter?"

"No idea. He already sent someone else. Abe Ferencz. Do you know him?"

"Heard of him." Ferencz had also been an agent way back in the early years, along with his partner, Thomas Donne. "Is he still alive? What is he?" The Bureau employed a fair number of NHSs— nonhuman species, such as Crespo—and some of them had very long lifespans.

"He's human, but kind of a special case. He's sort of come out of retirement recently." Crespo's expression was sorrowful. "God, I miss Thomas. Abe used to call him a mensch and Thomas would pretend to be annoyed, and…. When Tom died, Abe was a little lost for a while. Poor guy."

"Did a monster get him?"

Crespo snorted. "A monster called lung cancer. But he was ninety, which is a good run for a human, and he and Abe had a lot of happy years together."

"Oh." It was stupid to be envious of a dead man, but still….

"Anyway, Abe tried to recruit the Portland guy but it didn't work. So I guess now you're up."

"If he's so vital, why doesn't the chief go there himself?"

"Because Charles is tied up in something else. Besides, can you really picture him as an effective recruiter?" Crespo grinned and raised his eyebrows.

He did have a point. Chief Grimes was creepy, although Achilles couldn't explain why. He rarely raised his voice or showed much emotion at all, and yet being near him felt like hanging out with a loaded gun that had the potential to fire on its own without warning.

"Okay, fine," Achilles conceded. "Then why don't *you* go?"

"I told you. I'm working on another job."

Achilles tasted bitterness, like cold day-old coffee. "Right. You're needed for the important stuff, while I'm playing PR."

"Oh for fuck's sake. I'm heading to Wyoming, where I'm apparently going to flap around with an empath and an ex-cowboy on my back, like a goddamn flying *pony*, in hopes of tracking down some mysterious signal from some mysterious source that the empath thinks he sensed last year. Would you prefer that assignment?"

"No." Achilles sighed. "Wouldn't a flying pony make you a pegasus or something?"

"I am a dragon, not a mythical horse, and neither the cowboy nor the empath is Bellerophon."

Achilles, who was less knowledgeable about Greek mythology than his name and ancestry would suggest, didn't know who Bellerophon was. But he did have to admit that Crespo had a point—flying was not within his skill set.

While Achilles considered what to say next, Crespo seemed to let his temper ebb. His eyes faded to a more traditional green and he spoke more softly. "I told you—talking to the Portland guy *is* important. Maybe getting him on board is more critical than anything the rest of us are doing. No way to know."

Suddenly, Achilles was exhausted, every pain in his body intensified, and a few new aches popped up for good measure. He wanted to crawl into bed and pull the covers over his head, which he realized wasn't the most mature response but he didn't much care. "I can't," he said, voice almost a whisper. "I'm done."

Crespo didn't get up and leave, but he also didn't argue. He leaned back against the couch cushion and gazed at the big framed print on the wall near the TV. It was an abstract piece, various-sized blocks in soothing blues and greens coming together as if they were about to construct something good and solid. It was one of the few pieces of art that Achilles owned, except for the small selection of tasteful male nudes in his bedroom.

"Spanos, why did you join the Bureau?"

Achilles didn't have to think about his reply. "Chief Townsend recruited me."

"Which is significant. If he thought you would make a valuable agent, then you are."

"Whatever." Achilles followed Crespo's lead and leaned back, then partially closed his eyes. "I was twenty-two, holding down three or four crappy jobs and trying to get a college degree. What he was offering sounded a lot better than flipping burgers for minimum wage."

"So you signed up for a steady paycheck? Really?" Crespo gave him a knowing look.

"I—"

"You wanted to be a hero. Townsend said you would be."

That was way too close to home. Achilles could remember the excitement of it all, the promise that he could be someone. The assurances that he was wanted. "Well, he was wrong," he said with a snarl.

"That old bastard was never wrong about his hunches."

"If I'm such a hero, how come I worked for the Bureau—*bled* for it —for almost twenty years and now things are, as I keep hearing, spiraling down a shithole?" He was yelling. Achilles wasn't usually much of a shouter, but today was clearly an exception.

"Life's not a movie, man. You don't fight a few glorious battles, win the big one, and then ride off into the sunset while the credits roll. Life is *constant*. Day to day. I've been through… hang on." He took out his phone and tapped at it for a moment. "Fuck. Fifty grand. I've seen over fifty thousand days start and end. Some of them were beautiful: sitting on a porch with my aibek, smelling the evening breeze, watching the sun set, knowing that pretty soon we'd head inside, eat dinner, and fuck like bunnies. Some days, my friend, were goddamn awful. The thing is, no matter what kind of day it is, as long as you survive it, the next day will come."

"I don't understand what you're saying." Achilles was tired of lectures with metaphors. Riddles. Movies. He was just plain fucking *tired*.

"Forget about trying to save the world, my friend. None of us can. But each of us can save a little bit of it, for a minute or a day or a year. And that's always going to matter." Crespo stood suddenly, gaining his feet with more grace than Achilles had ever possessed, even when unmauled. "I have to head to Wyoming now. *Neigh*. Call Charles when you see the light... but don't wait too long. Not everyone has fifty thousand days."

He touched his fingers to his forehead in a little salute, mumbled something about replacing a couch, and left.

Achilles didn't move.

* * *

One week later

"THERE." Achilles surveyed his kitchen with satisfaction. The stainless appliances and granite countertops shone, and the mahogany-look flooring glowed warmly. No fingerprints, crumbs, or smears to be found. The two linen placemats on the little table—where he rarely ate—were perfectly aligned. He'd even cleaned the windows, and the sun beamed inside without any hint of the smoke from last month's fires. Not that Achilles had anything to do with putting those fires out, but the results were satisfying nonetheless.

He'd spent the whole day vacuuming, dusting, and scrubbing the entire condo, erasing all evidence of the neglect caused by his convalescence. And truthfully, he was pretty sore. The wound on his torso still pulled when he moved the wrong way.

But his home was spotless.

He felt pretty good about that... until he got tired of admiring his work and asked himself what he was going to do next. He'd watched more than his fill of TV lately and had spent way too much time scrolling on his phone. He'd already had a light workout at the fitness center and wasn't up for more exercise. He wasn't hungry.

"Grindr?" But he knew the answer even before the word left his mouth. He wasn't in the mood for a hookup. It would mean explaining his wounds, or at least making the effort to hide them.

A book. He had a small shelf full of them because he'd always been a bit of a reader. But lately all fiction had seemed too contrived, all non-fiction too uncomfortable.

Standing in his beautiful kitchen—which he rarely used because he wasn't much of a cook—he was fully aware that his current issue was more than momentary indecision. This was an existential crisis. The same one he'd been having ever since the bear shifter had— No. It had started before that. But until now he'd been able to back-burner it.

Not anymore.

"What do I want to do?" he demanded of the refrigerator, which didn't answer, even though it was state of the art and Wi-Fi equipped. Achilles had a Bachelor of Arts in criminology and a couple decades of experience as a Bureau agent. He was fluent in English, Greek, and Spanish and could get by in a couple of other languages. Surely all of this qualified him for some profession aside from law enforcement, which he wanted to avoid.

Hell, he could always go back to flipping burgers.

Without consciously deciding to do so, he fetched his phone from the living room and hit the number for the West Coast HQ's main line. "Achilles Spanos," he said when someone picked up. "I'd like to speak with the chief."

"Just a moment," replied a deep voice he didn't recognize.

If it had taken more than a moment, Achilles would have hung up and turned off the phone. But mere seconds later, a familiar voice came through. "Grimes."

"I'll go. But *then* I quit."

Grimes didn't hesitate and didn't sound surprised. "Come by now and pick up your badge and gun. We'll get you on a flight to Portland tonight." Then he hung up.

While Achilles changed into a suit and packed an overnight bag, he wondered who was in charge of travel arrangements now. Agents usually took care of it themselves or, if it required extra coordination or finesse, Holmes did. But Holmes was off doing… whatever he was doing. Did that mean Tenrael had taken over that duty? "A demon travel agent." Achilles, who might not be as level-headed as he hoped, chuckled at that image.

The agent on reception duty at HQ barely glanced up as Achilles walked through the lobby, and the three other agents he encountered simply exchanged brief greetings with him. If anybody had noticed his absence, they didn't comment on it. They must have known about the bear-shifter incident, must have taken part in honoring Agent Bautista, but they might not even be aware that Achilles had been hurt too. Unlike Achilles, Bautista had a lot of buddies. He'd been a good person.

There was no sign of either Grimes or Tenrael in the chief's office, but Achilles recognized the dark-haired person seated behind the desk in the outer office. The pointy ears were a dead giveaway. "Hi, Henry. They pulled you in for this?"

"It's keeping me busy. Dash is on assignment in Honolulu." Henry made a face. "I'm not fond of airplanes. I don't mind booking flights for others, though." He slid a paper toward Achilles. "Your flight, car, and hotel info. I'll text it to you also."

Achilles put the paper into his pocket without looking at it. "Thanks."

"Are you healing well? I heard you were pretty torn up."

Pleased at both the question and the indication that *someone* knew, Achilles nodded. "I have some ugly scars, but I'm fine. Thanks."

Henry shook his head sadly. "It's too bad. I used to get attacked by Termites if I went outside. Horrible creatures," he added with a shudder. "But it didn't take me long to heal afterward. Humans have it much worse."

"Well, we don't have to worry about Termites," Achilles pointed out.

Henry was… a house spirit of some kind. Nobody seemed sure about the details, including Henry himself, but maybe it didn't really matter. He was a good person who spent a lot of time working with Diana Afolabi, the Bureau archivist. Sometimes he also accompanied his partner, Dash Cooke, on missions, but apparently not when they involved air travel. The two of them had been involved in the death of Chief Townsend a few years ago, but the higher-ups had cleared them of wrongdoing. Everyone else decided not to ask too many questions about what the hell had happened.

While Achilles was thinking about all of this, Henry unlocked a desk drawer. Without a key, it seemed, but whatever. Smiling pleasantly, he pulled out a handgun and a badge and set them gingerly on the desk. "I'll be on call if you need anything, Achilles."

That brought a surprising amount of comfort.

Achilles swung by the armory to pick up an assortment of the Bureau's special ammunition. He decided to leave his own car in the HQ garage and instead took a Lyft to Hollywood Burbank, where a sour-faced TSA agent scrutinized his badge and ID before letting Achilles and his gun through security. Bless Henry, because Achilles had only a short wait before boarding.

Two hours later he deplaned at PDX, which had recently been remodeled. It was a nice airport, although he had a bit of a hike to his rental car—an exertion that emphasized he still wasn't completely healed. Walking while dragging a suitcase wasn't anywhere near comfortable.

Once Achilles was seated in the rented Camry, he had a decision to make. It was nearly eight p.m., so one option would be to find something to eat and then check in to his downtown hotel. He could do the recruiting gig in the morning. Or he could simply drive to the guy's house now.

"Let's just get it over with." Besides, at this time of day, he probably had a good chance of finding the guy at home.

Henry had sent Achilles a file with the man's name and address, along with some basic information about him, and Achilles—blessed with a good memory—had spent the flight reviewing and memorizing everything. Now he punched the address into the car's navigation system and set out.

Traffic was light at this time of night, and since Achilles didn't care about speed limits, it took less than twenty minutes before he parked in front of an old brick apartment complex on Southeast 30th. The street itself was fairly dark, all the parked cars empty. Achilles started shivering as soon as he got out of the car; living in Los Angeles, it was easy to forget that winter existed elsewhere. At least it wasn't raining.

He tromped up a few concrete steps and found himself in a grassy courtyard that might be nice under other circumstances but currently felt forlorn. Apartment 7 was right in the middle of the building. Before knocking, Achilles paused to rehearse what he was going to say.

Dee Martell? I've got an offer you can't refuse. No, that was a bad idea.

How about *Here's the chance of a lifetime!* Nope. That made Achilles sound like a pyramid-scheme salesman.

I'm Agent Spanos from the Bureau of Trans-Species Affairs. I'd appreciate it if you'd hear me out for a few minutes. I've been told it's really important. Okay. That would do, he supposed.

He took a deep breath and knocked.

Nobody answered.

He knocked again three times, harder each time, with no response. Then he took note of the sales circulars overflowing the little metal mailbox attached to the wall. And the fact that no lights were on inside. Most important, the back of his neck felt tingly, very much as it had right before the bear shifter attacked.

"Shit."

Putting expediency above good sense, Achilles tried the knob... and the door opened.

He stepped inside to discover a coffee table with a half-empty glass of water, an open pizza box—the contents congealed—and a chipped plate holding a slice minus a few bites. A small pile of shoes, jackets, and other clothing lay on the floor to one side. There was a palpable sense that nobody was home.

Achilles had arrived too late.

CHAPTER 4

The bench sat atop a rise along the edge of the beach.

"Sweetheart, you need to chill out," said the pretty woman sitting next to Dee. "I'm half your size—do you really think I'm going to attack you?"

Dee took a few deep breaths and frowned at her. "Size doesn't matter."

She threw back her head and laughed, her long blonde hair resplendent in the sunshine. More than just pretty, she was stunning. She looked like someone in an advertisement, her skin glowing, her expensive blouse and skirt arranged just right, her teeth white and perfect. More than that, she looked like someone who spent her days shopping in boutiques, nibbling in twee cafés, browsing the arts section in bookshops, meandering down long sandy beaches like the one currently in view.

"You're funny," she said and patted his knee. "I like you."

"No, you don't, and you can stop pretending you do. I'm nowhere near your league. I can't even buy tickets to your league. But you've dragged me all the way from Portland to San Diego, and you clearly want something from me. Also, you scare the shit out of me."

Dee wasn't normally this honest. But for the past three days his mind had been like a glitter-filled cloud. It was as if he'd been taking some really strong drugs, except he was sober as a judge. Which probably meant he'd finally fallen over the edge into insanity—not that he'd ever been all that far from the edge—and he didn't understand what was going on. Maybe if he was straightforward, some of the confusion would untangle.

The woman, who'd said her name was Ashley Dunn, gave him an indulgent smile. "That's sweet of you to say. And I *told* you what I want. Some of your magic."

"I don't know what that means. Why did you bring me here? What the hell is going on?"

Gazing placidly out at the waves, she acted as if he hadn't said a word.

Dee could have stood up and walked away. Theoretically. And yes, that would have left him stranded a thousand miles from home, but he'd been in worse predicaments. He would manage somehow. Yet he remained seated, just as he'd stuck with Ashley over the past days, believing she truly did have something to offer him. An opportunity he'd never have again.

He also believed that whatever that thing was, it would come at a steep price.

The sun felt good on Dee's head and neck. Temps here were in the sixties, which wasn't hot but was a lot warmer than back in Portland. And the water was pretty. He hadn't spent a lot of time near the coast, which was a little puzzling because he liked the ocean. It was beautiful, mysterious, and potentially deadly. Which, now that he thought of it, also described Ashley.

Dee had been having a surprisingly good day right before she showed up. A real estate developer had bought a charm several weeks earlier in hopes of speeding up the city's permitting process, and apparently he'd mentioned his success to a couple of buddies. One of them, a real estate agent trying to sell a mansion in the West Hills, had eagerly shelled out five hundred bucks for one of Dee's charms. And on the very same day, another of his pals had paid a thousand dollars for a charm that would improve his kid's score on the law school admission test. That gave Dee enough cash to cover the rent and even splurge on a large Italian Combo from the pizza place down the street.

And then a beautiful woman had knocked on his door.

People like Ashley Dunn didn't just come a-callin', and Dee never gave his address to clients. But he'd let her in anyway and listened to her little spiel about needing his help, and somehow within a few minutes he'd stuffed a few things into his suitcase and climbed into her Lexus. That night she drove them only as far as Eugene, not chatting at all along the way, and checked them into a nice hotel. Separate rooms. She'd ordered in a good dinner for him and then disappeared. The next day got them to Ashland—another nice hotel—and the next to Sacramento. And now here they were in San Diego, and he felt as if he'd been inside a dream or in a fugue state and was completely clueless.

"Did you… enchant me somehow?" A stupid question, except if he could work magic, it stood to reason that others could too.

Ashley chuckled and shook her head. "No, sweetheart. Let me tell you something important: I can't make anybody do anything that they don't want to do."

"Um… what *can* you do, then?"

After regarding him for a moment, she twisted around to face the road instead of the beach. Cars rolled by at a steady pace, the traffic constant but not heavy. As Dee watched, an SUV with surfboards on a roof rack pulled over to the side, then two young men got out and started getting the boards down. Ashley didn't pay any attention to them. But when a city bus appeared a moment later, her lips curled upward and her eyes narrowed.

Suddenly the bus accelerated sharply. It narrowly missed the SUV as it took the curve much too fast, and then it flew onward, cutting in and out of lanes to pass other vehicles. Brakes screeched and horns blared, but the bus zoomed away without slowing down.

"What the fuck?" Dee exclaimed. "That driver's gonna cause an accident."

She gave a slight shrug. "Maybe."

"Did you…. How did…. Did *you* make that happen?"

"I planted a teeny little idea in the driver's head. Just a suggestion. It wouldn't have had any effect if he hadn't *wanted* to do it. If he was perfectly content just toddling along, my itsy-bitsy nudge would have gone nowhere. But I guess somebody had a need for speed."

Dee's heart was speeding too. He began to stand up, but Ashley pulled him back down. "Chill," she said.

"People might die."

"People might. But we're all going to die. There's nothing you can do about it, and anyway, it's not your problem."

He felt sick—but he remained on the bench and didn't even take out his phone. "How did you do that?" he rasped.

"It's a talent I have. I can be persuasive when I want to be." She fluttered her eyelashes in a parody of coquetry, but then her expression shifted and became more intense. "I brought you here to discuss *your* talents, not mine."

"I can't do… that." He shuddered as he gestured in the general direction of the departed bus.

"Maybe not. But that's why we're interested in you—we like to have a variety of skill sets among us."

He was going to ask who *we* was, but then he remembered his other recent visitor, Abe Ferencz. "Are you with the, um, Bureau of Trans-Species Affairs?"

Ashley snorted in an entirely undignified way. "Hardly. I guess you could say we're competitors. Although that's like saying a certain megalithic tech corporation owned by the world's second richest person is a competitor of some kid cranking out zines on a vintage mimeograph machine. The Bureau is small potatoes and old, old news."

Even though he didn't want to hear the answer, he asked, "What business are you in?"

"The only one that matters, baby. Here's the deal. Every once in a while, that kid with the mimeo might stumble on something interesting. Something potentially profitable, right? And then the megalith looks into it. That's what's happening now. The Bureau noticed you, and we want to see if you're worth noticing." She spread her hands as if it was as simple as that.

The logical part of Dee, or maybe the part with a sense of self-preservation, wanted to tell her that the Bureau was mistaken, he wasn't interesting, and if Ashley could give him enough cash to make his way home, this would be the end of things.

But there was another part too, and it wanted very badly to be noticed. It wanted—*Dee* wanted—to be something more than a broke-ass ex-con with a few minor magic tricks up his sleeve.

"So, sweetheart," Ashley said, "what can you do?"

"Charms. I make charms."

She cocked her head instead of scoffing, and that was already a win of sorts. But also scary. "Tell me more."

"There's not much more to tell. They're good luck charms and the like. I mean, they're actually just rocks or sometimes little trinkets I find at thrift shops. Costume jewelry, maybe. But clients say they want better luck or improved health or something like that. Some clients are pretty specific, and others just sort of want their lives heading in a better direction. I tell them the charms can do that for them. They pay me."

"And do they work, Dee?"

He hesitated before answering. "Yeah. They usually do." He didn't mention that the charms also disintegrated into dust after use, because that seemed extra weird.

"Huh." She squinted off into the distance, clearly deep in thought, while Dee wondered whether he should have done more to upsell his talents. He also wondered whether Ashley had used her talent to get him to spill his little secret. If so, and if she'd been telling the truth earlier, then he must have wanted to tell her. And yeah, he probably had. His clients didn't know that Dee created the charms he sold. He always tried to give the impression that he'd found a stash of enchanted trinkets somewhere. It was a small relief to finally tell someone the truth.

"Okay, Dee. How do you make these charms?"

He gnawed on his lip until it hurt. "It's something my mom taught me."

It was, in fact, possibly the only thing she'd ever taught him, and it was one of his few memories of her. They had been sitting on the weedy grass in the backyard of the little house they were living in at the time. Her black hair, long and frizzy, was held back by a colorful scarf, and she had several shiny earrings in each lobe. She had a book, and Dee had a small plastic car that he'd gotten in a Happy Meal. It must have been summer because Dee wore nothing but a pair of shorts and his skin was sticky with sweat. He'd been... what? Four or five years old.

"I want a puppy," he'd complained.

His mother had looked up from her book. "Too much work."

"But I want one."

She'd looked at him for a moment—really *looked*, the way she rarely did. Then she took the toy from him and held it tightly in her hand. "Say it, then, Deedee. Say you wish for a dog."

He'd decided this was a new game. "I wish I had a puppy."

His mother had closed her eyes for a few seconds before handing back the car. "Make a wish, baby."

"I already did. I wish I had a puppy."

"But I'm not taking care of the thing," she'd said.

Confused, he'd stared at the toy, still just a piece of plastic, warm from her hand and his. Then the car had crumbled into colorful dust. His throat had felt tight, like he might cry, but he fought it because his dad might find out and call him a crybaby and say that only pussies cried.

With a strange expression on her face, his mother had taken out one of her earrings and passed it to Dee. "Hold it tight, Deedee. Man, I wish I could escape." She let out a long breath. "Think about my wish. Tell the earring—in your head, not out loud—that you want my wish to come true."

That was really weird, and although Dee was sniffling, he did as instructed. His hand had tingled, which alarmed him so much that he dropped the earring onto the grass. His mother had grunted her displeasure, wrapped her hand around the bit of jewelry, and repeated: "I wish I could escape." Then she returned to her book. Dee hadn't seen what became of the earring.

The next afternoon, a stray dog wandered in through the front door of the house when somebody left it open. A scrawny little thing with scraggly yellow fur, it had gone straight to Dee and curled up at his feet. Dee named him Happy Meal.

Under ordinary circumstances, Dad would have immediately kicked Happy Meal out. But not that day; Dad was distracted. Because not long before Happy Meal appeared, a man had pulled up in front of the house in a noisy truck. Dad, Mom, and the man had yelled at each other really loudly, and then Mom had gotten into the truck and the man had driven away with her.

Happy Meal stayed with Dee for five or six years before dying. Mom never came back.

Ashley interrupted his reverie. "How come your mother knew how to do this?"

"No idea."

"Shit." Ashley tapped her leg for a moment, then bent and picked up a small stone. It was just a bit of gravel, tracked there from a parking lot or broken off from the walkway, probably. She pressed it into Dee's hand. "Show me, baby."

He was still thinking about his mother and the way her hair wouldn't stay neatly tucked in the scarf, no matter how many times she adjusted it. He couldn't quite remember her face, though. His father had claimed that Dee looked just like her, but there weren't any photos to confirm this.

"What do you wish for?" he asked roughly.

Ashley gave a wicked grin. "A tidal wave to come and wash all those people away." She waved at the men, women, and children sitting on the sand or strolling on the beach.

"No." He didn't know if he was capable of something that dramatic and had no intention of finding out.

"Spoilsport. Okay. I wish…." She looked up at the sky and then grinned. "I wish it would rain. Hard."

Dee had never attempted anything on that scale. But she was batting her eyelashes at him, likely trying to influence him to obey; and the thing was, he wanted to. He'd never tried anything like this because nobody had ever thought to ask. Now he wanted to know if he could. He wanted to flex his wings. What if he truly was that powerful?

Besides, rain wasn't going to kill anyone.

Holding the bit of rock so tightly that it bit into his palm, Dee sent a silent message. *I want Ashley's wish to come true. I want it to rain.*

The familiar tingling ran through his hand and up his arm, but this was stronger than he'd ever experienced before. It was like an electrical shock, only nice. Really nice, in fact. His cock hardened and his breath came in gasps.

Then the sensation suddenly ebbed and he dropped the stone into Ashley's waiting palm.

Her pupils were wide and her face flushed, as if she shared Dee's arousal, and she was licking her lips. "I wish it would *pour*," she shouted.

For a few moments, nothing happened. Dee was both relieved and deeply disappointed. But then a bank of dark clouds appeared over the horizon. They rushed in, gathering moisture from the ocean as they went, until they swallowed the sun. The beachgoers all looked up and then started scurrying around to gather their belongings and reach the steps that led up to the parking lot. The temperature dropped sharply, making Dee shiver.

And then the rain began.

Just a drizzle at first, but within seconds it escalated to a shower and then a full-fledged downpour. Dee and Ashley were drenched, but she didn't seem to care. She leapt up from the bench and danced around, face lifted skyward, her blonde hair turned wet-dark.

Although Dee was appalled—at himself, at Ashley, and at their results—he found himself laughing: guffaws and hoots that were audible even over the deluge and that felt good in his chest, as if his lungs had finally been released from tight bindings. He watched as families struggled to climb the stairs and as rivulets formed in the soil between the sidewalk and the small eroded bank leading down to the sand. The rivulets widened to small streams. Little chunks of dirt broke off at the edge, tumbling down and out of sight. On the road, cars splashed through deepening puddles. Somewhere in the distance, sirens wailed.

"It's beautiful!" Ashley yelled.

Dee found himself wondering how much more rain it would take to erode away the entire cliff and send nearby houses tumbling into the surf. To wash vehicles off the road. To—

"Make it stop," he whispered. Then he repeated it much more loudly: "Make it stop!" He didn't know whether he was addressing Ashley, the gods, or himself.

Somebody listened. The torrent shut off abruptly, the clouds melted away like sugar on the tongue, and Dee and Ashley stood in the bright sunshine. He could see clouds of vapor as the moisture evaporated from their bodies and clothing.

"That was amazing!" Ashley skipped over to him, pulled him into a wet hug, and kissed his cheek.

He was shaking. "What are you? What am I?"

Instead of answering, she grabbed his hand and began towing him to the car. "We are *definitely* interested in you, baby!"

CHAPTER 5

On the other end of the phone line, Henry sounded exasperated. "We *can't* send someone else, Achilles. Everyone's out on assignment. HQ's like a ghost town. I actually put in a call to East Coast HQ to see if we could borrow some people, but they're maxed out too."

Sitting in his rental car in Portland, Achilles groaned. "But somebody's gotta go after him. I'm no Townsend, but my hunches are usually valid. And I have a feeling that something bad is going down with Dee Martell."

"I'm not saying I don't believe you. I'm saying I can't do anything about it. Except tell you to find him."

Someone was walking down the nighttime sidewalk with two dogs, both of them wearing glowing green collars. The dogs themselves were almost invisible in the darkness, so it looked as though the person was accompanied by a pair of tiny flying saucers.

"I was supposed to quit," Achilles said.

"And I'm supposed to be furniture shopping with Dash. We're redecorating the living room. But he's in Hawaii and I'm here." Henry sighed. "Look, Chief Grimes left me instructions about you. He said that if you ask for it, I should make sure you have whatever support you need. Except manpower."

Had Grimes known that things would turn out this way, or had he simply prepared in case they did? It didn't really matter, Achilles guessed. "Fine. Fine. I'm going to pad my expenses and nobody better complain."

"You won't hear a peep from me."

Shit. How to even begin? Achilles felt a few moments of blank-minded panic before remembering that he was a detective—duh—with twenty years of experience. He'd tracked down all sorts of things over that time. "Can you get someone to put a trace on Martell's phone?" Technically, this should require a warrant, but the Bureau generally seemed to find a way around that.

"Sure. I'll ask Con to get on it, and one of us will call you when he's successful."

Achilles thanked Henry and ended the call. After procrastinating for a minute or two, he got out of the car and returned to the apartment, where he spent a while poking around. The only interesting items he found were a wooden box full of miscellaneous junk jewelry and other trinkets, and an unopened packet of THC gummies. Martell lived simply, it seemed. A few changes of casual clothing, a small assortment of thrift-store furniture, some basic groceries.

In addition to a small shelf of books, there was also a little stack beside the bed, all from the local library. Four of them were novels in a variety of genres, but one, surprisingly, was a book of poetry. Yeats.

Achilles took photos of everything. He really yearned to throw away the pizza and wash the dirty dishes, but for all he knew, this apartment could turn out to be a crime scene. He let them be.

Only when he gave a jaw-cracking yawn did he realize that he was exhausted. Today's journey shouldn't have taken that much out of him, but he was still recovering. He needed some food and a bed.

Henry had booked him a hotel downtown, the room a study in bland corporate pleasantness. There was an on-site restaurant off the lobby, so instead of exploring the local culinary offerings, Achilles went down and ate a giant burger and a lot of fries. When he returned to his room, he sat at the window and watched cars cross over the Willamette River.

The buzz of his phone startled him.

"Agent Spanos? Con Becker here."

Achilles relaxed a little. Agent Becker worked in the basement of HQ—everyone called it Antarctica due to the frigid temperatures—and analyzed physical evidence. He was also a tech wiz who conducted a lot of training sessions and sometimes helped out with investigative needs. Some nasty injuries he'd received long ago precluded him from going out on most assignments, but he was smart, level-headed, and damned helpful.

"Hey, Becker. You traced my subject?"

"Yeah; sorry it took a while. Sort of swamped here."

Glancing at his watch, Achilles saw that it was past eleven. "Are you still at work?"

"Yeah. I haven't left here for… gee, four days? I have a cot set up and everything."

Achilles, who was going to sleep on a nice bed soon, needed to stop feeling sorry for himself. "That stinks. Sorry."

"It's what we signed up for, I guess. Anyway, I'll text you the coordinates for your subject."

"Where is he?"

"Imperial Valley."

Achilles blinked. "Southern California? Almost in Mexico? What the hell's he doing down there?"

"I guess that's what you're going to figure out, Agent Spanos. I'm also going to send you a link to a fancy little app we've developed. It'll allow you to continue tracking him if he moves—as long as he has his phone and it's getting service."

Well, it looked as if Achilles' visit to Oregon was going to be very brief.

* * *

AFTER A PEACEFUL, if too short, night on a comfortable bed, fancy donuts for an airport breakfast, and a cramped flight, Achilles was once again in a rented vehicle. This time it was a really nice SUV because he didn't want to go ranging through the desert in an econobox. For all he knew, Martell was planning to hide out somewhere among the cactuses and dirt roads, and four-wheel drive seemed like a good idea.

The desert had always felt weird to Achilles, partly because he'd spent his childhood in the very different landscape of the Midwest. But one of his first assignments as an agent—back when he'd been far too green to go on solo missions—had been dealing with aliens in Arizona. Not the human kind, who politicians liked to use as scapegoats and who were none of the Bureau's business. These had been refugees from another planet, trying to survive in an extremely remote part of an Indian reservation. They hadn't been dangerous, but they had certainly been unusual, and they'd cemented Achilles's association of the desert with strangeness.

As he drove, however, Achilles decided that maybe this location was good for him right now. It made him feel disconnected. As if neither the chaos depicted in the news or the apocalypse Grimes had warned about had anything to do with him. He breathed more easily than he had since the bear shifter, and he even found himself singing along with his playlist.

"You're not on vacation," he reminded himself more than once. He should be focusing on the job.

According to the file that Henry had sent, most of Martell's background wasn't noteworthy. Like Achilles, he was forty-one. He had a criminal record going back to his teenage years, but they were nonviolent crimes like larceny and possession. He'd moved around the country, done a little jail time now and then. At times he'd held various minimum-wage jobs.

Mostly, however, he supported himself by selling good luck charms, which nobody at the Bureau had cared about until recently, when it had come to someone's attention that the damned things actually worked. There was no explanation in his file as to how the guy managed this, nor was there a precise description of what he was capable of. But Grimes wanted him on board.

Martell had already refused one offer to get to know the Bureau more closely, and Ferencz's brief report had been included in the file. The report summary had said it all: *I don't think Martell knows exactly what he can do. He's not willing to join us just yet. He's not doing anything dangerous—but keep an eye on him.*

All of that was fine, but it didn't explain why Martell had suddenly disappeared. It didn't sound as if his encounter with Abe Ferencz should have been enough to spook him. And even if he had decided to make a run for it after chatting with Ferencz, he wasn't likely to have left so suddenly, with his pizza half eaten and his door unlocked.

But if the Bureau was interested in Martell, perhaps other parties were as well. Other parties whose intentions were less benign. Achilles didn't know who those people might be, and he wasn't sure he wanted to know. Sometimes ignorance truly was bliss.

Yet here he was, trying to find out what Martell was up to and why, heading into the middle of nowhere, which according to the app that Henry had sent, was Martell's last known location as of the previous night.

Still piloting the SUV through miles of sand and widely spaced low scrub, Achilles instructed his phone to make a call. It rang only once.

"Afolabi here." Her voice always soothed Achilles, not just because it was pleasant, but also because she knew things. And what she didn't already know, she could almost always find out. The Bureau might spend a lot of time training agents on how to use various weapons, but when it came down to it, information was the most powerful thing they had.

"Spanos. How are you doing?"

"Very busy. Just like everyone else. I'm happy to hear you're well enough to return to work."

He decided not to inform her that his return hadn't been entirely voluntary. "I'm sorry to hit you with more. But I've got a subject who, according to my briefing, can create actual lucky charms."

"Like the leprechaun?" She sounded skeptical.

"Yeah, only not the sugary cereal. Do you know how someone could go about doing that?"

Her answer came promptly. "Magic."

"That's… that's ridiculous."

"Agent Spanos, you were taught this years ago. *Magic* isn't pulling rabbits from hats and it's not a fairytale. It's simply a term we use for forces we don't yet understand."

Yes, that was what he'd been told, but he hadn't easily accepted that lesson. He believed in things he could see, hear, and feel. Most civilians might not realize that creatures such as vampires, merpeople, and shifters were real, but it was damned hard to deny their existence when they were biting you or attempting to eviscerate you with their claws. Magic, on the other hand, felt way too woo-woo.

"If magic is a thing, why haven't we researched it?" he asked.

"We have, although not sufficiently. There is some promising work suggesting that much of it involves focusing or harnessing forces of will, which can be quite strong despite being intangible."

"Okay, fine," he conceded. "How come this particular subject can do that harnessing and most people can't?"

"I don't know, but I'll look into it. I'll let you know what I can find. But unless it's urgent, I might not get to it for a day or two. We have agents on the way to Fairbanks with a reported Amarok sighting, a family of bakeneko near Milpitas, a possible kishi in Seattle, a… well, you get the point. Can it wait?"

Achilles considered. It would certainly be nice to have this information before dealing with Martell, but it wasn't critical. "Yeah, okay. Just call when you've got something, please."

"Of course."

He thanked her and ended the call, then glanced at his GPS. Martell's location was less than half an hour away. Although the road pavement continued to be cracked and scarred from heat and the shoulders sandy, the rest of the overall landscape had changed. The earth was covered with oasis-like patches of greenery laid out in neat squares. Despite getting only a few inches of rain each year, this valley grew a lot of the fruits and vegetables Americans ate during the winter.

"Huh. What if magic is like irrigation, with metaphysical canals carrying those forces of will?" He'd have to ask Afolabi about that the next time they chatted.

Soon he reached the outskirts of El Centro, where fast-food joints, taco shops, and gas stations squatted under the unrelenting sun. He considered stopping to grab something to eat but decided to get the business with Martell over with as quickly as possible. After leaving town, he found himself in an even more alien landscape, with endless sand dunes undulating in all directions. It reminded him of pictures he'd seen of the Sahara. "What the hell is he doing *here?*" he wondered for the zillionth time.

He was astounded that his phone continued to get reception out here, as did, apparently, Martell's. Maybe Con or someone else at HQ had worked their own brand of magic to make that happen. If so, Achilles was grateful.

He almost missed the turnoff, which looked more like a path than a road: simply tire tracks leading across packed sand and disappearing behind a medium-sized dune. Access for off-roaders and campers, he supposed, although he didn't see anyone else as he wound deeper into the wilderness.

Until he drove around a particularly tall dune and discovered a mansion.

It was so bizarre, so unlikely, that his first assumption was that he was seeing a mirage. He stopped the SUV, blinked several times, and even rubbed his eyes, but the mansion remained.

It was flat-roofed, two stories high, and glaringly white. A row of enormous columns topped by ornate gilded capitals created a deep front porch, and a line of palm trees surrounded the house on three sides. A Lexus SUV was haphazardly parked in front.

Realizing he was gaping, Achilles shut his mouth, then pulled in near the Lexus, cut the engine, and got out. He checked to make sure his gun was in its holster, and after a few deep breaths, he marched to the front door. The lion's-head knocker was bigger than Achilles's head.

"Here goes," he muttered. And he knocked.

It took a long time before the door opened, and when it did, a woman wearing a sundress smiled at him. "Are you lost, honey?" She looked familiar, although he couldn't place her.

"No. I'm looking for—"

"This is private property, and I'm going to have to ask you to leave."

Achilles had never been much attracted to women, but this one was an exception. She had vivid blue eyes and sunshiny hair, and it looked as if she worked out regularly.

He cleared his throat. "I just need to—"

"You need to go." When she smiled, she showed very straight white teeth.

And dammit, he wasn't even supposed to be here. He'd intended to remain in his nice condo until he was fully recuperated and then maybe take a vacation before planning the rest of his life. The Bureau could go screw itself.

"Sorry," he mumbled.

He turned, walked back to his SUV, and drove away. If he drove fast, he could be home in less than four hours.

CHAPTER 6

*D*ee sprawled on a couch in a vast room with gold-veined marble floors, white walls, and a fresco painted on the ceiling. Actually, the couch was more of a chaise lounge, and although its ornately carved and gilded frame was not to his taste, it was comfortable and big enough for him to sprawl. He'd been on the couch all day, yet he felt enervated and sore, as if he'd spent hours doing hard labor. He wondered whether Ashley would bring him some cold water. Or maybe ice cream. Had she conjured up any frozen treats?

She sauntered back into the room, her face slightly drawn.

"What was that noise?" he asked, although he didn't particularly care.

"Nothing." She sat down in the throne-like chair beside him and scooted around a bit, making herself comfortable. "All right, babe. We've established that you can do some pretty good things. I mean, this house is great. Needs more furnishings, but we're not staying long anyway."

The thought of moving made him groan softly. "What are we doing here anyway?"

"I told you. This is me taking you out for a little test drive. Kicking the tires and all. Seeing if you're worth an investment." She winked.

Dee spread his arms. "I made all of this out of nothing. Of course I'm worth it."

"Well, technically I made it. With my wishes. You just made the wishes work." She waved away his attempt to argue the point. "Anyway, yeah, this is cool. But we're in the market for more than a construction guy."

"Who's *we?*" Dee had asked this many times already, in many different ways, and had yet to receive an answer. He didn't actually expect one now.

"What if… I wished to be the country's first woman president? Could you make that happen?"

He frowned. "I don't know. But I wouldn't. We're supposed to be a… democracy." He couldn't say the last word with any conviction, considering recent politics. Man, what if that was how the current guy got elected? Somebody with Dee's talents helped him make a wish. That would explain a lot, but it was also deeply unsettling.

"You need to think *big* if you're gonna work with us. Don't you want to be valuable? Play a role in the changes to come?"

"I don't know." He wasn't sure of anything anymore. She was using her skills to push him to do things he wouldn't otherwise; he knew that for a fact. But they were things he wanted, in a way. He felt as if he'd been confined in a tiny box up until this point, and now he'd been let out and encouraged to flex his muscles. It felt wonderful. Being powerful was a new sensation for him, and it fit him comfortably.

"Can't we just make your dream house wherever you want to live? Or you could win the Mega Millions lottery. Or—"

"Can you create life, babe?"

"Uh…." He pictured creating life the typical way—fucking—and wouldn't mind the actions at all. It had been a long time since he got laid, especially by someone as hot as Ashley. He had no intention of becoming a father, however. He'd be shitty at it.

Ashley hopped out of the chair, glided the few steps over to him, and handed him one of the pearls she kept in her pockets. She had a whole necklace's worth of them, and she'd been doling them out one at a time. "I want plants," she said, leaving him both slightly disappointed and slightly relieved.

That seemed harmless enough. "Okay." He concentrated as he squeezed the pearl, enjoying the tingle as it raced through his body, almost as good as sex. When the tingle faded away, he handed the pearl back.

She mumbled something that he couldn't be bothered to decipher, then wiped the pearl dust from her hands. Almost immediately, greenery sprouted through cracks in the marble floor and snaked up the walls, bringing with it a thick, jungly odor. He couldn't help grinning as he watched. This wasn't the kind of vague, tiddly stuff he did for paying clients. This was real magic, *his* magic. And it was possible that nobody else in the world could do this.

Within less than five minutes, the walls were completely covered, while more vines hung like swags from the ceiling. The leaves were broad, bright green, and arrow-shaped, some of them so big that they could have been used as umbrellas. There were clusters of little star-shaped flowers too, tucked in here and there.

Ashley nodded approvingly before handing him another pearl. "Animals," she said.

That made him uneasy. Vegetation was one thing, but creatures that could feel?

"I wish for animals." She sounded a little angry.

And, well, he was pretty curious to see whether he could manage it. So he did his thing and Ashley did hers, and soon afterward hundreds of colorful snakes slithered along the vines.

"Snakes?" he croaked unhappily. He needed a nap, but no way was that going to happen in this room. Not now.

"I was in the mood. They're pretty, aren't they?"

"I'm not a big fan of snakes."

"But these are yours! You're like their daddy. And we made so many of them."

He glanced up, saw a snake with scarlet and sapphire scales looking down at him from a low-hanging vine, and shuddered. "Are they, um, venomous?"

Ashley huffed and gave him another pearl. "Fine. I wish the plants and snakes were all gone."

This time, the electric thrill he experienced while holding the pearl was even stronger. But when he gave the pearl to Ashley, he felt so depleted that he doubted he'd be able to stand. He watched while she made her wish. The room seemed to do a weird shimmy, as if he were looking through warped glass, and then the snakes dropped to the floor with sickening thuds. They lost their colors and dried to nothing but ashes, reminding him of the fireworks he used to play with as a kid. The vines also turned gray and disintegrated. Soon even the fine residue disappeared, leaving the room as pristinely white as before, the cracks in the marble gone.

"That was pretty good." Ashley's hands were on her hips as she surveyed their surroundings with approval.

Dee began to shake as he realized the repercussions of what he'd just done. He'd created life—and destroyed it—using nothing but his talents and will. Wasn't that one definition of a god? A minor god, perhaps, but still....

"I want mammals this time," Ashley announced. "Puppies? Or, no. Something fierce, but I also want to control it. A lion, do you think?" She looked at him as if expecting input.

And… Dee wanted to say yes. Because creating something like that would be amazing, and he could even picture himself scratching the creature under its chin and throwing a ball for it to chase, as if it were a house cat. But if he made the lion, what would Ashley demand next? A human who she could also boss around? Dee had a gut feeling it was exactly what she'd want.

"Not now," he said. "I'm worn out." That was the truth, at least.

"If you're going to be useful to us, you need to be stronger. You should exercise your magic like a muscle."

"Useful *how*? For gods' sake, who is *us*?"

She laughed and returned to her chair, arranging her limbs gracefully. "The world could be so beautiful, but it's fucked up. You know that, right?"

Images slid through Dee's mind of things he'd seen in jails and on the streets. Of recent news headlines. "Yeah."

"And who fucked it up?"

"I don't…. Um, corporations and politicians and billionaires and—"

"People, babe. They wear different hats, but they're all *people*. People who beat their kids or abandon them, right?" She cast him a significant look. "People who steal and fight and greedily gather every crumb they can while ignoring the starving. Who turn away from other people—or worse, attack them—because they look different or love different or believe different. They dump toxins into the environment, wage war, commit genocide. They—"

"I get it. People suck. But there are good ones too."

She shook her head. "They're good when it's easy or benefits them, that's all."

Dee had, on occasion, entertained somewhat similar thoughts, although he'd never been quite that pessimistic. "You haven't answered my questions."

"People have been making bad decisions for far too long. I'm a member of a… well, we're not really an organization, per se. An entity, let's say. Our goal is to gather power for those of us who deserve it. Those of us who are strong, who are special. We'll make sure that people stop fucking up, once and for all, and the world will be ours."

She sounded entirely sure of the goals and her likelihood of success. Dee had never been that certain about anything, and he envied her. "How do you plan to do this?" he asked.

"We recruit anyone of value. Some folks are a little harder to convince, but I don't think you're one of those." She winked at him. "And once we're strong enough, we work together to eliminate any opposition. Permanently. We're almost there."

Dee felt chilled. "Are you talking about genocide?"

"You're thinking small, honey. It's really just another step in evolution. It's like… when your kitchen gets invaded by ants. What do you do? You get rid of the little shits because that's *your* kitchen. It was made for you. And you don't stop to feel sorry for the bugs. Besides, in a way you're doing them a favor. Their dumb little struggles are over." Ashley shrugged and recrossed her legs.

Her little speech was terrifying—and yet also, somehow, oddly appealing. Why should Dee care about billions of people, none of whom had ever given a damn about him? And here he was with his rare and powerful talents. Maybe he *was* more evolved than ordinary humans. Maybe it did make sense to hand the keys over to extraordinary individuals.

No more scrambling around for rent money, trying to please idiots who wanted love charms, wondering how he was going afford his next meal. No more jails. No more… being alone in the world. He'd never asked for much but had rarely gotten anything. It was his turn to *get* something, dammit.

Besides, if he refused, he was pretty sure he wouldn't get to simply walk away. He'd end up one of those squished insects.

"How about you?" he asked after a long pause. "Why did you decide to join the cause?"

She nodded as if she approved of the question. "I'm not like you. I can't grant wishes. In fact, it used to be I couldn't do anything all that amazing. But certain people saw my potential and asked me to join. I grew so much stronger when I did, and I got all sorts of nice perks. So now I have superpowers too."

Dee couldn't help but wonder: if he joined, would he become more powerful too?

Then he remembered that nothing came for free. "What's the price?" Hesitantly, he added, "My soul?"

Ashley laughed. "It's not like that. You'll see. Anyway, even if you had a soul, are you really using it?" She lifted an eyebrow. "Maybe it's time to trade it in."

This conversation was exhausting him almost as much as magicking the pearls had, and now his head began to ache. "I need to rest."

"Just do one more thing for me. Then you can have a nice long nap. I want that lion you promised me."

He hadn't promised her anything—he was fairly sure of that—and he doubted he had it in him right now. Just keeping his eyes open felt like a Herculean task. "Later."

Ashley's expression hardened. "Listen up, bub. I don't think you understand the situation. I call the shots, not you. And you're still very much in your trial period. Don't blow it."

Fuck. It would be easiest just to give in. Dee held out his hand for a pearl. "Give it over."

Looking smug, she reached into her pocket. But she stopped when a loud pounding came from somewhere outside the room. "Seriously?" she snapped. "I didn't come all the way out to the middle of nowhere for constant interruptions."

Dee yawned.

Ashley stood and jabbed a finger in his direction. "You want to sleep? Fine. Have forty winks while I do all the work."

She stomped away, and Dee fell asleep before she'd left the room.

CHAPTER 7

Achilles did not take kindly to being fucked with.

He hadn't wanted to rejoin the goddamn Bureau, and he hadn't wanted to drag his carcass up to Portland and then out into the middle of a desert, and he abso-fucking-lutely hadn't wanted someone screwing with his brain. Because that was what had happened—he was sure of it by the time he'd driven halfway back to El Centro.

And look, he didn't give a shit if some crazy zillionaire decided to build an ugly mansion somewhere it didn't belong. The Bureau most likely didn't give a shit either. Idiotic architecture wasn't within the scope of their jurisdiction.

But apparently the Bureau *did* give a shit about Martell, who, according to the fancy-tech info, was inside that ugly mansion. The Bureau also gave a shit about anyone fucking around with other peoples' minds. That sort of thing was very much under their jurisdiction. And Achilles, when it happened to his head, cared especially much. It was bad enough when monsters wanted to gut, exsanguinate, or poison him, but mind control was a giant step too far.

As these thoughts stampeded through him, he realized that he needed to turn the damn vehicle around. Which he did, abruptly, squealing tires and all.

Achilles wasn't a complete dimwit. While he sped back to the mansion, he instructed his phone to dial HQ. Henry picked up on the first ring.

"Have you found the subject?" Henry asked. He sounded tired.

"Maybe. But things got complicated." Achilles gave a quick rundown of what had happened. Talking about it didn't make him feel any better.

"The woman forced you to go away?"

"Not… exactly. She suggested it, and it seemed like a perfectly good idea. For a while."

"How did she do that?" At least Henry wasn't criticizing Achilles for being so weak.

"No idea. Look, I'm on my way back there. Can you maybe have Afolabi dig into this in the meantime?" It was unlikely she'd find information so quickly, but it was worth a shot. "And I don't suppose you can send me some backup?"

"Gods, Achilles, there's nobody. You don't even want to know what a mess things are. The chief and Tenrael are in DC, meeting with the East Coast chief, and…. Well, none of that's your problem. But you shouldn't go back into that situation alone."

That was excellent advice. But Achilles was pissed off, impatient, and itching for a fight. He also felt somehow responsible for Martell, though for all he knew the guy was a perpetrator rather than victim.

"I guess I'm being stupid today, Henry. Look, Con Becker knows where I'm going and can track me. If I don't check in with you in a couple hours, let him know, okay?"

After a moment, Henry responded, sounding doubtful. "I guess. Be careful, okay?"

Despite everything, Achilles smiled. It felt nice that someone was a little worried about his welfare. "Thanks. Talk to you later."

He half expected to drive down that road and find the mansion gone, but it was still there—both improbable and, now that he took a closer look, vaguely foreboding. He'd been to genuine haunted houses that felt more welcoming. But he parked the SUV, quickly checked his weapons, then marched to the door and knocked, hard.

It took a few moments, but the door swung open and the woman glared at him. "I told you to leave."

Achilles put on an expression he thought of as Neutral Thug. "Ma'am, I need to ask you a few questions." He took a step forward, nearly into the doorway.

"You're not the police. Now go." She frowned and made a shooing motion.

Something about her actions triggered a memory, and suddenly Achilles recognized her. A couple of years ago, she'd been on TV and social media a lot. He couldn't quite recall her name—Allison Something, maybe? Alissa?—but he did remember that she'd been a congresswoman from a Southern state. She'd spouted a lot of right-wing conspiracy theories, then there was a fraud-and-bribery scandal, and she'd finally lost her incumbent seat in the next election. Beat by someone who hated everything she stood for.

None of which explained what the hell was going on now.

As she frowned at him, he felt a little tickle in his brain. Like when he'd forgotten something important and was on the verge of recalling it, or maybe like when he had a sudden craving for a gooey cheeseburger. A little voice whispered, *Let's go home.* Which sounded like a reasonable idea, and he almost backed away.

But instead he took another step forward. "Ma'am, this is important."

She looked pissed off. "This is my house. You're trespassing. Go away."

"I very much doubt that you have legal possession of this property." He paused, considering whether to divulge his identity. It was risky, especially without backup. But Christ, unless he pulled out his gun—which he didn't want to do—he was going to be stuck arguing with her forever.

"Ma'am, I'm Agent Spanos with the Bureau of Trans-Species Affairs. I need some information."

Most civilians had never heard of the Bureau, which preferred to keep a low profile. But her eyes widened in recognition. Then a smile that he definitely didn't like appeared on her face. "Really?" she purred. "This is my lucky day. Come on in, Agent Spanos."

He shouldn't. Not with her unknown powers and his nearest colleague hours away. But he felt the tickle again, and this time he gave in to it and walked through the door.

She closed it as he glanced quickly around the ostentatious foyer. Nobody else seemed to be in the room, but a pair of intricately carved doors were straight ahead, one of them slightly ajar.

"Why are you here, agent?" she asked sweetly.

"I told you. I need some information. Let's begin with—"

She made an odd little motion with her fingers, and Achilles was racked with pain. It hurt worse than being gutted by the bear shifter, and every nerve in his body shrieked in agony.

He might have shrieked too; he couldn't tell. His last awareness was collapsing to the hard floor as the world went dark.

* * *

GODDAMMIT, they needed to let him out of this fucking hospital and—

No.

As awareness gradually dawned, so did the realization that he was not in a hospital bed. Not in a bed at all, in fact, but rather on a cold, hard surface that felt like very firm rubber. There was no light, and he couldn't tell the difference between eyes closed and open. He briefly panicked, thinking he'd gone blind, but when he pressed gently on his eyelids, he saw some sparks. He hoped that meant his eyes still worked.

His pain receptors still worked, that was for sure. They sparked and sizzled all over his body like earthquake aftershocks, and for a long time all he could do was curl into a ball, moan, and ride them out.

By the time they ebbed away, he was exhausted. But at least he wasn't dead. He surveyed his body by touch, and even though he was somewhat dismayed to discover that he was naked, he was also relieved that there were no new additions to his decades-long collection of wounds.

Although it was nice to know that he wasn't actively dying, his heart raced, his breath came in short gasps, and he was both sweaty and chilled. All of these things were familiar, however. He'd been in many terrifying situations and had years of training on how to deal with them. He remembered a phrase, repeated often by one of his Bureau instructors: *A little fear will keep you alive; blind panic will kill you.* Achilles laughed a little hysterically, because at the moment he *was* blind.

"Stop it," he ordered brusquely. "Get those cortisol and epinephrine levels down pronto." He began deep breathing exercises, at the same time mentally reciting the opening lines of *The Iliad* in ancient Greek. *Sing, Goddess, of the wrath of Achilles.* He'd devised that little trick back when he was a brand-new agent, and although it was silly, it still worked.

Eventually he calmed down enough to assess his surroundings, not that there was much to assess. He couldn't hear anything but the noises he made. When he shouted, his voice didn't bounce back as it would in an enclosed space. The air temperature was comfortable despite his lack of clothing, and the only scent he could catch was a very faint plasticky odor.

Where the fuck was he?

Achilles slowly rose on legs as wobbly as a newborn colt's. He shuffled forward, hands held out in front of him, legs carefully testing each footstep before he put full weight on it. He encountered… nothing. Just the floor below him. When he jumped toward the ceiling, he wasn't surprised that he touched nothing overhead.

He walked for what felt like a very long distance, although he had no good way to judge. For all he knew, he was walking in circles. He shouted now and then, but never received a reply. Eventually, deciding that these activities were fruitless, he sat down and wrapped his arms around his legs.

This situation was scarier than the goddamn bear shifter. At least Achilles had known exactly what the shifter wanted—to tear him to bits—and what weapons the bastard had at his disposal. Fighting massive claws and teeth might be difficult, but it was way more manageable than trying to fight nothingness.

Then a horrifying new thought capered into Achilles' consciousness like a murderous clown: what if none of this was real? What if that former congresswoman could use her brain-zapping powers to lock him in his own hallucination? Achilles feared losing control of his mind more than he feared vampires, basilisks, or ghouls. More than he feared anything, in fact.

"Well, this isn't helping." His own voice was a comfort, even if it was slightly rough from his previous shouting. "Focus instead on what you know. Remember what Townsend once told you: information is power. Right now, information is your only weapon, so use it."

Okay. So, he knew to a high degree of certainty that he wasn't dead. Furthermore, nobody had killed him when he was unconscious and vulnerable, which suggested that his captor—or captors—had an interest in keeping him alive. He had some value to them. If he could figure out what that value was, he might gain some leverage.

He also knew that both Henry and Con Becker were trustworthy. If he didn't check in as promised, they would notice and take action. They'd be able to track him to that stupid mansion in the desert. Achilles had a strong sense that he wasn't there anymore, and of course he no longer had his phone on him, but at least the Bureau would have a good start on finding him, and he'd never personally known any chief who would leave an agent hanging.

The rest of Achilles' knowledge was spotty. He assumed that the former congresswoman was at least partly responsible for his plight, and she clearly possessed some unusual talents that the Bureau tended to frown upon: The power of suggestion. The ability to cause agony simply by wiggling her fingers. There might be more. It was entirely unclear what role Martell played in all of this—was he an accomplice or a victim?—whether other parties were also involved, and what the ultimate goal was.

Achilles acknowledged his own goal: to remain alive until the cavalry arrived. And if he could find out some details along the way about what the hell was going on, all the better.

CHAPTER 8

"Up and at 'em. We gotta scram."

Dee blinked groggily at Ashley, who stood with arms akimbo, looking down at him. He was still sprawled on the chaise lounge, with no clue how long he'd been asleep. He still felt slightly weak and shaky, as if he were at the tail end of the flu. "What?" he croaked.

"It's time for us to move on. Sooner than I wanted, but oh well." She didn't look unhappy. If anything, she emanated a smug satisfaction, like the cat who'd eaten the canary.

"Move where?"

"I'll tell you when we get there. Come on." She waved her hands impatiently.

Dee slowly stood and looked around. "I'll get my stuff." He'd shoved a few items of clothing and some toiletries into a suitcase when Ashley had collected him from his apartment, but he couldn't recall what he'd done with it when they'd arrived here. Most likely he'd simply handed everything over to Ashley.

"You don't need it, babe. We'll get you something much nicer, something that shows off that nice bod and handsome face. You've kept yourself in decent shape for your age."

He started to bristle but decided he didn't have the energy. He also didn't really care about any of the items he'd brought. Except one. He patted his jeans pockets, which were empty. "Where's my phone?"

"You don't need that either."

"But—"

"I'll get you a new one. One that doesn't have a cracked screen—and that isn't letting anyone track you."

That shook away the last of his sleepiness. "Track me? Who the fuck—"

"I'll explain on the road."

She took his hand and towed him out of the room, down a long hallway, through the entry foyer, out the front door, and into the chilly night. The light from the mansion windows allowed him to see a dark-colored SUV parked in front. He pointed. "Whose is that?" It hadn't been there yesterday when they'd arrived, and its presence seemed ominous.

"I'll explain that too." Then she bundled him into the passenger seat of the Lexus, started the engine, and zoomed away.

"Look, Ashley," Dee said after several miles of speeding through the fathomless desert. "You've given me nothing but puzzles and evasions. You want my help? Fine. Then tell me who you are and what the fuck is happening."

She glanced at him. "Or what, honey? You'll bail out right here on the highway?"

He growled, mostly at himself for getting into this helpless position. "I'll stop giving you charms."

"No, you won't. I can be pretty persuasive." Ashley laughed, but it didn't match her grim expression. "Anyway, I'm gonna spill all once we arrive. What I can tell you now is that the Bureau of Trans-Species Affairs has been following you, probably using your phone. One of their agents showed up at my door while you were sleeping. That was his car you saw."

"What happened to him?"

Ashley didn't answer at first, which gave Dee plenty of time to imagine all sorts of things. He could picture Abe Ferencz, that handsome older man in the old-fashioned suit. And he could imagine Ashley doing all sorts of nasty things to him. Dee already knew that her regard for human life was casual at best, and if she'd decided that the Bureau agent was a threat? Not good at all.

However, Ferencz and other agents weren't Dee's responsibility. He'd never asked them to contact him, and he sure as hell hadn't given them permission to track him. Furthermore, they'd assumed the risk of harm when they signed up to be federal agents.

Still, he didn't feel good about this.

Finally, Ashley spoke. "Don't get your panties in a twist. He's fine. In fact, I'll introduce you two when we reach our destination. And you can stop swiveling your head around like that. He's not in the car."

Great. Another mystery. Although it was admittedly a relief to know that there was neither a corpse nor a trussed-up fed stuffed into the back.

Ashley patted Dee's knee. "I kept my promise and told you a couple of things. Now just kick back, and when we arrive you'll hear the rest. Meanwhile, I bet you're hungry. I'll stop for munchies as soon as we hit civilization."

Dee opened his mouth to argue, then shut it and slumped back against the seat. Clearly she was going to divulge only what she wanted to, when she felt like it. There was no use wasting his energy pestering her. Besides, part of him was pretty sure he was better off not knowing.

He turned away from her and stared out the window, where there was nothing to see but darkness. After several miles of that, with the sound of the engine and tires murmuring in the back of his head, he fell into a trance that felt a bit like being stoned. Since he had nothing external to concentrate on, his focus turned inward in a way that was rare for him.

He thought about how passive he'd been since Ashley had walked into his apartment. Although he wanted to use her powers as an excuse, that would be lying to himself. The truth was that he'd spent his entire life being passive, as if he were a bit of wood floating down a river. The water carried him wherever it willed, sometimes bashing him against rocks and sometimes submerging him, and he never attempted to fight the current. He didn't know why. Maybe if he'd gone to a shrink, he'd have an answer.

And now here he was, capable of doing these incredible, inexplicable things, and he'd never *done* anything about it. Never explored to discover exactly what he could and couldn't do. Never really questioned why he possessed these abilities. Never thought about the possibility of using his gift for more than earning a few bucks.

"What's wrong with me?" he whispered.

"Nothing that we can't fix, babe." And Ashley gave a little laugh.

* * *

DEE AWOKE ACHY AND HUNGRY, eyes crusted and skin feeling grimy. "Where are we?" he asked, blinking as the sun shone through the windshield.

Ashley grinned. "Our new home. Come see."

He moaned as he extricated himself from the car and stood upright in what felt like the first time in years. Then he moaned again as he stretched mightily, his joints creaking and popping in a noisy chorus. His vision finally cleared enough to see where they were parked.

More desert. But this was a different desert, rocky instead of sandy, with scrubby brush and scattered evergreens close by and jagged orange hills in the distance. The car was at the edge of a road that barely merited the term, the tarmac cracked and degraded into barely more than gravel. The air was cold despite the sun, and there were a few traces of old snow on the ground. Apart from the road, there were no signs of civilization.

"Let's get cracking," said Ashley, interrupting his surveillance. She handed him a pearl. "I want a house."

Doing his thing to the pearl took only a moment. It was coming easier to him now, much easier than before Ashley entered his life, and the electric, almost erotic thrill was stronger. This morning, he felt as if he could move mountains.

And in fact, he sort of did. Because when she clutched the pearl, closed her eyes, and mumbled a wish, the earth in front of them rumbled and shifted, creating a slope where none had existed before. Then the air shimmered and seemed to pixelate. When it normalized, a flat-roofed multilevel concrete-and-glass mansion sprawled in front of them. The water in the vast swimming pool was an ethereal blue.

Ashley clapped her hands in delight. "That's great! I'll bet I'll need to make some adjustments inside, though. C'mon."

He followed her dutifully, just as his dog, Happy Meal, had followed him during childhood. The entryway had a high ceiling and an enormous glass chandelier; the floor and walls were white marble. The air smelled faintly of flowers.

Ashley seemed to know the floor plan. She took Dee's hand and led him down a long, echoey corridor, through an outdoor breezeway that spanned an artificial stream, and into a vast great room with a kitchen and several sleek white couches. She pushed him onto one of the couches and demanded another wish, which she used to create a lavish brunch of fruit, french toast, bacon, and eggs.

"Eat up," she commanded.

The food was… not quite right. Not awful, but off, with a slightly chemical taste that he couldn't place. Even as he ate, Dee wondered where wish-food came from—hell, where anything Ashley wished into existence came from—and whether the food had accurate nutritional properties. Maybe it would slowly poison him. He ate a lot anyway.

So did she, much more than he would have thought possible. Sometimes her food dripped onto the couch or floor, gaudy blackberry purples and egg-yolk yellows against the white, but she didn't seem to care.

When they finished eating, she wished away the leftovers and dishes but didn't do anything about the spills and stains. She sat primly on the couch opposite his, legs crossed and hands folded in her lap.

"It's like this," she said. "I used to be nothing. I grew up without much of anything. Like, d'you know what car my daddy bought me when I turned sixteen? A used Toyota! Seriously."

Dee, who had been on his own by sixteen and had rarely owned a vehicle of any type, held his tongue.

Ashley, who didn't seem to notice his disdain, continued. "But I always knew I had it in me to be someone great. I didn't have any magical powers or anything, not back then. It was just little ol' me. I got married when I was eighteen, and Cody and I worked really hard at his daddy's construction company. His daddy also introduced me to politics—he was a state senator—and I got super interested. Eventually I ran for US Congress and won." She flipped her hair back and raised her chin.

"Congratulations." Dee had never paid much attention to politics, even less so in recent years, when the shitshow had grown worse. The whole damn thing was too depressing to consider. "And I appreciate the bio, but this isn't—"

"Patience, baby. So Congress was great. I had a ball in DC, meeting with all these movers and shakers who had to bow to me because they needed my vote. I was moving up! But then…." Her expression darkened and she stared at the floor. "I wasn't doing anything different than the rest of them. Hell, some of those good ol' boys were doing way worse. But they resented me. They had it in for me! So I had to step down. It wasn't fair."

Looking at her now, Dee could almost envision her as a young child. Spoiled, perhaps, but also deprived of something fundamental—love or attention—and that absence had dug a hole in her psyche that could never be filled. He felt that himself on occasion.

After a pause, she returned her gaze to him. "Things were rough for a little while. There were some court cases. We owed a lot of money. Cody was talking about leaving me. Then a gentleman showed up at my door, told me that he knew I was special, and explained how things could be different. I could have the kind of power those assholes in Washington could only dream of. I jumped on board and haven't regretted it even once. Not even at the beginning, when I had to…. Well, let's just say Cody met an untimely end. Oopsie." She flashed an impish grin.

"You murdered your husband?" Dee wasn't even surprised at this revelation.

"He was in the way. And he wasn't like me—he wasn't someone who matters. He wasn't important."

Dee spoke carefully. "Your prize for joining this mystery man was supernatural powers?"

"Not a prize, honey. My tools."

The magically created food sat heavy in Dee's stomach, and he tasted the bitterness of bile at the back of his throat. "Tools for what?"

"Changing the world. Right now we're focused on growing our ranks—with the right kind of people, of course. People with lots of money, with political influence, or with special abilities. Like you. It's not so much the size of our group that's vital, but its strength. And right now we're *so* strong… and getting more so every day."

She stood, walked over, and settled so close to him on the couch that she was almost in his lap. She settled a hand on his thigh. Maybe she was trying to seduce him, but the only sexual high he was interested in nowadays was the thrill he felt whenever he created a charm. That sensation was more addictive than any drug he'd tried.

"We're gonna reshape the world," Ashley said. "Because it sucks, doesn't it? And there's not nearly enough resources to go around. So many billions of nobodies living here like parasites. If you don't get rid of fleas, honey, they can eventually suck a body dry."

Dee didn't believe that most of humanity were parasites. He knew, on an intellectual level anyway, that he was no more worthy than any of them. But Ashley had a point about limited resources, and if something didn't change soon, humans would face a mass extinction, along with countless other species that were blameless. Why not speed things along while the planet was still salvageable?

"What's your group?" he asked. "SPECTRE? LexCorp? KAOS? Demons?"

Ashley laughed. "The first three are fictional. And as for demons, you'd think they have potential for us, but it's like trying to organize cats. Impossible to get them to direct their energies where they'll do the most good."

"Demons are *real?*" Maybe he shouldn't be surprised by anything at this point.

"Yep. Demons, angels, and a zillion other things that most people assume exist only in fairy tales. But my group, we're humans. Just ordinary old *Homo sapiens*. We make our little pushes online, in board-rooms, in government offices. Sometimes we hardly need to lift a finger. We set those parasites against each other until there's nothing left but *us*. The cream of the crop."

He wanted time to think about what this meant, exactly, but Ashley hopped up and clapped her hands. "C'mon. I'm gonna show you something really cool."

She set off down a hallway lined with gilded mirrors. Dee, gods help him, followed.

CHAPTER 9

Time was a funny thing, Achilles thought. It was supposed to be linear—the past, the present, the future—and unless you were zooming through space in a sci-fi story, it was supposed to elapse in even increments. But a week could fly by in the blink of an eye when you were caught up in something exciting or when a deadline approached, and a minute could last an eon when you were eager for some event. Or you could simply lose track of time altogether, your mind and soul connected to it by no more than a tenuous thread.

That was Achilles' situation now. He knew he'd been in this lightless place for a while. But he couldn't begin to measure how long it had been. He'd dozed fitfully on the hard floor, wandered aimlessly, then sat and dozed some more. He didn't get hungry or thirsty. All of his scars, old and new, ached.

His body wasn't the only thing to betray him; his brain attempted to fill the emptiness with nonstop memories of everything he'd ever fucked up. It was like the opposite of a Greatest Hits compilation. All the stupid decisions he'd made; the times he'd been too weak, too slow; the wise actions he'd failed to take and the poor actions he'd implemented. Santiago Bautista's death was in there, in Technicolor, but so were dozens of others. Agents, NHSs, and bystanders meeting their ends in terrible ways that he hadn't prevented. Loved ones being let down. The grand finale of this trip down Misery Lane, of course, was walking straight into a trap when he hadn't wanted to be working at all.

He tried to steer his way toward more pleasant memories, he really did, because wallowing and self-flagellation would get him nowhere. Somehow, though, it was just a lot easier to focus on the negative.

As he lay flat on his back and attempted to get slightly more comfortable, his thoughts inevitably strayed to the one place they were strictly forbidden: Orson Davis, whose parents had named him after their favorite movie director—and who had lived briefly but fiercely in Achilles' heart. Surprisingly, Achilles didn't now find himself regretting what had happened between them or grieving Orson's loss. Instead, he smiled in the darkness and was grateful to have had Orson at all.

It's not immortality, son. That was what Chief Townsend had said to Achilles not long after Orson died, when the loss was as fresh and raw as a claw gouge in the belly. *But it's a cousin to it. If someone is important to you, a part of them stays with you even after they die.*

At the time, Achilles had listened sullenly to the lecture, knowing it was all bullshit. Orson was dead and gone, his body nothing but ashes and his spirit, according to official Bureau training, moved on to somewhere else.

"You should've listened to Townsend," Achilles scolded himself firmly. "The old man was never wrong."

If a part of Orson persisted as long as Achilles was alive to remember him, that was an extra incentive to not die. Which meant he needed to figure out what the hell was going on and formulate a plan for survival.

He rose to his feet and began to pace in hopes of stimulating sharper thinking. And he talked out loud too, because the silence was oppressive.

"What do you actually *know*, Spanos? Start with that. Okay. Well, I know that the former congresswoman possesses magical powers— nature and extent unknown. I assume she's hostile 'cause this place ain't the Ritz. But I also assume she has some use for me since she hasn't killed me yet."

Yes, good. Not a lot, but it was a place to start. Magical powers weren't common, thank goodness. The Bureau frowned on them and kept close track of those who possessed them but didn't actually provide much training on the subject. He racked his brain, trying to recall anything he'd heard that resembled his current situation.

Then it came to him so suddenly that he stopped in his tracks. "Owen Clark."

He should have thought of this earlier because it had happened barely over a year ago. But he hadn't been involved in the case, and after it wrapped up, Agent Clark ended up being reassigned to Wyoming. Achilles hadn't seen or spoken to him since. But Bureau agents liked to gossip, so at least the bulk of the story had reached Achilles' ears.

Clark had been sent on assignment to Wyoming, where he'd met up with a civilian who had strong empathic skills. The civilian had sensed something spooky at an abandoned coal tipple. Clark went off to investigate—solo, just like Achilles—and had gotten himself captured, also just like Achilles. The captor was human, more or less, according to the rumors, but spooky as fuck. He'd tried to get Clark to join his evil enterprise and, when Clark refused, tortured him. By inflicting pain through mystical means.

Like the congresswoman.

There had been more to the tale, something about portals, but Achilles hadn't paid much attention. He regretted that now. Clark had been rescued via the intervention of the empath. Together they'd killed the bad guy. Achilles wished he'd also paid more attention to the details of how they managed that.

Unfortunately, Achilles didn't know any empaths. And unless Henry and Con could track him down, nobody was going to come riding to his rescue. But at least Clark's adventures suggested that these opponents weren't invincible, which was promising. They also hinted at a possible motive for the congresswoman to capture

Achilles: to recruit him. So probably the best thing he could do now was decide how he was going to handle it when she tried.

Achilles sat back down and concentrated. This might not save his life, but it sure beat watching reruns of *Spanos Screws Everything Up*.

* * *

A BRIGHT LIGHT blazed on so suddenly that all Achilles could do was cry out and cover his eyes with his arms. He was just as blind now as he had been in the darkness, and the onslaught hurt, but change was an indication that new events would unfold. He did his best to steel himself for whatever came next.

Which did no good whatsoever when crushing agony again tore through his body, so terrible that he couldn't even draw breath to scream.

The pain ebbed very slowly. As it did, he became increasingly aware of voices.

"…lift him up here. He's too heavy for me." That was a woman's voice, Achilles thought.

A man's voice followed. "Jesus, Ashley. Jesus. He…. You…."

"Help me, goddamn it!"

Hands on Achilles' body. And because his nervous system was still experiencing aftershocks of the torment, touch hurt too. He groaned and tried to get away, but nothing seemed to be working properly, as if his brain were trying to distance itself from the mess. The hands raised him up and then set him roughly on a cold, hard surface. After a binding of some kind clicked around one wrist, he made another attempt to move but was too weak. Within moments, both wrists and ankles were fettered to whatever surface he lay on.

And the conversation was still ongoing. The man said, "You didn't tell me you—"

"Did you think it was all cuddles and rose petals?" snapped the woman. "You know what our goal is."

"But I don't—"

"Shut up, Dee. I'll explain it to both of you when he's capable of listening. Which'll be soon. Bureau agents can take a licking and keep on ticking. Look at this scar collection." A hand—the woman's, Achilles presumed—trailed down a few of his newest wounds.

Then they stopped talking, although it sounded as if one of them was breathing harshly. Achilles moaned and slowly pried open his eyelids. Blessedly, the light was at reasonable levels, and his vision gradually came back into focus.

He was on his back, still naked, arms and legs slightly spread. The ceiling was plain white and perhaps twenty feet above him, although it was hard to tell from this angle. Two people stared down at him. One was the congresswoman—Ashley, he presumed. The other was a fortyish man with hazel eyes and a disordered mop of curly dark hair. Ashley beamed as if she'd just opened a wonderful gift, while the man seemed pale and shocked.

"Martell," Achilles rasped. Speaking fucking hurt, and his voice came out weak and broken. But hey, at least he'd found his target.

The man twitched and gave Ashley a guilty look. "This isn't right."

"Says who, babe? Look, he showed up on his own—that wasn't my doing. But he could turn out to be a nice bonus. I just needed to make sure he was in a position to listen carefully."

"You're… torturing him."

Ashley heaved an aggrieved sigh. "Honey, do you know what these Bureau people do to people like you? People who are special? They murder them, that's what. And those victims are the lucky ones. The unlucky ones get locked up in teeny tiny cells in the middle of nowhere for the rest of their fucking lives. Isn't that so, Agent Spanos?"

It wasn't exactly a lie. While Achilles had never killed any humans who used occult methods in dangerous ways, he knew that other agents had. In fact, Santiago had said that during his assignment before the bear shifter, he'd shot a necromancer who'd been attempting to raise a personal army of the dead. And on a few occasions Achilles had been to the prison that Ashley alluded to, deep inside Nevada. It was true that the inmates were kept in solitary confinement and, with only one exception that he knew of, were never released.

But her statement also wasn't exactly the truth. "Not all of them," said Achilles.

That brought another sigh. "You people are brutal for your purposes; I can be brutal for mine. Only difference is, I'm better at it." She fluffed her hair.

"You won't win." Achilles hoped he looked more convinced than he felt.

"Oh, honey, we already have. All we need now is to get a few little details in place. Which I'll be happy to explain. I'm even going to offer you a way out. Let's call it salvation." She chuckled. "But first, a teensy reminder of what I can do."

She made an odd gesture with her raised hand. Before Achilles could say anything else, the pain flooded back.

CHAPTER 10

Dee was going to puke. That was what he felt like, anyhow, but he couldn't seem to do anything but gape stupidly at the naked man writhing in front of him. The man—a Bureau agent—shrieked through a throat that sounded ruined, and his heavy muscles bunched and strained against his bonds. The metal fetters held, but Dee was seriously worried that the long, fresh-looking wound on the agent's torso would reopen.

The torment seemed to go on forever. Ashley watched with a combination of mild interest and impatience, while Dee simply stood there like a nauseated statue. Eventually the pain must have receded, however, as the agent's struggles subsided and he lay there, sweaty and panting, eyes closed.

"Are you back with us, Agent Spanos?" Ashley asked sweetly. "Or Achilles, I guess. I think we can be on a first-name basis now."

Spanos cracked his lids, shuddered, and then opened his eyes more widely. "Water," he croaked, barely loud enough to be heard.

Ashley seemed to consider this for a moment before shrugging. "In a bit. Listen up first. You too, Dee."

Pretending not to notice the way Spanos glanced at him, Dee grunted a reply.

"Okay," said Ashley. "Dee's already heard a good chunk, and I bet the Bureau's filled you in on their version of the situation, Achilles. So I'll keep it short and sweet. There's a contest going on, and my side's gonna win because survival of the fittest and all that jazz. We've *been* winning for a long time already. But we want to speed things along and get to the finish line, so we're recruiting folks who can help. Dee's of special interest to us." She patted Dee's shoulder, making him shiver.

Then she continued. "But a Bureau agent falling into our laps, that could be a nice little bonus. One of my colleagues tried that last year and it didn't turn out so well, but he was an idiot. Plus it turned out that the agent had some unexpected help. I'm way smarter, though, and you're all alone here, Achilles. I'll make it simple for you. Join us or die… verrry slowly, and praying desperately for the end."

Spanos stared at her silently. Dee couldn't read his expression.

When the standoff continued to an uncomfortable extent, Dee shifted his feet. "Why don't you just use your power? Like you did on the bus driver?"

"Told you. I can't make anyone do something unless they want to, somewhere deep in their heart at least. And my suggestions don't last that long." She tapped her chin thoughtfully. "I guess I could *wish* for him to make a sensible choice, but I'm not sure whether you could pull that off. It's a lot easier to build a mansion or create snakes than to permanently affect human will."

Affect human will. Dee was appalled at the idea of doing that. But a part of him was intrigued. Imagine the things he could accomplish if he could control other people's thoughts and behavior. Especially if he could do it from a distance. He could end wars. Or start them. Of course, if Ashley was correct in her pronouncements, all of that was moot because soon there would be very few people left to control.

"Jesus," Dee muttered.

Spanos huffed a broken laugh.

Ashley startled both men by slapping Spanos's bare flank. "I have things to do. What's it gonna be?"

After swallowing a few times and clearing his throat, Spanos spoke. "If I say yes, will you trust me?"

"I like the way you think, agent. That's smart. And no, of course not. I'd need some proof. We can start with you sharing some Bureau info. Names and home addresses of other agents would be a good beginning. But actions speak louder than words, so I'll need you to do some things a good little Bureau agent would never dream of. You know, like raping and murdering a few innocent civilians." She rubbed her hands together gleefully.

Spanos swallowed again. It sounded painful. "Why don't you join us instead?"

"Oh, come *on*, Achilles! You're not even trying."

"Sure I am. Redemption."

Ashley waved a hand dismissively. "You can redeem coupons, not people. And I'm perfectly happy right where I am, thanks very much. On the winning side."

"You're trying to convince yourself you'll win, but you don't really believe it."

Her lips thinned and she wasn't beautiful at all. In fact, for a split second she barely looked human. But then she put on her confident smile again, as if it were a familiar mask, and nodded. "I can see you need some time to ponder. Okey-doke. Just remember: this thing I'm about to do? It's a playful tickle compared to what's facing you." She gestured and immediately Spanos started to thrash and scream.

"C'mon, baby," she said, turning to Dee. She had to speak up to be heard over the noise. "Let's have a drink."

"But he's—"

"It'll help him decide." She took Dee's hand and led him from the room. He went docilely, aware that she was probably influencing him to obey. Also aware that he truly wanted to get the hell out of there.

Even with the door closed, Dee could hear Spanos all the way down the long hallway.

* * *

THE DRINKS that Ashley had mentioned turned out to be a pitcher of margaritas for her and a glass of orange juice for Dee, both manufactured via wishes. She insisted they have them poolside on the patio as the afternoon sun disappeared behind the mountains. She didn't seem to notice the chill settling into the air, even though she wore a flimsy sundress.

"I like the desert," she announced. She reclined in a lounge chair, her legs crossed at the ankles and her margarita glass in hand. "Not too many people, so it's cleaner."

"Vegas is desert," Dee pointed out. Not that the subject mattered, but arguing about it was better than thinking about the helpless man inside the house.

Ashley was in a jolly mood, however, and only chuckled. "True. But I like Vegas. I go there sometimes for fun, just to nudge people into making worse decisions. It's super easy."

Worse decisions. Dee had made a lot of bad ones in his life, but lately he'd really been scraping the barrel. "I wish you'd never showed up at my door. I wish I didn't have this fucking talent."

"Honey, you grant wishes, not make them. And you should be on your knees thanking me. You should be grateful you're not one of the unwashed masses, the vast herds of sheeple. You get to be one of the survivors." She squinted at him. "Have you ever been a winner before? I bet not. Well, you're gonna love how it feels."

She was right—he'd never won at anything. But it sure didn't feel very good right now. Of course, Dee probably felt worlds better than Agent Spanos did. "Won't other agents come looking for him?"

"They'll try. But I brought him here via a portal, and no way they can track that. I destroyed his phone and yours. Maybe they'd eventually find some way to track him down, but we'll be long gone by then."

Sipping at his bitter juice, Dee felt an unexpected pang of guilt, an emotion that rarely visited him. It was his fault that Agent Spanos was being tortured and forced to make a terrible decision. Not that Dee had endangered the guy purposely, but Spanos got dragged into this because he was trying to recruit Dee. Unless he was trying to incarcerate or murder Dee, in which case Dee didn't feel sorry for him at all.

Ashley finished off her margarita and refilled the glass. "You're brooding, and that's not going to do you any good. Look, the key is to reject that BS moral code they've been shoving down your throat since you were born. Why should you buy into it? Has it ever helped you? Has *anyone* ever helped you? Until me, that is."

Dee had to think about this. His mother abandoned him without even a goodbye. His father bullied and beat him. If any other relatives existed, they'd never shown their faces. Teachers had called him sullen and slow. Social workers, on the few occasions he'd interacted with them, had assumed he was destined for failure. Cops, lawyers, and probation officers had been even worse. On the rare occasions that Dee had tentatively reached out for friendship, he'd been rejected. And lovers? They'd been eager to go once the orgasms were over.

Nobody had believed in him. Nobody had cared for him or about him. Hell, until the Bureau took notice of him, Dee could have dropped dead and the only people to notice would have been those inconvenienced by his passing.

So, yeah. Why should he give a shit about anyone but himself?

He wasn't a complete idiot, however. He knew that Ashley—and presumably her people, whoever they were—didn't care about him either. They just wanted to use him. Maybe that wasn't so bad if he used them back. If his powers made him valuable, he could demand a place of rank and privilege.

Once he'd helped them wipe out most of humanity.

Only... maybe that wasn't really going to happen. Ashley seemed convinced, but she could be wrong.

Gods, he didn't want to be making these choices.

As darkness fell, Ashley finished off the rest of the pitcher and got well into a second one. Dee mostly just sat there, staring up at the stars. A coyote howled somewhere, the sound faint yet haunting. Dee felt cold, empty, and brittle, like a seashell long battered by the surf. And he was tired.

"I'm going to sleep," he announced. He hoped that Ashley had conjured a bed somewhere.

She responded with a small grunt, but her eyes were closed. Her empty glass slipped from her hand and fell to the concrete, where it shattered, but she didn't react to that either. Dee couldn't tell whether she was passed out or just didn't give a damn. He went inside.

The floor plan was a maze of long hallways, seemingly random stairways, and endless empty rooms with white walls and big windows. Every surface was hard and unforgiving, every corner sharp. At one point, Dee pulled a pearl from his pocket and tried wishing for a bed, but he knew it wouldn't work—and it didn't. He could grant other people's wishes but never his own.

When he found himself outside the room where Spanos was chained, Dee wasn't surprised. It was possible he'd been searching for it all along. With a glance over his shoulder to make sure Ashley wasn't following, he opened the door and stepped inside.

The overhead lights were exceptionally bright and must have been uncomfortable for Spanos, who could do little to shade his eyes. Of course that was probably not his biggest complaint at the moment. The whites of his eyes were bloodshot, his newest scars raw-looking, his olive-toned skin pale. He was probably a handsome man under ordinary circumstances, but now his dark hair was tangled and he reeked of sweat and urine.

"Water," he croaked.

For a moment, Dee hesitated in confusion. But then he realized that he still held the empty juice glass and that he'd passed a nearby bathroom. He ducked out of the room long enough to rinse and fill the glass, then returned and held it to Spanos's mouth. Spanos could barely lift his head, so most of the water spilled, but at least a little made its way down his throat.

With a heavy exhale, Spanos allowed his head to fall back onto the table. Then he fixed his gaze on Dee. "Where are we?"

"Arizona."

"Shit." Spanos closed his eyes.

Dee was accustomed to awkward silences, but this one was exceptionally painful. He didn't know why he'd come to this room, and now he couldn't seem to make himself leave.

"Free me." Spanos didn't sound as if he expected Dee to comply.

"I can't."

Spanos's gaze was bright and intense. Feverish, really. "What kind of person are you?"

That was an excellent question, one that Dee had carefully avoided asking himself for his entire life. So instead of answering, he offered an inadequate and overused excuse. "None of this is my idea. I hardly even know what's going on."

Somehow Spanos managed a wry smile. His teeth were blood-stained. "Just following orders."

Dee clenched his jaw and started to leave. He felt like a coward. He *was* a coward. That was the kind of person he was. Now he'd go find a bed in this goddamn place and blot out the world with some sleep.

Somehow, however, he found himself turning back, crossing the room, and looming over Spanos, who stared at him without visible hope. "My name is Damnation," Dee said quietly. "I guess my parents never expected much out of me except trouble. And I guess they were right. But look what being the hero gets you." He pointed at one of Spanos's manacles. "Achilles, right? Big hero, but didn't he die at the end?"

"I don't believe in destiny. Or heroes. I believe in making the best decision you can and, if you fuck up, doing what you can to fix it." Spanos made a strange sound that might have been a laugh. "I guess I should thank you two for allowing me that realization." He turned his head away and closed his eyes.

After a few moments, Dee left, closing the door softly as if trying to avoid disturbing the room's occupant. Then he wandered for what felt like freaking eons until stumbling into a room that contained a couch. Not a bed, and he had to curl up to fit, but it was softer than the floor. He tried to sleep.

The couch fabric, however, was a screaming green that he could almost feel through his skin, and there didn't seem to be a way to turn off the bright overhead lights. Ashley's home design skills clearly left something to be desired.

Dee lay there on his side, two phrases echoing in his skull.

What kind of person are you?

Do what you can to fix it.

CHAPTER 11

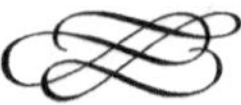

*A*chilles floated in some strange place beyond hunger and fear and pain. Well, not beyond them exactly. They were still with him, but only as vague shadows. What he mostly felt was empty.

The only spring he and Orson had spent together, Orson had invited Achilles to his parents' house for Easter dinner. Orson's family was Protestant, while Achilles' was Greek Orthodox, so the event had felt like a cultural expedition. Before the meal, Orson's mother showed off the eggs she'd decorated for the occasion: chicken eggs she'd hollowed and then decorated with intricate designs in blue and white wax.

Now, Achilles was like those eggs. There was an image of a man on his outside, but nothing inside, and he was very, very fragile.

But he wasn't yet dead.

Perhaps an hour or so after Martell left—it was impossible to accurately judge time—Ashley had tottered into the room smelling strongly of citrus and alcohol. She could barely stand upright and slurred her words when she greeted him, but being drunk didn't stop her from making that gesture and sending Achilles into throes of agony. Two, three, four times, never quite letting him pass out, never quite allowing the pain to ebb completely away. She didn't say anything while she did this, and when his vision was clear enough to make out her expression, it was entirely neutral.

Eventually, still without saying anything, she left. Alone and fettered, Achilles had cried for a while. And now he did… nothing much. He breathed, in and out. He blinked his eyes. Sometimes he licked his cracked lips or flexed his fingers. He wished he could scratch his damnably itchy nose.

"You didn't come up with a plan," he scolded himself, but without heat. When he'd been in that dark, formless place, he'd reviewed the little he'd known about his situation, and had sincerely tried hard to come up with a reasonable idea about what to do once he was plucked out of that place. But he'd drawn a blank. He'd never been great at strategizing, which was one reason why he was a follower rather than a leader.

Uncounted hours of captivity and several rounds of torture hadn't brought him any closer to an idea. He had, however, unequivocally decided on one thing: he wouldn't give in to Ashley. "I can take it," he whispered to himself. Whatever she dished out. Maybe all those years of being attacked were coming in handy; they'd toughened him up. "Hooray for being the monsters' chew toy."

There was one other thing he could do now, aside from persisting. From what he understood, when Agent Clark and his empath had been in a similar situation, hope had been what defeated their captor. Ashley and her compatriots had cruelty, greed, and indifference on their side, but those could be countered with their opposites: empathy, generosity, and hope. While Achilles wasn't optimistic about his own survival, he could at least strive to believe that the balance would soon shift in favor of his side. And as he'd been reminded by several people lately, sometimes even the smallest effort could make a huge difference.

"I *have* made a difference." True, he hadn't saved the world. But there were some people and NHSs alive today because of him. "I'm glad I worked for the Bureau. Encounters with bear shifters and all."

As the door to the room opened, he steeled himself for more pain.

But instead of Ashley, it was Martell who entered, carrying a clear plastic water bottle. His expression was unreadable as he walked over, and without a word he helped Achilles raise his head so he could drink without spilling. Getting some liquid into his body felt so wonderful that Achilles groaned, causing Martell to back away. "It's just water," Martell said defensively.

"You could do me a favor and poison me." Achilles wasn't joking.

"No." Martell looked down at the floor. Although he was Achilles' age, at the moment he looked much younger. He also looked as if he'd been running hands through his slightly frizzy dark hair, which was now in snarls. Oddly, Achilles almost felt sorry for him.

"I'm here because of choices I made," Achilles said. "You, not so much, I think."

Martell looked up quickly. "Yes! I never asked to have any goddamn supernatural powers. I didn't seek you people out—you showed up at my door."

"If you're hoping I forgive you, I don't. But you go ahead and tell yourself whatever it takes to face yourself in the mirror."

"Could you? Face yourself, I mean?"

Achilles thought about this seriously because he had nothing better to do and it took his focus away from the dismal situation. "Yes."

"Do you believe you'll go to heaven and I'll go to hell?"

Maybe this guy had been doomed the moment his parents saddled him with that stupid name. Hell, maybe Achilles had been doomed when his parents decided to honor their heritage by naming him after a mythological warrior.

He shook his head. "I don't have an opinion on that." He was confident that *something* happened to a person after death, because the Bureau sometimes dealt with ghosts. But he'd never given the matter much thought.

But now the issue was a lot more relevant to him, and Martell looked uncertain, so Achilles continued. "I do believe in redemption, though. That someone can fuck up royally but still end up a good guy. Not because I think a god is keeping track somewhere, and not because I believe that doing good deeds today erases yesterday's bad ones. I just think that people can reform. Is this why you came here—to discuss ethics and religion?"

"I came to give you a drink of water."

Achilles huffed. "Well, you did that."

Martell continued to stand there, brow furrowed. He was working out a problem in his head, but Achilles didn't know what—or how the potential solutions might impact him. And gods, Achilles was utterly exhausted and yearned to close his eyes and just... check out. He'd never been one to give up, though. Even his resignation from the Bureau had been short-lived.

"You didn't choose to be here," he said quietly, "but you have options now. Make the right choice, Martell."

"What kind of person am I?" Martell answered in an odd, mechanical tone.

"That's up to you to decide."

Achilles was sure that Martell was going to walk away. No, dammit. *Hope* was one of Achilles' few remaining weapons, so he'd hope for a miracle.

After a long pause, Martell reached into his pocket, pulled out something too small for Achilles to make out, and stared at the object in his palm. "Wish," he whispered.

"What?"

"Make a wish, Agent Spanos."

Achilles firmed his jaw. "I want to be free."

Martell nodded, curled his hand into a fist, and closed his eyes. His entire body shuddered and his face flushed; a small moan escaped his throat. Then he opened his eyes and pressed the object into Achilles' right hand. The thing was small and smooth, like a pea, but hard. And it was almost hot enough to burn.

"Make a wish," Martell repeated.

What the hell—might as well. "I wish to get the hell out of here. Alive and intact."

A quick electrical thrill ran through Achilles' overtaxed nervous system. It teetered on the edge of pain but didn't quite topple over, and then it was gone. The item in his hand crumbled to dust… and the chains at his ankles and wrists disappeared.

He wanted to sob with relief, but it was far too soon for that. He was still inside a building, possibly somewhere far from assistance, and he was so weak that he wasn't sure whether he could even stand on his own. But dammit, he'd go down fighting.

"Help me," he demanded.

Martell took a step back and then, thank all the heavens, came forward and steadied Achilles as he got off the table and onto his feet. At which point Achilles promptly collapsed to the floor with a swallowed curse, little dignity left as he swayed on his knees, panting and naked. Luckily, pride had never been one of his major faults.

Without a word, Martell tugged him upright and settled Achilles' arm around his shoulders. In fact, he bore a good portion of Achilles' weight as they struggled out of the room and down a long, glaringly white hallway. Although Achilles had lost some muscle mass since the bear-shifter mauling, he was still heavy, and although Martell wasn't a small man, Achilles couldn't have been an easy burden. Martell grunted slightly with the effort—they both did—but he didn't complain.

Goddammit, there were stairs—but at least they were descending. Achilles doubted very much that he could have walked up even half a flight. Not only was his body weak and shivery, but he was light-headed. Twice he started to fall, but Martell caught him each time.

Another long hallway at the bottom of the stairs, then a turn into a third. With the dizziness, Achilles felt as if he were trapped in an Escher drawing. He half expected to find himself walking upside down. But at last they entered a high-ceilinged room with a sweeping grand staircase on one side and, on the other, what appeared to be— thank the gods—a tall exterior door.

Which would have been a lovely sight if Ashley Dunn hadn't been standing in front of the door, hands on hips, head slowly shaking.

"I expected better of you," she said, apparently addressing Dee.

Achilles growled, "Get out of the way."

She ignored him. "I get it, babe. He's real pretty, even all beat up like this. You can fuck him, if you want. I wouldn't mind watching that. Just dump him on the floor, and we can get him all tied up."

"No," said Martell.

"Aw, c'mon. You know you want to. It'll be fun." She had a playful smile, as if she were enticing Martell to eat an extra dessert.

Achilles said, "Don't." He was gratified that it sounded more like an order than a plea. It seemed that he hadn't abandoned *all* of his dignity.

Martell looked at Dunn and then at Achilles, his eyes weirdly absent of emotion, then suddenly shrugged out from under Achilles' arm. Achilles folded to his knees, while Martell shuffled to her side, head hanging, shoulders drooping.

"That's a good boy," Dunn crooned. She raised a hand toward Achilles, fingers crooked. But just as the first wave of agony hit Achilles, Martell launched himself at Dunn, taking them both to the floor with a crash.

They thrashed together, he roaring something wordless as she screeched like a wounded harpy. With pain still echoing through him, Achilles got onto all fours and crawled over to them, because he'd already abandoned his dignity, hadn't he? And no way did he want that monster zapping him again.

When the bear shifter had gutted him, Achilles had lain there, bleeding and helpless, watching Santiago die. At least this time he could *try*.

Every cell in his body hurt, and his movements felt like wading through molasses. When he reached them, Achilles wedged his arms between the two struggling bodies, stiffened one hand, and with as much force as he could muster, jammed his fingers into Dunn's neck.

She made a terrible strangled gasp and stopped fighting, instead clutching desperately at her throat. Even if she had the vulnerabilities of an ordinary human, the damage he'd done to her trachea might not kill her. But it was the best he could do in the current circumstances, and at least it would slow her down.

"Get us out of here," Achilles said to Martell, who'd let go of Dunn and was staring, wide-eyed. "Now."

Luckily he obeyed, hauling Achilles upright. Although Achilles did his best to help, Martell had to pretty much drag him out the front door and down a gravel walkway. Which would have hurt Achilles' bare feet if he wasn't already overloaded with negative sensations. It was dark outside except for the lights from the house, and the air was cold. He couldn't make out any details around them.

Martell brought them to a stop, which wasn't good. "Find help," Achilles ordered. Talking was hard. "Phone."

"I don't…. There's nobody for miles. I don't have a phone."

Shit. But surely Dunn hadn't brought them here on foot. "Car."

"Over there. But I don't have the keys."

Achilles wanted to cry. Couldn't anything just be goddamn *easy*? He was capable of hot-wiring some vehicles; it was one of the varied skills the Bureau taught. But some cars were almost impossible to hot-wire, and he was currently in no shape to do it himself or even talk Martell through it. Still, maybe they could do the wish thing when they got in the car. And sitting there seemed like a better idea than tottering here in the open, in the cold. "Just take us there."

Once again Martell was obedient. Achilles stepped on something thorny along the way. And despite Martell's shared body heat, Achilles shivered hard enough to rattle his teeth. For all he knew, Dunn was preparing to fly outside like a vengeful spirit in a horror movie, her fingers ready to inflict more agony.

"Hurry," Achilles gasped. He saw the car maybe twenty yards away.

Martell was panting. "Trying. You're heavy." Which was true enough.

They'd closed half the distance to the car when an earthquake struck, or at least that's what it felt like. The ground shuddered so violently that they were knocked down. Before they could regain their footing, the house and car disappeared with an enormous boom that stole the air from Achilles' lungs and left his ears ringing.

Then he and Martell were alone in the dark. On their asses in the middle of nowhere.

The world wobbled again. Achilles felt himself toppling onto his side but couldn't stop it… nor could he prevent the engulfing wave of nothingness that washed over him.

87

CHAPTER 12

pparently cars and mansions could instantly poof away. Maybe it had something to do with them being created by wishes; Dee didn't know and was currently in no condition to find out. He needed to concentrate on the much more immediate mystery of how to get to safety.

Had he been alone, he would have jogged to the road, which wasn't far away, and proceeded as fast as he could back to civilization. It might take him a day or so, but eventually he'd reach a place with some traffic and he'd wave someone down.

But he wasn't alone. A naked, battered, and unconscious Bureau agent lay at his feet. Dee wanted to tell himself that Spanos was not his responsibility, but he knew that was a lie. The guy had been dragged into this mess because of Dee, and until a few minutes ago, Dee had done nothing to help him. Had, in fact, aided Ashley in her torture.

Evidently Dee had at least the ghost of a conscience and a dusting of ethics, because he couldn't bring himself to simply abandon Spanos.

That didn't leave him with many options, however. Even if the agent regained consciousness, he wouldn't make it to the end of the driveway, let alone to a main road. Dee could fetch help, but that might take a day or two, and in the interim Spanos would be defenseless. Despite that nifty ninja move he'd made on Ashley, she could still be alive somewhere and might return. Or her pals could show up instead. Those coyotes that Dee heard howling and yipping nearby might decide that Spanos made a tasty meal. Or hell, the guy could simply die of hypothermia.

Dee shook Spanos, hoping to rouse him enough to make a wish, but got nothing. Not even a moan.

Well, fuck.

Finally, Dee did the only thing he could think of. He smoothed a nearby patch of soil as best he could, dragged Spanos there, and lay down with him. Lay down pressed tightly against him, in fact, protectively spooning the agent's back, Dee's shirt draped over their torsos. When was the last time he'd held someone in his arms? He honestly couldn't remember, but it had been years.

There are so many stars, he thought. And then he fell asleep.

* * *

HE SLEPT POORLY, which wasn't much of a shock considering his bed was the bare desert ground and his arms were full of a naked, mostly unconscious man. But his wish-giving efforts and recent events had exhausted him so much that he did get some sleep, which was nice. Also, nobody nasty showed up and nothing came out of the darkness to eat them.

When he opened his crusty eyes shortly after daybreak, his companion was staring at him. "We have visitors," Spanos said softly.

Dee startled and might have bolted, but Spanos held him with surprising strength.

"It's okay. Just don't make any sudden moves."

Grumbling under his breath, Dee took a cautious look around. Four dogs surrounded them, their stances cautious and curious but not seemingly aggressive. No, wait. Those weren't dogs. "Wolves?" His voice came out in an embarrassing squeak.

"Coyotes. Big ones. I think maybe...." Spanos cleared his throat before speaking loudly. "Um, hi. I'm with the Bureau of Trans-Species Affairs. We could really use some help right now. Please."

"What the—"

"Shh. Wait."

While Dee watched, baffled, the coyotes exchanged a series of small yips. Spanos unwound himself from Dee and worked his way into a seated position, an effort that clearly took effort and caused him pain. Even sitting, he swayed slightly. Dee sat up as well and draped his dusty shirt over Spanos's shoulders.

"Thanks." Spanos flashed a ghost of a smile. "My record with shifters hasn't been great lately, but the Bureau has good relations with the coyote clans."

Before Dee could ask what the hell he was talking about, one of the coyotes stepped slightly apart from the others and howled, raising the hair on Dee's nape. The other coyotes joined in. The sound was still echoing when the first coyote rippled, like a heat illusion on a sun-baked highway.

Then suddenly it wasn't a coyote at all but instead a nude man on all fours, panting.

Dee was paralyzed with shock and fear—even his lungs stilled—until Spanos lightly touched his shoulder. "It's fine. Chill."

Although Dee wasn't much reassured, he managed to take a gasping breath followed by a more normal one. He watched as the man smoothly stood upright and looked at them, head cocked curiously. He looked to be in his mid-twenties and a little shorter than average, with a lean, sinewy build. His skin was light brown, and he had a mop of tawny head hair as well as healthy thickets on his chest, groin, and legs. His amber eyes looked intelligent. "What are you doing here?" he finally asked in an entirely normal voice but with a slight twang.

"Long story," Spanos replied. "I'm not in any shape right now, but I will share when I can. Please, I need to contact the Bureau. It's urgent."

"You're hurt."

"Nothing that rest, food, and water won't cure."

"Who's he?" The strange man pointed at Dee.

"Civilian. He saved my life."

Taken aback by that brief description, Dee blinked. He hadn't thought of it that way, although upon reflection he supposed it was true. Spanos hadn't mentioned that Dee's rescue efforts had come rather belatedly.

The man glanced at the remaining coyotes and then nodded. "I'm Boone of the Gerard Pack. We signed a treaty with the Bureau. We'll help."

Spanos briefly closed his eyes as if in prayer. "Thank you," he said when he'd opened them again. "There are some really nasty types after us. I don't know if or when they'll return."

Dee had been so distracted by the coyotes, by whatever the hell was going on here, and by being called a hero that he'd almost forgotten about Ashley and her cohorts. He glanced around nervously, and although there was no sign of anyone else nearby, he couldn't bring himself to relax.

Boone and the coyotes seemed fairly calm, however. At least as far as Dee could tell. "How can we help?" Boone asked.

"I need a phone." Spanos answered immediately, as if he already had a plan in mind. Maybe Bureau agents always had plans in mind, contingencies for whatever disasters they encountered on the job. If so, Dee envied them. He rarely had a plan for anything, and even now was just standing there, useless.

Except maybe he *wasn't* useless. "You could wish for a phone," he said to Spanos.

After seeming to consider this for a moment, Spanos shook his head. "It's best if you didn't do your... thing right now. Might attract the wrong kind of attention."

Although Dee wasn't sure what that meant, he didn't argue. Anyway, he wasn't sure how well his skill would work right now; he felt drained. So he listened while Spanos and Boone quickly worked out a strategy. Obviously, neither Boone nor his companions were carrying phones, and even if they were, cell service here was nonexistent. The coyotes' home was over the crest of a neighboring mountain, quite some distance away. It was obvious that Spanos couldn't walk that far, especially over such rough terrain.

It was decided, then, that the coyotes would head home. It would take them a fair amount of time to get there, and in the meantime, Boone would take Spanos and Dee to a sheltered location nearby, where they'd wait for someone to fetch them with a vehicle. Dee was a little hazy about who would be driving that vehicle but didn't ask. He'd find out eventually, if everything went as it was supposed to.

The coyotes barked a few times and then trotted away, leaving Dee with two nude companions. "How far to shelter?" he asked, looking doubtfully at Spanos, who seemed ready to collapse at any moment.

Boone shrugged. "About a mile."

"I can't carry—"

"I'll walk," Spanos interrupted. "Let's go." He tried to stand, fell on his ass, and waved Dee away. When he tried again, he made it upright but swayed in place.

"Lean on me," said Dee. This time, Spanos accepted the help, resting an arm across Dee's shoulders. Boone took the other side, and they began their slow, painful way up the slope. They stopped after only about a hundred yards because Spanos's bare feet had begun to bleed. Dee's shoes were too small for the agent, so he ended up providing his socks for protection.

By the time they reached a small canyon, Dee and Boone were bearing all of Spanos's weight. Dee wasn't sure whether he was even conscious. Atop the canyon were two small structures of stacked stone. One of them was partially collapsed and the other mostly intact. Boone took them to the latter one, where they ducked inside via a low doorway. The interior was empty and there was no roof, but the ground was sandy and level. They carefully laid Spanos down.

"I'll get supplies," said Boone and was gone before Dee could question him.

That left Dee alone with Spanos, who had curled onto his side and looked like death warmed over. Dee had to give the guy credit. Judging from the freshness of some of his scars, he hadn't been in tip-top shape even before Ashley got her claws on him. Then he'd faced torture, dehydration, and threats of a fate worse than death. But at least as far as Dee could tell, he'd held himself together. He'd calmly devised a plan when the coyotes showed up. And when it became clear that he still had a miserable walk ahead of him and would have to wait even longer for real help, he hadn't complained. If Dee had been in his shoes—or lack thereof—he would have bitched nonstop.

"Is there anything I can do for you?" he asked. He waited a moment, and when Spanos didn't answer, Dee cleared his throat. "You could wish—"

"No."

Dee didn't blame him. Look where the fucking wishes had gotten both of them so far.

It was still chilly out, and now that they weren't moving, Spanos had begun to shiver again. Well, at least Dee could address that without magic. "Do you want me to lie next to you?" he asked. "Body heat?"

"Yes."

The ground in here was only marginally more comfortable than where they'd spent the night. But it felt oddly good to lie with Spanos's back pressed to Dee's front and Dee's arms wrapped around him. The shivering faded away.

"You're warm," Spanos murmured.

"My normal body temp is slightly over a hundred degrees. Always has been. One of several metabolic quirks. I don't often get medical care, but when I do, I always have to tell them about the weird shit— uh, not the wishes part—and they act like I'm nuts until they see for themselves. Once when I was in jail, the doc was talking about studying me, and I really didn't want that. Luckily, I got released before he did anything. I'm no guinea pig."

Dee wasn't normally a babbler; he rarely had anyone to babble to, in any case. But now, rambling felt like a good way to distract Spanos from his miseries and distract both of them from worries about Ashley and her pals. Also, Dee very much needed to not notice that a man's naked ass was nestled tight against his groin. If there was a Hell and he wasn't already bound for it, getting turned on by helping a person in distress was surely a ticket to eternal damnation.

Damnation. He snorted. He'd never known whether his name was his mother's idea, his father's, or a joint decision. It had earned him scorn and jeers from teachers, classmates, and various authority figures, which wasn't fair. He hadn't chosen it. He'd occasionally toyed with the idea of having it legally changed, but that would involve interacting with legal types and a court, neither of which he was eager to do.

He used to wonder whether his name had been intended as an omen, or a warning. Maybe it was a comment by his parents on being saddled with a kid; neither of them ever said so, but he'd always had the impression that he wasn't wanted. Maybe his parents just thought the name sounded cool.

"Do you have family, Agent Spanos?"

Spanos gave a rattling laugh. "Might as well be Achilles at this point. And no."

"Why not?"

"Attrition and disinterest." Spanos—no, Achilles—didn't explain what that meant, or whether the disinterest was his own or other people's.

Dee decided to change the subject. "That guy, Boone... he's not, um, human?"

"Coyote shifter."

"Is that like a werewolf?"

That brought another weak chuckle. "That term's considered rude. But yeah."

Objectively, Dee shouldn't be shocked to discover that creatures out of horror films truly existed—not after what he'd seen, and not considering what he could do himself. But it was still deeply weird. "It's not a full moon, I don't think."

"That part's bullshit. And you won't turn into one if they bite you. That only works with vampires. Some kind of virus, I guess."

"Vampires?" Dee looked to the sky, as if Dracula might suddenly flap down through the open ceiling despite the sunshine.

"Gnomes. Dragons. Demons. Merpeople. Harpies. Sasquatches. And hundreds more, most of whom you've never heard of."

"And your job is to kill them."

"No," Achilles said with more strength than Dee would have thought he could muster. "My job is to protect everyone from monsters—human and otherwise. I'm not doing too great at it right now, though."

"Well… you're not dead. And you didn't give in to Ashley." As pep talks went, it wasn't great. But Dee had never given one before and it was the best he could do.

Achilles laughed again, coughed, and sighed. "I guess that's something." Then he went quiet, his breathing uneven. Dee wasn't sure whether to continue talking or let the guy rest. Hell, he wasn't sure of *anything*.

That wasn't true. He *was* sure that freeing Achilles had been the right thing to do, even if it got both of them killed. At least if he ever got a chance to face himself in a mirror again, Dee wouldn't turn away. He was weird at best and had more than his share of flaws, but he wasn't the kind of person who would help torture someone else.

That was good to know.

CHAPTER 13

$\mathcal{A}$ numbness had settled over Achilles. He should have been relieved, because it meant the pain no longer ate at him, but instead he found it unsettling. Before, he'd been hollow, and now he felt barely connected at all. He imagined his spirit—his soul, his anima, whatever it was—as a bit of gray fluff, attached to his corporeal self by nothing more than a slender strand of silk. The only thing keeping him together was the warm body behind him and the strong encircling arms.

Achilles hadn't expected Dee to release him from those chains. And he certainly hadn't expected him to get Achilles to safety and keep him as comfortable as possible. Honestly, Achilles had spent much of his life assuming the worst of people, so it came as a huge surprise to discover that someone was better than his initial behaviors implied.

When all of this was over—assuming Achilles survived—he'd see a shrink. Maybe a therapist could help him work through his low expectations.

He was still thinking about this when a coyote trotted into the building with a backpack held in its teeth. It dropped the pack, shivered, and became a grinning man. Boone, of course, and he looked pleased with himself.

"No phone. Sorry. But there's water bottles, food, and some stuff to keep you warm. It's too bad you can't grow fur."

As Achilles licked his parched lips, Martell—no, Dee—helped him sit up and lean back against the stone wall. Then Dee attacked the backpack, pulling out the promised bottles along with an assortment of packaged protein bars, trail mix, snack chips, and candy. There was also clothing: a pair of olive-green sweatpants, a matching sweatshirt, a knitted cap, and a pair of thick socks. Dee helped Achilles dress. It was maddening to be so weak, but warm clothing certainly made him feel better.

"Where did you find all of this?" Dee asked.

Boone, who apparently didn't care about his own nudity—shifters rarely did—plopped down to sit cross-legged. "Visitors' center. We're inside a national monument because of the adobe ruins."

"Why didn't you just have the rangers call for help?" Dee demanded.

"They closed the monument to the public a few days ago and fired all the rangers."

Achilles paused before taking a sip from a water bottle. "Why?"

"Feds, man. They're doing all sorts of crazy stuff. Our clan leader heard they want to lease out the land for mineral rights." Boone scowled. "We run on these lands. Hunt on them. We always have. If men come in with machinery, clawing away at the earth…."

"I understand. I'll speak with my boss about it, although I can't guarantee anything. A lot's going down right now."

Although Boone remained man-shaped, for a moment he didn't look at all human. Maybe it was something about his eyes. But he nodded gravely. "I understand. I can smell it in the wind. It's bad."

Well, lovely—a confirmation that Achilles didn't especially welcome. But he continued to sip the water and nibble at the snacks. He was ravenous and wanted to gobble all of it, but he knew better. The last thing any of them needed was him puking his guts out. Or worse. Anyway, although he was still in sorry shape, he felt a lot better now that he was hydrated, had a little food in his belly, and felt warmed by the soft clothing.

"The Bureau owes you a debt for your help," Achilles told Boone. "And I owe you a debt as well."

Boone's expression softened and he looked pleased.

After Achilles decided he'd eaten enough, he lay back down, using the now-empty backpack as a pillow. He pretended he didn't miss the comfort of Dee's embrace. The sun was high overhead now, although there was still a chill in the air, and the sky was a clear blue. Dee and Boone quietly rustled some of the snack bags, but the only other sounds were bird calls. Achilles could imagine the roars of excavators and backhoes, the stink of diesel exhaust, the gaping holes in the ground like wounds that would never heal. Countless plants and animals killed instantly or withering away through loss of habitat. And a thousand years of human history carelessly wiped out. Not the biggest atrocity the world was facing right now, but also not negligible.

"Where are all your scars from?" Boone asked through a mouthful of Doritos.

During a training session, Agent Becker had mentioned that coyote shifters respected scars as marks of having survived something dangerous. Becker himself was disfigured from his encounter with aliens, but he always wore his scars with pride.

"They're from a lot of things," Achilles said. "I think my first happened when I was eight, messing around with a pocket knife. My most recent ones came from a bear shifter."

"Bears," Boone growled. "They're worse than cats. Stupid and brutal."

"Well, this one wasn't very pleasant. But I've met other bears who were really decent."

Judging from Boone's snort, he didn't believe it. But Achilles lacked the will or energy to argue. He closed his eyes and drifted, somewhere between awake and asleep, the soft conversation between Dee and Boone gently washing over him. It reminded him of when he was a little boy and his parents and their guests would continue talking well after Achilles' bedtime. He could hear their voices coming up through the air vent in his bedroom, quick banter in Greek and frequent laughter, and he'd found it comforting. What would his young self make of Achilles now?

* * *

Darkness had fallen, along with the temperatures, and Achilles was shivering again despite his sweatsuit, hat, and socks. Boone and Dee huddled close against him, which helped a little, but this coldness seemed to emanate from Achilles' core. He wondered whether Dunn had changed something within him—created an infection, either biological or metaphysical—but he decided there was no use worrying about something he could neither assess nor control right now. At least his stomach felt settled enough to eat a couple of protein bars, a Snickers, and a packet of peanut butter crackers.

Suddenly, Boone sat up straighter. "They're here." He leapt to his feet and started stuffing trash into the backpack, an action that Achilles admired. Some of the current feds might not want to respect the history of this place, but Boone was doing his best to preserve it.

"I don't hear anything," said Dee.

Boone shot him a grin. "'Cause you have those stupid human ears. Doesn't it drive you nuts not to hear anything? Not to mention your useless nose."

A look of comprehension passed over Dee's face. "Oh, right. Coyotes."

Achilles decided against giving Boone a lecture on ableism. He knew that many NHSs found human limitations weird or pitiable, and he also figured that it was good for humans to be periodically reminded that, as a species, they were far from perfect.

Less than a minute later, Achilles heard engines. With Dee's help, he got to his feet, but he had to lean against the wall in order to remain upright. His feet were torn up from trekking through the desert in socks, his legs weak from being immobilized while chained to the table. Now a headache threatened to add to the party. But hey, he was standing, and that was something.

Boone hurried out of the building and returned a moment later with a woman and two men, all of whom had the look of coyote shifters. The newcomers took a moment to goggle before Boone urged them into action. Then everyone went outside—Achilles leaning on Dee for support—where a trio of ATVs awaited. Apparently it wasn't going to be a comfortable ride out of here, but it was better than walking.

Perhaps not surprisingly, coyotes drove ATVs like maniacs, hurtling through the roadless dark with seemingly little consideration for topography or the laws of physics. Achilles, seated behind one of the men, clutched him for dear life and kept his eyes tightly closed. He knew that coyotes could see well in low light and that their reflexes were faster than humans'. And presumably this crew was well acquainted with the local landscape. If he hadn't been exhausted and aching, he might have found the ride exhilarating; but as it was, he was terrified he'd lose his grip and go tumbling off a cliff.

He was deeply relieved when the vehicles skidded to a halt in a small valley. There were only a few lights here, so he couldn't make out the details of the surroundings, but he had the sense that the entire coyote clan was gathered: thirty or so people, some in human form and some canine. One of them, a middle-aged woman in jeans and a plaid shirt, approached him before he had a chance to peel himself off his driver.

"I'm Jackie," she said without preamble. "This is my pack."

Achilles dredged his memory for coyote etiquette. "Pleased to meet you, ma'am. I'm Agent Achilles Spanos from the Bureau of Trans-Species Affairs, and that's Dee Martell. I apologize for not bringing gifts. We're… in pretty desperate straits. And I'm incredibly grateful for your clan's assistance."

"My mother made an agreement with your agency twenty years ago. We keep our promise. What do you need?"

Achilles wanted to sob with relief. "A phone, please."

"No cell service here. But I got a landline, so come on in."

Achilles dismounted from the ATV… and promptly collapsed onto all fours. Dee—whom he was growing ever more fond of—rushed over and helped him back to his feet. Jackie told her clan members to stand back, then led Achilles and Dee to a small adobe house where an elaborately carved front door stood ajar. The interior was dark, and she switched on some low lighting as she took them into a tidy kitchen that looked as if it had escaped an Ikea showroom. Well, coyote shifters had to buy home furnishings *somewhere*.

After glancing at Jackie for permission, Achilles sank onto one of the white-painted chairs arranged around a small table. She brought him a corded black phone that was probably older than he was.

"I'll give you some privacy," she said and left the room. She'd be able to hear everything perfectly well from there, but he appreciated the gesture.

It took a moment to remember the phone number; he was accustomed to simply pressing a contact name on his cell. Henry answered after a single ring.

"Bureau. Who's calling, please?"

"Hi Henry. It's Spanos. We've got—"

"Oh my *gods*, Achilles! Are you all right? We've been searching for you."

Achilles hadn't expected otherwise; the Bureau didn't willfully abandon its agents in times of need. But it was still really nice to know that the effort had been made despite busy times, and it was also soothing to hear Henry's genuine relief.

"I'm all right now. Mostly. But I urgently need to speak to the chief, please."

Henry didn't hesitate. "Of course. He's out in the field but I can patch you through. When you're finished with him, please have him let me know whether to call off the search."

"You can do that now. I'm found, sort of. I mean, I know more or less where I am."

"Assuming this is really you," Henry said, slightly primly. "What if I'm talking to somebody who's impersonating Achilles, and the real Agent Spanos remains in distress somewhere?"

Achilles sighed. "If I were an evildoer looking to impersonate a Bureau agent, I'd pick one more interesting than me. But fine. I'll tell the chief."

"Thank you. And assuming you truly are Achilles, I'm very glad to hear from you."

Silence followed for a minute or so. Dee sat opposite him but didn't say anything. He looked haunted, which wasn't a surprise considering his part in recent events. Achilles wondered what was going through his head.

"Spanos! Are you safe?" Chief Grimes, who rarely showed emotion, sounded worried.

"Yes. And this really is me, by the way. I don't know how to prove that to you, though."

"Never mind that. What happened?"

Achilles tried to marshal his thoughts, but his brain was sluggish. "It's a long story. Bad shit. But Martell is here with me, so there's that. I'd much rather discuss this in person, and I'm not in great shape at the moment. Can you send help to get us back to HQ?"

"There is no HQ," Grimes growled.

"I…. Pardon?"

"No HQ and, technically, no Bureau. The feds shut us down yesterday."

Achilles' stomach plummeted. "But—"

"The agency no longer exists. You are free of all obligations and duties. If you continue to pursue our mission, you'll be doing so without official authorization and without payment. Do you wish to disengage?"

Although Achilles felt dizzy, he was certain of his answer. "No, sir."

"Just a short time ago you were insisting on resigning."

"Things have changed."

"So they have," the chief said grimly. Then he continued in a gentler tone. "I'm glad to keep you. We need you."

Those were good words to hear. "I'm glad I can help. I'll need a couple of days to recuperate first, though."

"Give me your location and I'll come collect both of you. Do you need medical attention?"

Achilles did a rapid self-assessment. "I don't think so." Rest, a good diet, and exercise should do the trick. "Um, I don't have an address, but I'm a guest of the Gerard Pack in Arizona. They saved my skin, chief."

"I'll be there tomorrow."

"Good." A bit of the tension in Achilles's body ebbed. "Oh, and can you tell Henry to call off the bloodhounds? This really is me."

Grimes made a sound that might have been a chuckle. "Done. See you tomorrow."

After hanging up the phone, Achilles gazed at Dee. "I'm going to have to tell him everything you did—the good and the bad."

"And the ugly?" Dee shrugged. "I figured." He didn't seem especially distressed. Maybe he'd already made peace with this.

"What I'd really like now is to wash up, eat something that's not from a vending machine, and sleep somewhere that's not literally rock hard. You'll be okay?"

"I'll stick around, if that's what you're asking. But I have a question. You said something earlier about being sorry you didn't bring gifts. Why?"

Apparently it was time for a brief lesson on coyote etiquette. "It's traditional when visiting a coyote shifter to exchange presents. They don't have to be a big deal, but they should demonstrate some degree of thought and consideration for the other party. Jackie is being very kind to overlook our faux pas." He meant that sincerely.

Dee chewed his lower lip, cast a quick glance at the doorway, then leaned forward and whispered, "I could give them a wish."

Although Achilles was not sure that encouraging Dee to use his talent was a good idea, he was intrigued that he'd offered. He was also a little curious about the whole process; he hadn't been in any shape to note details when Dee freed him. And, well, they did owe Jackie's pack. Big time.

"If that's what you want to do," said Achilles in a normal voice. "And there's no point in whispering. Coyotes have stellar hearing."

"We sure do!" Jackie yelled from the next room before sauntering in. "Let's get you settled, Agent Spanos, and then we'll see what your friend can do."

Achilles slowly rose to his feet. "Um, you heard what my boss said. The agency you signed a treaty with doesn't exist."

"Bull. I don't care what those assholes in DC are doing—we promised to be on your side."

"Thank you." Achilles gave her a broad smile. It was far too early for optimism, but the hope in his heart had grown a little stronger.

CHAPTER 14

$\mathcal{D}$ee found Achilles—now cleaned up, fed, and tucked into bed in one of Jackie's bedrooms—to be achingly handsome. Even when Dee was young, he'd never had much sexual interest in anyone. He had sex occasionally, but rarely got very into it. He'd always needed to connect with someone emotionally before really *wanting* them, and that connection had never happened.

Until now. At the worst possible time with the worst possible person: the man whose torture Dee had facilitated. Still, he couldn't help a stab of longing as he made sure that Achilles was comfortable.

"You should get some rest too." Achilles spoke through a yawn.

"I will, soon." Dee turned off the light and exited the room, leaving the door slightly ajar.

Jackie waited for him in her living room, settled into an armchair with a beer in hand. "Want one?" she asked, lifting the can.

"No thanks. Alcohol and I don't really get along." He took a seat on the couch. Like everything in the house except the kitchen, it was old and worn, but also clean and comfortable. Dee liked it. Hell, he liked the coyotes, who seemed like forthright, loyal people… who would all be destroyed if Ashley had her way.

"Thanks for the first aid supplies," he said before his thoughts got too maudlin. He'd helped disinfect and bandage Achilles' ankles and wrists torn by the manacles and feet torn by the desert floor. Achilles would need more medical care, Dee figured, but this would suffice for the time being.

Jackie laughed softly. "Pack members are always getting banged up on runs and hunts or from just plain being rambunctious. And we can't exactly visit a human doctor, so we make do." She sat up straighter. "But my son's going to medical school. He'll be the first coyote doctor."

"You must be very proud of him."

"Yes indeed." She took a long swallow of beer, sighed contentedly, and cocked her head. "What was that about wishes?"

He didn't especially want to talk about this, but he had been the one to bring it up, and refusing would be rude. "It's, uh, something I can do. Grant wishes. I mean, not for *everything*. But, like, good luck or fertility or things like that." He wasn't going to mention the sorts of things he'd done for Ashley. He didn't even want to think about those.

Jackie looked intrigued. "How come you can do that?"

"No idea."

"What *are* you, anyway?"

He blinked at her. "Pardon?"

"Well, you ain't human. I can smell that for myself. But I don't recognize… whatever you are."

Dee stared. *Not human?* What the hell did that mean? Achilles had mentioned a few things, like wolf shifters, vampires, and merpeople, but Dee was fairly certain that he wasn't any of those. What else was there? Demons. Achilles had said something about demons. Gods, what if Dee was one of those? It would explain the name his parents had given him. Did that mean they were demons too? But he didn't feel especially… demonic. He'd done some really shitty things at Ashley's request, but he hadn't enjoyed them.

That was a lie. He *had* enjoyed the process at least, if not necessarily the outcome.

He swallowed bitter bile. "Until a short time ago I didn't even know that the things I'd heard about in fairy tales were real. I've always assumed I was human."

She shrugged, seemingly unconcerned. "Doesn't matter. I was only curious."

Thankful that she was willing to drop the subject, Dee pushed the question of his identity deep into the closet where it belonged. "So anyway, I'm really grateful for your pack's assistance. If I can, I'd like to give you the gift of a wish."

For several minutes, Jackie sipped her beer thoughtfully. Most people who came to Dee for charms wanted the same things: money, love, admiration. He doubted, however, that Jackie would ask for any of those. She appeared content with her existing lifestyle, and she had the love and admiration of her pack. Probably she wanted people to leave her pack alone and not mess with their traditional land, but that was likely beyond Dee's abilities.

Coyotes were predators, so maybe she'd ask for excellent hunting skills or sharper teeth or something like that.

Finally, Jackie finished off the can and set it on the end table. "You know, we love to sing. We do it while in either of our forms, and it's pretty important to our culture. My sister Tammy? She used to have the most beautiful voice. But we're getting old, you know, and she just can't sing as well nowadays. Do you think you could fix that? It'd sure make her happy. Make all of us happy, 'cause we loved to hear her."

And to think that until recently, he would have called Jackie and her pack monsters.

"I think I can do that," Dee said. He glanced around for something to use as a charm, since he was out of Ashley's pearls. He wouldn't have been comfortable using those anyway. When his gaze fell on the empty beer can, he smiled.

While Jackie watched closely, he stood and picked up the can. He concentrated as he held it, and the now-familiar thrill ran down his spine, making him feel warm and tingly. Reminding him how handsome Achilles was, and how nice it had felt to hold him. Which was *so* not relevant.

With some effort, he turned off his internal power and handed Jackie the can. "Just hold it and make your wish."

She looked skeptical. He didn't blame her. But she clutched the can and closed her eyes, and in a clear voice said, "I wish my sister Tammy could sing as well as she used to." She made a surprised little yelp when the can crumbled to ashes that then fell onto her lap.

"I don't know how permanent this is," Dee warned.

"Don't matter. Even if it's for a few hours, it'll be real nice for her. For all of us." She stood and brushed her hands clean. "You can have the other bed in Achilles' room. You need anything more to eat?"

He answered with a jaw-cracking yawn, making both of them chuckle. "No thanks. I'm going to catch some shut-eye." Tomorrow Achilles' boss was going to arrive, and gods only knew what that would mean for Dee.

"All right. Sleep well. I'm gonna go find Tammy."

Thirty minutes later, tucked comfortably in bed, Dee listened to Achilles' soft snoring and, from outside, the sounds of coyotes accompanying a human voice in song. Dee fell asleep smiling.

* * *

"No! Gods, stop it! Don't!"

Dee woke so suddenly that he nearly fell out of bed, and for a moment he sat twisted in the blankets, heart racing. Then he remembered where he was and who else was in the bedroom, and he realized that Achilles had been doing the shouting and thrashing around. It was too dark to see what was going on, so Dee reached over and switched on the light that sat on the little table between the beds.

Achilles cried out again, jerked upright into a seated position, and then groaned and clutched his belly. "What's wrong?" he demanded, squinting from the light.

"Nothing," said Dee, his heart settling into a more normal rhythm. "Sorry. I think you were having a nightmare."

Achilles let out a long sigh and his shoulders relaxed, although he still gripped his midsection. "I'm sorry I woke you."

"It's okay."

Dee turned off the light and lay down again. He heard Achilles make small pained noises as he did the same. Now both of them were very clearly awake, lying just a few feet apart in the darkness, and it was awkward.

Finally Achilles spoke. "If I do it again, just throw something at me."

"You've been through a lot these past days. I wouldn't be surprised if Ashley haunts my dreams too." Dee shuddered at the idea.

"I wasn't dreaming about her."

Achilles sounded so bleak that Dee wasn't sure he should say anything else. He wasn't accustomed to comforting others and had rarely been comforted himself. But the silence felt oppressive, so finally he ventured a quiet question. "Then, what?"

"The bear. He got to me first, and I couldn't do anything but lie there and bleed while he killed another agent, Santiago Bautista. He was a good man." A ghost of a chuckle. "But honestly, there's a cast of thousands waiting to ruin my sleep. I've seen so many fucked-up things."

Dee had experienced a few horrible things too, although probably not as many as a Bureau agent. The odd thing was that Dee never had nightmares. Ever. Not even when he was a kid. In fact, he never had dreams at all, at least not that he could remember when he woke up. He'd always figured that this was another quirk of his weird brain, maybe related to the same brain chemistry that made him avoid alcohol. Possibly a mental illness so rare there wasn't even a name for it.

Now, though, he wondered if the cause wasn't something else entirely. Like not being human.

"Look," Achilles said. "Tomorrow's going to be a bitch of a day. I'm going to try to get more sleep. I feel like I could sleep for a week."

"When this is… all over, you could take a vacation." People did that, right? Even Bureau agents.

But Achilles gave another humorless laugh. "It's never all over. We might win this battle. I hope we do. But there will always be more battles in the future. We're Sisyphus, man."

"So then what's the point of fighting?"

"Well, maybe we can't win, but I don't want to lose. Besides, I guess we can find meaning in the struggle. Glory, even. When I die, I'll know that at least I tried." Then he yawned, rustled around a bit, and was silent.

Dee lay quietly and thought about his words for a long time.

chilles was settling in at the breakfast table. Although he still felt like shit, it was a big improvement over how he'd felt the evening before. A decent night's sleep in a good bed could work wonders, even if that sleep was interrupted with nightmares.

If he *did* survive all of this, he should probably talk to the Bureau's shrink. Except, he remembered with a start, there was no Bureau anymore and thus no Bureau shrink. The enormity of Grimes's news hit him, belatedly but hard. The Bureau had been around for a century, and he'd always thought of it as immortal and omnipotent. Yet apparently some clown had killed it with a few pen strokes.

"But it lives," he muttered.

Across from him, Dee looked startled and froze with a forkful of food halfway to his mouth. "What?"

"The Bureau is the undead. Not a zombie or a vampire. Maybe it's like one of Ferencz's spirits."

"I don't know what you're talking about."

"Never mind. Thinking aloud."

Achilles and Dee had awakened shortly after dawn and discovered that Jackie had rounded up clean clothes to fit each of them. After they dressed, she'd cheerfully cooked them a big meal of pan-fried venison steaks with a sauce made from dried berries. It tasted amazing. Dee and Achilles were both working on second helpings as she watched with approval.

"A good appetite's a sign of good health," she said.

Achilles smiled at her. "Thanks to you, I'm doing a lot better. I'm really indebted to you."

"Last night my sister sang as well as she did when she was young. Better, even. I figure we're even."

Although her statement puzzled Achilles at first, he quickly worked out that she was referring to the wish Dee had granted. Dee seemed pleased about it too, with a shy smile that transformed his face from plain to beautiful. Achilles hadn't seen him smile before, and he guessed it didn't happen often, even when the world wasn't ending.

After they finished their meal—and just as Achilles was wondering whether he had the energy to help wash up—there was a commotion outside. Jackie quickly ducked through the side door. When she returned a moment later, she didn't seem alarmed. "Your boss is here. And he brought… a friend?"

"Does his friend have big black wings, by any chance?"

"He sure does."

Grinning, Achilles stood. His feet hurt, but bearably so. "Let me go make some introductions."

"Wings?" Dee asked as they made their way outside. "Is it a… a bird shifter?"

"No such thing. Some sort of issue with the mass conversion." Honestly, Achilles didn't really understand the science behind shifters or anything else he dealt with on the job. He also didn't understand the science behind cell phones and airplanes, but he trusted them to work, just as he trusted shifters to change capably between their forms.

The sun pierced sharply through the cold morning air, making Achilles shiver despite his borrowed clothing. Seemingly all the members of the pack—some in human form and some as coyotes—were gathered in a circle around an SUV. Two figures waited beside the car.

One of them, tall, thin, and pale, wore old-fashioned wool trousers and a white button-up shirt. The other had bronze skin and small horns and wore nothing at all, his glossy black wings fanning gently behind him.

"Holy shit," Dee muttered, skidding to a halt.

But Achilles grabbed his arm and towed him along. "Allies. That's my boss and his partner. Neither of them is human, at least not entirely. I'd trust either of them with my life." He often didn't understand Grimes, just as he'd rarely understood the former chief, but it was like not comprehending the science behind the things in his life. He simply knew they worked.

Dee sort of dragged his feet but did come. The crowd parted to let Achilles, Dee, and Jackie pass.

"You look like shit, Spanos," was the first thing Grimes said.

"Thanks."

"I'm glad you're alive."

Achilles dipped his head. Then, mindful of etiquette, he turned to Jackie. "This is Charles Grimes, chief of the West Coast Bureau, and Tenrael, his partner. Chief, Tenrael, please meet Jackie of the Gerard Pack, and Dee Martell."

Tenrael gave Jackie a regal bow, and Grimes nodded toward her. "Ma'am. To be completely honest, I'm no longer chief of anything, although I'm continuing the Bureau's work. Do we have your permission to remain briefly on pack lands?"

Despite her casual clothing, Jackie looked every inch a leader as she nodded back. "We welcome you and grant you permission. We continue to consider ourselves your allies."

"I'm grateful for that, and also for the help you've given to my agent. His work is important to me. *He's* important to me. So thank you."

Maybe this was all just a load of political sweet talk, but Grimes's words warmed Achilles' heart. He was important.

Tenrael reached into the SUV's back seat via an open window, pulled out a paper accordion file, and held it toward Jackie. "A gift for you," he said with another bow. He was very good at bowing, managing to be graceful, powerful, and respectful all at once. The wings helped.

She took the file but seemed puzzled until Grimes explained. "That contains the contact information for a lawyer who'll be sympathetic to the pack's cause. She's a shifter herself, in fact—dog. The Bureau rescued her and several others from a really bad situation when she was a pup, and although she's never been an agent, she works on our behalf now and then."

"Dogs aren't bad," said Jackie. "We've had a few join the pack now and then. My cousin married one. But I dunno about lawyers."

"I understand. This is just in case you need an attorney. If encroachments on your land become intolerable, maybe she can help. The folder also contains some relevant paperwork about your land. Our tech guy was able to download it before we got shut down."

Yay, Becker, Achilles silently cheered. The guy could work wonders.

Now Jackie clutched the folder to her chest. "That's real nice of you."

"We owe you a great deal. The lawyer's fees are paid in advance, by the way, so no worries about that."

She smiled widely, and several members of the pack quietly expressed their approval as well. Achilles was impressed with the chief's ability to get this gift accomplished in a short period of time while so much else was going down. Or maybe it had been Tenrael's doing; he was an efficient demon.

Afterward there was a short conversation between Jackie and Grimes, mostly about how the pack was doing. Achilles lost the thread of it. Despite a decent night's sleep and good food, he wasn't in anywhere near top shape, and all of him hurt. Especially his feet. He wobbled a little and might have fallen if Tenrael hadn't darted forward to steady him.

Grimes looked slightly chagrined. "Sorry, Spanos. Ma'am, we're going to get out of your hair now. But thank you again, and good luck." He sighed. "We may need to call on your help again sometimes."

"We'll be glad to give it."

Achilles and Dee had just a moment or two to give their own thanks before Tenrael and Grimes herded them into the SUV's back seat. Tenrael took the front passenger spot, although he didn't seem especially pleased about it. Car seats were likely uncomfortable for people with wings.

It wasn't until they were out of the little valley and winding down the other side of a hill that Achilles realized that, aside from good-byes to Jackie, Dee hadn't spoken. And Grimes hadn't addressed him at all. Dee was folded in on himself, his gaze on the floor rather than the scenery, his expression bleak. Achilles wanted to talk to him about it… but not with their front seat audience.

"Where are we headed?" he asked Grimes instead.

"Not far. A temporary refuge where we can debrief and you can get some rest."

That sounded good, if not very specific. Then Achilles asked a question that had been haunting him since the previous evening. "The other agents…. Everyone else…. Are they safe now that the Bureau—"

"Nobody's safe now," Grimes interrupted. "But we're not in any more danger than we were before. The Bureau has always operated with minimal direction from Washington. We mostly took their money. And luckily, Townsend stuck a lot in reserve."

Of course he did. The former chief always seemed three moves ahead of everyone else. Until he got killed. Achilles suspected there had been something strategic about that as well.

He slumped in the back seat. He didn't like strategizing and wasn't good at it, as evidenced by his inability to get himself out of the recent mess. If Dee hadn't decided to help him, Achilles would still be in Dunn's talons, experiencing torture or worse. He might even have given in eventually and agreed to help her side, although he hoped that wouldn't have been the case.

"Are you ill?" Tenrael asked. He'd twisted in his seat to stare at Achilles with his intense red eyes.

Realizing that he was shivering again, Achilles tried to get hold of himself. "No. Just…. Sorry."

"You have been through great difficulties lately."

"You could say that. But, I mean, so have lots of people." Achilles couldn't meet that gaze anymore and turned to look out the window instead. But he could still feel Tenrael's scrutiny.

"Do you know the circumstances under which I met my master?" Tenrael asked.

"No." Bureau agents liked to gossip, so Achilles had heard plenty of stories about Grimes and Tenrael, but didn't know which—if any —were accurate. New recruits tended to be weirded out by the two of them, not to mention by the nature of their relationship: Tenrael referred to Grimes as his master and preferred to kneel at his feet when possible. But to Achilles, the devotion between the two of them had always been obvious, and he figured that if Tenrael and Grimes were comfortable with their bond and its power arrangement, then the hows and whys of it were nobody else's damn business.

"When my master found me, I was also undergoing great difficulties. I'm very old, Agent Spanos, and I have endured many things, but those years were…." Tenrael swallowed. But then Grimes murmured something to him that Achilles didn't catch, and Tenrael smiled and continued. "Those years were worth it for the joy I have experienced since then. But the point I wished to make is that I was changed by the things that happened to me. I am no longer the same being I was before. But this can be a good thing, yes?"

Psychological counseling from a demon—that was a new thing for Achilles. And he wasn't at all confident that he'd been improved by any recent events. However, he also didn't want to argue the point, so he simply shrugged. "Maybe."

That seemed to satisfy Tenrael, who faced forward again. But then Dee cleared his throat. "Um, excuse me? I don't know if I'm being rude by asking this, but what *are* you?"

Tenrael chuckled. "I am a demon."

After a few moments of speechless gaping, Dee shook his head rapidly. "I'm sorry, but did you say you're—"

"A demon. Yes."

"But…. I thought…. Aren't demons, uh, evil?"

Jesus. "Aren't humans?" Achilles snapped. "Ashley Dunn, for instance—is she a demon?"

"No, but—"

"Don't be a bigot. Judge a person by what they do, not whether they have horns or fangs."

Under other circumstances, Achilles might have been more patient with Dee. When Achilles had first joined the Bureau, he'd had many of those same biases; most new agents did, at least if they were human. But in Dee's case, he'd experienced human malevolence with his own eyes, and had been personally helped by coyote shifters. He should know better.

And also Achilles was tired and aching and, if he was perfectly frank with himself, scared shitless by the future. Patience wasn't currently on his agenda.

But napping was, so he closed his eyes and did his best to tune out the world.

* * *

ACHILLES STARTLED awake when the SUV came to a halt. The sun was high overhead, so they had likely been on the road for only a few hours. Although they were still in the middle of the desert, this landscape was different. Flatter, although with some peaks and mesas in the distance, and devoid of tall plants.

Grimes had parked in a gravel lot flanked by a pair of odd-looking buildings made of rounded stones. The buildings were each the size of a large house but irregularly shaped, with small windows placed seemingly at random. There were also several dozen colorful banners affixed to each of the houses. The banners contained irregular patterns of squiggles.

"What is this place?" he asked apprehensively.

Grimes opened the driver's door. "Refuge."

Whatever that meant.

Achilles dutifully got out of the car and limped after Grimes and Tenrael, Dee trailing behind him. When they neared the building on the right, a section of stones slid to the side, revealing an opening that took them into a dark, narrow hallway. Tenrael's wings brushed against the rock walls on both sides. If Achilles' feet hadn't been hurting so badly, he might have been slightly claustrophobic, but as it was, he mostly concentrated on forward momentum.

They took a sudden right and were in a large, sunlit room with tables and chairs in the center and a half-dozen simple beds along the walls. There was also a small kitchenette and an enormous television.

Oh, and an alien.

Achilles' life was weird enough that the sight of the extraterrestrial made him sigh with relief. He'd met these people once before and knew they could be trusted.

A couple of decades ago, when humans first started encountering this species, they called them orcs. They did bear a certain resemblance to the Tolkien creatures and, due to a cultural misunderstanding, had eaten several humans. Eventually, however, in a mission involving Con Becker and Isaac Molina, the orcs' true identities had been discovered: they were refugees from another planet who gained knowledge by consuming others. They'd simply been trying to assimilate to their new home. Luckily the Bureau was able to work with them to find less lethal ways of learning, and since then their presence had been benign.

"What the hell?" breathed Dee, who really ought to be getting used to this sort of thing by now.

Achilles shot him a glare. "I'll explain later. But they're friends, okay?"

Dee's nod was uncertain, but he held his tongue.

Perhaps for the sake of her guests, this alien had chosen to wear human clothing: a pair of black capri leggings and a loose emerald-hued shirt. No shoes, however; she probably couldn't, due to the large claws on her toes. Her smile revealed several rows of very sharp teeth.

"Welcome," she said, clawed hands held upright with the palms facing her. That was her people's first step when greeting someone, and Grimes, Tenrael, and Achilles mirrored her. As did Dee, albeit somewhat belatedly. She came forward for the next step, which involved exchanging a small cheek lick. Dee almost balked at that, but Achilles gave him a subtle poke and Dee went along with the program. When you thought about it, licking was only a small step away from cheek kissing, and lots of humans did that.

Formalities over, their hostess started a conversation with Tenrael in her language, which he apparently spoke well. That wasn't a huge surprise—languages were one of his specialties—but it was interesting to see that his talents extended to non-Earth tongues as well.

While they chatted, Grimes led Achilles and Dee to a cluster of armchairs and loveseats near the kitchenette. Achilles was grateful to get off his feet, and even more thankful when Grimes brought him a glass of water.

Dee couldn't hold back any longer. "Who *is* that? And where are we?"

"We have more pressing matters to discuss," said Grimes. Then he relented slightly. "Our hosts are immigrants from a distant planet. Their home was destroyed, and they—"

"Aliens?" Dee hissed.

Achilles, who was next to him, gave a kick. Which hurt his already-sore foot but also shut Dee up.

Grimes looked pained, like a schoolteacher dealing with naughty students. "There are only a few hundred of them, living in small settlements in several countries. They mostly want to keep to themselves and preserve what they can of their culture. This particular group was given special license to homestead on tribal land in exchange for sharing some of the technologies they brought with them. I guess the tribal leaders are working with the immigrants to find more efficient methods of storing energy and generating water."

That was a long speech from Grimes, who rarely gave them. Quite a bit of what he said was news to Achilles and would have been interesting to explore if other matters weren't more important. But he did have a question. "So what's this place?"

"Their home. They live primarily underground, but they keep this space for visitors from the tribe. And now they're letting us use it.

Spanos, you can stay here until you're fully recovered. Now tell me what the hell happened. You start, Martell."

Dee had clearly never done this before; his account tended to ramble and stray, and Grimes had to ask a lot of questions. The farther that Dee got into the story, the grimmer the chief looked. Tenrael quietly joined them midway through—the alien had left the room by then—and knelt beside Grimes, expression stony.

Finally, Dee got to the point where Achilles showed up—in chains—and Grimes held up a hand to stop him. "Spanos, can you please speak now?"

"Sure." He began with showing up at Dee's place in Portland and discovering him missing, explained how Henry and Becker had helped him track Dee, and then described his initial encounter with Dunn, when she'd promptly sent him packing.

Grimes' scowl had grown even deeper. "She could manipulate the will of a Bureau agent so easily?"

"Well, mine, yeah. Maybe if someone stronger had faced her—"

"You're as strong as any agent."

Achilles paused at the unexpected and unsolicited praise. He hadn't thought that the chief considered him especially useful. "Anyway, she didn't exactly manipulate my will. I mean, I *wanted* to leave. I'd already tried to quit, remember? She just gave me an extra push."

"But you returned to her."

"When I realized what she'd done, yeah." Achilles considered for a moment. "I was really pissed off at being manipulated. And really concerned about what was going on. I shouldn't have gone by myself, but...."

"But you knew that we're shorthanded and you felt the need to act quickly."

Once again, Achilles paused. This was empathy, coming from Charles Grimes. Not that Grimes was an asshole, but he wasn't exactly the touchy-feely type. Hell, Tenrael was generally better at relating emotionally to agents than Grimes was, and wasn't that weird.

The next part of the story was hard to tell. "Anyway, I did go back.

And she… zapped me. Just sort of wiggled her fingers and I was in so much pain I couldn't even scream."

Tenrael spoke for the first time in a while. "A similar thing happened to agents Clark and Gale last year."

"Yeah? And did they get transported to some type of terrifying liminal space? 'Cause that's what happened next."

Grimes paled. Which was quite a feat, considering how white his complexion normally was. His breathing grew harsh. "Liminal space? Explain," he barked.

So Achilles did, in as much detail as possible, even though he would have preferred not to think about it at all. Grimes listened, his lips pressed so thin it must have hurt. Achilles didn't understand why this particular part of the tale upset the chief so much, but he continued. He didn't gloss over Dee's initial acquiescence with the torture, but he also made sure to describe how Dee had facilitated his escape, likely putting himself in grave danger.

There was heavy silence. Achilles was exhausted; Dee was hunched over as if expecting a blow. Grimes and Tenrael stared at each other silently, as if they could communicate telepathically. For all that Achilles knew, maybe they could.

Then Grimes abruptly stood. "I need to talk to some people. Both of you stay put. Get some rest. There's food over there." He pointed at the kitchenette.

He and Tenrael started to leave, but Dee surprised them all by jumping up and planting himself in front of them. "Hang on. All of this started because you guys were so eager to get your hands on me. And now you've got me, but you're acting like I'm barely an afterthought, and you won't let me ask any questions."

"Bigger fish to fry," Grimes said through clenched teeth.

Dee threw up his hands. "I get it! End of the world as we know it. And I fucked up big time. But Jesus, I can grant *wishes*, and I don't know why, and there are demons and aliens and werewolves, and I don't understand…." His voice tapered off and he covered his face with his hands.

It was possible that Grimes' expression softened an infinitesimal amount. "I know why you can grant wishes. One of my agents has been doing research, and she's reasonably certain she knows what you are."

Exhaustion forgotten, Achilles leaned forward. This should be interesting.

Dee uncovered his face and stared at Grimes. His expression was a study in mixed emotions: hope, fear, anxiety, eagerness. "What am I?" he whispered.

Grimes shrugged as if it weren't particularly important. "She's pretty sure you're a genie."

CHAPTER 16

A *genie.*

Chief Grimes said some things after that, but Dee couldn't hear through the roaring in his ears. Grimes and Tenrael swept past him, but Dee remained rooted in place, his brain short-circuiting. A moment or two later, Achilles gingerly walked over—Dee noticed, even through his fugue—and led him to an armchair, which Dee collapsed into.

For what might have been a long time, nobody said anything. Finally Dee managed a few words. "Like, in a bottle? And blue-skinned? Or with the pink crop top and gauzy, um, harem pants?" He realized that he wasn't making much sense, but then his life, his very existence, didn't make much sense anymore. Not that he'd ever followed a traditional path to begin with, but somehow over the past year he'd veered from odd into pure fantasy. Or horror—he wasn't certain which.

"It's that guy's fault!" he shouted suddenly, startling Achilles, who'd looked ready to doze off. He probably met genies all the time.

"What guy?" Achilles asked groggily.

"The… guy with the New York accent. And Yiddish."

Achilles nodded. "Ah. Abe Ferencz. How is anything his fault?"

"I was doing fine until he showed up at my door." That was an exaggeration, because Dee had not been doing fine. He'd been flat broke, in danger of getting evicted, and out of weed. But still.

"That's how it goes. Life flings shit at you like a pissed-off chimpanzee. But Ferencz didn't make you what you are—you know that, right? The world's a mess right now, and sooner or later *someone* was gonna come knocking."

Dee was aware of all that, but he really wanted to place the blame somewhere, and it didn't seem fair to dump it on Achilles, given his recent experiences. Dee slumped back and massaged his temples. "Fine. I mean, totally not fine, but…. Tell me about genies."

"I only know about the Disney one."

"What?" Dee stared at him in disbelief. "But you're a Bureau agent."

"Sure, but I didn't know you guys really existed. They never mentioned genies during training, and I've never met one before. That I know of, anyway." Achilles didn't seem particularly concerned. "Do you have family you could talk to?"

Dee couldn't help but scoff. "I haven't seen Mom since I was a little kid, and…. She could grant wishes too. Dad OD'd when I was thirteen. As far as I know, he didn't have any special powers. Do you think maybe he was human? Can genies and humans…"—he waved his hands vaguely—"interbreed?"

"No idea. But humans can and do have children with other NHSs. Shifters, for instance. The chief's an example of that—one of his parents was an angel."

An angel. Dee's capacity for shock was depleted by now, and anyway it wasn't important at the moment what Grimes was. But Dee still couldn't help but comment. "He doesn't seem all that angelic."

Achilles laughed. "No. But then he's the only angel I've ever met, so maybe they're all like that. More into scowling than harping." He shrugged. "Lots of lore is BS. You certainly don't live in a bottle, and you granted Dunn a lot more than three wishes."

Good points. But then, Dee had no way of knowing right now what *was* real. It did occur to him, however, that the genies in stories were often bound to human masters. Dee had never had a master, unless you counted Ashley, and he'd been able to escape her clutches once he made an effort. Yet while he was with her, he'd experienced an odd comfort in being… used. More than comfort: pleasure. Like a border collie that had finally been given access to a herd of sheep.

"I can't think about this right now." He stood and looked toward the kitchenette. "Are you hungry?"

"I could eat."

To Dee's considerable relief, Achilles didn't press him for more information. In fact, Achilles might have even dozed off while Dee dug around in cupboards to see what was available. It turned out that there were no animal products, but he found pasta and tomato sauce and cooked up a couple plates of spaghetti.

Achilles didn't seem inclined to walk to the table, so they ate while sitting in armchairs instead.

"Thanks," said Achilles when he was done, setting the empty plate on the floor beside his chair. "That hit the spot."

Dee knew they should be discussing his newly discovered identity or the impending apocalypse. Or both. But he didn't want to talk about either right now, so he sidetracked instead. "How come you haven't called anyone except Chief Grimes?"

"What do you mean?" Achilles asked through a yawn.

"I don't know if the, um, aliens have phones. Oh gods, that's a movie, isn't it? But anyway, the coyotes did. And your boss must have one too. But you haven't used them except to call him."

"Who do you think I should be calling?"

"Family? Friends? You were missing for several days, and they must be worried."

Sadness flashed across Achilles' handsome features and then was gone. "The only people who might be worried about me work for the Bureau, and I'm sure word's gotten around that I'm not dead yet."

Dee decided to ignore that ominous final word and focus on the rest. "Are agents required to cut themselves off from the outside world?"

"We're federal agents, Dee, not monks. We *were* federal agents, anyway." A sigh. "Look, it's hard for us to have close outside connections. Not forbidden, just hard. We can't really talk much about our job to most outsiders, we travel a lot, and we're often in the kind of dangerous situations that would make loved ones freak out. Also, connections like that, well, I guess they can be a source of strength, but they're also a vulnerability. Most of the people that get recruited are like me—unconnected."

Dee was unconnected too, and he had always thought of that as an anomaly. Now he felt an unexpected kinship with Achilles. "Did you ever have family? A girlfriend or wife?"

"My parents were immigrants. The rest of the family stayed in Greece, so it was just us. They died a couple of decades ago, and my sister and I, we never got along. And if you must know, I did have a fairly serious boyfriend. Orson. But that was a long time ago. We broke up, and he died a few weeks later." Achilles said all of this without showing any emotion, but his delivery was almost too flat, as if he were tamping down hard on whatever he felt—or didn't want to feel.

But Dee couldn't resist another attempt. "And no boyfriends since then? A handsome guy like you?"

Now Achilles gave him an odd look before answering. "I told you —that's really hard in the Bureau. Most agents end up with other agents, or at least someone who's… a part of our world, you know? Like, one man who headed our lab for years, his partner is a Sasquatch. They're retired now."

Dee wondered if being a genie—or at least half genie—qualified him as a part of Achilles' world. But he didn't ask. Instead he gathered the dishes and took them to the sink. After he finished washing up, he found Achilles asleep on one of the beds.

Dee sat down in the armchair and clicked on the TV.

* * *

A few hours later, a demon entered the room. Tenrael, of course, with his magnificent dark wings and scary-ass red eyes. He was still naked, which nobody else had commented on or even seemed to notice. Maybe demons never wore clothing. A shirt would be nearly impossible with those wings, but pants would work. Anyway, he was intimidating as hell.

Dee suppressed a slightly hysterical laugh at his own unintended pun.

"I apologize for neglecting you," Tenrael said to Dee, but quietly, since Achilles was apparently still asleep. "The news you brought us has raised pressing issues."

Fair enough. "That's okay. This place is comfortable." The chair he was sitting in, for instance, was amazing.

Tenrael set a blue plastic box onto a table. "First aid," he explained, then gestured toward Achilles. "If he requires more intensive medical care, we can send for a doctor."

Dee glanced at the sleeping form and then shook his head. "I think he'll be okay. I mean, I'm not a paramedic or nurse or anything, but…." He let that thought trail into obscurity. It was a little hard to converse with Tenrael.

But as a new thought struck him, he straightened in his chair. "Hey, uh, do you happen to know anything about genies? Because I don't."

That was compassion in those demon eyes; Dee was sure of it. And because of that, he didn't flinch away when Tenrael approached and crouched down in front of him. Close up, Tenrael wasn't any less frightening or less impressive, but he was somehow more real. A *person* who had, according to his own account, endured some awful things… and survived. Had even fallen in love.

"I have met genies a mere handful of times over the millennia. They have always been few and reclusive, and my business did not intersect with theirs."

Those two sentences raised a whole host of questions, but Dee tried to concentrate on the most immediate matter. "Are they evil?"

"No more or less than humans. Like humans, genies may be led by others into acts that are immensely harmful. But also like humans, they may choose a more admirable path."

"My… my powers…. How strong are they, really? What are the limits? What difference does it make that I'm only half genie?"

"That I cannot tell you. And I'm afraid my master has directed our researcher to concentrate her efforts on other issues at the moment."

Dee nodded in understanding. His identity crisis didn't outweigh doomsday. But it was time for a confession. "I'd like to help you guys. I really would. But I'm not a hero like Achilles. I'm afraid I'll be tempted to do bad things again." No, worse than that. "I'm afraid I'll give in to that temptation."

Before responding, Tenrael seemed to think for a moment. "Everyone I have known at the Bureau has possessed darker urges, myself and my master most definitely included. Quite a few of them have followed those urges at times, sometimes with disastrous results. But this is nothing more than what human philosophers call free will. It is the daily battle each of us must face, and we must win that battle before we can begin to fight larger ones. I believe that free will is one of the things that makes the world beautiful. It means every single person has the power to help tip the balance toward good."

Tenrael, apparently satisfied with his speech—which Dee was going to need to mull over for a long time—stood and patted Dee's shoulder. Then he turned and left the room, folding his wings tightly as he passed through the doorway.

"I'm not a hero," said a sleepy voice.

Dee saw that Achilles was still lying down, but now he was looking at Dee.

"Sorry," said Dee. "Didn't mean to wake you."

"Yeah, 'cause I've gotten only, what, fifteen or sixteen hours of sleep in the last twenty-four?" Achilles sat up, started to stretch, and winced. "Would you mind bringing me the first aid kit?"

Dee brought it over, along with a glass of water, which Achilles downed in one long gulp. "Thanks."

"You are a hero, though. You save people. Save, uh, NHSs. You're trying to save the world."

Achilles scoffed and ran fingers through already wild hair. "I do my job. I'm okay at it—other agents are way better. I've fucked up royally a few times."

"You didn't give in to Ashley under torture."

"I might've, eventually." But Achilles looked pleased at the acknowledgement. Then he ran a palm over his bristly chin. "Gods, I probably look like a Sasquatch's runty cousin. Do you think you could find me a razor?"

Dee went off to root through cupboards, thoughts of heroes tumbling in his head.

CHAPTER 17

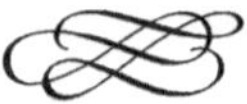

Neither Grimes nor Tenrael returned that evening, although aliens came by a couple of times to make sure everything was okay. That made Achilles want to know what they called themselves—*aliens* felt slightly rude and derogatory—but he couldn't really ask since he didn't speak their language. Anyway, the bed was great, there was plenty of food, and Dee didn't seem to mind waiting on him hand and foot. Due to the combination of meals, plenty of sleep, and the first aid kit, Achilles felt fairly decent come nightfall, and he joined Dee on a small couch in front of the TV.

"There were big protests everywhere today," said Dee as he flicked through channels. "I saw it on the news."

"That's heartening."

"The president and his people, are they allied with Ashley's group, do you think?"

Achilles shrugged. "Dunno. It's possible that they've signed on to the same program as her. It's also possible that they have no clue about her gang, and their BS is just helping to feed the fire. Or maybe there are a couple of key advisors who are in on it and the president is clueless, a handy means to their end. Same results in any case."

"There are a couple of his buddies that I'd be willing to bet are like Ashley."

"I'm inclined to agree," said Achilles. He'd never paid much attention to politics, preferring to keep his attention on things that he could influence in some way. He understood NHSs better than he did those people in DC.

Dee was quiet for a while, although Achilles had the sense that his mind wasn't truly on *The Drew Barrymore Show*, which was what he'd paused on. Luke Wilson was the guest. After a while, Dee rubbed the back of his neck. "That extraterrestrial who greeted us, did she— Um, are they a she? And if so, is she pregnant? The way that they sort of cradled their belly a few times made me think so."

Achilles remembered what he'd been taught. "Like humans, they have multiple genders and multiple sexes. Individuals shift genders and sexes at various points in their life, although I have no idea what the rules are for that. If there are any. And I don't speak the language, so I don't know the proper terminology. I think it's more complicated for them to get pregnant than it is for us. Takes more than two to tango. But there is one sex that carries the fetuses and breast-feeds them when they're born, and the Bureau tends to use she/her pronouns for them. And yeah, I think she is." The idea made him smile; it was a sign that the survival efforts were succeeding.

But Dee was frowning. "If Ashley's group wins, our hosts here, they'll be wiped out too, right? Not just humans?"

"A lot of species will be—human, NHS, and otherwise."

"That sucks."

Achilles was inclined to agree with that as well.

Which turned his thoughts in a pretty depressing direction. He was casting about for something cheerier to talk about when he noticed that Dee was staring at him rather intently.

"What?" Achilles demanded.

Dee's cheeks colored but he didn't look away. "You're really good-looking."

"You mentioned that before." Achilles tried hard not to blush in response. "Is that a problem?"

"No. And you're gay."

"Is *that* a problem?"

"No."

This was a weird conversation, but it beat thinking about the end of the world. "Then why are you bringing these things up?"

"Because...." Chewing his lip, Dee looked down at the remote in his hand. He kept his gaze trained downward as he continued. "I'm not.... I can appreciate a pretty face of any gender. But I hardly ever want to get physical with anyone. I mean, I've had sex before. Maybe a dozen times? Mostly because it seemed like something I should want to do, but the reality was pretty meh."

Achilles used to enjoy sex a lot, although in recent years it hadn't often felt as if it were worth the hassle. So he could sort of understand. But he didn't get why Dee had raised the issue. "To each his own," Achilles said.

"Sure. Except that now I, uh...." Dee swallowed audibly. "I keep thinking about what it would be like to kiss you." He faced Achilles again, scowling. "Have you put a spell on me or something?"

Bursting out laughing hurt, and it probably wasn't the best response, but Achilles couldn't stop himself. "Are you *serious*?"

"You can't believe I'm thinking about kissing you?"

"No, that's plausible, if a little unlikely under the circumstances. I meant the spell part. You're the magic guy. I'm the most ordinary human on the planet. I can't even do card tricks."

Dee made an exasperated noise. "Then how come I want to kiss you?"

He was so serious about this that Achilles tried to be too, even though this was a truly dumb thing to be worrying about when everything else was falling apart. "Maybe it's due to the Florence Nightingale effect? The fact of almost dying tends to get the juices flowing. Or maybe it's simply because I'm really hot." Achilles waved away Dee's protest at the last part. "Look. If you want to try a kiss and see if it gets your motor running, go for it. Just watch out for my bruises and things."

In fact, the experiment sounded like a good idea to Achilles. Well, not a *good* idea precisely, because even a hint of a fling was probably unwise with someone who'd almost helped end the world and who'd also just found out he was a genie. But common sense be damned. Dee was good-looking, and sleeping in his arms had felt nice—and weirdly safe. Also, nobody had kissed Achilles in a long time, and for all he knew, he might die before sunup.

"Carpe diem," Achilles said by way of explanation.

"Right." Dee took a deep breath and dove in for what Achilles expected to be a harsh and messy kiss.

But it wasn't. Dee was gentle about it, at first barely brushing their lips together. And even though their bodies were angled awkwardly and aches still echoed in Achilles' body, the contact felt good. There was something absurdly sweet and innocent about it, as if they were a pair of teenagers trying this for the first time, not a middle-aged ex-agent and a genie.

Dee pulled back slightly, eyes wide with surprise. "Oh."

"Oh?"

"I liked that."

Achilles smiled. "Me too."

"I want to try it again."

"By all means." Achilles spread his arms to demonstrate acceptance.

The second kiss was firmer and more lingering but still tender. Lips closed, no tongue. And this time Dee tentatively reached up to thread his fingers through Achilles' hair. That particular kind of contact had always been Achilles' little kink, sending him from first gear straight to third, as if his scalp was an erogenous zone.

"How do you manage," Dee asked, kiss ended but face still close, "to have such soft hair after days of ill treatment in the desert?"

"Maybe it's my superpower. You grant wishes, I have good hair. Notice too that's it's not thinning or going gray, and my hairline's not receding."

It was one of the first times Achilles had heard Dee laugh, and it was nice to know that he was responsible for that. Just then an epiphany hit Achilles. "Dumb jokes are a form of hope. So are soft kisses and fresh shaves and bowls of pasta. I think they all count, they all help. In a small way, sure, but if you accumulate enough grains of sand you can build a giant dune."

"Or create a whole desert." Dee waved toward a window, although it was too dark outside for the landscape to be visible.

"Deserts are surprisingly diverse in terms of flora and fauna. A fair number of NHSs make their homes in deserts too."

"Yeah." Dee moved back a little but didn't break eye contact. "Is sex hope too?"

"It can be, sure. There's a reason people get horny after facing and surviving death. Was that a proposition?"

"Maybe? Would you even consider having sex with someone who's not, um, human?"

This time Achilles managed to suppress the laugh. "Not a problem. I've been with a few friendly NHSs over the years. There was this vampire once, for instance—"

"Male?"

Taken aback, Achilles blinked. "Uh, yeah. I may not be picky about species but I'm at least a Kinsey five."

"How do vampires get hard-ons if they're undead and their blood isn't circulating?"

"I have no idea. If we survive all of this, and once things calm down, you can ask our archivist, Diana Afolabi. She probably has a file on the subject somewhere."

Dee seemed to mull this over for a moment before giving his head a small shake, perhaps to clear his thoughts. "Okay. So fucking a genie?"

"Never tried it before. Would be amenable." But when Achilles shifted slightly, the resulting twinge was enough to reconnect him with reality. "But not tonight. I'm not physically up to it. Besides, I'm not sure how our hosts feel about that sort of thing and I don't want to be rude."

Dee looked disappointed, and Achilles didn't want him to think he was just making up excuses. So he patted Dee's knee, even though it hurt Achilles' chewed-up wrist. "If we come through this and you still want me, I'm yours. It'll give us an extra incentive to win."

"Hope for sex is hope?"

"Definitely."

Later that night, as they lay in separate beds, Achilles regretted being an adult about this. He heard Dee's soft breaths and remembered what those little puffs of air had felt like on his nape. Gods, Dee was *warm*, like a comfortable seat in front of a crackling fire, like a bellyful of hot soup. Like a fever.

Achilles sighed, rolled over to face the wall, and tried to sleep.

* * *

"You look better this morning," Grimes pronounced, sweeping into the room as Achilles and Dee ate breakfast. Dee had grumbled about a lack of sausage, eggs, and cheese, but had made a tall stack of pancakes instead, along with sliced strawberries and scrambled tofu with salsa. Achilles was definitely making up for those missed meals.

But now the chief and Tenrael were hovering nearby, so Achilles pushed back his plate. "I feel better."

"Good. I don't think it's safe for you to go home now, but you can stay here indefinitely, or we have some other safe houses if you'd prefer to be closer to civilization."

"I'd *prefer* to be on assignment," said Achilles, fully aware that he'd attempted to resign from the Bureau just a short time ago.

Grimes looked at him with something that might have been sympathy, and when he spoke, his voice was softer than usual. "I know. But you need more time to heal, and things are, well, a little chaotic at the moment."

"Is this your polite way of telling me I'm fucking useless?" Achilles wouldn't normally have been quite so blunt, but technically Grimes wasn't his chief anymore. And whatever patience Achilles had once possessed was long gone.

"I'm not a polite man."

They glared at each other for a moment, but Achilles was the first to back down, in part because he knew he wasn't at his best. He wanted to be a help, not a liability.

Dee, who'd been watching this interchange with interest, spoke into the silence. "What about me? Do I go to the safe house too?" Judging from his expression, he knew what the answer was going to be. Achilles knew too. Dee was potentially too valuable to sit on a shelf.

"You're coming to San Francisco with us," Grimes announced.

"Why?"

"We need to ascertain exactly what you're capable of."

Dee set his jaw. "I'm not going to do any testing. No floods, no houses in the desert, no snakes."

"No," said Grimes, shaking his head. "None of that. Our archivist is conducting more research on genies and hopes to be done soon. We'll go from there."

That answer seemed to mollify Dee a bit, and although he still looked unhappy, his posture relaxed. But Achilles, who was clearly not a part of this particular discussion, decided he wasn't in the mood to keep his mouth shut. "What is it you want him to do? Because I'm guessing he can't just give you world peace or something like that."

Grimes didn't look as though he intended to answer, which would be just like him. Tenrael, however, had been standing slightly behind him, wings furled. Now he took a step forward and set a hand on Grimes's shoulder. "You should tell them."

Everyone was silent during what surely qualified as a pregnant pause. Tenrael didn't remove his hand. They were quite a sight: the thin, pale man in the suit; the darker more muscular demon wearing nothing at all. Both of them quietly fierce and, in Achilles' estimation, as solid as the ground beneath his feet. Maybe more so.

Finally, Grimes gave a jerky little nod. "Last year, Agents Clark and Gale encountered a... being who we believe was allied with Ashley Dunn and her compatriots. During this encounter they learned that our enemies are capable of creating portals between places. Also during this encounter, Gale sensed an entity trapped and held captive between these portals. We believe you were also trapped in such a space, Spanos. Perhaps the same one, but more likely another space of the same nature."

Achilles shuddered. He didn't want to think about that place. Being there had been worse than the physical torture.

"For the past months, Clark and Gale have been trying to find this captive or gain access to them so they can be freed."

"Oh!" said Achilles, remembering. "Ralph Crespo was helping them."

"Yes, but they haven't been successful. What I'd like is for you, Mr. Martell, to get me there."

"And back," Tenrael added gently.

Light dawned in Achilles' beleaguered brain. "You want to wish yourself into Dunn's black hole so you can do a rescue mission."

"Yes."

Dee spoke up. "Why? I mean, I get it—this person is stuck somewhere awful. But you guys keep saying how busy you are, and I've seen for myself that there's a Big Nasty waiting to take a chomp out of everyone. And you seem like a pretty important guy. Why use limited resources and risk your life over one person?"

That was an excellent question, and Achilles gave Dee an approving look.

Grimes's scowl deepened. "Because," he said, "I suspect that captive is my father."

CHAPTER 18

$\mathcal{D}$ee was trying very hard to keep up with the conversation. It wasn't that he was especially stupid, although he'd never claimed to be a genius. It was simply that everyone else in the room was accustomed to missions and nefarious plots and forays into weirdness, and Dee wasn't.

Anyway, although he now understood what Chief Grimes wanted, the father part confused him.

But Achilles didn't seem befuddled. He leapt to his feet, winced, but remained standing, fury plastered on his face. "What the fuck?" he bellowed. "The world is teetering on the edge, what's left of the Bureau is short-staffed and in disarray, and *you're* worried about a family reunion? *That's* what you're using limited resources on? Look, that black hole place sucks, but not as bad as mass genocide. Oh, and by the way, Dee's not an agent, so he's not at your beck and call for personal service."

"You're not an agent anymore either," Grimes snarled back. "None of us are. And I don't need you to—"

"Master." Tenrael's hand was on Grimes's shoulder again, and although he'd spoken quietly, his voice held a definite firmness that contrasted with the subservient term.

Grimes turned his head to look at him. "What?"

"Perhaps you should explain who your father is."

"All right," said Grimes in a considerably calmer tone. He reached over to stroke Tenrael's feathers, either to thank him or to calm himself. Maybe both.

And as Achilles, with a disgruntled expression, retook his chair and Grimes seemed to collect his thoughts, a realization hit Dee. A person could submit to another not out of fear but out of love and the desire to submit. And the relationship between those people, rather than involving the brute imposition of power, could be a delicate dance of strength and weakness. Contrary to initial appearances, Grimes and Tenrael weren't unequal; they'd found a way to strike a balance.

And hadn't Dee been told already that it was all about balance?

A yearning encompassed Dee with such ferocity that, had he been standing, he would have fallen to his knees. As it was, he had to swallow a moan and, briefly at least, squeeze his eyes shut. *That* was what he wanted—no, what he *needed*: to have a master who loved him and who Dee loved back. Someone who wouldn't just use him, as Ashley had, but who would respect him. Someone who would help Dee be a better and more complete version of himself, and who would be similarly helped by him.

How had Dee gone four decades without knowing this about himself?

But Grimes was about to speak, and this wasn't the best time for earth-shaking self-revelations.

"My father is an angel," Grimes said finally. "I never met him, and my mother never spoke of him. I know his identity only because of certain things I inherited from him."

Dee thought he might be referring to his extremely pale coloring or his oddly-hued eyes. But then Grimes shrugged out of his suit jacket, letting it fall negligently to the floor, and then swiftly removed his tie, shirt, and undershirt. When he turned his back to them, Dee saw a pair of long, ugly scars, red lines that paralleled his spine.

Achilles caught on first. "You had wings." His anger had fled.

"Not like Ten's. Mine were small. Useless. I had them removed when I was eighteen. But I know they were once there, and I know what they mean."

When Grimes turned toward them, his face was set, no emotions visible. "My father disappeared before I was born. For a long time, I assumed he'd deserted my mother. And me. I was furious at him because of this. And then one day, circa.... Christ, Ten, when was it?"

"It was 1942," Tenrael answered without hesitating.

"Right. In 1942, that bastard Townsend gifted me with one of his cryptic pronouncements. I remember the exact words. We were talking about wounded angels needing time to heal—I'd been hurt on a mission—and he said, 'Maybe what looks like abandonment might, in fact, be something else.'"

"So he knew what happened to your father?" Dee asked, now caught up in the story. He also wanted to ask how old Grimes was, but didn't.

"Hell if I know. He wouldn't explain himself then or in any of the following decades. I've tried to let it go, but as you might imagine, it's always been at the back of my head."

Dee could imagine this perfectly well. One of his parents had disappeared too, although under marginally less mysterious circumstances, and he'd spent a good chunk of his life wondering what had happened to her. Was she alive somewhere, or was nothing left of her but crumbling bones? Had she regretted abandoning him? Had she planned to return for him someday?

"How do you know that the prisoner who was sensed by the agent is your father?" Dee asked.

"I don't. It's conjecture. A hunch." Grimes spread his arms. "Yet I know it's him. And Spanos, this isn't me wanting to meet my father. Well, I suppose there's some of that too. But I've been waiting over a century to meet him, and I could wait more. He's an *angel*, though. Not half like me. Imagine how valuable he could be to our cause—or how dangerous he could be if the other side were able to use him."

Of course, Dee had no idea what angels were capable of. He wasn't even sure what they truly were, and whether they were literally holy creatures like in religious texts or just another kind of NHS. Tenrael, after all, was a demon, but he wasn't trying to drag anyone to the depths of hell. Assuming hell existed.

But maybe it didn't matter whether angels were superheroes. Because Dee had been told that the balance was precarious. It might take nothing more than a small breeze to tip things irrevocably one way or the other.

Before he could speak up—and he wasn't sure what he was going to say anyway—Achilles sighed. "He's been in that place since before you were born?"

"Perhaps," Grimes said.

"How long is that?"

"I was born in 1897."

While Dee did the math, Achilles swore under his breath. His complexion, normally warm, had gone sickly pale. "Almost a hundred thirty years of… nothingness? I guess maybe an angel could survive that physically. But what about his mind?"

"I don't know," Grimes said quietly.

This was a lot more uncertainty than Dee was comfortable with. Nobody knew for sure whether Grimes's father was held captive in the black hole. If he was, nobody knew whether he'd be willing to help, and if so, what he could do. And to top things off, it seemed uncertain that he'd possess the mental capacity to do anything at all.

Oh, and even assuming everything was great with the angel, Dee had no idea whether his own powers were strong enough for someone to wish their way into—and out of—the black hole.

But hadn't both Abe Ferencz and Achilles lectured Dee about the power of hope? It was time for Dee to hope, dammit. Possibly for the first time in his life.

"I'll do my best to help," he announced.

Everyone stared at him. And a funny thing happened: they all looked at him with relief and admiration. They—a hero, a half-angel, and a frigging demon—were regarding him as if he were someone worthy. Dee sat straighter in his chair, confident for one of the first times in his life that he'd made the right decision.

Well, that kiss the night before had been the right decision too. He was also sure of that.

Grimes gave him a small smile. Dee had the definite impression that the guy smiled very rarely, but this one seemed genuine. "Thank you, Mr. Martell."

"You might as well call me Dee. But you know my real name is Damnation, right?"

"Were either of your parents capable of foreseeing the future?"

"I doubt it. They'd both have made better choices if they could."

Grimes smiled again. "Then we won't assume that your name is a prophecy."

"I'd like to assume the same about my name, please," Achilles chimed in. Dee must have looked puzzled, because Achilles explained. "In the *Iliad*, the Fates say that Achilles will live either a long uneventful life and be forgotten after he dies, or a short one where he's remembered as a hero. I'd prefer Option C."

Dee, who had no clue why his parents had saddled him with Damnation, now wondered what Achilles' parents had been thinking. Was it a common name among Greeks even nowadays, a nod to their heritage, or a wish for their son's future? Dee might ask him sometime, if he got a chance.

In the meantime, he needed to say something else. "There's a complication. We're not at all sure I have enough juice to grant your wish. If I can't do it at all, I guess we'll figure that out pretty quickly. But what if I get you there and then the magic sort of fizzles out and you're trapped?"

Grimes frowned. "I'm willing to risk—"

"Master. You do great harm to our cause if you cannot return. We need you. *I* need you as well."

"Jesus," Grimes muttered. "Okay, then Dee can give me two wishes, one for each leg of the trip."

Dee had already considered this. "I've never granted someone more than one wish at a time. Ashley tried to do a couple of doubles, just small things, and it didn't work. I'm guessing that transporting you to the black hole is not a small thing."

"Then give me a one-way ticket and I'll figure something out when I'm there."

"Your father is an angel and he's had over a century to figure something out, but he's still there. Apparently."

"I don't care!" Grimes snapped. "I'm not going to just walk away from this. I can't. I'll—"

Achilles got to his feet again. "What if someone else wishes that the chief—and the prisoner—would be zapped back here?"

"Unlikely to work," said Dee. "It's really hard for a wisher to affect a third party so directly, and when they try, the results aren't pretty." He was thinking specifically of several love charms gone very wrong, to such an extent that he'd refused to make any more even when he was broke.

"Well, fuck," said Achilles, which summed things up succinctly.

Dee, however, had a solution. "I'll go with the chief."

Now everyone looked shocked. Dee was slightly stunned too, even though he'd made the decision himself just a few moments ago. He was not the type to throw himself at danger. But he didn't regret making the offer.

Achilles limped over to Dee's chair and squatted so he could look into his eyes. "You don't need to atone for past sins. It doesn't work that way. And Dee, you do *not* want to go to that place."

"I don't want to," Dee agreed with a sigh. "But I'm going to. And not to atone. It's the right thing to do, and I want to help. I really do." He chuckled. "Maybe I'll be the one with the short but storied life."

Achilles stood up straight and looked away, as if the entire subject pained him. Surely he couldn't be that concerned about Dee's welfare. Dee was nothing to him... even though Dee was slowly coming to accept that Achilles was definitely not nothing to him.

And then Achilles crossed his arms and made a soft grunt. "Okay, well, not to steal Dee's thunder or anything. But Chief, you're staying put. I'm joining Dee for the rescue operation."

CHAPTER 19

Interestingly, both Grimes and Dee loudly opposed Achilles' plan to dive into the black hole, but not because they thought he'd fuck things up. Grimes kept insisting that he couldn't ask anybody else to undertake such a hazardous mission, and Dee kept saying that Achilles was being a reckless idiot. To which Achilles replied, in turn, "You're not asking, I'm telling," and "Takes one to know one."

The only one who didn't say anything at all was Tenrael, who stood there with his wings slowly fanning, his red eyes bright. Only when the three-way argument had devolved into snarls and curses did Tenrael step into the middle, his arms held out to silence them.

"Agent Spanos's plan is the most logical. He is the only person we know with experience in this so-called black hole, so he will be less disoriented and quicker to act when he arrives there. And Charles, your skills would be put to better use by continuing to organize what remains of the Bureau."

"Also, I'm more expendable," Achilles added, almost cheerfully.

But Tenrael shook his head. "Nobody is extraneous or expendable."

Grimes swore once more, but the wind was clearly gone from his sails, and Achilles sat down again, trying to suppress a triumphant grin. Winning meant that he would willingly return to the worst place he'd ever been, and quite possibly something awful would happen to him. He felt pleased nonetheless.

"Let's go," he said to Dee. "What's something you can use as a charm?" He looked around for something suitably small, but before he had a chance to find anything, it was Grimes's turn to cross his arms.

"Not now. Give yourself another day to heal. And in the meantime maybe Agent Afolabi can find useful information about genies. Anything to make success more likely."

Everyone agreed that this made sense. Grimes and Tenrael departed, leaving Dee and Achilles staring at each other across the table.

After a while, Dee said mildly, "That was a damn fool thing to do."

"Funny—I was just going to say the same to you. But it's my job. What's your excuse?"

Dee lifted his chin. "It's not your job anymore, is it? Nobody's paying you for this."

"Do you think I became an agent because it pays well?" Achilles snorted. "I'm not exactly living in poverty, but I could have found lots of careers that would have made me richer—and where I'd more likely survive to enjoy my retirement savings."

"Why did you join the Bureau, then?"

This was sending the conversation off-topic, and Achilles wasn't sure he wanted to talk about this. He'd never discussed these things with anyone except Townsend, back when Achilles had first been recruited. He'd tried to tell Orson once, when he'd been high-pressuring Achilles to quit the Bureau. But Orson had refused to listen, claiming that Achilles' past was irrelevant to their future. It hadn't been the only thing that doomed their relationship, but it played a major part.

Now, though, Dee genuinely seemed as if he wanted to know the answer to his question.

"It's all because of a fucked-up childhood. I mean, isn't it always?" Achilles tilted his head back to stare at the ceiling, hoping the lack of eye contact would make it easier to speak. But it didn't, and it also made him feel like a coward, so he faced Dee again. "My parents were immigrants. It's an old story: they came here with nothing, worked like dogs, and eventually saved up enough to open a little shop. Very basic. They sold sandwiches, pastries my mama baked, a handful of food and sundry items they imported from the old country. There weren't a lot of Greeks in our town, but they'd all gather at my parents' place, sitting around little tables with cigarettes and cups of coffee, gossiping."

He paused for a moment, remembering the scents that had surrounded him since birth, the way the conversations had ebbed and flowed like the Aegean Sea, the hands that had reached out to tousle his hair or feed him a small treat.

"My parents worked incredibly long hours, seven days a week, and they made it crystal clear that they were doing this for our benefit: my sister's and mine. In exchange, we were supposed to be… legendary. They named my sister Atalanta. She was—"

"A mythical hunter." Dee grinned. "I read, sometimes."

"Right. Sorry. Anyway, my sister—she's six years older than me—fulfilled all their expectations. Straight A's. Never got in trouble. When she wasn't studying, she was helping out at the shop or doing chores at home."

"That's a lot to ask of a kid."

Out of habit, Achilles almost denied it. He and Atalanta had been trained to see these expectations as natural. But he'd known even as a child that there was something wrong with them. His parents had made him feel stifled, as if they'd stuffed him into a too-small suit.

"Atalanta didn't seem to mind. She was really proud of what she did. My parents were proud of her too. Me, on the other hand…. I wasn't a rotten kid. But I didn't push to do my best in school. I fooled around when I was supposed to be studying. I'd sneak away from my chores to go hang out with friends. When I hit my mid-teens, some-times I'd get stoned or drunk. I was a disappointment."

His parents had made sure to tell him that, likely in hopes of inspiring him to reform, but it had only made him more stubborn.

"It got worse. When I was sixteen, I got caught fooling around with another boy. My parents freaked out. They weren't all that homophobic in general, I guess, but I was their only son. I was supposed to marry a nice Greek girl and have kids to carry on the family name."

Achilles wished he could pace the room, or better yet, take a long run outside. But his feet needed to heal and outside wasn't safe, so he remained at the table, toying with his empty water glass. If he was supposed to feel better by getting all of this off his chest, it wasn't helping. He felt as if his lungs were being squeezed.

Dee looked concerned. "Did they kick you out?"

"No. There was just yelling and tears at first, and then… silence." He'd preferred the yelling. "So all of this is sort of backdrop for what eventually happened, I guess."

Achilles stopped, truly not wanting to continue. Dee remained across from him, though, paying close attention but not seeming to judge, and not even urging him to continue. Just… waiting to listen. In a way that Orson never had.

"It was the summer after I graduated high school," Achilles said, his voice sounding too loud in his own ears. "Atalanta was out of state in med school. She'd gotten a full-ride to Stanford for under-grad. I, on the other hand, barely made it into a state university—with no scholarship—but at least I was going to college, which molli-fied my parents a little. I was supposed to spend the summer working at the shop so my parents could take a break now and then, but I was being flaky about showing up on time. I'd stay up too late, oversleep…."

Getting mauled by a bear shifter was less painful than reliving this memory.

"One particular day…. It was a Tuesday in July. One of those days when it's already hot when the sun rises, and moving around feels like wading through syrup. I was supposed to be at the shop by 10:30, but I stayed in bed and ignored the phone when it rang."

Actually, he'd spent the morning alternately dozing and lazily jerking off. He'd seen *Gladiator* a few weeks earlier, and visions of buff

Romans had been dancing through his head ever since. That was more information than Dee needed, however.

"I figured it was no big deal. Mornings were quiet. The lunch rush didn't start until just before noon, and my parents' friends usually showed up mid-afternoon." Achilles took a deep breath and let it out slowly. "A few minutes before eleven, a guy walked into the shop and pulled a gun."

"Shit," said Dee.

"The robber was just a kid. A dumb one, because there was hardly any cash in the till at that time of day. The rest, well, my parents didn't have security cameras, so the cops had to piece things together the best that they could. They figure Mama was in back and my father up front, and Baba refused to hand over the money. Which makes sense. They'd worked so hard for so long. Every penny was hard-earned. Mama probably heard them yelling and stepped through the back-room door, and the robber panicked and shot her. Baba pulled his own gun then—he kept it hidden near the till—and shot the robber. Who managed to pull the trigger once more before collapsing. By the time police arrived, all three of them were dead on the floor."

Achilles hadn't seen this himself, for which he was grateful. But he'd gone to the store later, after the bodies had been taken away, and had seen the damaged fixtures and the dried blood. He could picture the scene plenty clearly. He often saw it in his nightmares.

"Do you blame yourself for this?" Dee asked.

"If I'd been there when I was supposed to be…. I don't know what would have happened. But I think it would have turned out different-ly." Achilles realized that he was gripping his glass almost tightly enough to break it, so he forced himself to relax. "Atalanta totally blamed me. And I decided I'd honor my parents' memory in a way that I never had when they were alive, although I wasn't sure exactly how. Then when I was close to graduating college, Townsend—he was Bureau chief then—showed up at my door and offered me a job."

Dee nodded slowly. "A job where you could be legendary."

"Something like that."

"I get it." Dee nodded again. "I mean, you can tell what low expectations *my* parents had for their son, Damnation. But I get it."

Achilles' lungs loosened. "So why did you volunteer to go into the black hole?"

"Dunno. It's nice to feel needed, though." Now it was Dee's turn to look away.

Achilles knew for a fact that the wall to Dee's left was not fascinating, so he waited a few beats and then said, "You're critical to this mission." Which was the complete truth, because without Dee, how the hell was anyone going to rescue the prisoner?

Dee's cheeks pinked. "I guess genies are as bad as humans, throwing themselves to the wolves in hopes of satisfying their egos." Then he sighed. "Also, I watched the news last night after you went to sleep. It's bad. The kinds of things you read about in history books, and you shudder and think *Thank God I live in the USA*, only that doesn't work anymore. I don't know if going into the black hole will solve anything, but I have to try."

"I think that's a pretty fair description of a hero," said Achilles.

"But you haven't told me why you're going. You said it's your job, but I bet the chief could find lots of other things for you to do. He said so himself."

Well, what the hell. Achilles had already spilled most of his guts this morning—without the help of any bear shifters—so he might as well spill the rest. He held Dee's gaze.

"I'm going because you are. Because I want to do my best to keep you safe."

CHAPTER 20

*D*ee had virtually no experience with emotionally close relationships. Nevertheless, he was fairly certain that when someone gave you their difficult backstory, including one of their deepest regrets, and then admitted that they were risking their life to keep you safe, it was appropriate to react with physical contact. Especially when you had kissed that someone and could still almost taste them on your lips.

So although Dee froze in astonishment after Achilles' announcement, his inaction lasted only a few seconds. Then he shot to his feet fast enough to knock over the chair, rushed around the table, and threw himself into Achilles' arms. Fortunately, Achilles had fast reflexes, and he caught Dee without major mishap to either of them. He did, however, grunt softly, which reminded Dee that Achilles had fresh scars on his torso and had been recently tortured.

"Sorry," he said as he tried to pull away.

But Achilles held him fast. "I'm fine."

"You're hurt. And this is an awkward position."

Achilles put his mouth so close to Dee's ear that Dee could feel the warm puffs of breath. "I'm fine," Achilles whispered softly. "This feels good."

Which was true, despite everything. It had been only a couple of days since Dee had spent a night and day with Achilles in his arms, and now that strong body felt familiar. Like home territory. Dee felt as if Achilles could do anything he pleased to Dee—could disassemble him atom by atom, if Achilles wanted—and Dee would take pleasure in it because serving Achilles was what he was made to do. Which were stupid and dangerous things to be feeling, but he felt them nonetheless. And he wasn't sorry.

"Hope sex?" Dee asked… hopefully.

Promisingly, Achilles paused before responding. Then he sighed, a motion that made Dee's body move too. "Still not a great idea."

"I guess not."

"But… if this isn't too weird…. Maybe we could just lie down together and… cuddle?"

That idea hadn't crossed Dee's mind, but now that Achilles had made the suggestion, it seemed like an excellent one. "I'd like that."

The beds were only a few yards away, but a little stumbling happened as they decided which bed to use, settling on the one that Achilles had slept in. They were both wearing jeans and T-shirts, thanks to the generosity of their hosts, and they remained fully clothed as they climbed onto a mattress that wasn't really large enough for two big men. They ended up spooned on their sides, the wall against Dee's back and Achilles against his front, and a thin soft blanket covering them to their shoulders. This time they sighed in unison as soon as they were settled.

"I haven't done much of this," Achilles said after a time. He sounded wistful.

"I haven't done any. It's nice."

"Yeah."

Silence for a while, but neither of them was asleep.

Finally Achilles spoke. "If you had a genie available to you, what would you wish for?"

Dee's mind went blank. He'd never given much thought to his own wants and desires, aside from the basic needs of life and maybe some cannabis now and then. What he wanted had never seemed especially significant, since he probably wouldn't get it anyway. "No wishing for unlimited wishes, huh?" But that question was mainly to stall for time.

"Nope. Ya gotta play by the rules."

"You tell me yours first."

"I already got my wish. You freed me."

Oh. That was a nice thought. "Okay.... Assuming my hypothetical genie is constrained by the same rules I am, I guess I'd wish for a nice home. A permanent one."

Achilles nodded, his hair tickling Dee's face. "I've got a condo in LA. I don't know if I'll see it again. It's a nice one." Then he yawned.

They stayed like that for a long time, quiet but awake, pressed together in their tiny, imaginary safety zone. As content as anyone could be when the world was in the process of ending.

* * *

"Sorry about the exposition dump," said Achilles when he woke up. Dee hadn't fallen asleep—except for the arm that was trapped under Achilles—but he'd been content to listen to Achilles' deep, even breathing and to bury his nose in soft curls.

"It wasn't a dump," said Dee, extricating his arm. He was still pinned against the wall.

Achilles slowly sat and stretched, then ran a hand along his cheek and grimaced. "I need a shave."

"There are razors in the bathroom. You know, I never grow a beard or mustache. I always assumed it was another weird biological tic—I have several—but now I wonder if it's a genie thing."

"We can ask Diana Afolabi to research it."

Dee scoffed. "I think she probably has more important things to worry about than genie facial hair."

Achilles' grin made him look years younger. "She can add it to her list for later."

The rest of the day was spent mostly relaxing and eating healthy snacks. They found a deck of cards and played for a while, but since Dee always won, Achilles eventually abandoned the game, laughing. One of the aliens brought a totally random selection of paperbacks. Achilles dipped into parts of, variously, a murder mystery set on a cruise ship, a romance between a starship captain and an android, and the autobiography of an actress neither of them had heard of. Dee, meanwhile, worked his way steadily through a collection of Greek tragedies. Sometimes the two of them simply chatted about unimportant things that nonetheless mattered a lot: their favorite foods, places they'd visited, books and movies they'd enjoyed.

As days went, it was entirely unremarkable. And if Dee had been given the chance, he would have wished for it to last for a month.

An hour or so after sundown, two of the aliens arrived and led Dee and Achilles outside. "What's happening?" Dee whispered to Achilles, worried, although their hosts seemed happy and relaxed.

"No idea."

Together they walked about a hundred yards into the desert, their footsteps muffled by the soft soil. There was no moon tonight and no artificial lights, but the aliens could apparently see just fine and made sure that Dee and Achilles stayed close.

When they stopped, one of the aliens pointed up.

Dee gasped. "The stars!" Maybe it was a dumb thing to say, but it was all that he could manage. With no clouds, haze, or light pollution, the glitter of the night sky was breathtaking. There was the long, speckled streak that he assumed was the Milky Way, and for the first time he understood how the galaxy got its name.

He'd seen stars before, of course. But he'd rarely been anywhere that granted a view like this. And, well, he hardly ever looked up. What a loss if he'd died before having this experience! It made him feel infinitely small yet at the same time larger than life. Because nowhere in all this immensity was there anyone else exactly like him. Somehow it helped him believe what the Bureau had been telling him: everyone mattered.

"Beautiful," said Achilles, followed by something in what must have been Greek.

One of the aliens said something in her own language and then pointed one clawed finger at a spot near the periphery of the Milky Way.

"Your home?" Achilles asked softly, and when she cocked her head, repeated, "Home?" Then he gestured toward the building where they'd been staying before directing his own finger in the same direction she did. "Home?" he said again.

She smiled and said something that was pretty close to "home" only with more fangs. Her expression turned somber after that, and she moved her hands in a way that suggested something exploding. Her companion made a low ululating sound that was especially mournful under the vast sky.

For several minutes, they all stood silently, a tiny memorial service for a lost planet.

"Hey, Dee? Do you think I could have a small wish on their behalf? I don't want to drain your battery, but—"

"Yes. Go ahead."

Achilles bent, picked up a small jagged stone, and handed it to Dee. "I wish for something small but meaningful to our hosts. Something to remind them of home. Is that too vague?"

Dee, who was already working on it, shook his head. The familiar tingle danced through his nervous system, making his heart race and skin flush, making his cock hard, to be honest. He wondered whether the aliens or Achilles could see that in the darkness but then decided he didn't care. He was smiling when he returned the stone to Achilles.

Achilles repeated his wish right away. Nothing happened, except that the stone crumbled to dust and Achilles brushed off his hands. He looked around expectantly, which made Dee realize that Achilles *trusted* him. Expected that he'd be able to accomplish things.

Dee himself was feeling doubtful, however, and was about to trudge unhappily back to the building. If he couldn't even do this much, how could he possibly help to save the prisoner in the black hole? But after only two steps, he nearly tripped over something, and when he stopped to peer at it, he saw… a potted plant?

He couldn't see details very well, but the plant didn't look familiar. He picked up the pot and held it toward the aliens. "Uh, is this yours?"

They came closer to inspect it and then hissed in surprise. They spoke to each other very fast, with evident excitement, before bursting into what sounded like a celebratory song. The female took the pot and cradled it in her arms as if it were a baby. "Home!" she exclaimed.

This felt good.

When they were alone again in their borrowed room, Achilles set a hand on Dee's shoulder. "That was a nice thing you did for them."

"It was your wish."

"Which would have been useless without you."

They slept together that night, again with no sex, but with a speck more hope in their hearts anyway.

CHAPTER 21

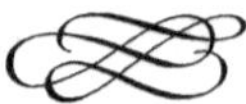

The chief and Tenrael arrived early, just as Dee and Achilles were finishing breakfast. "Want some?" Achilles asked, gesturing at the small feast that Dee had prepared. If they survived this, Achilles was going to cook him some of the Greek dishes his mother used to make, because despite her long hours at the shop she had insisted on preparing big family dinners. Achilles hadn't made any of those things in years.

Grimes scooped up a couple of strawberries and popped them into his mouth, nodding with approval. Then he looked solemnly at Achilles and Dee. "Are you still willing to do this?"

"Yes," they replied in unison.

"I should probably tell you that things are looking increasingly grim. I've lost touch completely with the East Coast Bureau. I don't know what part, if any, they're playing in recent events. Due to proximity, they've always had a closer relationship with everyone in DC."

Achilles regretted eating such a big meal. "Is East Coast working *with* DC now? Are they… opposing us?"

"I don't know." Grimes winced. "I've also lost touch with some of our own agents. It's possible they've just decided to disengage, now that we're not official. Or it's possible…." He stopped mid-sentence and looked away.

"Why are you even telling us this?" Dee demanded. His hands were fisted atop the table.

"Because I think you both deserve to go into this with open eyes. Or choose not to go at all."

"I'm going," Achilles said stubbornly. He'd already decided he couldn't live with any other decision. "But Dee, you don't have to—"

"I'm going."

Achilles managed to be both relieved and unhappy about that. Dee's presence would greatly increase his own chance of getting out alive. But he cared about Dee, who'd turned out to be much more complicated than Achilles had initially suspected. He hadn't needed a shrink to tell him that his experiences with his family and Orson had made him extremely reluctant to form close emotional bonds with anyone, but all of that had apparently flown out the window over the past days. Dee's welfare was important to him, beyond the general sense of responsibility he felt for everyone in his jurisdiction.

Grimes still stood beside the table, looking as if he had something more to say but didn't want to, while Tenrael waved his wings in a way that somehow seemed mildly reproachful.

"Spit it out," Achilles finally grumbled.

Grimes let out a breath. "Agent Afolabi was unable to find much information on genies. Except that they prefer the term djinn, apparently. Sorry, I've been using the wrong word, Dee."

Dee snorted. "I don't care about that."

"There's really not much about them in our records. She thinks it's because they originated in Asia and North Africa and not many immigrated here. Maybe some of the agencies abroad have the information we need, but nobody trusts us right now, and I don't blame them."

"So we don't know anything," said Dee sourly. "Like, magic tricks I might have up my sleeve and don't even know about."

"She mostly confirmed what we already know. She did find out one interesting thing, however. It's about you personally."

"What?"

"Your mother came to the United States about five months before you were born. She was from Bosnia. It was actually part of Yugoslavia then, but— Anyway, did you know this?"

Dee was frowning and shaking his head. "No. She never talked about it. She wasn't very chatty. I don't remember her having an accent either, but to be honest, I barely recall her voice." This was obviously a painful subject, and Achilles wished he could comfort him. Not with Grimes here, though.

Then Dee's eyes widened. "Wait! Five months…. The man I thought was my father was definitely not Bosnian. I'd be willing to bet he never stepped foot outside the US." He swallowed. "So he…."

"Jack Martell was not your biological father," Grimes said.

"Then who was?"

"We don't know. But it's entirely possible that both of your parents were djinn. In which case your abilities may be stronger than we'd assumed."

Dee looked as if he couldn't decide how to take this news. It could mean their mission had a better chance of success. But it also meant that he'd just had a fairly shocking revelation about his parentage.

"He must've known he wasn't my dad," Dee said quietly, probably to himself. "He was a son of a bitch, but he kept me fed and housed after she abandoned me." He looked up sharply. "What happened to her?"

"Another thing we don't know. Afolabi couldn't find any records of her after her marriage to Martell."

Silence filled in the room until Achilles huffed. "Do you have any more bombshells to drop, Chief? 'Cause I'd like to get this over with."

"Okay. Let's—"

Tenrael startled all of them by whirling toward one of the doors. Grimes spun too, hand inside his jacket and, no doubt, on a weapon holstered to his chest. Achilles didn't have any weapons—they'd disappeared during his encounter with Ashley Dunn—but he leapt to his feet and tensed himself in readiness. If he had to, he could throw dishes or use his fists. Dee shrank back in his seat, looking bewildered.

Three aliens burst into the room, all speaking rapidly in their own language. They were clearly upset, but it took Tenrael a few moments to understand them. "Vehicles approaching," he finally translated. "Not likely friendly."

Shit.

Fortunately Achilles and Dee were dressed and ready to go, and neither had any personal items to worry about. They abandoned the kitchen and rushed after Grimes, followed by Tenrael and the aliens, down a hall and out a door into the glaring morning sun. A black Jeep was the only visible vehicle and their apparent destination. They climbed in and, without even a chance to thank their hosts, they were off. Eschewing the road, Grimes piloted them straight across the desert, bumping over rocks and roaring down hills. It was not a comfortable ride.

"Are they safe?" asked Achilles, referring to the aliens.

It took a few moments before Grimes responded. "Maybe. They have tunnels. And I suspect that right now, the four of us are more interesting to our foes."

That would need to be reassurance enough since there was little that any of them could do to protect their hosts. Achilles imagined masked men in ICE uniforms swarming the place—demanding papers from people who were definitely aliens and likely undocumented—and unsympathetic to explanations that they were refugees. A ridiculous scenario, yet eerily possible.

"Townsend promised to help them," he said, knowing it was hopeless.

Tenrael turned his head to look at them. "They understood the risks and they know the forces that oppose us."

Maybe Achilles would have argued about this, but Dee, who was looking out the back window, made an alarmed noise. "They're following us." Sure enough, two dark shapes were barely visible through the dust kicked up by the Jeep's tires.

"I'm aware," Grimes said, driving faster and more erratically, zooming over ridges as if he didn't think gravity applied to him.

Achilles held onto the grab bar for dear life. The jostling was uncomfortable to his wounds and his ears were ringing. "We could wish ourselves somewhere else," he suggested.

"No," Dee said firmly. "I don't trust my ability to be a transporter beam for four people and a Jeep. I don't know where we'd end up or in what kind of shape. And I need to save my battery."

Fair enough. Achilles didn't want to end up like that scientist in *The Fly*. And he wanted to get into the black hole and back out again. But he also didn't want to fall into Dunn's clutches again. "Where are we going?" he shouted over the roar of the Jeep's engine.

Grimes didn't answer, which could have meant he was too busy to chitchat or he didn't think Achilles needed to know. Or, less happily, it could have meant that Grimes himself didn't know where they were going. Perhaps he was just speeding aimlessly through the desert until they crashed, ran out of gas, or got overtaken by their pursuers. Tenrael didn't say anything either, and he looked tense, although that could have partly been discomfort from his wings being squashed against the car seat.

Which got Achilles thinking about Grimes' wings, or lack thereof. It had never occurred to him that Grimes might once have possessed them, but now he wondered what past trauma those scars represented. Unlike Dee, Grimes must have grown up knowing he was different, that he was something… not quite human. But both of them must have felt isolated. As had Achilles himself, even though, as far as he knew, his DNA was one hundred percent *Homo sapiens*.

That thought brought the idea that Dee could have his DNA tested —if he wanted—if things ever got back to normal. The Bureau had those capabilities in the Northern California lab. It might answer at least a few of Dee's questions and would likely also prove interesting for research's sake.

All of these thoughts were convenient ways of distracting himself from current facts: his body hurt, the Jeep didn't seem to be getting anywhere but deeper into the desert, and the two dark shapes behind them were now considerably closer.

Dee leaned close and spoke just loudly enough to be heard. "Are you used to things like this?"

They slammed together as Grimes made a sharp left-hand swerve, and then bounced high enough to bash their heads into the ceiling. "I guess," Achilles answered, rubbing his scalp. "Not a ton of high-speed off-road chases, but uncomfortable near-death adventures, sure."

"Let's just hope it's only near-death."

As if on cue, somebody started shooting at them. Bullets shattered the rear window, spraying them with pebbles of safety glass. Dee yelped, and Achilles shoved Dee's head as low as his tall frame and the enclosed space allowed.

"Anyone hit?" Grimes shouted as he continued his evasive maneuvers.

Dee shook his head, and Achilles was about to answer *no*, when another bullet grazed his right shoulder and burrowed into the seat in front of him. Tenrael made a pained grunt.

"Ten!" Grimes didn't sound panicked—quite—but he certainly wasn't calm.

Tenrael gave Grimes' leg a quick pat. "You know I am very difficult to kill."

"But not impossible."

This was true. Achilles tried to rally his brain to recall exactly how durable demons were—he'd certainly been trained on the matter—but realized his shoulder stung. A quick inspection indicated that even though he was bleeding, he wasn't in mortal danger. Also, his arm remained fully functional, which was important.

"Fuck." That was Grimes, who, in Achilles' experience, rarely swore. Hearing him do so now wasn't heartening. Achilles decided to play ostrich and not lift his head to see what, specifically, was troubling the chief.

More gunshots, this time apparently not hitting anyone or anything important, and then Grimes turned the wheel so sharply that they very nearly overturned. "Can't outrun them," he explained. "Prepare to bail out and take cover."

"Unbuckle!" Achilles yelled at Dee, unfastening his own seatbelt.

A moment later, the Jeep came to a shuddering stop. Achilles, who'd been ready for it, flung his door open, grabbed Dee's arm, and hauled him out. They both hit the ground running, which was better than Achilles had hoped for. There was no time to assess the situation, but years of training and experience kicked in, and Achilles dragged Dee up a steep incline of jagged rocks and behind a mansion-sized boulder. Grimes and Tenrael were right behind them.

No chance to strategize. When Grimes tossed Achilles a gun, Achilles caught it. That left Grimes armed with a nasty-looking knife, Tenrael with his teeth and claws, and Dee with nothing at all. "Hunker down!" Achilles barked at him. "Stay behind us!" He gave him an almost-gentle shove to encourage him to obey.

The pursuing vehicles stopped at the bottom of the hill. Heavy footsteps and grunts approached fast.

"Shoot first, ask questions later," Achilles muttered to himself. He didn't like guns, but he was grateful to have one now.

As soon as the first person appeared around the rock, before Achilles even had the chance to see who it was, he pulled the trigger twice. He'd always scored well while practicing at the range, and now his target made a muffled scream and collapsed, unmoving. That must have made the others hesitate, because nobody else showed their face and the sounds on the other side of the rock stopped.

Grimes looked at Tenrael—who was ignoring the blood streaming down his own torso—and pointed upward. Tenrael nodded and took to the air, as graceful as any bird despite his mass. Achilles, who'd never seen him fly, wished he had the opportunity to gape, but now wasn't the time. In any case, Tenrael rose only high enough to peek over the top of the boulder, then landed lightly on his feet back on the safe side, holding up three fingers on his left hand.

The low number was a slight relief, although if the pursuers could do Dunn's magic-finger pain thing, the promising odds might not matter. Achilles wondered the range of Dunn's little trick.

Noises started on the other side of the rock, weird shuffling and groans. Before Achilles had a chance to consider what that meant, a trio of bodies rushed around the edge. Large, furry bodies. Achilles shot again, emptying the magazine, and although one of the attackers joined their fallen colleague, the others continued forward with ground-shaking roars.

Bears.

Out of ammunition, Achilles did the only thing he could—he fell back, leaving Grimes and Tenrael between him and the bears but standing in front of Dee. He picked up a rock, ready to throw it if needed. In dire straits, even caveman weapons were better than nothing at all.

The chief and Tenrael collided with the bears. Between the swiftly moving bodies and the demon's wings, it was hard to follow the action, but there was a lot of roaring and growling and snarling. Not all of it from the bears. Achilles set his jaw and tried not to remember the sensation of claws ripping him open or the sight of Santiago Bautista dying a few feet away.

One more howl echoed against the boulder, and then the combatants were still. Achilles held his breath until Tenrael and Grimes separated from their opponents and stood upright. Grimes' clothing was shredded and they were both covered in blood—their own and the bears'—but they wore matching feral grins that were both terrifying and wonderful to see.

"You're bleeding," Dee said from behind Achilles.

Achilles laughed. "'Tis but a flesh wound."

"I'm sorry I was so fucking useless. I don't—"

"Fighting isn't your strength. That's fine. I wasn't ready to go hand-to-hand with bears either, you might have noticed."

Breathing heavily, Grimes and Tenrael walked over to them. They all watched as the corpses shuddered and reshaped into four naked human-shaped bodies. Three male and one female.

"What the fuck?" Achilles said, disgusted. "They have bear shifters on their side? And with guns?" Because shifters of any species tended to look down their snouts at human weapons.

"Apparently." Grimes wiped his blade on his trousers and tucked it away. He also took the handgun from Achilles. "Good shots," he said drily.

Achilles, who was trying not to think about the fact that he'd just killed two people, made a face. His killings were clearly justified, but that didn't mean he was comfortable with them. He never was. He hadn't even been happy to see the bear that had killed Santiago collapse under another agent's hail of bullets. Relieved, certainly, but not happy.

"This is going to sound stupid," Dee said hesitantly. "But compared to Ashley, these guys didn't seem that scary."

Grimes gave a quick headshake. "They want you alive. They'd be pleased to have Spanos too. And not just for strategic reasons—they're undoubtedly furious that you beat Dunn."

"They don't want you two?"

"I'm sure they'd be delighted with either of us. But they didn't know who was accompanying you. Maybe they know now. We need to get you somewhere safe and get this over with." Grimes looked at Tenrael and they had some kind of silent conversation with their eyes. "San Francisco?"

Tenrael nodded. "I'll go ahead and let them know." He leaped up, flapped away, and was soon barely a speck in the sky.

CHAPTER 22

"Let who know?" They were back in a vehicle, this time with Dee alone in the back seat.

But Chief Grimes, again behind the wheel, didn't answer—which wasn't exactly a shock—and Achilles, in the front passenger seat, only shrugged. From what Dee could see, Achilles looked drawn—maybe from pain, or exhaustion, or anxiety, or the aftermath of the battle, or maybe from all of the above.

After Tenrael had flown away, the sight of which under other circumstances would have left Dee stunned, Grimes had urged the rest of them to move quickly. They'd abandoned the four very human-looking corpses and, after some quick touchups from a first aid kit in the Jeep, had chosen one of their pursuers' Toyotas. Which was fair enough, since the pursuers had shot up the Jeep, and anyway none of them needed a vehicle anymore. The key fob was in the center console, and Achilles did something to the Toyota that he said would disable tracking. He also collected all of the bear shifters' cell phones, extracted their SIM cards, and crunched the phones to bits.

Dee felt a little as if he'd walked into a *Mission: Impossible* movie, only with demons and were-creatures. And genies—no, djinn.

Once everyone was buckled in, Grimes drove off cross-country, quickly but not as death-defyingly as before. They arrived at a road about forty-five minutes later, which eventually took them to a highway that finally delivered them to something resembling civilization. They took turns washing up in a McDonald's bathroom, and then Dee—at the moment, the least disreputable-looking of them—ducked into a Walmart with Grimes's money and came out with replacement clothing for those pieces that were bloody, ripped to shreds, or covered in desert grime.

"Get comfortable," said Grimes as they got rolling again. "We've got a long haul ahead of us."

Achilles suggested that they take turns driving, and once that was settled, everyone was quiet. Dee slowly processed everything that had happened over the past days. He'd been through some rough spots in his life—some of which had landed him in jail—but none of them held a candle to recent events.

But not everything had been awful; there was Achilles.

Dee began to laugh. At first it was a small chuckle, but the more he tried to suppress it, the more insistent it became, until Achilles twisted around and looked at him with concern. "Are you having a breakdown? Do we need to—"

"N-n-noooo," said Dee through guffaws, tears rolling down his cheeks.

"Then what—"

"I want to live!"

Achilles was still clearly puzzled, understandably so, but it took several minutes before Dee got himself sufficiently under control so he could explain. He wiped his eyes with the back of his hand.

"Sorry. I haven't lost my marbles. It's only... when Abe showed up at my door, I was barely skating by. Hell, for most of my life I was barely skating by. There was no real reason for me to get out of bed each day. If I'd been hit by a bus while crossing a street, my last thought would have been, *Well, at least that's over with.*" That part wasn't really funny—he knew that—but he laughed anyway.

"And?" Achilles prompted. He still looked worried.

"And now if I got hit by a bus, I'd be really pissed off. I mean, evil people are sending homicidal were-bears to catch us, the entire world is close to spiraling down the drain, but now I want to live. I really do. And that feels... good."

Maybe he *was* losing his marbles after all.

But Achilles smiled. "Hope. You're feeling hope."

Grimes, who'd been silent throughout this interchange, briefly caught Dee's eyes in the rearview mirror. "There's a seesaw. Do children still play on those? On one side is hate, rage, greed, prejudice, cruelty, apathy... all of those ugly, heavy things that live within each of us and within our society as a whole. But on the other side is hope. Love. Empathy. Openness. Joy. Generosity. Kindness. Every one of us struggles to keep the heavy things from overbalancing the light ones. It's hard work. But it feels so good when the light prevails."

Dee frowned. "Do *you* struggle? You're an angel, right?"

"Half." Grimes's laugh was bitter. "And sometimes I think I struggle more than most. Ten says if I live another couple of centuries, maybe I'll gain a little more... solidity. But he may be overly optimistic."

"Then what are those of us with ordinary lifespans supposed to do?"

"The best you can, Dee. The best you can."

* * *

THEY DROVE all day and into the night, and although the terrain varied, it was desert for a good chunk of the way. They stopped a few times at gas stations in towns too small to deserve the name. They'd gas up the Toyota, grab snacks, and swap drivers. By the time they hit the Central Valley, where it was too dark to tell whether the fields were green, Dee felt as if he'd been in motion forever.

Charles—they'd been calling Grimes that for the past several hours now—took the final shift. There was little traffic at this hour, even once they got close to San Francisco, and skies were clear. As they zoomed over the western span of the Bay Bridge, Dee marveled at the beauty of the water and city below.

"Looks different now," mused Charles.

"Compared to what?" Achilles yawned through the final word.

"My first visit, almost a century ago. I nearly died here once, in the forties. Merfolk."

Achilles nodded as if that made perfect sense, while Dee tried to process another new nugget of information. "Did they lure you into the water with their singing?"

"Something like that. And then they bit me. They're venomous."

That would have put an interesting twist on the Disney movie. "I thought you were immortal."

"I'm not. And at the time, I was more vulnerable than I am now."

Although Dee would have liked to hear more of the story, he didn't ask.

Off the bridge and now in the city proper, their route twisted and turned on surface streets, going uphill and down, until they reached a neighborhood with century-old houses of wood or stucco mixed with apartment buildings and newer glass-and-concrete boxes. In most cities, this might have been a comfortable working-class neighborhood, but Dee, who'd occasionally lived in San Francisco for short periods, knew that these modest homes would probably sell for well over a million bucks.

Charles pulled the Toyota to a stop in front of one of them, apparently not caring that he was blocking the driveway. But he didn't cut the engine. "Townsend knew for years that things were… working up to what we have now. He refused to tell me many details, the old bastard. Something about free will. But one thing he did say was that he'd been developing a safety net of sorts. A network of people we could rely on when things went bad."

"Like the coyotes and the aliens," Achilles said.

"Yes. And like the gentlemen you're about to meet. One of them was an agent for a while, so you probably know him, Achilles. Clay White."

Achilles made a startled noise. "He got kicked out of the Bureau after a colossal fuck-up. Children died."

"Yes. But Townsend retained contact with him, and White and his partner agreed to help if needed."

Dee was uneasy. There was clearly something that Charles wasn't telling them; Dee could tell by the way Charles stared resolutely through the windshield.

"Can we trust him?" Achilles apparently shared some of Dee's trepidation.

"Townsend thought so. And we don't have much choice."

They all sat in the car for a few moments, until the front door of the house swung open. Silhouetted in the light from the interior was a large winged figure. Charles immediately turned off the car and got out, swiftly followed by Achilles. Dee hesitated only a few seconds before following.

In the dark it was hard to discern many exterior details of the two-story house, but it had wood siding and was probably painted white or light yellow. A flight of steps led up to a small front porch and the open door, and to the left was a bay window with closed curtains. Tenrael stepped aside so that Charles and Dee could enter; he nodded at Dee, and Charles gave Ten's arm a stroke as he passed.

"You can fly that far and that fast?" Dee asked. "Even after being shot and mauled?"

Tenrael gave him a very sharp-toothed grin.

They were in a hallway with wooden wainscoting and old-fashioned wallpaper. Tenrael slid open a pocket door and ushered them into a living room where two men stood, waiting for them. One was very tall and muscular, with close-cropped blond hair, a square jaw, and a scowl. Wearing dark slacks and a white shirt, he looked like an extra in a mob movie, one of the main star's hired goons. The other man was shorter, slender, with reddish hair and high cheekbones. He was dressed like the front man in an emo band.

"White," said Achilles, nodding at the big guy.

The man nodded back. "Spanos." Then, maybe a little reluctantly, he gestured toward the other man. "Marek."

Marek looked amused, as if he was used to White's gruffness, and stepped forward. "You are welcome in our home, Achilles Spanos and Damnation Martell." He had an accent, maybe Eastern European.

"You have had a long and difficult journey. Please sit down." He waved toward a couch.

It all felt really awkward, but Dee sat and then so did Achilles. As their hosts regarded them, Charles and Tenrael remained in the hallway, speaking softly. Although neither White nor Marek seemed hostile, there was something sharp and considering in their gazes. Dee felt a little like a sheep being sized up by a pair of wolves.

"This is a nice house," Achilles said suddenly.

Dee agreed. The living room was tastefully furnished, showing respect for the age of the house but with nods to modern comfort. It wasn't one of those places that felt staged for a magazine shoot.

Although White didn't loosen at the compliment, Marek looked pleased. "We like it very much. For a long time it belonged to two Bureau agents, but when one of them passed away, his husband sold it to us. It has a strong sense of history for such a young building."

That was an odd thing to say, considering the house must have been over a century old.

Before Dee could comment, however, Charles and Tenrael entered the room, both looking serious. "I'm sorry, gentlemen," Charles said. "But we have to go. There's an urgent issue in Seattle. But you'll still—"

"We'll do what we promised," Achilles interrupted. "We'll try our best to bring out whoever's in the black hole."

"And you'll contact us once you've succeeded?"

That made Achilles smile. "You'll be the first to know."

Everyone stared at one another, maybe in silent acknowledgment that this could be their last meeting, and then Charles and Tenrael left. Which meant Achilles and Dee were alone with their weird hosts.

"I heard you died," Achilles said to White.

White rumbled back, "I did."

He lifted his lips to show an impressive set of fangs. Marek, still grinning, did the same.

Dee's heart lurched. "Vampires?" he squeaked. Achilles had mentioned their existence, but Dee hadn't expected to meet any in the undead flesh—let alone be their houseguest.

White nodded, confirming the answer to Dee's question. Achilles looked neither surprised nor alarmed. Dee realized that White might not be intentionally scowling; in which case, he clearly had the world's most intense resting bitch face.

"Don't worry," White said. "We've already eaten." When Marek laughed, Dee guessed it might have been intended as a joke. Maybe.

But White was giving Dee a quizzical look. "You smell weird. What are you?"

Jackie the coyote chief had mentioned something about that too; apparently he didn't even smell human. He wondered which creatures could sense that. As far as he knew, the aliens hadn't caught on to it. Or maybe they simply didn't care.

Marek gave White a friendly shove. "Please excuse my Clay. He has all the subtlety of a charging rhinoceros. Your scent is actually quite pleasant, Mr. Martell, and—"

"Dee."

"Dee. And your identity is none of our business. If you'd like to share, however, I'd be interested. I'm quite old, and I don't think I've met anyone like you."

Achilles didn't say a peep, and Dee appreciated having the choice whether to self-disclose. And why not share? "I guess I'm a genie. Um, djinn. Full or half, I'm not sure."

The response was satisfying in that he'd managed to surprise a pair of vampires, who both looked slightly stunned. They looked at each other and then back at Dee, and they probably would have asked more questions if Achilles hadn't stood up. "Guys, this is tons of fun and everything, but we have work to do. Maybe we can play Twenty Supernatural Questions after we've finished laughing in the face of death?"

"I thought the Bureau frowned on the term *supernatural.*" White's voice was a growl and the corners of his mouth remained turned down, but the spark in his eyes suggested he might have been making a joke of some kind.

Achilles huffed. "There *is* no Bureau anymore. Didn't Tenrael tell you?"

"Motherfuckers."

Dee assumed this meant the people in DC who'd made the decision. If so, he was inclined to agree. Everyone he'd met who was associated with the Bureau was odd and dangerous, but none of them had forced him to do anything against his will. And Achilles, at least, was a genuinely good person. Dee was confident about that.

He stood up and moved next to Achilles. Dee felt as if the two of them were partners, and it turned out that it felt really great. "I'm ready."

After smiling at him, Achilles turned back to the vampires. "Did Tenrael tell you what we are going to do?"

"Risk your fool lives," answered White.

"Exactly. Dee is going to take us into this… place. We've been calling it the black hole. I was there once and it's not a top vacation destination. But he'll get us there, we hope. And we'll find someone who's being held prisoner there, we hope. And we'll return here with the prisoner. We hope."

Dee had the sense that Achilles' repeated use of *hope* didn't just represent the uncertainty of their success, but also acted as a sort of prayer. According to Achilles, hope was powerful. And Dee knew the lore about a set of three: third time's the charm.

But Achilles wasn't quite done explaining. "I don't know how long we'll be gone. It's impossible to measure time in that place, and I'm not sure whether it runs at the same rate as here. If we do bring this person back, I'm betting they'll be traumatized. No idea how badly. Oh, and at our *last* safe house, they sent a quartet of bear shifters after us, so you'll want to keep an eye out for something like that."

None of this appeared to rattle their hosts. White cracked his knuckles a few times as if preparing himself for a rousing fistfight, and Marek simply smiled. "Our home will remain a refuge for you as long as you need it."

"Thanks."

Then Dee had an idea. "I'd really like to grant you guys a wish, but I can't right now. I need to conserve my juice. Think about it, though, and after we get back, as soon as I'm able…."

"That is very generous of you," Marek said solemnly, and he gave a small bow that didn't seem the least bit ironic.

"Can I ask one more favor? I need a couple of small tokens to turn into charms. It can be anything, really, but they'll be destroyed when Achilles uses them."

Marek trotted away immediately. Dee heard him run upstairs and, a moment later, run back down. When he returned to the living room, he held a closed fist toward Dee and passed him the contents. Two small pieces of amber. "They remind me of my homeland," Marek explained. "I like to keep a few pieces around."

It felt right to do this with something more valuable than a bit of gravel or a thrift-store trinket. And unlike Ashley's pearls—objects produced as a result of a creature's irritation—these pieces of amber were meaningful to the donor.

Dee put one in his pocket, held the other in his hand, and nodded at Achilles. "Go ahead."

Achilles squared his shoulders. "I wish for you and me to safely travel to the black hole location where that prisoner is. Is that specific enough, Dee?"

"I think so." Dee clutched the smooth stone, closed his eyes, and felt the magic surge through him.

CHAPTER 23

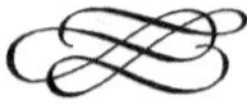

"Achilles?" Dee sounded close to panic, and the hand clutching Achilles' tightened enough to hurt.

Despite the pain—and his own deep unease—Achilles squeezed back. "Yeah, this is it. As far as I can tell, anyway. You did it, Dee."

"I'm…. Can we rest for a minute? I know we're not safe, but…."

"But that was hard work. Of course." Achilles lowered himself, gently tugging Dee along, until they sat side by side. As before, there was an absolute absence of light. Sounds carried oddly—Achilles hadn't registered that during his first visit since it had been just him. Even though he knew that Dee was only inches away, it sounded as if he was across the street.

Dee shuffled a bit nearer until their knees touched. "My clothes are gone."

"Oh. Mine too." Last time he'd assumed that Dunn had stripped him before sending him here, but it appeared that wasn't the case.

"That means my pocket's gone. And the amber that was in it. The one I was supposed to use to get us home."

Shit. That was an unwanted complication. Achilles kept his tone light because there was no use spreading his own fears to Dee. Not when there was nothing they could do about the situation. "We'll figure something out."

"Okay." A noisy, shuddery exhale. "Sorry. I feel like I've run a marathon and gone a week without sleeping."

"You transported two grown men to… I don't know… another dimension? That's a huge feat. You've earned a rest."

Dee sighed again, this time longer and quieter. "What do we do next?"

"You catch your breath. Just, um, don't dawdle over it, okay? I don't like this place."

"I'd give it one star on Tripadvisor."

Laughter might have sounded weird here, but it felt good. For what might have been ten minutes—or might have been a century, for all Achilles could tell—they sat there silently. Holding hands, knees touching.

"Hey, Dee? Tell me something joyful you've experienced."

There was a long pause. "Happy Meal," Dee whispered.

"Hamburgers?"

"No. That was the name of a dog my mom gave me—a wish she granted me right before she walked out of my life. He was just a mutt, but he was the most wonderful dog in the world, you know?"

Achilles gently squeezed Dee's hand. "That's a great memory. Thank you." He meant it. Thinking about Dee as a lonely little boy, finding someone to give him unconditional love… that made the darkness feel less oppressive.

"How about you?" Dee asked. He sounded less exhausted.

"Eight years ago. I had an assignment sort of near Seattle. Someone had seen something weird in the woods and the Bureau got notified, so Townsend sent me to see what was what. It was out in the rain in the middle of nowhere, wet and cold and just… green stuff dripping everywhere. I was in a pissy mood. Then I came to this clearing and…." He stopped, smiling at the memory but unable to convey how magical it had been.

"There were these little creatures. If they stood still, they looked like mushrooms. But they had tiny drums and whistle things and they were dancing. When they saw me they rushed over and spoke to me, but I couldn't understand a word. They weren't hostile, though. They seemed welcoming. And soon they were dancing around me, and it was so *weird*, I started dancing too. Carefully, so I didn't step on anyone. After a few songs they wandered off into the forest."

"What were they?"

"No idea," said Achilles with a chuckle. "Agent Afolabi looked them up but drew a blank. Townsend didn't know either, which was incredibly rare. But I hear some strings were pulled and that stretch of land was bought by a private conservancy. I hope they're dancing still."

It was Dee's turn to squeeze his hand. "So you rescued them."

"I don't know about that. If so, indirectly. But the world… sometimes it sucks so bad. But it's also full of wonders."

"I'm ready now," said Dee.

So was Achilles.

Together they stood. There was no point in wandering around blindly, so they just had to hope that Dee's magic had placed them conveniently close to their target.

Achilles took a deep breath. "Hey!" he shouted. "Hello! Are you here? We'd like to help you." His call rolled away as if they stood on a vast plain.

Nobody answered.

"Together?" Dee offered.

"Good idea. One, two, three. Hello! Are you here?"

The two of them together were greater than the sum of the parts. Not only was the shouting louder, but it had more depth. It felt more real.

This time, a response arrived like a whisper carried on a breeze. "You here."

"What direction was that from?" Dee asked.

"Can't tell." Achilles said much more loudly, "Call again!"

There was a pause, then, "Call again," weaker this time.

Dee made a frustrated noise. "What if that's just an echo?"

"It's all we've got." But they needed more info to locate the source.

From somewhere in the far reaches of Achilles' brain, an idea surfaced. "Sing-along time."

"What?"

Achilles cleared his throat and bellowed. "The other day!"

"Day."

"I met a bear!"

"Bear."

"What the hell, Achilles?" That was Dee, not the… whatever.

"Some things are easier if you sing. And boy, I've met some bears." He continued the song, which he'd probably learned during some school event as a kid. "Out in the woods!"

"Woods."

"A way out there!"

"Out there."

When Achilles repeated the stanza, Dee joined him… and so did the faint third voice. So he continued. "He looked at me!"

"Looked at me."

It was coming from ahead and to the right. He was almost sure of it. Joined with Dee—physically and vocally—he walked slowly in that direction, singing the whole way and listening for responses. And they grew stronger. Soon the third person was repeating the entire line, loudly. They sounded male.

Dee and Achilles got to the end of the penultimate stanza— "Caught that branch, on the way back down!"—and the answer came right *there.*

They tripped over something and landed in a heap on the ground. Achilles felt around frantically and nearly sobbed when he touched someone who wasn't Dee. This someone was cold as the grave, skin stretched tightly over bones, and…. "Feathers!" Achilles exclaimed. His heart was beating too quickly and he could barely breathe.

The someone was in a ball, cowering.

"Get it together, Spanos," Achilles muttered to himself. Then he set a gentle hand on what he hoped was the person's shoulder. "I'm Achilles. This is Dee. We came here for you."

"I'm lost," the person whispered.

"But we found you."

"I'm broken."

"I've been broken too. Friends helped me heal. We can help you." Achilles hoped very much that this was true. "What's your name?"

The answer, when it came, was barely audible. "Ish."

Although the Bureau had given Achilles a fair bit of training on demons, there had been little discussion about angels. That was because, with rare exceptions, angels kept to themselves. The Bureau almost never had to deal with them. So Achilles didn't know whether angels, like demons, had distinct names, and if so, whether Ish was one of them. That was something they could work out later.

"Okay, Ish. Just give us a minute and Dee's going to get us out of here."

"No charm," said Dee, sounding panicky again.

Right. That. There was nothing here but the three of them, all of them bare, and—

Something grabbed hold of Achilles' ankle and jerked, making him yelp with pain. It was cold and hard, like an iron band, and when he kicked violently, it didn't let go. He reached down to dislodge it but felt nothing against his hand even though he was now being pulled away from Dee and Ish. He tried to get to his hands and knees, but the force only jerked at him again, and when he scrabbled at the floor he couldn't get any handholds, any traction.

He was being dragged away.

He vaguely registered someone calling his name, but it was very far away. Unimportant. The futility of resisting hit him like a heavy, wet blanket, and he collapsed entirely. What was the point of fighting? He would lose anyway. They were all going to lose, and there was nothing a nobody like him could do about it. Gods, the despair was too much. He curled into a ball and felt his heart thudding slowly, uselessly, his lungs dragging in and out, the weight of every mistake he'd ever made pressing into him. He'd killed his parents. He'd killed Orson. He'd killed Santiago Bautista. And now he'd killed Dee as well, and—

Dee.

He wasn't sure whether he'd said the name out loud, but he definitely heard the response—"Achilles!"—and now a pair of hands grasped his upper arms.

"No use," Achilles moaned. But the hands were warm and strong. He *knew* those hands. Those fingers had threaded through his hair during a kiss, had applied antibiotic ointment and butterfly bandages to a bullet graze on his shoulder, had brought him water when he lay parched in chains. Had given him literal magic.

Achilles rose to his knees and took both of those hands in his. "Did I lose Ish?" he asked hoarsely.

"Caught that branch," Ish replied, very close.

The hopelessness didn't entirely flee, but now there was an equal measure of optimism in Achilles' chest. They *could* win this. Together. Because he was neither powerless nor alone, and when he gave his support to his formidable allies, they could work wonders.

When Achilles reached out with one hand—the other still had a death grip on Dee—he brushed against feathers. A desperate little noise escaped him as he groped until he found Ish's thin wrist and held that too. "Don't let go." Meant as a command to Dee, it came out more as a plea.

Achilles' brain felt slow, as dark as their surroundings, a machine whose batteries had nearly run out. It would be so much easier to give in to the inevitable and become the nothing he knew he was.

"Happy Meal," said Dee, quite clearly. "Dancing mushrooms. The starry sky in the desert."

Achilles was *not* nothing.

"Ish, can we have one of your feathers?"

"My feathers are the branch?"

"Yes, yes!"

"Take a twig."

So Achilles released Ish's wrist, but only long enough to yank a single feather from a wing—Ish didn't even twitch in response—and hand it to Dee. "Our charm," he explained.

When Dee laughed, the darkness momentarily lightened. Only a little, but even that much was a miracle. "Perfect. Make your wish, Achilles."

He had so many wishes, all of a sudden. One was paramount, however. "I want to return safely to White and Marek's house with Dee and Ish."

He waited, and after a minute or so Dee moaned. "It's not working. I can't do it."

"You can."

"I'm not strong enough."

"You are. You've rescued me how many times already? You saved me just now." Achilles put all his conviction into his words. Because sometimes if you believed in other people, then they believed in themselves.

Dee huffed, squeezing Achilles' hand while trying again.

"Can't!" Dee sobbed.

They were going to be stuck here forever. And without Dee, without Ish, with the battle lost, the war would be lost as well, and then—

"She'll be coming 'round the mountain!" Achilles bellowed.

"Um, what?"

Not bothering to explain, Achilles simply continued singing. Badly, but that hardly mattered. "She'll be coming 'round the mountain, she'll be coming 'round the mountain, she'll be coming 'round the mountain when she comes."

"She'll be… driving six white horses?"

"Fuck yes! She'll be driving six white horses!"

Together they yelled the stupid song, and as they did, a slight tingle began at their joined hands. It was weird but not unpleasant, and it grew as they continued through the verses. By the time they reached the final one—"We'll be singin' 'Hallelujah' when she comes"—Achilles' entire body felt electrified. He was sweating, his cock hard and throbbing, his heart racing so quickly it was a wonder it was still in his rib cage.

And then Ish joined the song. He didn't sing in English or any other language that Achilles had ever heard; his syllables sounded as wild and alien as the mushroom creatures' music. But Ish kept to the same tune as Dee and Achilles, and now a current ran *through* Achilles, from Ish in one hand to Dee in the other. Achilles twitched with it, literally dancing with pleasure and pain, until they all reached the song's final word.

"Got it!" Dee shouted triumphantly.

This time, all three of them laughed, and the darkness brightened as if dawn was on the verge of breaking. That lasted only a moment, which was long enough for Achilles to see Dee's beautiful, almost ecstatic face.

Then Dee pressed the feather between their clasped hands, Achilles repeated his wish, and a supernova exploded.

CHAPTER 24

*D*ee had been run over by a freight train. That's what it felt like, anyway, and although he didn't think anything was broken and he didn't seem to be bleeding, he couldn't move. Untangling his body from the other two nude bodies was far more than he could manage. He couldn't even pry his eyes open.

But he could hear.

"Holy *shit!*" exclaimed a gravelly male voice.

Another male voice, smoother and more refined, responded. "What is *that?*"

"I think… he's an angel."

The response from the smoother voice came in a Slavic-sounding language and had the cadence of a prayer.

Then Achilles, who was mostly underneath Dee, groaned. "Help Ish. Please."

Dee managed to get his eyes open in time to see a familiar pair of vampires stepping toward them. The vampires were naked, which was a puzzle to be worked out later. Clay White, who was the bulkier of them, scooped Ish into his arms as if he were a child and carried him out of the room. Which was, Dee now realized, a tastefully decorated living room.

He'd managed to transport all three of them back to San Francisco, exactly as Achilles had wished.

"Oh, thank fuck," he said. And then blacked out.

* * *

"You are goddamn amazing, Damnation Martell."

Achilles sat on the living room floor, staring at Dee, who was laid out on the couch like an invalid. Dee was naked under the soft plaid blanket; Achilles wore sweatpants and a gray T-shirt, both possibly borrowed from White. Which implied that vampires wore sweatpants, an image that made Dee want to break out in hysterical giggles.

Instead he asked, "How's Ish?"

"Sort of comatose. I've never seen any living creature look that awful. But he is alive. And he's out of the black hole. Thanks to you."

Dee took a few deep, shuddering breaths. "Now what?"

"Now you rest."

That sounded like an excellent plan. Dee felt as if he could give Rip Van Winkle a run for the record. "Is Ish really Charles's dad?"

"Dunno. Chief'll be back from Seattle tomorrow. We were gone for five days."

"*Five days?*"

"They feared we might be gone for good. And when we did return, Clay says we popped back in with, like, a sonic boom."

Dee turned this over in his head for a moment. "I'm hungry."

"Yeah. I ordered a whole lot of delivery because our hosts' diet doesn't quite suit us. Want me to bring you some Korean fried chicken and/or pizza and/or pad Thai?"

"All of the above," Dee answered, laughing.

"I got donuts too."

But the conversation had sapped the last of Dee's strength, and his lids slid closed. "In a little while," he mumbled.

Achilles tucked the blanket slightly higher under Dee's chin. "I'm here to serve you, Dee. Your wish is my command."

* * *

They had arrived in San Francisco midmorning, which explained their hosts' nudity: the vampires had been fast asleep at the time. Apparently vampires—these two, at least—eschewed pajamas. It was well after dark by the time Dee felt capable of prying himself off the couch, and even then, it was all he could do to totter around in jeans and a sweatshirt that Achilles had somehow procured for him.

"I hate being so weak," Dee complained as he sank back onto the couch after a bathroom visit.

Achilles sat next to him. "I know what you mean. I was laid up for a while after the bear attack—the *first* bear attack—and I hated it."

"Who took care of you?"

"The Bureau has—*had*—its own little hospital wing. Top-notch care by people who are used to treating weird injuries and weirder patients. But it's still a hospital, and I hate those places. I got out of there ASAP."

Although Dee was glad that Achilles had received proper medical treatment, he didn't like the sound of the rest of it. "So who took care of you once you were out?" He was pretty sure he knew the answer.

And sure enough, Achilles shrugged. "I managed okay on my own. I always have. You too, right?"

"Until recently, I never had to. I hardly ever get sick, and I spent forty years with nobody trying to kill me. When I made charms, they were little ones. Not enough to drain me."

Achilles, who was looking pretty drawn himself, nodded and leaned back against the cushions. Dee wanted to ask what had happened to him in the black hole, but Dee had raised the subject twice already today, and both times Achilles had shuddered and shaken his head.

Maybe it was time to distract Achilles with a different painful subject. "Orson," Dee ventured.

Achilles looked sharply at him. "What?"

"Tell me about him."

"Ugh." Achilles lolled again, closed his eyes, and kept them that way. "He was a really good guy. Smart. Working on a grad degree in some kind of biomedical thing that I totally didn't understand but knew was important. We met right after I graduated college and started Bureau training. He was… I don't know. Wholesome. *Normal.* He had a supportive family who were nice to me, a cat named Scan— because CAT scan, ha ha ha. He liked to play video games, go snow- boarding, and yell at the TV."

Dee felt a small pang, but couldn't tell whether it was jealousy, envy, or both. "What happened to him?"

"On one of my very first assignments, my partner and I had a surprise run-in with an anzu. Injuries ensued. I detoured by that hospital I was telling you about and came home late, after some treat- ment for third degree burns. I mean, they were just small ones. I wasn't very close to the anzu when it spit fire. But Orson freaked out. Gave me an ultimatum—the job or him."

Well, Dee knew how that had turned out. "He shouldn't have forced that decision on you."

"No, I get it. He couldn't deal with constantly worrying that I'd die. So… he died instead."

"From the anzu?" Dee asked, horrified even though he didn't know what one was.

"No. From Los Angeles. A couple weeks after we broke up, he was driving back to my apartment to pick some stuff up—it had been *our* apartment—and got in a wreck. He was a good driver, too. The other guy wasn't."

Achilles was clearly trying to be flippant about the whole thing, as if it didn't matter anymore, but the pain on his face said otherwise. Dee patted his knee slightly awkwardly. "Thanks for sharing with me."

Achilles started to say something, stopped, and then shot to his feet. "I should check on Ish."

"Can I come too?"

"Can you make it upstairs?"

"Yes," Dee said with far more certainty than he actually possessed.

In fact, it took him about a thousand years to climb the single flight, but he managed. Achilles came up right behind him, as if prepared to catch him should he fall.

The upper story looked as if it hadn't been changed much since the house was constructed. There were some built-in cabinets and drawers, a bathroom, and two bedrooms. The one to the right overlooked the street and was likely the one where Clay and Marek slept. The other currently contained a bed, a chair, a dresser, a vampire, and an angel. Until Dee and Achilles entered, at which point it also contained a hero and a djinn.

"How's he doing?" Achilles asked Marek softly. Clay had left the house soon after dark to fetch dinner for himself and Clay. Dee hadn't been brave enough to ask what that errand entailed.

Marek, who'd been sitting in the chair, stood. "He rests."

There was more whispered conversation, but instead of trying to follow it, Dee tiptoed forward. Ish lay on his side, his back slightly curled and a blanket pulled up to his waist. His skin was nearly as white as the sheets, as was his long, matted hair. His eyes were closed, pale lashes over razor-sharp cheekbones, and his mouth hung slightly open, revealing razor-sharp teeth. One hand was loosely curled near his face, which lent him an air of innocence sharply at odds with his skeletal features.

And his wings…. They were as enormous as Tenrael's but with snow-white feathers. They were terribly ragged, however, the flesh torn and swaths of feathers reduced to nothing but naked barbs.

"Hi," Dee said, because he felt as if he should say something. "It's Dee. You're among friends now."

Maybe he imagined it, but he thought that perhaps Ish's eyelids fluttered a little.

Then his own exhaustion hit him like a wave, and he came damned close to swooning like a Victorian maiden. Fortunately, Achilles noticed and acted fast, catching him before he fell and then half carrying him down the stairs. Dee made it to the couch and was asleep before his head hit the cushion.

CHAPTER 25

Marek and Clay generously offered Achilles their own bed, but he didn't want to be far from Dee and so he slept fitfully in an armchair instead. Not that he expected Dee to run away—he wasn't capable of it right now—and not that their current situation felt especially dangerous. Achilles simply wanted to be near.

He woke up before Dee and crept into the kitchen, where he found Clay sitting at the table with a mug of red liquid. "I picked up a few groceries if you want 'em," Clay said.

"Thanks. Is Marek still on angel duty?" Achilles made a vague gesture upward.

"He's fascinated. Someone his age, it's hard to find something completely new. But you brought us Ish *and* a genie. Congratulations." Clay flashed one of his rare grins.

The groceries in question turned out to be a slab of bacon, a dozen eggs, and a fresh loaf from Acme Bread. There was also a thermos of coffee, which was an extra-nice touch. Achilles fried up a healthy serving of food and joined Clay at the table.

"Jesus, that smells good," Clay moaned.

"I'd offer you some, but…."

The habitual scowl returned. "Yeah."

Vampires could consume blood from any mammal and a few non-mammalian NHSs, but according to what Achilles had been taught, anything else made them violently ill. "Do you want me to eat this somewhere else?"

"No, it's fine. I can enjoy the scent, at least."

"Vampire limitations must be frustrating at times."

Clay's big hands were wrapped around his mug, dwarfing it. "I mostly don't mind. I was a night person before. And if Marek hadn't turned me, I'd be dead. Now I won't go bald, my knees and back won't give out, and as long as I avoid sunshine, decapitation, and wooden stakes, I'll be around a long time. It's worth the trade." He gazed at Achilles from under his brow. "I bet you've also given things up to be where you are."

"Yeah." And if, right after the bear mauled him, someone had asked Achilles whether it was worth it, he'd have said no. His answer might be different today, however.

They sat in silence for a long time, nursing their respective drinks. It was a cozy kitchen. Abe and Thomas must have updated it in the fifties, and since then very little had been done. The current owners, of course, didn't do any cooking. It was a wonder they'd even possessed the basic cookware and cutlery that Achilles had needed to prepare breakfast.

But Abe and Thomas had lived here a long time; from what he understood, they'd been together for decades. Abe, who was aging very slowly due to his weird association with the dead, had watched his partner get old, fall sick, and die. From what Achilles had heard, Abe was heartbroken when Thomas passed. But even then, Abe didn't give up. As he told Achilles once, "I'll keep fighting the good fight, boychik. I still have to face myself in the mirror, don't I?"

"Grimes is here," said Clay, seconds before the doorbell rang. Vampire hearing was a wonder.

When Charles entered the house, he looked uncharacteristically disheveled and his pallor was even more pronounced than usual. One of Tenrael's horns was broken. "It will grow back," he said when he caught Achilles staring.

"What the hell happened in Seattle?" Achilles demanded. They were all crowded into the vestibule, and he smelled gunpowder on Charles's clothes.

Charles shook his head. "It's bad. But I need to see—" He stopped and visibly calmed himself. "Thank you for what you did. Is Dee all right?"

"Just tired. He was fucking amazing, Chief. He didn't just grant wishes—he saved my neck."

"And… the angel?"

Clay answered. "The same. He's upstairs."

Charles took off at a near gallop, Tenrael hard at his heels. Clay apparently decided to stay downstairs, but not Achilles. He didn't need to be there when Charles and Ish met, but he was curious as hell.

They all burst into the bedroom in a manner that would have startled anyone but a vampire. Marek, however, was already standing. He nodded at Tenrael and left the room.

Charles froze when he reached the bedside. He stood there, gazing down, looking more vulnerable and more human than Achilles had ever seen him. The resemblance between him and Ish was unmistakable now. They shared the same arched white eyebrows, high cheekbones, and slightly beaky nose. The same prominent chin. They were both ageless. And when Charles touched a tentative finger to Ish's wing, Ish's lids lifted to show eyes the same bottle-green as Charles's.

"I am Charles Grimm."

Ish stared at him silently before letting out a long sigh. "I failed your mother. I failed you."

And then Charles began to sob. It was far more than Achilles thought he should witness, so he gave a single pat to Tenrael's arm and then left the room.

Downstairs, Dee was sitting upright on the couch while Clay and Marek hovered nearby. "Is it him?" Dee asked. "Is Ish his father?"

"I think so."

Achilles sat next to him. He didn't know what Clay and Marek were thinking about, but he suspected that Dee's thoughts were running the same direction as his own: memories of parents long gone. Some wounds were incredibly slow to heal and would always leave a scar.

* * *

An hour later, Dee had eaten breakfast and the vampires had retired to their room. It had been interesting to see Clay and Marek together. Clay had always been dour, and becoming a vampire hadn't changed that, but in Marek's presence he seemed more comfortable in himself. And Marek, elegant and urbane, seemed as if he felt more grounded with Clay's earthy presence. An odd match, perhaps, but in Achilles' estimation, a good one.

Tenrael and Charles came down to the living room. Now Charles *really* looked like he'd been dragged backward through hell, but some of the perpetual iciness in his eyes had warmed. He sat in the armchair, and when Tenrael knelt beside him, Charles immediately reached over and stroked his wings.

Emotional support demon, Achilles thought, but he managed to suppress a smile.

"My gratitude to both of you," Charles began.

Achilles raised a hand. "It can remain unstated. We would have done it regardless of whether he was your relative."

"Is he going to be all right?" Dee asked.

Charles sighed. "He's… badly hurt. I need to find a place where he'll be safe as he recovers. But there are no safe spots now."

"I can make him one."

As Charles blinked in surprise, Achilles gave Dee a poke in the arm. "You're already worn out, man. You can't—"

"It's not so bad. The more I use it, the stronger I get. Like a muscle. Give me a couple hours and I bet I could manage."

Although Achilles wanted to be protective of Dee, he held his tongue. Dee was an adult and could make his own decisions; he didn't need a nursemaid, and it wasn't Achilles' place to tell him what to do. He couldn't help but wonder, however, just how much Dee would be

190

capable of with more practice. Charles was undoubtedly wondering the same.

"I'd be deeply obliged," Charles said. "But if you're going to fashion a place of refuge, it should be for you. And maybe Achilles."

Achilles made a noise. "Not me. I'm still in this, Chief." It was weirdly relieving to say so.

Dee clutched at Achilles' knee. "But… we won. Ish is free."

Oh no. Achilles hadn't been clear enough about this, just as he hadn't sufficiently explained to Orson how risky his new job was. He spoke slowly now, carefully. "People talk about it—*I* talk about it—like it's a war. Battles. Enemies. Casualties. But that's as much a fiction as"—he made finger quotes for emphasis—"the 'war on drugs' and the 'war on crime.' A real war, even a bad one, has a goal in sight. Has an end. The Bureau's duties don't. We will *never* win, although I guess we can lose big time."

"Then why bother?" Dee looked deeply troubled.

"Because… because making the effort counts. Every time someone tries to do good, even in a small way, it matters." Achilles wished he could articulate this better. He felt the truth of it even if he couldn't quite find the right words.

Unexpectedly, Tenrael came to his rescue. "An analogy. Imagine a plot of land. Perhaps a forest once grew there, perhaps crops were planted, but now it is barren. I plant a seed there—it is tiny. Charles also plants a seed, and Achilles, and Clay and Marek, and our friends from the stars, and the coyotes, and many others. Some of those seeds mature to plants that, in turn, produce more seeds. Now the land is lush with growth. Eventually, drought will come, or floods, or fire, or the climate may become inhospitable. The plants will die, the land is once again barren. For a time, however, there was growth. In the future there might be again. So we plant our seeds."

Achilles gave him a grateful smile before turning to Dee. "By the sound of it, something's royally fucked up in Seattle right now. We don't know whether Dunn's still alive, and even if she isn't, her buddies are still moving forward. There's shit *everywhere*, it seems like. Lots of Bureau agents are smarter than me. Lots are stronger. I don't have a single, solitary superpower. I'm not as young as I used to be. But dammit, I can still plant a seed. So that's what I'm going to do."

As he gave this little speech, Achilles had a realization. He wasn't continuing the fight because he wanted to impress anyone or receive praise. It wouldn't make up for anything in his past and it wouldn't make anyone love him. He'd probably end up with more scars, at the least, or quite possibly a grave. Nevertheless, he wanted to do this because, for fuck's sake, planting seeds was what he did. Who he was.

After a long pause, Dee nodded and then took Achilles' hand. "Could you maybe use a trowel?" he asked.

Forget about overextended analogies and the watchful presence of a demon and a half-angel. Achilles twisted, grasped Dee's shoulders, and kissed the ever-loving hell out of him.

CHAPTER 26

An agreement was negotiated without Dee's participation, which was fine with him. He was still recuperating from his magic and slightly stunned from that kiss. Achilles had kissed him like he meant it—not out of lust but a different sort of passion altogether. Which made Dee think that, while their time together might end up being cut short by death, it would still be worth it. While they could, they'd damn well bloom.

Consequently, Dee was thrilled to learn that he'd be given until tomorrow to recharge his battery, and that since the little house was now overflowing, Achilles and Dee would temporarily decamp to a hotel. Charles was concerned about the safety aspects of this, but Achilles argued that nowhere was safe right now, not even secret alien compounds in the desert.

An hour later, Dee and Achilles were gleefully checked into a room at a vintage hotel a couple miles away. It wasn't the fanciest place in town, but it was nice enough, in a quiet neighborhood, with an ocean view.

They were barely inside when Achilles kicked the door shut, grabbed Dee, and shoved him against the wall for another of those knee-shaking kisses. "Sorry," Achilles said, pulling back slightly. He didn't *look* sorry at all. With his wild hair and a feral gleam in in his eyes, he bore more resemblance to a satyr than his namesake hero. "If you have any doubts about this, I don't blame you. I won't—"

Dee shut him up by kissing him back.

"Does that satisfy your need for affirmative consent?" Dee asked when they came up for breath.

"It does."

For the first time in his life, Dee wanted someone. Not in a sort of general *it would be fun to fuck* sort of way. This was a burning need—almost literally, like a fire raging in his core—to physically unite with this particular person. He felt greedy in that he wanted to have Achilles. But also generous, in that he wanted Achilles to have him.

"The one time when being naked would come in handy," Achilles grumbled, fumbling at his clothes.

Dee's came off more easily—like magic—and he graciously helped Achilles with the last of his. Then they both stood there, feasting with their eyes. Dee didn't know what Achilles saw in him, although Achilles was hard, which was a good sign. When he looked at Achilles, he saw a Greek god turned man, with scars old and new, with some sexy facial stubble and warm brown eyes.

Suddenly it was Dee's turn to grab Achilles and pin him against the wall. "I need your consent too."

"Jesus, Dee, can't you tell I—"

"You could take me apart, piece by piece, and if I thought it pleased you, I'd only beg for more. You could consume me and I'd be glad of it. I don't know if this is because I'm a djinn or if it's my own personal quirk, and I guess it doesn't matter. I want you to own me, body and soul, and I want to grant all your wishes. Do you understand? Because we've known each other only a short time, and it's been a *weird* time, and I understand this may be way too much for you."

Achilles looked at him solemnly, and for a terrible moment Dee believed that Achilles would turn away. Then he reminded himself to *hope*, just as Achilles kept telling him. And as if the thought made it true, Achilles leaned his forehead against Dee's.

"I feel like I've been waiting for you for twenty years," Achilles said.

That was the most beautiful sentence that Dee had ever heard. The core of it all, he thought, was that Achilles didn't seem to value him for the magic Dee could do. Achilles saw in him a man of worth, a man who made good choices, a man who had a place in the world.

Dee sank to his knees and took Achilles' cock into his mouth.

Dee had given head only twice before. He'd never been especially interested in the act, but now he wanted it desperately. Wanted to kneel in front of Achilles, worshiping him in the most intimate way, making Achilles temporarily forget all his worries. Dee feared he wasn't very good, however, since he couldn't take all of Achilles' length without choking.

Then Achilles grabbed Dee's hair—hard, with both hands—and moaned deeply, and Dee decided maybe he wasn't so bad at this after all. He experimented with different movements of his hand, tongue, and lips, glancing up often to see what had the best impact. When he scraped his teeth ever-so-gently against tender skin, Achilles groaned and gripped Dee's hair even more tightly.

Looking up at Achilles' flushed skin, his wide-blown pupils, Dee realized that he could very likely come just like this, his own cock untouched, simply from the pleasure of pleasuring Achilles.

Before Dee could explore that intriguing idea, however, Achilles hauled him upright, dragged him to the bed, pushed him down, and threw himself on top. "Too rough?" he panted, cradling Dee's face in his hands.

"Take me apart, piece by piece," Dee repeated, meaning every word of it.

They groped each other roughly, thrillingly, learning new topography and making it their own. Achilles had firm muscles despite his recent misadventures. His skin, marred in places with divots, ridges, and furrows, was otherwise pleasingly soft. Dee wanted to burrow into him, make a living robe of him, taste him even in his dreams.

When Achilles probed a single spit-slick finger between Dee's cheeks, all that Dee yearned for was to engulf him. "Please," he begged, hoping that Achilles knew what he meant.

"I don't have lube. Or rubbers."

"Don't care."

It might have been foolish to proceed without either, but Dee was very much in a *carpe diem* sort of mood. For all he knew, gun-toting bears and evil ex-congresswomen would burst in on them five minutes from now and he'd never again have this opportunity. It was absolutely worth the pain and risk.

Achilles must have thought the same. He growled into Dee's ear, sounding very much like a bear himself, then rose up, but only so he could flip Dee over. When Dee hastily gathered his knees beneath him, Achilles gave his ass a couple of appreciative squeezes and then, with a happy sort of sound, used his tongue to wet and loosen the tight ring of muscles.

Dee clutched the bedcover and thought frantically of the least sexy things possible. Recycling collection schedules. American cheese. Stock market tickers. But not even software terms and conditions could calm him down, and by the time Achilles stopped tonguing him and instead pressed the tip of his cock slightly in, Dee was almost sobbing with need.

"Fuck me, dammit. Please. Gods, Achilles."

Achilles leaned down over Dee's back so he could whisper in his ear: "Well, when you ask so nicely...." Then he reared back up, grabbed Dee's hips, and pushed inside.

Dee literally saw stars. There was some pain, yes, because it had been a long time since Dee had done this, and Achilles was not being at all gentle. Dee didn't want him to be gentle. What Dee wanted was exactly what he was getting: deep thrusts making him burn, a bruising grip on his hips, soft words tumbling from Achilles' mouth in a torrent.

"Yes, Dee, beloved, good, so good, Dee...." There was also a lot of Greek, which Dee didn't understand, but it sounded poetic, as if Achilles had been possessed by the spirit of Homer himself. Except there were also plenty of English profanities, and those sounded entirely like Achilles.

Dee himself didn't say much. Couldn't say much, although he

managed some coherent pleas in between his whimpers and moans. He teetered right at the edge, trying his best not to fall.

"What do you need, Dee?" Achilles asked, still rocking his hips.

And *that* was enough. Dee tumbled, electrified and ecstatic, disintegrating into endless points of bright light.

* * *

DOZING IN ACHILLES' arms, Dee felt stupidly optimistic. He didn't *know* that they'd survive whatever was coming. In fact, if he thought about it logically, his doubts were many and entirely realistic. But he *felt* differently. Felt, in fact, as if they'd already won. Post-coital endorphins, probably, but nice nonetheless.

"Icarus," he said sleepily into Achilles' shoulder.

"Huh?"

"I flew too close to the sun."

"I'm not the sun." Achilles drew back a little so that they were face to face. "Did I hurt you? Are you having regrets?" His brow was drawn with concern.

Dee reached up to smooth the crease away. "You hurt me deliciously, and I have zero regrets. I don't mind being Icarus. I mean, it must have been glorious for him for a while, right?"

Achilles' expression relaxed. "This wasn't…. It's never been like that for me. Why do I feel like this about you? What's going on?"

"You're asking me?" Dee chuckled. But then doubt stabbed him. "Are you sorry? Do you wish I—"

"I wish you to be exactly as you are. I'm the opposite of sorry. Just… bewildered, I guess. But hey, if we're both destined to live a life of weird, at least for once the weird can be good. Spectacular, in fact." He waggled his eyebrows.

"You know, I made love charms a couple of times. Didn't want to because it's creepy, but I was broke. Anyway, they sort of worked at first. But pretty soon…. One client came back a couple months later, looking like she'd aged years. She said the guy fell for her, all right, but pretty soon they had nothing but shrieking arguments. So she left him, but now he was stalking her."

"Jesus."

Dee winced at old regrets and moral failings. "She told me that all her previous feelings for him had changed—like a chemical alteration —and now they were, well, synthetic. Like that artificial banana flavor."

"What did you do?"

"I let her wish the other wish away. For free," he hastened to add. "And it helped. He stopped stalking her. She felt less torn up. It definitely wasn't a happy ending, though. They both had to live with what they'd done."

Achilles was silent for a while, although he gave a small smile when Dee toyed with his tangled curls. Finally, he sighed. "If you're implying that what we have is influenced by magic, I wouldn't argue, although I have no clue how. But even if it *is* magic, it's not like your love charm. I can feel this—feel you—in every cell of my body. And it feels right. If magic got us here, well, I'm fine with that. I don't understand jet airplanes and I know they sometimes fall out of the sky, but when I have to get somewhere far and fast, I'm happy to use 'em."

"It feels right to me too," Dee assured him. "I just felt like I ought to say something. Caveat emptor?"

"I don't own you, Dee."

Dee looked at him earnestly. Imploringly, even. "But you could. I really, really wish you did."

Achilles' smile was blinding. "Always, your wish is my command."

Sex the second time was even better than the first. And the third time, late that evening, was somehow even better. So good, in fact, that Dee seriously thought it might kill him. It would have been a very happy ending indeed.

CHAPTER 27

*T*he following morning, Marek took one look at Dee and Achilles and burst out laughing. "I thought that Dee was meant to be resting yesterday."

Achilles blushed, which made him feel ridiculous, and pretended to be fascinated by a framed print hanging in Marek and Clay's living room. It showed a vast ghostly army marching across a field toward a large stone building.

But Dee simply chuckled. "I slept. In between."

Achilles turned to Charles, who was watching closely from the armchair, Tenrael kneeling beside him. "Yeah, I know it's not very professional." He lifted his chin. "But I don't give a shit because—"

"It's fine. It's good, in fact. Intimacy is one of our greatest weapons." He stroked Tenrael's feathers, and Tenrael nearly purred in response.

Dee, who looked slightly triumphant, took Achilles by the hand and towed him to the couch, where they sat pressed close together. Marek took a seat at the other end, while Clay leaned against a wall, muscular arms folded. "The good news," Dee announced, "is that I'm fully recharged. More than. I feel like I've been *turbo*charged. And I'm in the mood to grant wishes." He bounced up and down like an eager kid.

Actually, he'd been bouncy all morning, first waking Achilles with a blowjob and then practically ping-ponging off the walls while he waited for Achilles to shower and dress. Unlike Achilles, Dee hadn't needed any caffeine when they made a quick breakfast stop. Achilles, while somewhat more sedate, was feeling pretty buoyant himself, like a hot air balloon barely tethered to the ground.

"I'm going to need a couple small items to use as charms." Dee sounded like a stage magician.

"In a moment," said Charles solemnly. "I want to share some developments first."

Achilles tensed, not liking the sound of that. "Is Ish doing okay?"

"He's much the same. Dee, I asked Afolabi to do some more research on djinn."

"I thought she had a zillion more important things to worry about."

"She's… very busy. But you did a great service for us—for *me*—and it was important to thank you." Charles gave a half shrug. "And if you choose to remain with us, it would behoove us all to know more about your capabilities."

He probably also wanted to know about Dee's weaknesses but was wise enough to not say so. And Achilles wasn't about to butt in.

"Did she learn stuff?" Dee's tone was light, but Achilles could feel his tension.

"A bit. Most of what's recorded is folklore, so it's hard to know how deeply it can be trusted. In general, it appears that djinn are inclined to become subservient to humans—to a particular human."

Dee nodded. "We want a master."

Achilles had mixed feelings about this. On the one hand, well, he wanted to *be* Dee's master. Wanted it a lot. But he absolutely didn't want to force anything. He shifted uncomfortably on the couch.

"For what it's worth," said Charles, "I see nothing wrong with this." As if for emphasis, he tugged one of Tenrael's feathers, which made Tenrael smile. "It took me a while to realize this. But me being Ten's master doesn't make him weak. You've seen him and know he's not. If anything, willingly giving yourself over to someone takes a lot of strength. It makes me stronger too, though, because I have added responsibilities. So together, Ten and I are much more than we are apart."

Tenrael reached behind himself, plucked a feather, and handed it to Charles, who smiled and tucked it into his shirt pocket.

"I offered myself to Charles," Tenrael said. "I told him that he would be my heart and soul, and I would be his wings. And for nearly a century—a long time by human standards—it has been so. I would eagerly trade all the previous years of my existence for a single day with my master."

Achilles was not accustomed to discussing feelings, and this was beginning to seem more like group therapy than a strategy meeting, so he attempted a redirection. "Did she find out anything else useful?" When Dee elbowed him, Achilles elbowed him back.

Charles hesitated slightly before speaking. "She may have found some information about your mother, Dee."

Dee went very still. "Yes?" His voice sounded choked.

"A woman matching her description was selling charms in New Orleans four years ago. I'm sorry, but that's all we know. New Orleans is in the East Coast's jurisdiction, and we're not currently in communication with them."

"Oh."

Well, shit. Achilles took Dee's hand. "I can wish that you find her."

Dee opened his mouth, closed it again, and shook his head. "Not now. Things are already pretty complicated." He turned to Charles. "Anything else?"

"Not about djinn, no. I'm sorry. But there have been… other developments. I believe I mentioned earlier that I've lost touch with several agents. Well, we've found some of them."

An icy chill ran down Achilles' spine. "And?"

Charles's expression, usually stony, turned almost terrifying with anger, and he spat out his reply like poison. "Deported. Arrested by the feds, who claimed they're illegal aliens and sent them to a prison camp in Central America."

Achilles, who should have become accustomed to atrocities, found himself speechless.

After a heavy silence, Dee spoke. "But they are—or were—federal agents themselves. I don't understand."

"It's a pretext," snarled Charles. "Many of those who worked for the Bureau were, in fact, born outside of the United States. Others were born here but their paperwork is problematic."

Achilles did a quick mental tally. Henry, a house spirit, didn't have a birth certificate. Neither did Edge, a dog shifter. The coyote shifters probably didn't either. Ralph Crespo had been hatched somewhere in Europe. The aliens were literally aliens. Achilles didn't know when or where Tenrael came from, but it certainly wasn't the US. Charles and Abe *were* born here and might have had birth certificates, but both of them were well over a hundred years old and looked much younger, which would be an issue.

"In the past, I have seen governments behave in such a way," said Marek gravely. "It does not bode well."

Charles nodded. "I don't think any of us are safe right now, but you need to take special care. They may know you've been associated with us. I'm doing what I can, but I don't have much influence outside the US. Dammit, if Townsend hadn't gotten himself killed...."

"Master. He believed that the best course of action was for you to become chief. You should not assume things would be better under his command."

"I don't see how they could be much worse. At any rate, we already knew that Dee and Achilles were actively targeted. Now it appears that any of us might be seized at any time."

"I'd like to see them try," Clay growled, showing a mouthful of fangs. He'd been a fairly scary human, but as a vampire... well, Achilles was very glad they were on the same side.

Things got a little chaotic at this point. Charles tried to remind Clay that none of them were invulnerable, Marek was talking about despots from three hundred years ago, Tenrael continued to try giving

Charles moral support, and Dee was still expressing bewilderment that the feds could be this downright nasty.

"Hey!" Achilles shouted, leaping to his feet. "This is getting us nowhere. We need a plan of action."

That shut everyone up, which was gratifying, and then Dee stood too. "We can start with wishes."

Achilles gave him a quick kiss, because why the hell not.

Grinning, Dee turned Marek. "I promised one to you guys. If you want, you can wish for safety from the feds."

"No," Marek said slowly. "That would feel inequitable. But perhaps...." He glanced at Clay, who gave a firm nod. "The sun. Clay has not walked in the sun for a decade, and for me it has been... considerably longer. If we could have one day—"

"I can make it permanent," Dee said. "If you want."

Nobody questioned Dee's confidence, Achilles least of all. Not after what Dee had already accomplished. And when both vampires stared at Dee in wonder, Achilles felt as proud as if he were the one wielding fancy magic. This was *his* djinn.

The rest was simple. Marek handed Dee a silk handkerchief and Dee did his thing. Marek made a wish. Then everyone watched as Clay and Marek walked out the back door into the postage-stamp yard and turned their faces up to the bright sky. When Marek fell to his knees and Clay went to comfort him, though, everyone else returned to the living room to give them some privacy.

And Dee, whose jeans were sporting a noticeable bulge, blurted, "Excuse us!" and dragged Achilles into the vestibule, pushing him into a wall and plastering himself against him. "Wishes turn me on," he panted.

"Apparently," Achilles laughed. He grabbed Dee's ass and encouraged him to dry-hump Achilles' thigh.

"Can I...? Do you mind...?"

Deciding to do Dee one better, Achilles wedged a hand between them, unfastened Dee's jeans, and grabbed his eager dick. Although Achilles had usually preferred private locations for sex, he found this entire situation incredibly hot, especially when he squeezed and Dee whimpered. "Gonna make this quick and dirty," Achilles warned. Or maybe promised.

"Yes. Please."

Achilles was a man of his word. He maneuvered them so that Dee was backed into him, ass tight against Achilles' crotch, body pinned in place by Achilles' arm. While he worked Dee's cock with hard strokes, he licked his neck, nibbled on his earlobe, whispered obscene promises in his ear, and finally—maybe influenced by recent time spent with vampires—*bit* at the junction of neck and shoulder.

Dee came with a howl and collapsed back, shuddering. "J-Jesus fucking Christ. Let me—"

"Not now. You can owe me for later." Because while Achilles was also sort of desperate to get off, he thought a little bit of waiting would do him good. He needed to work on his patience.

Tenrael and Charles were waiting in the living room, Charles with a long-suffering expression. There was no sign of Marek and Clay, who were presumably still frolicking in the sunshine. Achilles couldn't help smiling at the thought of Clay White frolicking. Did magicked vampires have to worry about sunburns?

"Not sorry," Achilles announced, knowing that he and Dee had been perfectly audible even to human ears, let alone demonic or angelic ones. He didn't feel remotely apologetic.

"Is this… usual?" Charles asked. Despite his long-time career and hardboiled nature, he still had the vestiges of a person born during the Victorian era. Which was sort of charming, really.

"Kind of," Dee replied. "When I do my thing, it always feels sort of, uh, tingly. If it's a really *big* thing, like when we left the black hole, it's tingly while I'm making the charm, but then I'm so drained that I collapse afterward. Also…." He glanced at Achilles, seemed to consider for a moment, and then shrugged. "It's all a lot more when Achilles is near."

So was Achilles sort of his booster battery? Whether the effect was magical, physical, or psychological, Achilles liked it. He was a pretty ordinary guy, but if he could help make Dee even stronger, that was awfully damn special.

Charles looked intrigued too. "I'd love for you to have some discussions with my science people. Once we have the time… and I have science people again."

"Sure," said Dee. "As long as those discussions don't involve scalpels or probes."

"Perhaps we can…." Charles stopped and frowned in thought. "This just gave me a thought about where we might find refuge for Ish. Ten, what about Gunderson?"

Achilles recognized the name. "Art Gunderson? The guy who ran the lab?" Achilles had never met him in person because the lab was located in northern California, almost at the Oregon border. But they'd talked on the phone a few times before Gunderson retired. He'd seemed like a calm, steady sort of man. But he had to be close to eighty years old and was, as far as Achilles knew, entirely human.

"Why him?" Achilles asked, maybe somewhat too bluntly.

"His home is extremely remote. It's not approachable by land vehicle and is a strenuous hike on foot. Airplanes can't get there, and helicopters can't land." The corner of his mouth twitched. "Crespo can get in. I think he visits sometimes. Also, Gunderson's partner remains formidable."

"Not human?" Achilles guessed.

"Half Sasquatch. Dee, do you think there's some way you could get Ish to them? I can give you the coordinates of their cabin. Unfortunately, I have no way to contact them."

"So… you want me to just zap him there? Like, 'Hi guys, I'm a genie and this guy's a traumatized angel. Can you please babysit him while what's left of the Bureau tries to avert the end of the world?'"

Charles sighed. "Something like that."

Achilles wasn't sure what he thought about Dee acting as a transporter beam. Moving between dimensions, or whatever the black hole travel entailed, was one thing. But moving across physical space? He'd been taught that magic was simply stuff that science didn't understand yet—nothing more than unexpected bends in physics, chemistry, and biology—but this seemed like an especially big leap.

"I'll give it a shot," Dee said.

"What about what you said the other day?" Achilles asked. "The part where we didn't want to end up like *The Fly*?"

"I'm stronger now."

Achilles believed him.

They all tromped upstairs. Ish looked marginally less gaunt, and his eyes tracked them even though he didn't respond to their greetings. Charles knelt at the bedside like a penitent and spoke softly. "We're going to send you to a quiet place to rest. With friends. I will come back for you soon. I promise."

Ish lifted a hand and set it on Charles's. Although his voice was tissue-thin, the words were clear. "Your shadows are so deep and your lightness so bright. You exceed my hopes."

Charles covered his face and his shoulders shook.

Achilles tried hard not to think about his own parents. That was his personal baggage and not relevant now. Maybe when all of this was over, though, he might track down his sister and drop her a letter. Just to wish her well.

After a moment, Tenrael plucked one of his feathers and ceremoniously handed it to Dee with a small bow. "I very much hope that someday we have more time to speak," Tenrael said quietly. "You are an intriguing person." Before Achilles could decide whether he felt jealous, Tenrael turned to him. "When a person endures great hardship and deprivation yet goes on to care for others, as you have, that person is a hero."

"I haven't—"

Tenrael set a clawed hand on Achilles' shoulder and, smiling slightly, shook his head.

It really was time to move on; everyone knew it. Nobody bothered to try to talk Achilles out of joining this particular adventure, which saved a lot of wasted words. He was gratified to know they all trusted him to volunteer.

"I think Achilles should make the wish," Dee said. "If you don't mind, Charles."

Charles stood and backed away from the bed, then gestured them forward.

"Any special instructions?" Achilles asked him.

"If all goes well and you can make your way to civilization, call Henry on the emergency line. Con has made sure it's secure. But if you'd prefer to remain in sanctuary yourself—"

"No."

And that was that. *This is gonna be weird*, Achilles thought. Out loud, he said, "I wish that Dee and Ish and I can go to Art Gunderson's cabin. Safely." He intentionally left the means of transport vague, in case teleportation really was beyond Dee's skills. He didn't want to stretch the magic beyond its capabilities. Hopefully, the magic would come up with an alternative. Did magic itself have some kind of data-processing abilities, like AI? Maybe best not to think about that right now.

Dee did… whatever he did to grant wishes. He stared at Achilles the entire time, smile wide and cheeks flushed, and damned if Achilles' jeans didn't suddenly feel too tight. It appeared that he'd acquired a new kink.

He winked when Dee handed over the feather, then spoke to Ish. "I'm not sure exactly what's going to happen now. It might be really strange. But Dee came through for us before, and I know he will this time."

Ish said something in ancient Greek. Although Achilles had to struggle to understand him, he got the gist of it.

"I'm… cruel? I don't care about my comrades?"

With a ghost of a smile that made him momentarily beautiful, Ish shook his head. "The blind poet was mistaken," he said in English. "You care very much." Then he closed his eyes again.

Cryptic as all of that was, Achilles decided it constituted consent to be magicked. He gestured Dee to take one of Ish's thin hands, and he took the other. He gave a final nod to Charles and Tenrael—they both looked tense—and made his wish.

CHAPTER 28

Dee was a deck of cards, shuffled and reshuffled. A blizzard swirling across a plain. A sandy beach battered and stirred by stormy seas. A rubber band stretched allllmost to breaking.

And then he was a person again, kneeling in the dirt and puking his guts out, as Achilles did the same right next to him. Ish was there too, curled into a tight ball and possibly unconscious. Maybe angels didn't barf.

"I most sincerely hope," said Achilles, pausing to spit, "we never have to do that again."

"Amen."

"But you did it. None of us is a fly."

That seemed to be the case. Dee rose unsteadily to his feet and looked around. They'd landed—if that was the right term—on soil that was covered with layers of evergreen needles. Trees towered so high overhead that it was difficult to see their tops, while the understory was thick with brush and small greenery. He heard water burbling nearby. The air was cold enough to make him shiver.

Twenty yards away, in a small clearing, was a wooden cabin with solar panels on the roof and what looked like an early-spring vegetable garden in front. It was rustic but adorable, the sort of place where you could imagine Snow White and her entourage hanging out.

Instead, two Paul Bunyans with full gray beards came rushing from behind the cabin. The larger one was barefoot.

Achilles, who was evidently still dealing with the aftereffects of being magicked, shot upright and held up his hands. "Art Gunderson?" he yelled. "I'm Achilles Spanos."

That slowed the men slightly, but they still approached at a speed impressive for their size and apparent age. They weren't even out of breath when they got near enough to stop and survey their unexpected visitors.

"Spanos?" the one with boots asked uncertainly.

"Yeah. This is my… my partner, Dee Martell. And this is Chief Grimes's father. I promise I'll explain, but could you help us, please?"

The bigger man—Jesus, his insteps were *furry*—didn't even hesitate before scooping Ish carefully into his arms, turning, and heading toward the cabin. When everyone else started to follow, Dee stumbled. He would have fallen if Achilles hadn't caught him.

"You need to lie down for a while," Achilles scolded him. "Lean on me."

Dee swallowed his pride and obeyed, partly because he needed the support and partly because it felt good to lean on that strong body—and to trust that Achilles would support him as much as he needed.

They all went inside, and the interior was nicer than Dee expected. One room had a couch, a couple of armchairs, a table and chairs, and a neat little kitchen. Through an open door, a bedroom was visible. A flight of stairs led to an open loft with another bed and a bunch of overstuffed bookshelves. Most of the furniture looked hand-hewn, and while the walls and floor were bare wood, there was also a scattering of bright area rugs and woven wall hangings. And, somewhat inexplicably, a framed poster for a punk rock band called Steep Descent.

That was about as much as Dee managed to take in before sagging in Achilles' arms. He had the vague sense of conversation going on around him before Achilles half carried him up to the loft and guided him to the bed.

"Ish?" he asked before drifting away.

Achilles patted his arm. "He's fine. Rest."

So Dee did.

* * *

HE MUST HAVE SLEPT for several hours. By the time he shuffled down from the loft, low sunlight—barely managing to break through the forest canopy—slanted through the windows. The cabin smelled pleasantly of food, and although the man with the hairy feet was sprawled in an armchair, there was no sign of Achilles or the other man. Ish was just barely visible in the bedroom.

"Your guy and Art are outside having a confab. Help yourself to bread and stew. Oh, and I'm Jerry." He had a slight Southern twang and, congruent with his size, a deep voice.

"Thanks." Dee's stomach rumbled loudly enough to make both of them laugh. "I guess I'll take you up on that offer."

"It's venison, so if you're a vegetarian you're out of luck."

Dee was definitely not a vegetarian; he filled a big bowl and sawed off a hunk of what looked like homemade sourdough. He sat on the couch to eat. "This is delicious."

"We don't cook anything complicated, but we're pretty good at it."

"Do you… live off the land?" There wasn't exactly a neighborhood Safeway.

"Mostly. We carry in some stuff about once a month, but we hunt, gather, or grow the rest."

"I'm impressed. That takes a lot of work."

Jerry shrugged. "We're used to it. We have a pretty cushy setup here. Solar power. Running water. Composting toilet. We've got a place in town too, but we're not there much except during the height of winter. We need a big personal space bubble." He grinned.

"I'm sorry we invaded you without warning."

"Naw, you're fine. Biggest surprise us codgers have had in a while. We met an elf last year, but you guys have topped that one for sure."

Dee liked this man who, despite his size, seemed gentle and sort of goofy. He reminded Dee of a Newfoundland dog he'd once lived next door to. "Did Achilles tell you what's going on?"

"Yeah. Me and Art have never paid much attention to the news, but lately it's been so bad we've avoided it completely. We've got a ham radio, but that's just for weather reports, or if we have an emergency. I guess we're pretty chicken, hiding out here and pretending the rest of the world doesn't exist."

Dee swallowed a mouthful of bread dipped in stew. "From what I understand, you two put in your time and earned retirement. Me, I spent my whole life mostly ignoring everyone else. I'm only in the middle of things now because I got dragged in."

Jerry scrunched up his face thoughtfully. "You're not a regular human, right? Sorry—Art says my manners need work. Don't mean to be rude."

"I don't mind. I was kind of raised by wolves myself. Um, not literally," he added quickly. Then he thought about the coyotes he'd met. "Actually, wolves probably would have been an improvement."

That made Jerry chuckle. "You maybe heard I'm not a regular human either." He lifted one of his enormous furry feet and wiggled his toes. "I grew up among humans, though. Lots of 'em weren't nice. Even the ones that were, well, I always knew I wasn't one of 'em. Took me a while before I found a place where I felt like I belonged. And a person to belong to. You know?"

It was strange. Jerry's words didn't change anything about Dee's past or about his current situation. But just hearing them—knowing that he wasn't the only person to have experienced this and that someone empathized—somehow made it all feel less oppressive. "It all worked out for you?" he asked, needing a little more reassurance.

"We've had fifty years together. I won't say we never argue, 'cause we do, now and then. We've both had to compromise sometimes. But I think I'm the luckiest guy in the world."

A little of the tightness in Dee's soul loosened. "I don't know if we're getting fifty years. We just met, and now the world's going to shit...."

"Yeah, that's tough. Me and Art, when we first met, we just had a serial killer to deal with. Art got kidnapped and tortured and almost died; it wasn't Armageddon, though."

Dee snorted. "Achilles also got kidnapped and tortured and almost died—or worse. And here I was, thinking our meet-cute was unique."

Jerry stood, took Dee's bowl, and lumbered into the kitchen to dish up seconds. He also filled a glass with water and brought them both over. "You're only our second houseguests," he said, handing them to Dee. "Do you know Ralph Crespo and his husband Anton?"

It took Dee a moment to remember. "No, but I think I heard of them. Is Ralph, um, a dragon?" And here he was, living in a world where questions like this made perfect sense.

"Yep. Anton's a gnome. Great guys. Anyway, when they met, Anton was kidnapped and tortured and almost died. We could start a club."

They'd all survived, at least so far. Maybe a relationship begun in adversity wasn't doomed. They were all tough cookies, it seemed— good people to have as allies.

Maybe they all really did have a chance.

* * *

When Achilles reentered the cabin, cheeks pink from the outdoor chill, the very first thing he did was hurry to Dee's side for a quick visual inspection. "Are you all right? That last charm didn't take too much out of you? Did you get enough rest?" It was embarrassing and sweet.

"I'm fine," Dee insisted. "I checked on Ish a few minutes ago. He looks comfortable. He said some things, but I don't understand the language."

Achilles sighed as he sat down. "Probably Homeric Greek. He's sort of been stuck on *The Iliad* today."

"Achilles dies at the end."

"Not in the actual text. Lots of other people die, but Homer doesn't mention Achilles kicking it,"

"But we all know he's going to because of the prophecy."

Achilles made a dismissive gesture. "As far as I know, angels aren't oracles, so I'm not taking it as a bad omen. Hey, do you mind coming outside with me for a bit? Art and I have been talking, and I don't want to put you on the spot without discussing things with you first."

That was also sweet, although Dee worried about what Achilles was going to say.

He had to borrow one of Art's coats, which was ridiculously large on him even though Dee himself was not a small man. Then he followed Achilles out the door, through the garden, and to a picnic bench next to a firepit. "This is a really nice place," Dee said as he took a seat.

"Would you want to live somewhere like this?" Achilles looked a little worried.

"No. I'm not the wilderness type. Vacation, maybe. I never went to summer camp as a kid or did anything outdoorsy as an adult."

"And I'm kind of attached to takeout Thai and streaming video services. But yeah. Vacation. Sorry I sort of abandoned you in there."

Dee grasped his hand across the table. "It's fine. I enjoyed chatting with Jerry." Dee had told a few little tales from his life, while Jerry taught him about some of the local flora and fauna. He seemed especially fond of some nearby ravens and was confident he'd recently discovered a new subspecies of lizard. It was a balm to listen to someone so enthusiastic about matters most people would consider trivial.

Achilles, uncharacteristically hesitant, looked down at their clasped hands. "Art wasn't a field agent—not normally, anyhow—but he ran the lab for years. He's smart and knowledgeable and... I don't know. Analytical? He thinks carefully about stuff. None of those things are my strengths, so I'm glad to have him as sort of a sounding board."

"For what?" Dee wanted to know, although he dreaded the answer.

"I feel like, with our enemies, we've been purely defensive and piecemeal. Putting out their fires. Which makes sense, because that's what the Bureau has always done. And man, there's a lot of fires right now."

He paused again, and a large black bird—probably one of Jerry's ravens—landed on a nearby branch. It stared at them, ruffled its feathers, and uttered a long series of varied croaks and trills, some of which sounded as though they'd been borrowed from other bird species. It seemed to be trying to communicate something to them, although sadly neither Dee nor Achilles spoke its language. Dee remembered Achilles saying that there were no bird shifters and wanted to ask if Achilles was positive about that. Might Achilles wish to become a bird temporarily? And bring Dee along too? That would be pretty cool. Something to think about in the future. But he didn't say any of this aloud because he didn't want to sidetrack the important conversation.

"I think," Achilles said, "we need to be proactive. I know we can't defeat evil forever, but if we could at least face these particular antagonists head-on, maybe we'd get somewhere."

"Who *are* these particular antagonists? Aside from Ashley Dunn and some bears and maybe a good chunk of Washington, DC? Who's in charge?"

"That's part of the problem. We have no idea." Achilles' shoulders slumped.

"You could… wish that you knew."

Achilles widened his eyes. "Would that work? That seems too easy."

Dee felt it out. It was an odd sensation, a bit like checking to see whether a limb was asleep, only in his head. And maybe he was simply still drained from transporting them here, but nothing clicked. He knew that if he leapt off a cliff he wouldn't sprout wings and fly, and he knew that he couldn't help Achilles gain knowledge via wishing.

"Sorry," Dee said. "No."

But Achilles didn't act disappointed. "Everything has limits. Even superpowers. But, um, I had an idea for what might work. Art agrees that's it's viable. It's just incredibly dangerous."

Not so long ago, Dee would have refused point-blank without even asking what the plan was. Hell, he'd kicked Abe Ferencz out of his apartment, never considering even a simple talk with the Bureau. And that version of Dee, ironically, had nothing much worth protecting other than his own unhappy existence. Dee decided that he was glad that old Dee was gone.

"What do I need to do?" he asked. And then added, with a grin, "Master."

Achilles groaned. "Jesus. My libido wasn't this ramped up when I was eighteen—and I *never* had this many kinks."

"Are you upset about that?"

"The only thing I'm upset about is all the time we wasted not knowing each other." His expression grew more serious. "And that our best option right now will probably end up cutting our short time together even shorter."

"What's our best option?"

"Instead of running and hiding like scared rabbits, we draw them out. Then we see exactly who—or what—we're dealing with, and act accordingly. Knowing that once we *do* draw them out, we might very well discover we've bitten off more than we can chew."

The raven had commentary on this, although Dee couldn't tell whether it was supportive or derisive. Hell, maybe the raven knew who their enemy was, but neither of them could ask it. Maybe the raven wouldn't be all that helpful anyway; Dee recalled reading that in many cultures, ravens and crows were both creators and tricksters.

"It may be more than we can chew, but I'll bite anyway," Dee told Achilles. "Even if we can't destroy it, we can make it hurt. You?"

"My namesake chose a short life and glory over long obscurity. Me too, I guess. See, I was thinking about how we've been stymied by our weaknesses, but we have strengths too, and we need to use them. We can draw out the enemy by capitalizing on one of those strengths: we have something they really want."

As the raven croaked again, sounding as if it approved, Dee understood what Achilles was asking of him. It was, predictably, a big ask.

In some ways, bigger than any of the wishes he'd granted thus far. But the new and improved Dee was willing to say yes.

Sure, he now had a lot to lose. But he had the world to gain.

He looked steadily into Achilles' eyes and squeezed his hand. "Our strength is that we have a good bait to hook them," Dee said. "And that bait is me."

CHAPTER 29

*I*t wasn't unusual for Bureau agents to put their lives at risk in the line of duty. It was part of what they signed up for, and it was heavily emphasized during training. Achilles had never particularly minded that aspect of his job; he felt that the results were worth the effort—a sentiment that Orson had never understood. But over the years, after Achilles had witnessed dozens of deaths and had very nearly experienced it himself more than once, he'd reached a point where he felt as if the sacrifice was futile.

It didn't feel futile now.

But Dee wasn't a Bureau agent. He hadn't voluntarily chosen a life involving considerable personal threat, and he'd turned away when that life had been offered to him. But now he'd received it anyway, simply because of the characteristics he was born with, which also hadn't been his choice.

Dee was opting to join the battle. A part of Achilles grieved for him, and grieved, too, for the peace they'd likely never have together. Yet Achilles was also nearly overcome with pride that Dee was willing to take this great and hazardous step. *His* Dee.

"I love you," Achilles said. The nearby raven laughed, perhaps because Achilles sounded so puzzled about his own statement. He *felt* puzzled. But he was also positive that what he'd just said was true.

"You're a closet romantic, aren't you?" Smiling, Dee bent to kiss Achilles' hand. "I love you too. And I gotta tell you, man, I never thought I'd say those four words. The world is so much weirder than I suspected just a few weeks ago. And I'm happy to say it's weird in a lot of good ways."

Achilles glanced around, caught the raven's gaze, and imagined he saw encouragement there. "How recovered are you?" he asked Dee, waggling his eyebrows.

Dee's pupils dilated then and there, which was about the sexiest thing Achilles had ever seen. "More than enough."

Laughing, they chased each other a short way down a narrow trail, stopping beneath a particularly thick grove of trees. It was cold out. The ground was bumpy, slightly muddy, and likely full of slugs, spiders, and freshly sprouted poison oak. Their very kind hosts were back at the cabin with an angel in their bed, possibly wishing that Dee's transporter beam had landed somewhere else.

But dammit, Achilles felt as if he had finally found his person, and Dee apparently felt the same, and even if the entire thing was magically engineered, neither of them cared. They had each other and they had the present.

Achilles steered Dee to a broad-trunked tree and pushed him back against it. A little bit hard, yes, but Dee seemed to enjoy a firm touch. When Achilles pressed up against him, Dee embraced him tightly but then quickly moved his hands to Achilles' head, tugging his hair as they made out. Since Achilles also enjoyed a firm touch, this was delightful.

The raven, who was now definitely spying on them, called from overhead and was answered by a second.

"Bird peeping toms." Dee laughed into the crook of Achilles' neck. Dee's smooth cheeks were very warm. They kissed some more. Possibly for hours, because nothing else seemed as good, as important... no, as *vital*, in all senses of the word.

Achilles managed to work his hands past Dee's waistband, gripping the firm muscle and soft skin of his ass, feeling the tree's nubbly bark digging into the backs of his hands. Their cocks ground together, cushioned annoyingly by a few layers of fabric. And of course there were slippery tongues, hard teeth, soft lips… so many sensations that Achilles was drunk with them.

And then he wasn't just drunk—he was ravenous. He licked Dee's neck, opened the jacket, and pulled down the neck of the T-shirt enough to mouth his collarbone. And then, even better, he rucked up the tee so he could nibble Dee's nipples. Mostly tenderly, but sometimes not quite, so that still-pinioned Dee writhed and moaned and finally flat-out begged.

Those pretty words drove Achilles to his knees—potential mud and small forest creatures notwithstanding—to hastily unfasten Dee's jeans and shove them and his underwear down over his hips. And then wasn't Dee a sight! Front bare to the elements from upper chest to thighs, skin flushed and chest heaving, arms spread wide against the tree as if he were offering himself up to a forest god. Cock rampant. And eyes wide open, staring at Achilles as if he was the amazing one.

Not in the mood for teasing, Achilles dug his fingers into Dee's hips and took his cock into his mouth. He tasted good, warm and salty, and he made desperate little gasps with every bob of Achilles' head.

It would have been nice to continue like that forever, but Achilles was too greedy. He slid off, nipped at the point of one hip, rose to his feet, and spun Dee around to face the tree. Dee hugged the trunk like a lover and canted his ass outward. The damned borrowed jacket, too big on him, was in the way, so Achilles maneuvered it off of him. Feeling a little too guilty to just toss it aside, he draped it over a shrub before returning his attention to glorious bare skin.

He knelt again and, after a few moments of happily kneading and lightly slapping Dee's ass, used his tongue. When Dee's noises became even more insistent and he was pushing back so strongly that they were both in danger of tumbling to the ground, Achilles decided Dee was ready enough. He fumbled his own jeans open, hissing a little as the chill hit sensitive skin. Seconds after that, however, he was *in*, surrounded by welcoming heat and urged on by Dee's words, which were a garbled mix of pleas and commands.

Achilles grunted with every thrust. He felt strong. Feral, as if the trappings of civilization had fallen away from him entirely. He felt like a warrior, a demigod, a hero. And when Dee howled his climax to the ravens and the trees, Achilles felt like a lover too.

They both moved a bit stiffly on the short walk back to the cabin, but Achilles figured it had been worth the ache in his knees. Dee didn't look regretful either.

When they entered, Jerry and Art stopped mid-conversation to stare at them. Then Jerry guffawed. "The joys of young love."

"We're not that young," Dee pointed out.

"You're practically babies. And you're new. I was a virgin when me and Art met, but wow, those first few months—"

"Jerry!" Art looked lovingly exasperated. "They don't need to hear all the details."

Unrepentant, Jerry winked at Dee. "Lemme just say, we made up for lost time."

"Jerry!"

"Maybe," Achilles said, "it's a good time to talk business."

Everyone's expressions turned serious as Dee and Achilles took their seats. Achilles opened his mouth to speak, but Dee beat him to the punch. "I'm cool with being bait. I mean, otherwise I'm going to spend my life in hiding anyway, and if I can contribute to the cause, I'm all in."

"I guess you already know the risks," Art said.

"Yup."

"And you realize…. This is going to entail more than luring someone somewhere, having your allies bash them on the head, and then you get to sail on home."

Dee looked slightly offended. "Yeah, yeah, I get it. They're not going to send the head honcho to fetch me. Even assuming there is a single head honcho and not a… cabal. I figure that I'm going to have to pretend that I've had second thoughts about leaving them, so I can infiltrate and gain info. And then I'm going to have to escape so I can get the info out." He said it easily, as if he was describing a trip to Safeway.

But Art wasn't finished. He cleared his throat. "Do you also realize you're going to have to offer them something to demonstrate good faith?"

"Oh. Yeah, okay. I can grant a wish for them. I'm not sure what I'll do if they wish for something really destructive, but I guess I can deal with that if it comes to it."

"Um…" Art said, and Achilles remembered that Art had washed out as a regular agent because he was too soft-hearted.

Achilles decided to rescue him. "He means me, Dee. You're going to have to give me to them." He'd been hoping to avoid this discussion until the last minute, which was cowardly of him.

"No. No way." Dee glowered, arms crossed. "I saw what she did to you, and that place where she stuck you when she wasn't torturing you, and… just no."

"Look, I'm not even all that valuable to them. You're a huge treasure; I'm just a fun little toy. But you stole me from them, and they're probably extra pissed over that, and there's no way they'll believe you unless you hand me back."

"You're not a goddamn soccer ball!"

"I pretty much am." Achilles made sure to catch Dee's eyes. "Anyway, if you think I'm letting my djinn waltz into their hands without me, you've got another think coming."

"But they'll—"

"I know, Dee. I know. I'm willing to pay the price." And then a thought occurred to him and he gave a small smile. "You're the Trojan horse, Dee."

Dee didn't laugh. In fact, he continued to argue, but eventually he must have realized he couldn't win. After muttering darkly about suicide missions, he subsided into a scowling silence. Achilles and Art worked out the rest of their little plan: In the morning, Jerry would hike with them to civilization, where Achilles would call Charles and fill him in. No doubt Charles would be relieved to know that Ish had arrived safely. After that, Dee and Achilles would travel to Dee's apartment in Portland and wait for the bad guys to appear. Along the way, they'd devise a credible means to make the enemy believe that Dee was handing over a captive Achilles.

It wasn't a great plan, but it was what they had. And as for what happened once Dee obtained the necessary intel, well, he'd have to play it by ear. Achilles trusted him to figure something out.

* * *

THAT NIGHT, Achilles and Dee shared the guest bed, which was a little tight for two full-grown men, but they didn't mind. Although their hosts were left bedless—neither of them could have stretched out on the couch—they were happy to camp outdoors.

"You won't be too cold?" Achilles had asked.

Jerry laughed. "Not a problem."

And then it was morning and time to go. First, Achilles and Dee stopped in to speak to Ish. "You're safe here," Achilles assured him. "And we'll tell Charles where you are."

Ish looked at him with ancient eyes. "I am grieved that I am not stronger."

"You will be. Give yourself time."

"For humans, time is a great gift. I have previously not needed it." His gaze went vague and he said a few sentences in a language that Achilles didn't recognize. Then he seemed to focus again. "Remember your weapons, hero. Hope. Love. Joy. Empathy. Generosity. Kindness. Justice."

"Charles told me something very similar."

Ish managed a smile. "He takes after his mother. My hope lies with you; perhaps that will help."

Achilles, who figured an angel's support couldn't hurt, thanked him. As did Dee. Then there was a round of thanks and farewells to Art—including a kiss from Jerry—and they were off.

Under other circumstances, it would have been a glorious day for a hike. The sun shone brightly, warming the air. Spring blossoms and fresh greenery sprouted everywhere, birds twittered, squirrels chattered. Sometimes the trail took them through thick trees and sometimes it skirted ledges with spectacular views. The air smelled fresh, as if just breathing it could remove deeply lodged toxins.

But this wasn't a pleasure excursion. Achilles and Dee wore sneakers that weren't up to the task, and Achilles' feet still hadn't completely recovered from his barefoot desert tromp.

Jerry, he noted, wasn't wearing any shoes at all, and the terrain didn't seem to bother him. He also wasn't wearing a jacket—just jeans and a plaid shirt. Maybe he had a lot of insulating hair under his clothing; Achilles didn't ask.

After clambering up a particularly steep hill, both Dee and Achilles needed to pause to catch their breath and drink some water before moving on. "I got mauled by bears," Achilles muttered to nobody in particular. "And tortured. And shot. My cardio routine has suffered."

Jerry clapped him heavily on the shoulder. "It's not an easy hike. We chose our cabin spot because of that."

"But you and Art are getting kind of, um—"

"Ancient? Yeah, but this kind of life is in my blood. My father's people don't retire to subdivisions with golf carts and food delivery, you know? Even my mother's people—they're human—are pretty tough."

"Okay," Achilles acknowledged. "But Art?"

"Good genes. Both his parents lived to almost a hundred. I've always kinda wondered if his mom had some yeti in her. Okay, c'mon guys. We got a ways to go yet."

It took a total of four hours to reach town. Achilles had never been so happy to see pavement and cars. Jerry took them to a cute little bungalow near the city limits. It was atop a hill that gave it a sweeping view of the forest.

"The mansion," Jerry joked as he let them in. "Hot running water, even! Why don't you guys have a rest? I'll pop over and get you some food. Can pick up a couple of cell phones for you too, if you want."

Slightly stricken, Achilles winced. "We're flat broke. Those fuckers got my wallet, and—"

"Forget about it. Me and Art have a nest egg." Jerry gestured at the interior. "Make yourselves at home." Then the eighty-something man who'd just led them on a strenuous hike hurried back outside.

"If we survive this, I'm definitely improving my exercise regimen," Achilles said.

Although the bungalow was bigger than the cabin, it was still modest: two bedrooms, a 1950s-vintage kitchen, and a cozy living room. Also a lot of books, stashed just about everywhere. And there was a big bathtub, large enough for a half-sasquatch, in fact.

"Do you think Jerry'd mind if I had a soak?" Achilles asked.

"I doubt it very much."

That was enough encouragement for Achilles. Within moments he had his clothing off and the tub filling with steamy water. Dee stood fully clothed, hands on hips, apparently supervising. "How's your shoulder?"

"Fine."

"Your feet?"

"They'll be okay after a soak."

"Your other bumps and scrapes and gouges?"

Achilles had never had anyone who cared about his condition, aside from assessing whether he was healed enough to return to work. "Tolerable."

"You could wish yourself healed."

"It's not worth wasting your juice on. It'll happen naturally soon enough." Achilles glanced down at his midsection. "Unless the scars gross you out?"

Dee stepped closer and trailed a finger along some of the larger ones, making Achilles shiver. "They don't."

"Good."

"But I don't want you to get any more, if we can help it."

Achilles took Dee's hand and kissed the knuckles. "Agreed."

The bath was lovely. Achilles dozed off, in fact, and by the time he roused himself, the water had cooled, Jerry was back from his shopping, and Achilles' clothes had disappeared. He remained in the bathroom for a bit, listening to the quiet rumble of Jerry and Dee's conversation in the living room, before venturing out with a towel tied around his waist.

"Uh, hi?" Achilles crept into the living room, feeling ridiculous.

"New clothing and toiletries in there," Dee said, pointing at a bedroom. "Your other stuff's in the dryer. Jerry and Art truly do have all the modern conveniences here."

Hoping his dignity remained intact, Achilles hurried to dress. When he returned, Jerry was standing up. "Food's in the kitchen and Dee has your phone. Stay as long as you want; just take out the trash and lock up when you go. I'm gonna head back."

Achilles blinked. "But it's getting dark out."

"I see better in the dark than you do at noon. Art's always been a little envious of that."

"Well, thank you for… gods, for everything. You guys have literally been lifesavers. I don't know how long it'll be before Charles can get Ish—"

"Aw, he's welcome as long as he needs it. And we're happy to help. Nice to know we can still contribute to the cause. Oh! I almost forgot this." He dumped some keys and a wad of rubber-banded cash on the coffee table. "Take it. It's parked out front."

"Your *car?*"

"Ya gotta get to Portland somehow, right? It's nothing fancy, but it runs. We hardly use it, and it's really more fuss than it's worth. Hard to keep the battery charged when it sits there for weeks."

There really were no words to properly express his gratitude, so Achilles instead gave him a hug. Jerry happily—enthusiastically— hugged back, leaving Achilles slightly breathless and convinced that *sasquatch hug* would be a better phrase than *bear hug*.

"I can grant you a wish," Dee offered.

"Aw, that's real nice. Thank you. But I already have everything I want. I hope you guys get there someday too." After a final wave, Jerry was gone.

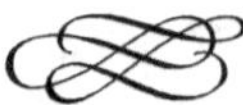

CHAPTER 30

*D*ee didn't pay much attention to Achilles' phone conversation with Charles, but he got the gist of it. Charles was relieved that Ish was safe, slightly astounded that Dee had been able to teleport them successfully, and cautiously approving of their new plan. He did try to give warnings about the likely outcomes, but Achilles overrode him, saying he'd already considered them. Charles wished them luck and asked them to report in regularly.

"Do you want to go now?" Dee asked after Achilles hung up.

"No. It's a long drive." He gave a small smile. "And Jerry bought food for us. Let's wait until morning."

That was good news. Not just because Dee was tired, but because it meant a little more time spent with Achilles—and a little more delay before leaping into the lions' den. "I'll make us some dinner."

"Really?"

"I'm capable of cooking."

Achilles shook his head. "It's just nice, that's all." He flopped down on the couch and poked at his phone for a moment before making a sour face and tossing it aside.

In the kitchen, Dee found the ingredients for a feast: a couple of enormous steaks, the fixings for a pair of loaded baked potatoes, a green salad, some seeded rolls, and two pints of fancy ice cream. The quantities likely reflected the oversize appetites of two oversize guys rather than what Dee and, likely, Achilles were accustomed to, but he was definitely not going to complain. In fact, he caught himself whistling while he prepped.

What would it be like to live a cozy domestic life with a partner? He'd never pictured that for himself. Not because he didn't want it, but because he assumed he would never have access to an existence like that. Now, though, playing at it for an evening, he could almost picture it. The irony, of course, was that now a tranquil little partnership was equally out of reach because he and Achilles likely wouldn't survive much longer.

But... wow. They had been able to spend a few days together. They'd had a lot of great sex. They'd proclaimed their love. Dee had discovered a comfortable space with another person, like finding an oasis in the desert. And along the way, he'd seen so many wonders and met beings he'd only read about in stories. Hell, he'd learned that he himself was one of those beings.

Oh. And at least fairly recently, his mother had still been alive. He didn't quite know how he felt about that. Best not to think about it right now.

They demolished their dinners as if they hadn't eaten in days, then sat beside each other on the couch, lazily noshing melting ice cream straight out of the carton. This house didn't have a TV, and neither of them had any desire to pick up a phone. They didn't even talk all that much. For the most part, they simply *were*, which turned out to be surprisingly pleasant. Dee didn't know what was going on in Achilles' mind, but his own was sort of blurry, one thought easily flowing into the next like chalk drawings in the rain.

They went to bed early. Not surprisingly, it was a big bed, taking up almost all of the bedroom. Maybe the mattress was firmer than ideal, but that hardly mattered. Not with Achilles spooned against Dee's back, smelling like soap and steak, the bristles of his beard tickling Dee's nape.

"You've introduced me to some pretty weird people lately," Dee said.

"True."

"But lots of these weird people... they've found someone to love. For a really long time, in some cases."

"Also true."

Dee thought for a moment. "And some of them... they're good guys, but they have some significant, um, character challenges."

When Achilles laughed, his breaths were warm against Dee's skin. "You could put it that way."

"It's hopeful, though, isn't it? That very imperfect people can still find True Love, capital letters and all."

"It is." Achilles snuggled impossibly closer.

They didn't have sex that night, but they both slept soundly.

* * *

THEY LEFT before dawn in the borrowed Jeep, which bounced around as if it had no shocks and gobbled gas at an alarming rate. Still, it was a vast improvement over traveling by wish. Achilles took the first shift driving, swearing as he laboriously kept under the speed limit. "Usually I drive as fast as I want, and if I get pulled over, I just flash my Bureau badge."

"You don't even have a license on you now."

Dee wondered what would happen if they did get pulled over. Neither of them carried any ID. And if the cops were in cahoots with the opposition, Dee and Achilles might very well find themselves deported. Or worse.

Instead of dwelling on these gloomy thoughts, Dee played with the radio. The mountainous terrain meant that stations faded in and out, and neither of them wanted to listen to anything religious or anything that covered current news, so finding something suitable was a challenge. When Dee managed to tune in a station playing old pop music, Achilles held up a hand. "Let's listen to this for a while."

"Whitney Houston? I wouldn't have guessed she was your jam."

"Not really. But my parents used to play top-40s radio at their shop. I think they thought it would help appeal to younger customers. It didn't, but it was sort of the soundtrack of my childhood."

Dee kept the station on until it faded away near the Oregon border.

* * *

IT WAS early afternoon when they arrived in Portland with Dee behind the wheel. Spring had arrived during his absence, and the trees in his neighborhood flaunted a gaudy surplus of blooms in pinks, whites, and yellows. Daffodils nodded in front yards. Because the sun was out, pedestrians strolled slowly with their children and dogs, and even the bicyclists seemed less hell-bent than usual.

Despite the fact that he was rolling into a trap of his own making, Dee found himself smiling. This place had been home for almost a year, and he'd missed it.

He parked the Jeep on the street in front of his apartment, gathered his few belongings as Achilles did the same, and led the way. "I don't have the key," he remembered.

"It was unlocked when I stopped by. Maybe still is."

And sure enough, it was. Dee allowed himself a moment of sadness —not a soul had even noticed he was gone—before entering. Then he made a face. "Ugh. It stinks." When Ashley had arrived, he'd stuffed a few things in a suitcase and walked right out the door, not pausing to take out the garbage or clean the fridge. Looking back on it, he couldn't recall what had been going on in his head at the time. And now, the fact that Ashley had messed with his mind made him angry.

Achilles pointed at the coffee table. "That pizza looks like it may have evolved far enough to come under Bureau jurisdiction."

"I'm gonna clean up, okay?"

"I'll help. Just... I should probably stay inside, away from open windows. In case anyone's watching."

Although Dee strongly disliked the idea of being spied on, he nodded and started gathering what used to be a decent pie from Baby

Doll, up on Stark Street. Achilles headed for the kitchen. It was a small apartment, so it didn't take long to tidy up. It was good to have the foul smell gone, but now the barrenness was more evident. Dee had lived with battered thrift-store furniture, well-worn thrift-store clothing, and a few items of thrift-store kitchenware. There was nothing inherently wrong with picking up what was cheap and expedient, but nothing in his apartment was there because he *liked* it. He'd accumulated stuff, but none of it was meaningful. Perhaps for some people, a lack of attachment to personal possessions meant they were approaching a Buddhist ideal. But in Dee's case, it just meant he hadn't bothered to give a damn.

"I bet your place is really nice," he said, throwing himself onto the couch next to Achilles.

"I like it."

"So what do we do now? Just sit around and wait for someone evil to show up?"

"Pretty much. It might help if you try to make it obvious you're home. Turn lights on. Walk to nearby shops. But right now, could you give me a wish?"

Dee's heart sped a bit. He felt like an addict who'd been offered a hit. "Sure. Hang on." He jogged into his bedroom, opened the dresser drawer where he kept his collection of baubles, and brought one back to Achilles.

"A hinge?" Achilles asked, looking mildly surprised.

"There's a salvage hardware store nearby. I sort of wandered in one day and bought a few things. I don't know why." At the time, he'd been skeptical that clients would be impressed with a charmed cabinet knob or coat hook, but he'd liked the feel of the pieces in his hand.

"Okay. I wish that I'll fall unconscious for one hour."

Dee, the hinge on his palm, blinked. "Why?"

"When they arrive, it'll look like I'm your captive. You'll have to come up with a cover story about what you did to keep me zonked out."

That made sense, but…. "You'll be completely helpless."

"Can't be avoided," Achilles said grimly. "If they can do that pain finger trick, I'm helpless anyway."

Remembering, Dee shuddered. "I don't like it. I don't like any of this. It's not fair." He wanted to throw a tantrum. Not that he'd ever expected fairness from the world, but what he and Achilles had to do now, that went beyond the pale.

Achilles, bless him, didn't tell Dee he was being childish and unreasonable. Instead he nodded solemnly. "If you want to back out of this, I won't make you do it. And I won't blame you."

"But there are no other options for taking these people down."

"No." Achilles paused for a moment, scratching his incipient beard. "Which isn't to say that someone smarter than me won't come up with a plan, but...."

"But so far nobody has. And time isn't on our side, is it?" Not waiting for an answer—because he knew what it would be—Dee clutched the hinge and invoked his powers. Even as much as he hated what he was having to do, the process still felt wonderful. If he hadn't met Achilles, he could imagine himself getting so addicted to this sensation that he would have done whatever he was told, consequences be damned. It was easy to not care about the future when the present made his nerves sizzle and his cock throb.

"Here," he said, a little roughly, shoving the hinge in Achilles' direction.

Achilles tucked it into a pocket. "Thank you."

Dee dithered momentarily, not sure whether he wanted to pick a fight, fuck, or burst into tears. In the end he decided on option four: he grabbed some bills from the wad that Jerry had insisted they take. "I'm walking to Safeway. Conspicuously. Want anything?"

"No thanks. Stay safe."

With a slight huff at the ridiculousness of that command, Dee stalked away.

* * *

THE NEXT SEVERAL days passed by in a weird limbo. It was like waiting for a really painful dental procedure: a part of Dee dreaded what was to come, but another part just wanted to get it over with.

The good thing was that he got a lot of rest and was able to charge his magic battery to a hundred percent. The bad thing was that he and Achilles were bored silly, although Dee was at least able to take walks and run errands. Achilles was stuck inside an apartment that suddenly seemed far too small. He did chores. He read books that Dee picked up at one of the nearby bookshops. He doomscrolled on his phone. He paced. He had short phone conversations with Charles and, occasionally, with a few other Bureau agents.

Achilles and Dee played cards—Dee nearly always won—and Achilles taught him some key phrases in Greek. They sorted through Dee's collection of charms, with Dee describing how he'd obtained each one.

They had sex two or three times a day. Sometimes hard, fast, and a little painful. Sometimes slow and gentle. Always very, very good. Dee worked on perfecting his blowjob technique. They grew to know each other's bodies so well that if Dee were given a bunch of clay, he was sure he could have sculpted an exact likeness of Achilles, the result worthy of any art museum's collection.

And sometimes, late at night, pressed together in Dee's bed with sweat cooling their skin, they simply *were*. Together. A single, united entity that existed apart from the rest of the universe.

"Caesura," Achilles murmured during one of these times.

"Is that Greek?"

"Latin. It's a pause between two phrases in a line of poetry." He said something in Greek and then continued in English. "Sing, goddess—caesura—of the wrath of Achilles the son of Peleus."

Ah. "We've had the singing part and now we're waiting for the wrath."

"Something like that. I don't want…. Anger has its place. Right now in the world, a lot of people are feeling righteous anger, and it's giving them strength to fight for good. But I don't think it's all that useful as a tool for me. Just look at the text of the *Iliad*: Achilles acted out of rage, and as a result so many people died. Including Patroclus."

Dee had never read *The Iliad* but knew the general story. "His beloved." He took Achilles' hand, which had been resting on Dee's flank, and kissed it. "Let's try not to die."

The next afternoon, Dee walked to Powell's bookstore, where he bought a translation of *The Iliad* and, just for the hell of it, a copy of Madeline Miller's *The Song of Achilles*. Because the route was lined with restaurants and food carts, he also picked up some pastries and a lot of Thai food, making a quick detour to a game shop before finally heading home.

"Food," he announced to Achilles, who was frowning at his phone. "Books. And a two-player board game that the clerk said is a lot of fun."

Achilles put the phone down. "Sounds as if you have an exciting evening planned."

Dee was about to suggest other things they could do to pass the time—he'd stocked up on lube as well—but someone knocked on the door. Hard.

Although his blood turned to ice, Dee didn't hesitate. He marched to the door and opened it only as far as the security chained allowed. A trio of people stood there. The one in front was large, hard-faced, and dressed like a Mormon missionary—dark trousers, white shirt, and navy tie. Dee couldn't get a good look at the others.

"What do you want?" he demanded.

The frontmost one took a half pace forward. "Damnation Martell." A statement, not a question.

The chain was not going to hold if he exerted any force on the door. Dee did his best to sound pissed off and aggressive rather than terrified. It helped that he channeled his father a little. "Who are you?"

"Acquaintances of Ashley Dunn."

His heart sped up a few more notches, and behind him he heard a slight rustle but didn't dare turn around to look. Although he didn't hear Achilles invoke the charm, a barely perceptible tingle on Dee's skin told him that Achilles had made his wish. Dee's heart increased its speed.

He didn't move, however, and made no motion to unlock the door, even though this was exactly what he and Achilles had been waiting for. An irrational voice in his head babbled away, insisting that he could still back out of this plan, that he and Achilles could run away somewhere and hide forever. Maybe if Achilles made the right wish? Maybe they could at least have another month, or week, or day.

One of the figures in the back made an impatient noise, pushed the front man out of the way, and stepped forward. It was an older woman, her long hair steel-gray and the corners of her mouth turned down. She was tall and thin and wore black trousers and a mustard-hued silk blouse.

"Dee," she said. "Enough nonsense. Let us in."

Dee unlocked the chain and stepped back, allowing his mother to enter.

CHAPTER 31

Achilles knew as soon as he heard the knock: it was time.

He pulled the hinge out of his pocket, where he'd kept it for days, and clutched it tightly. Oddly, he wasn't nervous or frightened. He'd made up his mind about what he was going to do, and at this point, the outcome was out of his hands. He'd done his best. Now it was all up to fate, or luck, or the brave and wise actions of his lover.

As quietly as possible, Achilles rolled off the couch and onto the floor, curling into a loose fetal position.

He whispered his wish.

It took effect immediately, paralyzing him and cutting off all feeling from his body. His vision dimmed and then darkened completely, his hearing began to fade, and unconsciousness pulled him inexorably into its fathomless chasm.

Just before he plunged completely, he heard Dee utter a single word.

"Mom?"

CHAPTER 32

She looked older. Of course she looked older; it had been nearly forty years since Dee had seen her. Her voice was the same, though, with the accent he'd never consciously noticed. And her golden-brown eyes, the same hue as his, they hadn't changed either, although there were wrinkles at the corners now. She was still thin and still smelled of cigarettes. Her hair, although no longer dark, was still frizzy and wild, reminding him of Medusa. And he still couldn't read any expression on her face as she stood in his living room, staring at him.

The big man and her other companion, a whip-thin thirty-something guy who looked like an angry greyhound, stood silently near the door as if to keep anyone from escaping.

Achilles lay curled on the floor, motionless, eyes closed.

Dee felt… nothing. A complete absence in his core, as if the black hole had settled there and swallowed all emotions.

"Mom," he said, because nothing else came to mind. The word tasted dry and bitter.

"You've caused much trouble."

"That's what you have to say to me, after walking away four decades ago?"

She shrugged. "You survived."

"You left me with that bastard."

Again, she showed no reaction. "He kept you alive even though you weren't his. Besides, they're all like that. Better for you to learn it while young."

He didn't know what she meant by *they*. Men? Humans?

Before he could ask, she clapped her hands briskly. "So do you want to tell me what's going on here?" She cast a pointed look in Achilles' direction.

Now Dee did experience an emotion: he felt like a chastened child and had to work hard not to cower. "He convinced me that what Ashley was doing was wrong. That I should rescue him and help his cause. We were on the run and it was goddamn miserable. I changed my mind—I've had enough of their Bureau crap. I came back here and waited for someone to show up. Didn't expect you, though."

"So why is he here?"

"I figured the people I took him from would want him back. I strung him along, made him believe I was helping him. He's going to stay unconscious for an hour."

Her lips thinned. "How?"

"More tricks." He forced a laugh even though his chest was hollow. "He wished for it himself. Thinks he's going to be a big hero."

"You fucked him into complacency?"

Dee didn't wince. "Yeah."

"Not a bad way to get what you want. It worked for a while with Martell."

That wasn't something Dee wanted to think about. He glanced at Achilles, motionless and vulnerable, and looked away. As he waited, the goons near the door shifted their feet.

Finally his mother spoke. "What did you hope to gain by handing him over?"

"I made a mistake. Look, I've seen for myself—the Bureau people are going to lose. The agency's been disbanded, they have zero resources, and even though some of them are still dumb enough to stay in the fight, they're losing people all over the place. The ones that are left, they're old. Isolated. They have no real weapons, and they're just scurrying around aimlessly, trying to put out fires. But the fires are everywhere, aren't they?" All of this was distressingly close to accurate.

For the first time, she smiled. "Everywhere, darling."

"I want to be on the side that wins. And Mom, I'm *strong*. I don't want to be a lowly peon who's just trotted out to do magic tricks." He crossed his arms and tried not to think about the fact that this was also distressingly close to accurate. "Take me to whoever's in charge. Not a minion like your two pals here. Not a screw-up like Ashley. I want the head honcho."

"That's a lot to ask, especially from a person who's turned traitor twice."

"A mother who abandoned her child with an abusive junkie is in no position to make judgments." He lifted his chin. "I did what I had to in order to survive. I still do. And I look out for myself because nobody else does." Also true, at least until recently.

She tapped her foot for a moment before responding. Then she turned to the men near the door. "Strip the agent and make sure he's got nothing on him. No jewelry, no *nothing* that could be used as a charm. Then tie him up tight and throw him in the trunk."

Dee had to feign indifference while the goons pulled off Achilles' clothing and then moved his body around. Apparently satisfied, one of them trotted out the front door and returned a short time later with an assortment of ropes and zip ties, which he and his partner quickly used to bind Achilles. They clearly had no qualms about this, although they didn't show signs of taking pleasure in it either. Dee wondered what they got out of it. He found it terrifying that how no matter how cruel the cause, there always seemed to be plenty of people eager to jump in and do the dirty work.

He took a look at the bag of Thai food cooling on the table, the books he'd just bought, and the game he'd hoped to play with Achilles.

He turned to his mother. "Okay. Let's go."

* * *

IT WAS A NICE CAR, big and sleek and black, although the nighttime dark made it hard for Dee to discern the make. The goons were up front—the greyhound driving—while Dee and his mother sat in the back seat. Achilles, of course, was in the trunk. The charm would have worn off by now, and Achilles must be very uncomfortable, but Dee hadn't heard him make any noise. He was probably too tightly bound to move, and the goons had gagged him with a wad of fabric.

Gods, what if he'd suffocated?

Dee didn't ask where they were headed. In fact, for the first hour or so, nobody said a single word. Which was weird, because he had about a million questions for his mother, and he would have thought that she'd have a few for him. But they sat there silently, strangers hurtling east along I-84, the Columbia River invisible in the dark.

They were well past the town of Hood River when Dee finally spoke. "Who's my father?"

"He was a djinn. Full-blooded, not half like me. His name was Kiril, and he was nothing like humans. He respected me." She narrowed her eyes at him. "Do you want to know what happened to him?"

"Yes." Even though Dee guessed it was nothing good.

"The Bureau," she hissed, followed by something that sounded like a curse word in another language. "He escaped his human master and came to this country to make a good life for me. And for you. But the Bureau found him and murdered him. Shot him down as if he were a rabid dog."

Dee felt sick. He didn't know whether to believe her. If she was telling the truth, then either his father was dangerous or the Bureau was less benign than Achilles had led him to believe. Neither of these were welcome scenarios.

His mother continued her story—which was Dee's story too. "When I didn't hear from him for a long time, I came to this country too, with you heavy in my belly and with an empty purse. I searched almost a year before I learned what had happened to my Kiril. By then I had a baby to feed, and as you've learned, djinn don't do well on their own. Martell... he was nothing like Kiril. He was a weak man.

But I was desperate, and he was willing to take you in even though you weren't his. I did what I had to do."

He could understand this. Without someone to… well, to master him, he'd been aimless his entire life and had skipped almost eagerly into Ashley's grip. And Dee hadn't even had a kid to worry about.

"Did Martell know you're a djinn?"

Her mouth puckered as if she'd eaten something sour. "No. Can you imagine what someone like him would have done with that knowledge? And, of course, it meant he didn't know about you either."

Had protecting Dee truly been one of her goals? That seemed unlikely since she'd left him with Martell, knowing full well that Martell was abusive. Memories of hard hands bubbled in the back of Dee's head like boiling sewage. He pushed them away as irrelevant now. But he couldn't push back his anger. "You left me with him. And you never came back."

"He was killing me!" She took a moment to collect herself. "Men like that, even if they don't know what we are, they suck at us like leeches until nothing remains but an empty husk. But I couldn't leave him, not with nowhere to go and a child weighing me down. Until you grew old enough to grant your first wish." She made a dismissive gesture. "The new one wasn't much better, but this time I was wiser. I saved enough money to be able to escape him on my own."

Tears stung Dee's eyes, much to his frustration. "Why didn't you take me with? Or return for me later?"

"Too hard," she said, almost lightly.

"Did you even love me?" He hadn't meant to ask, but the question escaped anyway.

Her hands were clasped in her lap. Long-fingered, like his, but with several bejeweled rings. She stared down at them for a long time before meeting his gaze and answering with a surprisingly soft voice. "I did the best I could. It wasn't very good, but I was young and had so little to work with."

Dee turned his head to look out of the window, even though there was nothing to see. He didn't forgive her. Couldn't. But she wasn't asking for forgiveness, and somehow that made him more sympathetic to her. When he was young, he'd made bad decisions too. He hadn't had a child, so those choices most often impacted just him, although sometimes others got caught in the mess too. He'd ended up in jail more than once. But like her, he had done the best he could with the little he had to work with.

With eyes closed, he tried to disengage from his emotions again. And, more importantly, from thoughts that did him no good right now: thoughts about his wretched little family, and thoughts about Achilles currently suffering in the trunk and headed for worse.

His mother, perhaps with a sense of what he was up to, made a sharp scolding sound. "Hold on to your rage, Dee. It belongs to you. If you're angry at me, so be it. But think of all the others who've wronged you. Your father who got himself killed before you were even born. Your stepfather who hurt you. The children who sensed you were different when you were young and bullied you—they did, didn't they? The society that never would have accepted you as you were. The goddamn Bureau that murdered your father and used you. *Feel* that rage, my son. Let it strengthen you."

He didn't know whether anger was her weapon or if it was used by whomever his mother worked for. But he felt the truth of what she said. Yes, he had been mercilessly tormented as a child. And yes, fury lay within him like lava held back by a layer of solid rock. It always had. He could fracture that rock, let the lava freely flow. With that fueling him, he could accomplish astounding things.

Dee kept his eyes closed and allowed his body to sway slightly with the motion of the car.

CHAPTER 33

$\mathcal{A}$chilles missed the warmth of Dee's body. The trunk of the car was cold, and he couldn't move even slightly in order to warm himself. His limbs, bound tightly for hours, screamed with pain, and his mouth was bone-dry from the gag. Old wounds made themselves known. And he was hungry, dammit.

Even though he'd known this was coming, even though he'd insisted on offering himself up, he couldn't rein in the self-pity. There had been so few occasions in his life when someone had cared for him —in any sense of the word—and so many times when he'd been hurt. He wasn't special. He couldn't fly, or grant wishes, or change his shape, or run through the forest barefoot in the dark. He didn't have extraordinary strength or speed or intelligence. He sure as hell wasn't immortal.

He was just an ordinary human being doing his best to help a world that had done very little to help him.

Feeling sorry for himself wasn't accomplishing anything either. *You're miserable enough as it is,* he thought fiercely. *Don't make it worse.*

He focused instead on his short time with Dee, who'd somehow managed to make Achilles *feel* special: strong, brave, heroic. Who'd called him *master,* and—although there was some humor there—had meant it. Dee, who'd welcomed Achilles' touch even when it was painful, perhaps understanding that sometimes it was the counterpoint that made pleasure even deeper.

Dee, who'd apparently just been reunited with his mother.

Achilles didn't know exactly what to make of that unexpected occurrence, but he knew he didn't like it. Hopefully that feeling was not due to simple envy or jealousy. He told himself that he trusted Dee to stick to the original plan and not lose sight of their goals.

But gods, he was so fucking *cold*.

Cut it out. Save your energy. Keep the blood flowing. Keep your shit together.

He followed his own stern advice as well as he could, flexing his muscles and moving his limbs to the minor extent possible. He steadfastly pushed negative thoughts into a tiny pocket at the back of his mind, where they undoubtedly had lots of company from past terrible experiences. If he survived this, it might be a good idea to talk to a shrink before that pocket blew wide open.

Good. A plan for the future. That was the type of positive thinking they'd encouraged in his training—even if the plan did involve doing something he'd avoided for years.

He actually had seen a therapist once, shortly after Orson's death and at the suggestion of a senior agent. But the visit hadn't made him feel any better-adjusted; if anything, it made things worse by uncovering wounds. He'd complained about this to Agent Guerrero, and she'd rolled her eyes. "It's not like taking out the garbage, Spanos. It's not a one-and-done kind of thing. Our pasts are embroidered into our psyches, and it takes time and work to change the pattern."

Back then, Achilles hadn't been willing to make those investments. Now he pondered how much the course of his life might have changed if he had. He would have been better adjusted, probably. He might have been able to form friendships with people and maybe even romantic relationships. He might not have ended up naked—again— and tied up in a trunk, on his way to be tortured—again. Or killed.

But then, it's possible he would have been mauled to death by a bear shifter.

Almost certainly, however, he wouldn't have fallen in love with Dee, and that would have been a shame. Despite where that path had taken him, he was grateful for their time together. Dee Martell was a marvel, and not just because he was a djinn, although that was certainly one contributor.

A weird sort of peace settled over Achilles. He didn't know what his future held, but he didn't regret the recent decisions that had put him here.

The drive was interminable. He dozed lightly at times, and sometimes distracted himself by mentally reciting bits of *The Iliad* or reviewing some of his old Bureau lessons.

Until, finally, the car stopped.

Nothing happened for a while, and he began to wonder if he was simply going to be left there to rot. That would certainly be an anticlimactic way to go. But then the trunk opened, and while he was blinded by the bright light, someone forced a cloth bag over his head. Then several hands hoisted him up and dropped him—not at all gently—into a metal cart of some kind, which was rolled swiftly along a smooth surface. The bag muffled sounds, making it hard to assess whether he was indoors or out.

They didn't go far. The cart came to a halt and he was dumped unceremoniously onto what felt like cool, smooth stone. Someone yanked off the bag, and Achilles squeezed his eyes shut against the light.

"Who are you?"

That was Dee's voice coming from behind him. Achilles opened his eyes a bit and saw a tableau so starkly lit from above that it looked like a stage setting. He was indoors, in a cavernous room with high ceilings supported by steel beams; spotlights shone down from the supports. The wall opposite him was all glass, but since it was still dark outside, all he could see were reflections of the interior. He lay on a floor of white marble. Sleek furniture was grouped here and there, all of it white or glass or chrome, looking expensive but not very comfortable.

And standing a few yards in front of him were a man and a woman.

The woman had to be Dee's mother; Achilles saw the resemblance immediately. She was nestled up against the man, embracing his left arm, and she looked very pleased with herself.

The man displayed no facial expression at all. He was white and fiftyish, with mousy brown hair that might have been a toupee or a dyed transplant. It was hard to tell from Achilles' position on the ground, but he thought the man was fairly tall. He was pudgy too, although his clothing seemed tailored to camouflage that. He wore jeans, a gray T-shirt, a navy sport jacket, and black loafers. He had an earbud in one ear and a phone in his hand.

There were other people in the room—Achilles could hear them breathing—but they were behind him, perhaps flanking Dee. Who repeated his question, this time more loudly. "Who *are* you?"

"You're in my house. Show some respect." The man spoke like a parent chastising a teenager, which Achilles imagined must have rankled Dee. Especially since his mother was hanging all over the guy.

"Give me a reason why I should respect you."

Nice answer, Dee.

Unfortunately, the response was predictable. The man did the nasty finger thing and agony erupted in Achilles' body. He couldn't even writhe and scream properly; all he could do was ride it out and try not to choke to death.

It was a short-lived blast, and Dee waited until Achilles was still again to speak. "Fear isn't the same thing as respect. And there's nothing especially worthy about attacking someone who can't fight back."

The man nodded a bit, as if impressed with Dee's backbone. "Fair enough. I'm Garrick Spurling. You're standing in one of my houses. And you're Damnation." He laughed. "Great name, by the way."

Dee's mother beamed.

"It's Dee," he said. "And I'm sick and tired of playing games. I already told her—I want to see whoever's in charge."

"You want to talk to the manager, Karen?"

"I want to talk to someone with real power. Not a flunky."

"Do you think a flunky would own a place like this?" Spurling spread his arms. "And this is just one. I've got penthouses in New York, San Francisco, and Miami. Mansions in LA, Austin, Maui, and half a dozen other places. Two yachts and three jets. I also have—"

"I don't care."

Spurling glared at Dee. Achilles was glad that, at least momentarily, nobody was paying attention to him. He still hurt like hell, his bladder was full, his mouth dry, but at least he wasn't being actively tortured. And he had the chance to get a good look at Dee's mother and Spurling.

She looked younger than her actual age, which must have been at least sixty. Her hair seemed untamable, a thick tangle of curls flowing past her shoulders. But the rest of her appearance was restrained—elegant, even—with an expensive blouse and slacks and a pair of black high-heeled shoes with wickedly pointy toes. It was odd to look at her face and see Dee reflected so strongly, although hers had a hardness that his lacked.

Superficially, Spurling seemed like an ordinary human man. A CEO of a tech firm, perhaps, whose third wife was younger than the children from his first marriage and who liked to talk about cryptocurrency and AI. Although Achilles was positive he'd never met the guy before, there was something weirdly familiar about him. Maybe his pale eyes, which, upon closer examination, were subtly off in a way that Achilles couldn't pinpoint. Even though Achilles claimed no special talents at reading auras, Spurling still registered as... blurry somehow. Or layered. Like a creature wearing a really excellent costume, or like one of those deepfake videos.

Spurling wiped away his scowl and put on a long-suffering expression instead. "It's late. Almost morning. Why don't you get some rest, and we'll chat after that. Irina, show him to a room."

"I'm tired of screwing around," said Dee, much to Achilles' relief. "I'm willing to play on your side, but only after I get the straight story about what's going on. Take me to your leader."

"This isn't a game, Dee, and it's complicated. You do realize that I came a long way to meet you? And Irina has been traveling for hours."

Don't give in, Dee. Don't leave me.

After a brief pause, Irina peeled herself away from Spurling and stalked to Dee, heels clicking on the hard floor. She had to walk around Achilles to do that, and she gave him a sharp kick in the shin as she passed.

"Come on, Deedee," she purred in an apparent attempt to sound maternal. "We'll get you something to eat first. Anything you want. Then after you've rested we can discuss all the opportunities ahead of you."

"I want—"

Spurling interrupted. "You're wasting my time. I'm a busy man with better things to do than stand here arguing. Irina, this one's useless." He gestured at Achilles. "I'm going to get rid of him, unless you want to add him to your collection."

Achilles' heart seemed to stop beating as he waited for her response. He didn't even know which option was the lesser evil. He really wished he could see Dee right now, if for no other reason than to get a final glimpse.

"I'll keep him," she finally said.

Spurling made a motion with his hand.

Achilles expected the usual agony, but instead, he was… narrowed. His body, still bound, first flattened out so impossibly thin that he couldn't breathe. There wasn't even room for blood to flow through his veins. He couldn't hear anything, and all he could see was a relentless white. And then he was pressed even thinner and couldn't remember anything except this excruciating state—he had no past, no name, no sense of anything but an eternal *wrongness*, no movement, no will, no—

He suddenly became full again. His limbs flopped free, his back arched, and he screamed and screamed into a fathomless darkness.

CHAPTER 34

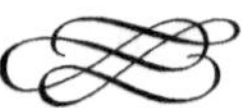

*I*rina. Dee must have heard Martell use his mother's name in the distant past, but he couldn't recall it, and he hadn't consciously remembered her name himself. For almost forty years she'd simply been Mother (missing) and nothing else.

But now Spurling had used her name—very casually, as if the name, too, hadn't been absent for most of Dee's life—and although this was the most unimportant detail in the world right now, it was all that Dee could think of. Which was so *wrong* when the man he loved lay bound and miserable right in front of him, and when that man's life was probably going to be stolen very soon.

If Dee tried to focus on Achilles, however, horror came at him like a tidal wave and he had to back away. That was his master there, his beloved, and Dee had simply handed him over and pretended it was no big deal.

His mother—*Irina*—gripped Dee's arm like a vice, her hands cold and hard. "I'll keep him," she said.

A moment later, Achilles was gone.

This was not the worst possible outcome, Dee reminded himself. *Keeping* implied that Achilles wasn't dead; he'd probably been sent to the black hole. And although that place was fucking awful, Achilles had survived it twice already, so maybe he could survive again.

Meanwhile, Dee had a job to do.

As soon as Achilles disappeared, Spurling walked briskly away and through a door, followed silently by the goons who'd driven them here. Dee, who hadn't used any magic in days, felt utterly exhausted.

"You should be polite to him," Irina scolded. "He doesn't know whether to trust you yet."

"I don't trust him either." He felt anger roil inside him, hot and bitter. Although he knew that anger was the enemy's weapon, he couldn't completely tamp it down. "Is he your new husband?"

She squeezed his arm hard. "Stop it. You know as well as I do that we need somebody. I've had to settle before, but not this time. And when you're the magic behind the power, well, then *you're* the power. And Deedee, this is the real thing."

He couldn't argue with that logic, although he did want to point out that power, like money, was a hollow goal. It didn't seem to matter how much people had, they always seemed to want more, until the need became as all-consuming as any addiction. But he stayed silent as she steered him through the room and down a long hall with bare white walls.

"Did you make this house for him?" Dee asked.

She didn't answer. Instead, she said, "You'll need a proper master. I'll speak to Garrick about it. The idea was that the Ashley woman would suit you, but your tastes seem to run to men. Not a problem. He'll find you one."

Dee was still shuddering at the concept of infernal matchmaking when Irina brought him into a bedroom. It had no windows, and the furniture was limited to a bed, an armchair, and a dresser, all of them as bland as something from a mid-range hotel—the sort that is found near highway interchanges and offers English muffins and bruised bananas for breakfast. Through a door was a small bathroom.

"Someone will bring you some food soon, and fresh clothes and a toothbrush," Irina said, patting the mattress.

"I don't even know what time it is." There were no clocks in the room, and he didn't have a watch or phone.

"It doesn't matter." She walked to the door but paused before leaving. "This is the best choice, Damnation. Nobody will look out for us but us." Then she left, shutting the door firmly. When Dee tested it, he wasn't surprised to find it locked.

"You made your own bed, Damnation," he said out loud. "Now lie in it."

Still clothed, he did just that.

* * *

AT SOME INDETERMINATE hour the next day, Irina came to fetch him. He'd been up for a while, pacing the small room like a caged animal. Today she wore a sleeveless black dress and black pumps, and her hair was starting to escape from an elaborately pinned updo.

"Where's Spurling?" Dee demanded, not caring how petulant he sounded.

"In a meeting. He'll join us later. Let's have something to eat first." She held out a hand as if he were a small child, but he ignored it and crossed his arms.

"I'm not here for a social call. I want—"

"I know what you want. In due time. These people do things on their own schedule. Besides, I want to chat with you a bit first."

Although he wasn't happy about this, he figured a tantrum wouldn't help. And he was curious to see what she had to say, especially since she hadn't been talkative during the hours they'd spent in the car. He followed her out of the room and down the same long, plain hallway as the night before. He repeated a question from the previous day.

"Did you make this house?"

She glanced at him from the corner of her eye. "No."

That left him wondering what she *had* done for Spurling. He decided that he'd rather not know.

After walking for what felt like an unreasonably long time, they came to a room that resembled an office break room. The overhead fluorescents cast a harsh light over white melamine cabinets, a wheezing white fridge, a cheap-looking sink, and a microwave and coffee maker. There was also a slightly battered table and six chairs with worn upholstery sitting in the middle of the scuffed vinyl floor.

"Sit," Irina ordered before spending ten minutes or so brewing tea and arranging food on plates. Dee thought about Achilles. Was he hungry and thirsty? In pain? Frightened?

By the time Irina handed Dee a dish with diced fruit and something that looked like a slice of quiche, his appetite had fled. He sipped some tea, though, and considered his scalded tongue a small part of his penance.

"Can you just tell me what's going on?" he asked her. "Nobody wants to give me a straight story and I'm sick of it."

"You can't simplify this situation. But you've been spending time with the Bureau scum, so I'm sure you have at least a basic sense of it, even if the perspective is warped." She hadn't eaten any of her food either, and now she looked down at her carefully manicured hands. "It doesn't matter anyway. It's not your fight. You're in this to get as much as you can."

Ah, so Irina wasn't so much evil as amoral, much as he'd always been. But he didn't think that was true for him anymore.

"Get what?" he asked.

She leaned forward and lowered her voice. "Everything. If you play the game right."

"Spurling said this isn't a game."

"Him." She waved a hand dismissively. "Let me ask you something. You thought that I'd created this house. You did something like that for Ashley, didn't you?"

He decided there was no need to lie. "Twice. So?"

"And you got that angel into the Bureau's hands. That was quite something. Garrick and the others pretend like that wasn't important, but I think it was. They're certainly angry over it."

Dee managed to suppress a smile. "Your point?"

"I couldn't have done either of those things. Yes, I can grant wishes, and some of those are quite useful. But nothing as big as that. Your powers, Deedee, are far stronger than mine. And that's because my mother was fully human, but you are three-quarters djinn. And there's one more thing you should know." She paused, clearly expecting him to ask for more.

But he was still digesting the first bit and contemplating what it signified. Did it mean he could counteract anything Irina did? And what, exactly, were the limits of his abilities? His current hosts might not even know.

Finally, he looked at her. "What should I know?"

Her smile was wide and her eyes sparkled. "You and I are the last djinn in the world."

"What?"

"There were never more than a few of us; we're not very fertile. And over the centuries, different regimes have sought us out and slaughtered us out of fear of what we could do." She shrugged. "Your father was the last full-blooded djinn, and I've told you already what happened to him."

A disturbing mix of emotions roiled through Dee. He was relieved that Spurling and his pals didn't have an army of djinn at their disposal. He grieved the loss of a father he'd never known and a people that, until recently, he hadn't even known existed. And he was thrilled to realize how exceptional he was. Assuming, of course, that Irina was telling the truth.

"This is why I gave you your name," she said softly. "A memorializing of our entire species, which has been damned for many generations."

Dee cradled his mug between his palms and tried to think. He wished that Achilles was here to help him make sense of all this, and that Charles was here too, promising to get his agents researching Irina's claims. He wished he could talk with Tenrael about what he'd seen of djinns over the centuries.

But Dee was alone now.

"Why are you telling me this?" he asked.

"So you understand your value and also the danger you're in. If they believe that you've truly turned your back on the Bureau, that you're genuinely willing to help their cause, they'll forgive you for Ashley and the angel. You're potentially too beneficial for them to hold a grudge. And they will give you nearly anything you could possibly want. Look at me—Garrick gives me human Bureau agents for my collection because I ask for them and he has uses for me. But Deedee, if they *don't* believe you, they'll destroy you. Because they can't risk having you act against them."

She leaned back in her seat, arms crossed, and solemnly watched him.

Dee wanted to ask her about her *collection* and the implications for Achilles but couldn't think of a way to do so without giving himself away. Her collection hadn't been the point of her little lecture anyway. Instead, she'd been giving him a warning.

"How do I convince them?" he asked.

"Show respect. Obey their orders. Put aside your personal desires. It'll be worth it in the long run. Imagine what you and I could accomplish together. But not yet. Bide your time."

Before he could decide how to respond to this, she rose to her feet. "Let's go talk to Garrick," she said briskly.

* * *

SPURLING WAITED for them in a modest-size room with a glass wall that overlooked a hillside covered in cultivated grapevines. A television with a gaming setup dominated one wall, but the set wasn't turned on. Spurling sat in a leather armchair, holding a highball glass full of amber liquid. A bottle of bourbon perched on the table beside him. Today he wore tennis shoes, khakis, and a green golf shirt with a pair of sunglasses hanging from the front placket.

Irina glided over, bent down to kiss his cheek, and then arranged herself on the arm of the chair, one hand lightly massaging Spurling's shoulder. Dee stood awkwardly as they both stared at him, then he moved to sit in the chair across from them. But that proved to be slightly awkward too, as it was too low and his knees stuck up.

"I trust you slept well," said Spurling lightly. He sipped his drink, watching Dee over the edge of the glass. "I don't have much time, but you can ask a few questions, if you want."

A few. Dee tried to decide what information would be most helpful to the Bureau, if he ever managed to get it to them. "Who's in charge and what are they trying to accomplish?" There. That was pithy enough.

Spurling drained his glass and refilled it. He didn't offer any to Dee. Maybe he knew from his experiences with Irina that Dee couldn't drink the stuff—assuming it was a djinn thing and not a personal quirk—or maybe the guy was just a jerk. In either case, he drained the refill before replying.

"The world's screwed up," he finally said. "Has been for a long time. I don't have to tell you that. Birthrates skyrocketing among people who shouldn't be reproducing, while the smart ones, the healthy ones, have hardly any kids. And instead of rewarding hard work and intelligence, we just give handouts. We've let ourselves drown in emotions and subverted the natural order of things."

Oh, great. Spurling was a racist on top of it all. Probably also a misogynist, judging from how he treated Irina. And a classist. Maybe a homophobe too.

"I want answers, not a lecture," said Dee, fighting the urge to squirm in the uncomfortable chair.

"This is an answer. There are some people who are working to improve things. Some guys, they're ready to give up on the planet altogether and move to Mars, but that's bullshit. This is *our* planet. So a few of us have formed a coalition. We've all got brains, money, power. The will to make things right again."

"And how are you going to do that?"

Spurling took his time with another refill. There was something… off about him. Not just what he was saying, but also his physical self. Irina had implied that he was human, and he certainly looked it. But then so did Dee. You didn't have to have horns or giant wings to be… something else. If a creature had suddenly come bursting through Spurling's chest like something out of a horror movie, Dee would have been grossed out and startled but not especially surprised.

Nothing burst out, though.

"Do you know what disruptive innovation is, Dee?"

"No." But he was pretty sure he was about to find out.

After flashing a superior smile and taking another long swallow of whiskey, Spurling set down the glass, apparently so he could motion with his hands while speaking. "Disruptive innovation is when something comes along and completely changes how people do things. Mass-producing cars—starting with the Model-T—was one. That replaced horses. Streaming services. Remember when we had to watch a TV show on a particular day and time or drive to Blockbuster to rent a movie? Smartphones. Online one-stop shopping with fast shipping, like Amazon. Do you get the gist of it?"

Dee nodded.

"Okay, well, those are all examples of marketplace disruptions. There are other kinds too. Back in the eighteenth century, Sir William Blackstone thought it would be a great idea to summarize several centuries of English court decisions—the common law—into a single multivolume set. Even our Supreme Court still cites his work. Several decades later, Sir Robert Peel completely restructured how policing works. We're still following his principles, at least theoretically. Disruptions can be political, social, environmental, religious…."

For every minute that Spurling was blathering away, Achilles was stuck somewhere, suffering. Dee balled his hands into fists and took a few deep breaths. "I get it."

Spurling leaned forward, his expression the most animated that Dee had yet seen. "What my partners and I are doing, kid, is disrupting *everything*. When we're done, the leeches will be gone. Survival of the fittest, right?"

Dee felt physically ill. The ideology didn't shock him, but he had the gut feeling that these plans weren't just possible, they were probable. And imminent.

"How?" he managed to ask.

"We have a variety of mechanisms in place. It's a multi-faceted approach. Disinformation, distractions, diseases, divisiveness." He spread his hands, palms up, as if to signal that this was no big deal. "We use our tools, large and small." He patted Irina's leg, rather hard, apparently to indicate that she was one of those tools. She beamed at him.

"I could be one of those tools." Dee phrased this somewhere between a statement and a question.

"Could be. Depends what you can do. Ashley indicated that you could do a lot, but you got rid of her before she found your limits. Hell, I guess the fact that you ended her tells us something already. She was a tough cookie." He chuckled, apparently not grieving the loss. Then he looked more serious. "Also depends on whether we can trust you."

"I told you—I've had enough of the Bureau. I don't really care about you guys either, but I do care about myself. And I figure my chances are better on this side."

Spurling's eyes looked ordinary enough, pale blue and a little watery. But they creeped Dee out. He felt as if there was a camera hidden behind them, as if someone—or something—was watching him too.

"Well!" Spurling clapped loudly, making Dee jump. "As it happens, we've got a little test to prove both your strength and your loyalties."

"A test?" He wasn't going to like this, Dee was certain of that.

"Yup. All you gotta do is grant me one wish. Damnation, I wish to start a war."

CHAPTER 35

*A*chilles was thinking about Orson, because why the hell not. Here he was again, stuck in the black hole, and this time feeling vaguely grateful because the alternatives were even worse. He sat on the ground—or was it a floor?—with arms drawn around his legs and his head on his knees, reminiscing about his time with Orson. It had been a short period, and especially toward the end, there had been a lot of friction related to Achilles' job. But there had been good times too, and Achilles focused on those. He hoped very much that in his final days, Orson had been happy.

When he ran out of those memories, Achilles turned instead to his sister, Atalanta. He hadn't seen her since shortly after his parents' funeral, when she'd shrilly accused him of being responsible for their deaths. He hadn't argued with her, mostly because he *felt* responsible, and also because he realized that she was hurt and grieving. But so was he. And he'd been the one who had to deal with the immediate aftermath of the murders, despite being still just a boy. He'd needed comforting and found it nowhere.

He and Atalanta had communicated via phone and letter a few times after, exclusively about the settling of the estate. And that had been it; not even Christmas cards. He hadn't known her address for years, and although he could have found her via his connections, he'd never tried. Maybe she still had the same phone number.

Now, like long-sealed boxes tucked away in an attic, he found some good memories of Atalanta too. She used to very patiently help him with his homework when he was young and their parents were at work. When he was reluctant to read, she took him to the public library and helped him find books he'd enjoy. When he acquired cuts, scrapes, and bruises during various childhood exploits, she provided disinfectant, bandages, and ice. Maybe that was when she'd first decided to become a doctor.

He'd loved her and his parents. Had loved Orson. And, mystifyingly, wonderfully, he loved Dee. If you wrote those names down, they wouldn't look like much. But all of those loves were important, and they'd left indelible marks on his heart and soul. Each one of them was worth remembering.

Sometimes Achilles walked in the black hole, blindly of course, and not really expecting to get anywhere. Sometimes he lay on his back, arms and legs spread, and stared up at nothing. Once or twice, he cried.

In fact, it was after a brief bout of sobbing that he wiped his eyes and scolded himself. "Wallowing won't do you any good." His voice sounded rough. Had he been screaming again? He couldn't remember.

He decided to pretend that the chief was there and Achilles was debriefing him on the results of his latest assignment. He'd done that dozens of times, most recently with Charles but for many years before that with Townsend, and he'd always liked that part of his job. It made him feel accomplished.

"I don't know what happened to Dee," he told the imaginary chief as he neared the end of his story. It was hard to say those words, but at least he was fairly certain that Dee was too useful for the enemy to murder. Plus his mother had shown up and was on the enemy's side, whatever the implications of that might be. "Spurling was going to kill me, I think, but Irina asked to keep me. For...." He tried to remember what she'd said, exactly. "For her collection. So Spurling zapped me to the black hole, and that was not fun at all. Way worse than when Dee did it. The first time, with Ashley, I was unconscious."

Wait. He thought back to what he'd just said. *Collection.* Didn't that imply that Achilles wasn't Irina's only prisoner? And Charles had said that he'd lost touch with several agents. Some had been deported, and maybe some had cut their ties to the Bureau, but it was possible that some were here.

Achilles shot to his feet, his heart racing. For the first time in… however long he'd been here, he felt something akin to hope. And hope, dammit, was a weapon.

"Hey!" he shouted. "Anyone here? It's Agent Spanos."

He tried several times, until his throat hurt, but didn't get any response. Dispirited, he sank to the ground again. During the drive to San Francisco, he and Charles had discussed what they knew about the black hole, which wasn't much. The Bureau had only learned about it recently, when agents Clark and Gale had obliquely encountered it in Wyoming. According to what *their* bad guy had told them, there were several black holes, reachable via portals. He could have been lying. But Gale was an empath, and when he was trapped in one of those liminal spaces, he'd sensed Ish in another. Which tended to support the bad guy's claim.

And if all of that was true, Irina could have multiple agents in her clutches, each one confined in a separate space, like different cages in a zoo. Inaccessible to one another.

Shit.

But the more that Achilles considered this, the less sense it made. Magic and the occult might not be well understood, but they weren't immune to the laws of physics. They just took advantage of loopholes that nobody yet comprehended. And one rule of physics was that using magic took energy. He'd seen that for himself with Dee, who was mentally and physically drained after granting a wish. Creating black holes—weird pockets in reality—undoubtedly required energy too, as did maintaining their connections to the ordinary world. Unless energy resources were boundless, which was rarely the case, conservation made sense. Which meant that there was probably just one big black hole with weird topography.

He hoped.

Achilles stood. This time, instead of shouting, he sang. He wasn't sure why that had worked with Ish and didn't know why he'd instinctively tried it. Maybe because music had its own magic.

Remembering the top-40 radio station his parents had favored, and the music he and Dee had listened to on the drive to Portland, Achilles began belting out "I Will Always Love You." Poorly, but who the fuck cared? He followed that up with "Baby Got Back" and "I'm Too Sexy." He was debating between George Michael and Mariah Carey when he heard… something. Very faintly. But it was definitely there.

He stopped breathing, closed his eyes—not that it mattered here—and concentrated. And… yes. There it was. He couldn't make out the words or even the tune, but he was positive that someone was singing, the sound coming to him like the tiniest breeze on a sweltering summer day.

Achilles started walking in what he hoped was the right direction, singing loudly as he went. For absolutely no rational reason, his brain settled on "Amazing Grace." And when he reached the end, he started back up again, still walking. Every time he reached the end of a verse he paused, and every time he heard the answering song. It wasn't in English, which was irrelevant, and the singer sounded male.

For the fifth or sixth time, he sang "I once was lost, but now am found." And before he could get to the part about blindness, the other voice came through loud and clear. Was that… Hebrew?

Achilles laughed as he sang "was blind, but now I see."

A moment later, he stumbled into someone. They clutched each other to keep from falling, and the other man said something that Achilles couldn't understand.

"Who *are* you?" Achilles demanded desperately, realizing he was gripping the other man's bare arms too hard but not willing to let go.

"Abe Ferencz, boychik. Who's this?"

Relief hit Achilles so hard that his knees buckled and he collapsed, dragging Abe down with him. It took a moment for them to untangle themselves and for Achilles to regain enough oxygen to identify himself. They sat, knees touching and hands clasped, each of them afraid to lose the other.

"Are you okay?" Achilles asked. "Are you hurt? How long have you been here? Is anyone else here?"

Abe's laugh was wonderful to hear. "I'm as well as possible under the circumstances. No idea how long I've been here. You're the first I've met. Who are you?"

Not as promising news as Achilles had hoped, but also not the end of the world. "Achilles Spanos."

"Oy vey! You too!" Abe clutched him harder.

They exchanged stories, with Abe going first. His tale was simple. Spurling had burst into Abe's house in Palm Springs, along with a couple of goons and Irina. They'd taken him to a nearby house and tortured him for a little while. "They wanted to know what I could do," Abe explained. "And whether I'm human or something else."

Achilles, who was a little fuzzy on those points himself when it came to Abe, prompted, "And?"

"And I'm nothing but an old man and useless to them. So they sent me here."

"For Irina's collection."

"And you, Achilles? How did you end up in this place?"

So Achilles explained, accompanied by grunts and other little sounds from Abe.

"A djinn!" Abe exclaimed when Achilles was done. "Who would have thought that, at my age, I could still encounter something new? But I'm glad to hear that Dee changed his mind after I spoke with him. Even if it's gone badly for you."

"This was my idea, so don't blame him for it. Abe, were you really not valuable to Spurling? I heard that you can, um…."

"I see dead people." Abe chuckled. "Yeah, I watched that movie. It's nothing like that for me, but yes, I can often converse with spirits. The schmucks who sent me here don't know that, though." He sounded a little smug.

"And there aren't any spirits here?"

"I'm not sure. Sometimes I sense… a whisper. An almost-scent. Not enough to connect to, which is just as well. Without access to booze, I doubt I could hold them off."

Achilles frowned in confusion. "What do you mean by that? Are they hostile?"

"Not necessarily. But some of them…. It's difficult to be without a body. So some of them try to shove themselves into one. Fortunately, they usually can't. The spirit of the living person takes up too much room. A few of us, though, we're susceptible. It's easier for us to be possessed, and I don't know why. A quirk of some kind. Alcohol helps keep the spirits out."

Although none of this had any obvious relevance at the moment, it was interesting. Better than collapsing in existential fear, at any rate. Also, something was nibbling at the edge of Achilles' mind, something he couldn't yet identify.

"What happens when a spirit takes over?"

Achilles felt Abe shudder. "It's not pleasant. It happened to me once, and I'd rather not talk about that. Some spirits are worse than others. Dybbuks, they bring no end of misery. But an ibbur can be benign, even helpful. Possession by an ibbur prolongs life and can bring strong powers." He snorted. "Still not necessarily nice for the host, though."

Prolongs life. Maybe that explained Abe's longevity. Of course, lots of Bureau agents were long-lived for a variety of reasons. Townsend, for instance, had remained seemingly unchanged for many decades.

That nibbling morphed into something more like a vigorous gnawing. "Chief Townsend. Was he—"

"Possessed by an ibbur. Yes." Abe sounded old and tired. "Originally Townsend was a chazer, a true pig of a man. But an ibbur, the spirit of a mensch, a righteous man, possessed him, and he became the chief you knew."

Well, that explained some things. Achilles wondered why Abe had never shared this tidbit of knowledge with anyone. Generations of Bureau agents had speculated fruitlessly about Townsend's secrets.

"Okay. So Townsend gets possessed by a good guy and he becomes… everything that Townsend was. But when someone gets possessed by a bad guy, a dybbuk, are they equally powerful?"

"They can be."

Shit. Oh, shit. "Spurling."

Abe sucked in his breath. "What makes you think this?"

"Just a hunch. I didn't spend a lot of quality time with the guy, but he reminded me of something. Not exactly the same, but similar. I couldn't put my finger on what, but now I know. He reminded me of Townsend."

"I interacted with him only briefly. Something was certainly off, but I didn't have a chance to evaluate it."

"I didn't have much time either. But the more I think about it, the surer I get."

Abe responded with what sounded like a string of curses in Yiddish, and Achilles added a few in Greek for good measure. Because Townsend had been very powerful and, even though they were on the same side, scary as hell. They both sat silently for a while.

"What are we going to do about this?" Achilles finally asked.

"You're asking me?"

"You have way more years of experience than I do. And you know much more about Townsend, which means much more about Spurling."

Abe made a dismissive sound and let go of Achilles' hands, but only so he could lie down beside him, Abe's elbow resting against Achilles' knee. "I don't know anything. I'm just a tired alta kocker—an old shit—who got careless." He sighed, loudly. "I didn't truly know that much about Townsend. I didn't like him, and to be honest, I felt guilty because I'm the one who made him. But Thomas and I, we avoided him as much as possible."

"He was really creepy. It was weird. I never knew whether to believe anything he said, or whether anything he did was what it seemed. But I also trusted him to be on the right side, ultimately. Although maybe he was willing to experience casualties along the way."

"I'd agree with that assessment."

Now it was Achilles' turn to sigh. "I wish he hadn't gotten killed. Thomas makes a good chief under ordinary circumstances, but he doesn't have Townsend's… spooky ibbur gifts."

At first Abe was very quiet, and then he sat up suddenly, startling Achilles. "Gotten killed," Abe echoed. "Tell me more about how that happened. When you're retired, the gossip isn't as good."

"Honestly, I don't know all the details either. It was kept kind of hush-hush." Achilles frowned as he tried to recall the most reliable information he'd heard, ignoring all the idle speculation. "So, Dash Cooke. Do you know him?"

"Met him once or twice. Handsome man. Not very chatty."

That was a concise summary. "I've worked with him over the years. He's the kind of agent who gets sent in when things really need to be obliterated, you know? Not much subtlety to him, but he can best anyone at the firing range." Achilles had always thought of him as a goon—an enforcer—which wasn't necessarily a bad thing. Sometimes a goon was needed to get a job done. "Anyway, he got an assignment in Sacramento. A poltergeist, supposedly, except it wasn't. It turned out to be Henry, a house spirit of a previously unidentified type."

"That seems an odd assignment for someone like him."

"Well, yeah. But you know Townsend. He always had his reasons." The import of Achilles' own words struck him as he said them. "This… this is significant. We're onto something. I don't know what." It felt good, though. A step up from despair. He probably should have followed this train of thought earlier, except that Townsend had done so many inexplicable things that it was easy to simply shrug and accept.

"What happened with Cooke and this house spirit?" Abe prompted.

"Cooke brought him to HQ. And I don't know whether the two of them became an item up in Sac or whether it happened in LA, but it happened. And the thing you have to know is that Henry is the sweetest, least dangerous person you could imagine. He dresses in bright prints and decorates offices and rescues spiders, for gods' sake." Achilles smiled at the memory. Then he grew serious. "But Townsend tried to kill Henry. Nobody knows why. Cooke shot Townsend to protect Henry. He was cleared of any wrongdoing, and last I heard he was still working for the Bureau. When we still had a Bureau to work for."

Abe gave a dry laugh. "So the mamzer caught the bullet. It sounds as if Townsend deliberately orchestrated his own death, *nu?*"

It kind of did. "But he never struck me as the suicidal type. And if he was, why drag Cooke and poor Henry into it? Why not just do it himself?" Achilles really wanted to pace, which always seemed to help him think, but he was afraid he'd lose Abe if they separated. He didn't want to risk not being able to reunite; that they'd connected at all might be a temporary fluke.

"These are good questions. The thing he became when Birdie possessed him—Birdie was the ibbur—was no longer human. I don't know if a name exists for such a creature. He was that thing for nearly a century, gathering power over the years. Perhaps it was physically impossible for him to end his own life—directly, in any case."

That made sense to Achilles. Especially since Townsend left clear directives for the future of the Bureau, including naming Charles as the next chief. Which implied that he'd known what was coming.

Instead of pacing, Achilles drummed his fingers on his leg. "Okay, so maybe after a hundred years or so, he was sick of it all and just wanted to retire. Like, *really* retire. I tried to retire myself recently, only less dramatically."

"That doesn't seem to have worked out well for you."

"Not really. I couldn't stay away, though. Not with Dee, and not with the stakes so high. Jesus, Townsend had been going on for years about how something really big and bad was coming down the line, but I don't know if he did shit all to prepare for it."

"Boychik, what if his death *was* the preparation?"

Achilles gasped. "Townsend knew he'd be more useful dead than alive! He sacrificed himself for the cause."

Abe patted Achilles' knee. "Seems to be going around, doesn't it?"

Shit. The key to this puzzle lay in figuring out *how* a now-dead possessed creature could help. "Can we assume that a lot of the other things he's been doing over the past decades—maybe stuff that doesn't seem to make much sense—those were part of his grand plan too?" A rush of anger filled his veins. "He's been moving us all around like goddamn chess pieces."

"He may have set up the game, but I think we've moved ourselves."

Achilles sneered. "Free will, huh?"

"Back when your... your great-grandparents were children, maybe, I held seances—they were in vogue then. I wasn't bad at it. Between the seances and my stage shows, I made a living. The seances were *my* game, nu? But I never forced any of my marks to do anything. I simply made educated guesses about how they'd behave, and I based my spiel on those guesses. Townsend did this on a larger scale."

If this was supposed to make Achilles feel better about being manipulated, it didn't. In fact, he was indignant on behalf of dozens of agents—maybe hundreds—whose personality traits and personal circumstances Townsend had capitalized on.

Except... recent events notwithstanding, things had eventually turned out well for a lot of those agents. They'd found meaning. In some cases, they'd found partners. Dash Cooke, for instance, was madly in love with Henry, whom he met only because of Townsend.

Achilles groaned. "I don't know what to think."

"How about if we deal with the moral crisis later and concentrate now on what to do? Can we use Townsend's death to our advantage somehow?"

Achilles wasn't smart enough for this kind of thing. He wasn't a master chess player and, unlike Abe, had no real experience in moving the pieces around. Hell, he had no extraordinary talents at all, unless you counted stubbornness. He couldn't fly or grant wishes or talk to dead people.

Wait.

"Dead people," Achilles whispered.

"Pardon?"

"There are a lot of dead Bureau agents."

"I'm aware," Abe said softly, his sorrow clear. He hadn't only lost a husband, Achilles realized. Abe, over the course of his long life, must have had lots of his Bureau friends die, whether in the line of duty or otherwise.

"What if they could help us?"

There was a long silence. Although Achilles couldn't see Abe, he imagined that his expression showed bewilderment. "They're *dead*," Abe finally said. Slowly and firmly.

"Right. But you told me yourself that Townsend became powerful after he was possessed by the spirit of a righteous man. So that dead guy did a lot, right?"

"Poor Birdie," Abe whispered. And then, more loudly, "How do you propose we do this? In this place especially?"

"I don't know." Achilles' mind was whirring like a food processor blade. He hoped the slicing and dicing would prove productive. "But we've got you, right? You can communicate with spirits. And, gods, I have to think that Townsend got himself killed for a reason. What if it was so he could rally the troops on the other side?"

"This...." Abe gave a lengthy pause. "Feels less impossible than it should. You're a persuasive man. But even if we weren't in this place, and even with my abilities, there's a wide gulf between the living and the dead."

Gulf. Abyss. Chasm.

A memory surfaced in Achilles' spinning mind, an assignment he'd been given during his early years in the Bureau. This one had taken him to a tiny community in Alaska, where most of the town clustered near the harbor. But there were a handful of houses halfway up a steep mountain, accessible by a single road. A few of the locals had gone missing, and there were reports of an unearthly woman in a white dress lurking nearby.

It had turned out that the woman was in fact an osenya, a creature from Eastern Europe who was known to seduce men and lead them to their deaths. She had probably arrived in Alaska along with Russian immigrants at some point. Achilles and his partner had trapped her and sent her to the Bureau's prison in Nevada—and Achilles didn't want to think right now about what had happened to all the inmates there, now that the Bureau was dissolved.

At first, he didn't understand why he was thinking of her at all, since she had nothing to do with the urgent current problem. But then it struck him. There was a deep gorge between the harbor village and the mountainside homes, and that was where the osenya lured her prey: she would stand on the bridge over the gorge and wait for someone to drive up to her.

"A bridge," Achilles said to Abe. Confidently, because he was once again relying on hope. "We need a bridge between you and Townsend. And I know someone who can build it."

CHAPTER 36

"*A* war," Dee said to Irina. Again. He'd already said it several times, and each time she'd simply shrugged. Which is what she did this time, without even looking up from the magazine she was reading.

After Spurling had dropped the bomb about what his test would involve, he'd announced that he had a meeting and left the room. Now Irina was arranged comfortably in the armchair, and Dee paced.

"He wants me to start a goddamn *war*," he growled, as if she somehow hadn't understood that point.

"What difference does it make? There are always wars happening somewhere. That's what humans are like. Anyway, all of that will end once we've achieved our goals."

"*Our* goals. Is this what you want?"

She raised her eyes from the page. They were as cold and hard as metal. "I told you what I want. As it happens, my interests—*your* interests, my son—align with theirs right now. Garrick would probably put this in business terms, so I'll try that. It's like... I used to use ridesharing services often. No need for that now, of course." She waved a hand at the room in general, maybe to remind Dee that Spurling was impossibly wealthy. "But back then, I noticed that the rideshare company had partnered with a streaming music service, so that when you got in a car your playlist would start up."

It was weird to think of her using Uber, and he couldn't begin to guess what music she listened to. "Your point?"

"Two companies with different products, differing goals. But by partnering, they could each increase their customer base and revenue."

He shook his head impatiently. "This isn't a lift home from a bar or a dank groove, Irina. This is—"

"This is *survival*," she snapped. "Our people are extinct, Damnation, all but me and you, and the humans did that. I'm going to do everything I need to do in order to ensure that we are not the end of our line."

A horrifying realization hit him and he sat down hard in the uncomfortable chair. "Are you planning some sort of… breeding program?" He shuddered.

She rolled her eyes and pushed her hair over a shoulder. "Don't make it sound so sordid. I'm too old to have more children. But if Garrick wished to have a baby with me—babies, plural—I think you could make that happen. And you can certainly father children of your own. We'll need to choose the mothers carefully, of course."

Dee felt as if he was going to be sick. It was probably perverse that Irina's plan hit him more viscerally than the ideas of war and genocide, but he couldn't help that. "I'm not a goddamn stud horse," he growled.

"Stop with the melodrama. What you are—or could be, if you behave—is the powerful father to an entire race. You could be *Adam*, my dear, only you'll never be expelled from paradise. We will create our own paradise." She smiled brightly, showing off teeth that were too straight and too white to be natural, and she held out a hand as if bidding him to take it.

But Dee sensed something shallow about her enthusiasm, a thin brittle shell masking something else. If he'd known her better, he might have been able to identify the deeper, truer emotion. All he could do now was bury his face in his hands.

Irina went back to turning the pages of her magazine.

How do I get out of this? How do I get information to people who can do some good with it? And gods, how do I get Achilles to safety?

Dee had no answers to these questions. He'd never had to strategize before. Hell, he'd barely managed his own life and certainly hadn't taken on responsibility for anything or anyone else.

Maybe his djinn nature was to blame. Irina said he needed a master; Charles had said the same. And Dee had felt the truth of this in his bones, in his soul—if he had one. He was destined to follow, to obey, to passively allow someone else to steer him.

Bullshit. That's just an excuse for doing nothing.

Face still hidden in his palms, Dee scowled at the voice in his head. Couldn't he get sympathy from himself, at least?

Sure, buddy. Add self-pity to the mix. That'll help.

Dee growled. He'd feel sorry for himself if he damned well wanted to. He'd ended up in this situation purely because he'd been born a djinn, and he'd done the best he could, and now—

For fuck's sake. Look at your mother, Damnation. She lost her people. Lost her husband. Got stuck in a new country with a useless brat and a son-of-a-bitch husband she only hooked up with because she had to support the brat.

Yeah, look at her. Sitting there in her fancy clothes with her stupid magazine, hooking up with a monster who made Martell look like an angel by comparison.

But she's finding a way to control her destiny, isn't she? It's a fucked-up way to be sure, but she's using Spurling at least as much as he's using her. She's not passive at all.

Dee groaned, mostly because he had to admit that the obnoxious voice was right. Irina *was* in charge of herself, sort of, and was getting what she wanted. Including, apparently, a private collection of Bureau agents to toy with. Whereas Dee was just sitting on an uncomfortable chair, spiraling nowhere except possibly into insanity.

And Achilles was still in the black hole.

Dee suddenly realized that a lot of his most immediate problems could be solved if he was in the black hole too. Because if the two of them were reunited, Achilles could make a wish, and then both of them could get the hell out of there.

Okay, then. How could Dee get into the hole?

He knew that this was urgent. Time passed differently in the black hole, so there was no telling how long Achilles had been there already, and what the experience had done to him. At any point, Irina might decide she felt like doing something even worse than collecting him. Or Spurling might opt to get rid of someone who he considered a nuisance at best and a potential threat at worst.

On top of that, Spurling clearly didn't trust Dee. If Dee didn't gain that trust quickly, Spurling would undoubtedly decide he was far too dangerous to keep alive. A djinn wasn't the sort of weapon you'd want to risk falling into the enemy's hands.

Plus, there was the big evil master plan. Dee hadn't caught the news for the past few days, but he had the impression that things were going very badly in the country and maybe the entire world. How much longer until the damage became irreversible?

Fine. So Dee had to do *something*, and he had to do it pretty fast. The problem was that, while he was a weapon, he couldn't wield himself. And he didn't have a Bureau agent's training, or much of an education, or any relevant experience.

He must have groaned again, because Irina made an annoyed sound. "If you're going to have a tantrum, Deedee, do it somewhere else."

She'd never had any patience for his shows of emotion, even when he was very little, and she'd almost never revealed her feelings to him. Even Martell, asshole that he was, had occasionally sympathized when Dee was upset and had even, on rare occasions, shared happiness over something like an extra-large paycheck or a TV show he liked.

Emotions were *important*, even if Irina didn't seem to understand that. Even the negative ones, but especially the positive ones. Charles had put it well during their drive to San Francisco, when he'd talked about the balance between things like hate and greed and things like hope and joy. *It feels so good when the light prevails*, he'd said.

Dee saw now that he had a tool after all.

"Irina," he said quietly.

She looked up, face composed. Waiting.

"My father—my real one, not Martell. Did you love him?"

Her mask slipped momentarily, briefly replaced with a startled expression. "What?"

"It's a simple question. I know his death caused you a lot of trouble. And it also got in the way of your plan to save our species. I'm guessing, though, that you two were together out of necessity. Only two djinn on the ark, so to speak. But what I want to know is whether you *loved* him."

It was possible that her eyes softened infinitesimally. Or it could have been a trick of the light. Her voice remained crisp. "I respected him, greatly. I admired many things about him. I don't know if I loved him."

Fair enough. "What about your family? Your parents? Siblings?" She'd never mentioned them at all.

She iced back up again. "My father, like yours, was murdered before I was born. My mother struggled to support me—just as I struggled with you. She died when I was very young. I had no siblings. I spent much of my childhood in institutions."

Although Dee didn't want to feel sorry for this woman, he did. Life had handed her one shitty deal after another, apparently. No wonder she hadn't been able to nurture him appropriately—she'd never learned how. Dee had heard about a series of studies in which infant monkeys were raised in isolation and, when later placed in the company of other monkeys, were basically unable to function. Barbaric experiments that shed light on human behaviors. And, it seemed, on djinns.

"I'm sorry," he said, in full honesty. "You should have had better."

Another slip of that mask, almost too fast to catch. "I survived."

"You thrived, by the looks of things. In some ways, at any rate. But are you happy?"

She looked away instead of answering.

Then he asked another question. The hardest one. "Did you love me?" He took a steadying breath. "You clearly made sacrifices to support me. But was that because you cared about me, or because you needed your Adam to survive?"

It hurt when she didn't respond. And he was going to drop this whole attempt, but then another memory surfaced. "Happy Meal," he whispered.

"What?" she asked, seemingly bewildered.

"The day before you walked away from me, you granted me a wish for a dog. It was the only wish you ever gave me. Why did you do that?"

"You were whining for one. I wanted you to shut up."

"No. I wasn't much of a whiner, I don't think." He'd learned very young that there was no point in it. "I remember that day. We were just sitting outside peacefully. It was hot out. I mentioned a puppy just once and then you... *poof*. You could have refused or ignored me. You didn't gain anything from me getting a dog. So why did you do that for me?" This question had never occurred to him before. It skewed things a little, but that might not be a bad thing.

Irina still didn't say anything. But there might have been a tiny movement of the corner of her lips, and she didn't look away.

Dee smiled warmly at her. "I think you did love me. Which is sort of amazing, really, considering your background. It explains why I'm capable of love too, because Mom, I *am*. And I have to tell you that love is hard. It hurts. There's a good chance that it doesn't end in a happily ever after. But gods, there is nothing like it." He held a fist over his heart. "It can make you feel stronger, happier, better. It can fill holes inside you. It can help you be so much better than you'd ever dreamed of."

He had to stop in order to swallow a few times and blink back hot tears. He might have given up on speaking altogether if not for the recollection of the way Achilles had looked at him. The way Achilles— his beautiful hero—had treated Dee like someone who mattered.

Dee got out of the chair and walked over to kneel in front of Irina.

Not like a supplicant, but like a caring family member. "I don't know how you feel about me now," he said. "But if I were to go along with Spurling's plans, I'd be broken. Ruined forever. I didn't used to think I had a set of morals, but it turns out that I do. Love helped me find those. And I'll die before becoming responsible for killing countless innocent people." Yes, those words were true.

"None of those *innocent people* would lift a hand to help you." She might have intended to sound harsh, but there was a hollowness behind her words. As if they were a mask too.

"That doesn't matter."

"You've been consuming nonsense. Love is just a word people throw around in order to manipulate others."

Dee kept eye contact with her. "I'm sorry you've experienced it that way. It's been different for me."

"I doubt that." Her mouth pursed as if she'd tasted something bitter, and she tapped her fingers on the magazine. "If you're worried about being alone, don't be. You can father offspring… remotely. And you can pick out any man you want for yourself, and simply wish for him to love you, and—"

"You know that doesn't work. True emotions aren't magic tricks. They're… they're a part of you. Forcing them on someone is like using AI to write poetry. You get words, and they rhyme and everything, but there's nothing *behind* them. They have no heartbeat." He wished he was handier with words himself so that he could do a better job explaining this. But he was fairly certain that Irina knew all of this already.

She didn't admit this, but she did stop trying to argue. He wondered how many people had bothered to sit down and discuss things with her, rather than ordering her around or keeping her in the background as an ornament. Until the Bureau dropped into Dee's life, few people had held true discussions with him.

Irina was tense, though, and he was afraid she was going to jump up and stalk away. He chuckled softly at his own foolishness and then threw everything he had into the pot. If he lost this bet, he lost… everything. But he hoped he'd win.

"Mom, there's a way for me to possibly save myself and the man I love. Maybe I'll save some other people too. But I need your help. And if you ever loved me—even a tiny bit—I'm asking you to help me. Please."

Then, heart beating fast, he got to his feet and walked out of the room.

CHAPTER 37

"You're an interesting fellow," Abe said. "More going on in your head than I'd guessed."

Achilles decided to take this as a compliment. "Okay, good, because I have additional ideas. I'm wondering if there might be more of us in this place. We should find out."

"So they can be part of our bridge, assuming we have a chance to construct it."

"Yeah." They'd already begun walking, arms looped together, which gave Achilles a sense of purpose even if they weren't truly getting anywhere. "I guess we should try singing. Why do you figure that works better than just shouting?"

"Prayers are sung. So are many enchantments. Maybe music has magical properties of its own."

That made sense. Achilles knew how well a particular song could evoke a specific memory, and of course nearly everyone had experienced how music affected emotions. Soldiers sang and so did work crews, and not just because it helped them keep rhythm. As far as Achilles was aware, music was universal to human cultures and to many NHSs. "You pick the first song, Abe."

"Anything in particular?"

"Whatever you think is appropriate."

After a brief pause, Abe started in. He had a very pleasant voice and knew how to project it well, probably a holdover from his days as a stage performer. The song itself, a plea for a soldier boy to return, wasn't familiar to Achilles. "My Thomas fought in the First World War," Abe explained after he'd finished. "Birdie—his first love—died in that war."

"Ah," said Achilles. "The same Birdie who possessed Townsend?"

"Yes."

Well, that was messed up. No wonder Abe had never trusted the old chief. "I think it's a good choice. Try again—I'll join in this time."

They'd sung it through four or five times, and Achilles was about to suggest they change their tune, when he thought he heard an answering voice. He stopped suddenly, forcing Abe to stop too, and listened closely. "Alternative Ulster?" he asked, confused.

Abe listened too and then let out a whoop of laughter. "Desmond Hughes!"

The name was familiar but it took a moment for Achilles to place it. "The librarian?"

"I think so."

When Achilles was first hired, Des Hughes had been the Bureau's librarian. He was a big man with an easy smile, a soft Irish brogue, and a sordid past that Achilles had never asked him about. Hughes had retired a few years later, along with his partner, Agent Kurt Powell. Achilles had barely known either of them and had no idea what had happened to them postretirement.

After another couple rounds of singing, Achilles and Abe found their way to another prisoner who was, indeed, Des Hughes, and who was pretty emotional about being discovered. "What in bloody hell is going on?" he demanded.

They tried to give him a quick summary, but he interrupted well before they'd finished. "Kurt. They've taken Kurt as well and I can't bloody find him."

Achilles gave his shoulder a reassuring pat. "We'll do our best to help."

Now all three walked arm-in-arm while belting out Des's Ulster song, and when someone eventually chimed back with "We Shall Overcome," they broke into cheers. Desmond was reunited with Kurt amid a healthy fall of tears. Then they were a marching choir of four. Achilles was beginning to feel downright positive. Whatever had caught him the first time he was here and dragged him into despondency might make a reappearance, but it hadn't yet.

Although Achilles had lived through a lot of strange experiences, this was near the top of the list: walking in complete darkness with several other people, all of them naked, all of them joined in song, all of them hoping to avert the worst disaster imaginable. None of them grew tired or hungry or sore. If anything, they gained energy as they went.

In time, three more agents joined them. Achilles was acquainted with them all, although he didn't know any of them well. One was an enthusiastic woman named Mazur, who'd joined the Bureau only a year or so ago, and the other two were a much more seasoned man and woman, Buhalis and Lu, respectively. Everyone was understandably relieved to be found and all were generally mystified about what was going on. With the exception of Abe, nobody had a particularly great singing voice, but that didn't stop them. Achilles noted that all were fully human and, with the exception of Abe, nobody possessed any special abilities. This was interesting in itself, given the Bureau's high proportion of NHS agents and employees. Finally they'd picked up Nathan Pandya, a man who'd joined the Bureau about the same time that Achilles had but who'd retired early due to a back injury.

"Is anyone left *outside* the black hole?" Achilles wondered aloud. He shuddered to imagine Dee still in the hands of the enemy, without a single potential ally remaining. Nobody in the group had any information to console him.

One piece of good news came to light, however, when they compared stories. It became clear that they'd all been captured within the same two-week period. Months might have gone by since then—no way to tell—but this was at least some evidence that not too much time had passed in the real world. And that there was a good chance that there was still a world left to save.

There wasn't much else to be positive about. Achilles felt as if he'd been here forever, and although it was nice to find other prisoners, he didn't sense that they were getting any closer to building a bridge. Abe still couldn't catch more than the faintest hint of spirits. And after they'd all been singing for a long time without finding anyone new, a sense of hopelessness started to settle in.

Kurt expressed the sentiment that all of them felt: "Can we just find the Tin Man, tap our heels together, and go home already?"

"None of us have slippers, ruby or otherwise," Lu pointed out. "And this isn't a movie. It's real life."

"This doesn't feel real at all. More like an endless fucking nightmare."

"The true nightmare happens if we don't succeed on this assignment."

"It's not a fucking assignment!" Kurt shouted. "Des and I retired years ago and we've been minding our own business. I'm seventy-three years old, dammit. Haven't I earned some rest?"

"You're but a babe," Abe butted in. "I'm over a hundred and thirty, and I haven't had any rest yet."

Things devolved into one big squabble. They stopped marching. Achilles, feeling defeated, sat down and sank his face into his hands. His body felt heavy, as if he were turning to stone. He was useless. This had been his stupid, half-baked plan because, even after a long career in the Bureau, he hadn't come up with anything more clever. Townsend never should have hired him to begin with. Gods, Achilles should have showed up at his parents' shop on time that day, and it should have been him that got shot.

The opposite of despair is hope.

At first Achilles thought that someone had whispered in his ear. But everyone else was still standing over him, arguing without any real point to it, like exhausted siblings stuffed in a back seat during a long drive. And then the voice spoke again, sounding scratchy and ancient like an antique record: *Hope. Love. They sustain us.*

Achilles rose to his feet. "Hey! Shut up, everyone. Let me listen."

Surprisingly, they obeyed. At first there was utter silence; Achilles couldn't even hear his own heartbeat. Then there was the hint of an exhalation, the trace of a throat clearing, and the slightest suggestion of a single word: *Act.*

"Someone else is here," Pandya announced.

"Then let's bloody well find him," said Des.

Lu began to sing "Over the Rainbow." None of them had the range for it except Abe, who didn't know the words, but they did their best as they resumed the trek.

"He's humming back!" Mazur exclaimed after a while. "But I don't recognize the song."

Abe chuckled. "Sinatra. 'Witchcraft.'"

The humming was quiet, but it grew louder as the group continued onward, arms linked. Just like Dorothy and her crew, Achilles thought. He figured he was probably the scarecrow. Then he tripped over something and nearly brought the entire chorus line down with him.

The something turned out to be a some*one*. Even though Achilles was literally on top of the person, their voice was still barely audible. Merely a thin whisper that hurt to listen to. And although Achilles grasped one of their hands in his own, the person made no attempt to get up.

"Are you hurt?" Still unable to see a thing, Achilles was hesitant to grope someone without permission, even if only to check for wounds.

"Who are you?" the person asked.

"Achilles Spanos. And I'm here with… a bunch of other Bureau agents. Who are you?"

"Bureau," said the person, followed by a drawn-out sigh. "Did you imprison me here?"

"No! Gods, no. We're stuck here too and trying to find a way out. Are you an agent?"

Another sound that might have been meant as a laugh. "No. I'm John."

Achilles settled into a seated position and heard the rest of the gang do the same. They all seemed to be waiting for him to act, which suddenly struck him as odd. How had he ended up leading this group? His only advantage over them—if you even wanted to call it that—was that he'd visited this place twice before. But he didn't really know any more than they did, and he certainly wasn't any more capable. Yet here he was, in charge.

Maybe the first order of business was figuring out why John was here.

"John, we were all Bureau employees at some point. That's why we got sent here. Do you know why you did?"

"I was a monster," John whispered. "Until Harry made me a man."

Before Achilles had a chance to parse this puzzling statement, Abe uttered what sounded like a string of expletives in multiple languages. And then he spoke gently. "Are you Harry Lowe's John?"

"I was once." John's voice was heavy with sorrow.

"Ah, tayerinker, then you still are."

"He's dead."

Achilles felt John's grief as acutely as if it had been his own. It tore at his heart and made his gut feel hollow. But Abe scooted closer. "I can assure you, John: love survives death. I've seen this myself more times than I can count. Felt it when I lost my own Thomas."

This time when John sighed, it sounded as if a burden had been lifted from him. "He's been gone so long. I lived on alone with memories for comfort, and our bookshop where we spent so many years together, and our Gavin, who was like a son to us. But they burned the bookshop and took me away, and in this place I can't feel him anymore."

On instinct, Achilles did something that was out of character for him and gently gathered John into an embrace. He did so carefully and loosely, so that John could easily pull away at any time. But instead John emitted a broken sob and clung tightly. Achilles could feel that John was heartbreakingly frail, nothing but skin stretched tightly over bones, and the skin crossed with myriad ridges of scars.

Which was funny, because after a moment John pulled away slightly and said, "You've been wounded."

Achilles, who'd almost forgotten about his own scars due to the burgeoning disasters, laughed a little. "Once or twice."

John hugged him then, as if Achilles were the one who needed comforting. "The Bureau kept me caged for a long time in a place not much better than this. But it was because of the Bureau that I met my Harry. And now you've come here to...?"

"We were all sent here against our will by people who are trying to commit atrocities. We're working to get everyone out."

"And to save the world," added Buhalis.

Desmond spoke next. "John? I think I read about you and Harry. I was a librarian. Well, first I was a prisoner too, although I daresay I deserved it. Originally you were, um...."

"Sewn together from fragments of dead men by a real-life Frankenstein. Yes. I was a monster. But Harry treated me like a man, and I became one. I was *strong*. We had a bookshop, a little family, a long life together."

Unlike Desmond, Achilles had never heard of John, but he was familiar with a few cases involving necromancers. Santiago had mentioned working on one. Fortunately, Achilles had never handled one himself, because the idea creeped him out. John wasn't creepy, however. He was just a person who'd lost everything and had then been abandoned in this little slice of hell. Either Irina and her pals hadn't realized he wasn't human, or they'd decided that he held no particular value except as part of her collection.

"John," he asked, "how did you get here?"

"A fire started in the shop—my apartment is there too, on the floor above. It was late at night. I was able to escape the building, everything in flames, everything *gone*...." He took a deep breath. "A man and a woman I'd never seen before were standing on the street corner, watching. They said some things to me—I was far too upset to understand—and then I was here. At first I thought I'd died, but then I grew so weak, and that made sense only if I was still alive. I didn't know—"

"Wait." Achilles was sorry to interrupt but was on the verge of an insight. "You were strong until you came here?"

"Yes. I aged, but not as much as a regular person. Not as much as Harry. He passed away just after his ninetieth birthday."

"And you said it was originally Harry's presence that strengthened you."

John gave Achilles' arm a gentle squeeze. "Not just his presence. It was his nurturing, his love. You see? I became *real* because he believed in me. And even after he was gone I had so many memories. So much of him was… was encapsulated in me."

That was similar to what Townsend had once lectured Achilles about: a cousin to immortality. *If someone is important to you, a part of them stays with you even after they die.*

"I told you," said Abe. "Love survives death."

"Not in this place. I lost Harry when they sent me here. I remember him, of course. But I can't feel him. I'm depleted."

This was another of those things that would be interesting for the Bureau to research someday, if the Bureau were ever reconstituted: John was apparently sustained by affection much the same way a vampire was sustained by blood. And that sustenance didn't require the physical presence of the beloved. What was more important right now, however, was that the black hole changed this.

"It's a weapon!" Achilles exclaimed, probably startling everyone. "This place isn't just a prison—it's a weapon."

"What do you mean, boychik?"

"Can't you feel it? We're being… bombarded with despair, the opposite of hope. Right, John?"

John squeezed him again. "Yes."

"It's why we all had that stupid argument before. Why we're all tempted to just lie down and give up. Why an angel—a genuine goddamn angel—couldn't find his way out. Why John withered away. And I think it's why the stupid songs work to unite us. They counteract the despair. People sing the blues because it lifts their burdens a little." This was important information. Achilles *knew* that to the depths of his being, even if he didn't yet understand why it was important.

Kurt said, "So you're telling us that if we don't get out of here soon, we're all going to be destroyed. Or close enough that the difference doesn't matter."

Achilles shook his head impatiently even though nobody could see. "Almost all of us spent months, even years in Bureau training. And a good chunk of that time was learning what makes NHSs tick so we can deal with them. So we can kill them, if necessary. Sorry, John. I don't mean—"

"I understand."

"The better we understand something, the better we can handle it. Now we understand this place better. Abe and I, we have an idea of how to get us all out and maybe save a lot of people. We just need one crucial ingredient: a djinn named Damnation. So we're going to wait, and we're going to hope like hell that he shows up. And while we wait, we're going to stay strong by using all of our weapons. We're going to generate all the hope we can. All the love and joy that we're capable of."

"Do we have to keep on singing?" Lu sounded a little plaintive.

When Achilles laughed, it felt wonderful. Like the first breaths after being underwater for too long. "We can take a break, I think. John? Would you like to tell us about Harry and your bookshop and Gavin?"

"Yes," said John. He sounded better already. "I'd like that very much."

CHAPTER 38

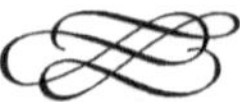

*D*ee knew he ought to be grateful.

For three days he'd been left alone in Spurling's mansion. Midway through the first of those days, a pair of expressionless and mostly silent thugs had shown up in Dee's minimalistic room, scaring the crap out of him. But all they'd done was lead him down the hall to a different, larger bedroom before closing him inside. This one had a comfortable bed, a sitting area with a view of the vineyards, and an expansive bathroom with high-end towels and toiletries. Several sets of clothing were in the closet and dresser. And there was a giant TV. It was, he supposed, like being held prisoner in a very expensive hotel.

It was many orders of magnitude better than where Achilles now was—assuming he was even alive. Just thinking about that made Dee's heart thump and his throat feel thick.

The room had a small fridge that contained assorted nonalcoholic beverages, and several times a day, unspeaking minions appeared bearing trays of delicious food.

But Dee didn't feel grateful. He was angry—at everyone, including himself—and worried. He was so lonely that he was surprised when he looked in the mirror and his skin wasn't withered like a dried apple. He was sad and scared and apprehensive. And he was also bored out of his mind.

He tried asking the minions for a book, but they ignored him. That left him with little to do except stare out the window at the unchanging vista or watch television. And gods, that was awful—nothing but bad news followed by worse. Smug politicians spouting lies, rich men spinning webs to make themselves richer, ecosystems collapsing, children dying, freedoms disappearing, diseases spreading, prisoners calling out for justice, educational institutions failing.

Dee wondered sometimes how much of what he saw was the direct result of Spurling and his pals. It didn't really matter, though, whether they were creating catastrophes or merely delighting in them. That Yeats poem that Abe Ferencz had told him to read kept echoing in Dee's brain: *Things fall apart; the centre cannot hold.... The best lack all conviction, while the worst are full of passionate intensity.* A poem written in the aftermath of a war and a pandemic.

On the third day, with the sun already setting behind the nearby hills, Dee paced his gilded cage, *the best lack all conviction* circling through his skull the way his body circled the room. But then he stopped suddenly. "That's not true," he said out loud. "The best have plenty of conviction." Achilles, willing to give up his freedom and his life for even the smallest chance of making a difference. Charles and Tenrael, fighting for decades. Clay and Marek, Art and Jerry, all of the other Bureau agents and former agents still doing whatever they could even though the Bureau itself was gone. The coyote shifters and the aliens. And hell, the people he saw on TV, holding signs in protest marches, calling out their elected representatives, filing lawsuits. He was sure there were many more that didn't make it onto the news, all of them *holding* conviction that even the smallest gestures mattered.

"I'll hold it too," he promised himself, hands curling into tight fists as if hope were something he could physically hold on to. As if hope was a magic charm.

A short time later, Dee sat on the love seat, watching an influential female politician give a TV interview blaming immigrants for soaring retail prices. The interviewer nodded gravely, never questioning any of her assertions. One or both of them might be on Spurling's side, Dee thought. They both had odd, shifty eyes. Or maybe that was just something to do with the TV signal.

The door suddenly flung open, startling Dee. Two beefy, bearded men wearing dark suits and white earbuds stepped inside. "Come with us," they ordered in unison.

"Why?"

They took a synchronized step in his direction. "Your presence is requested."

"What if I say no?" Dee crossed his arms. He didn't know why he was being so difficult, except that a tiny bit of rebellion felt good. Even if it was pointless.

They again spoke together. "We'll drag you if we have to."

"What are you guys? Robots?" He wouldn't put it past Spurling's gang to create sophisticated androids. That might even be a trick that Irina could pull off, although Dee wasn't sure about that. But no, one of these guys had a little dot of what might be mustard on his suit lapel, so he was probably not mechanical. Unless androids had to eat too.

Jesus, Dee was losing his mind in this place.

Meanwhile, the two were stomping closer, and it occurred to him that even if they weren't robots, they weren't necessarily human. In fact, he wouldn't be surprised if either of them turned out to be a bear shifter.

Since Dee had no desire to end up nearly gutted like Achilles, he rose and shuffled to the corner to put on his shoes. He did it as slowly as he could get away with, and behind him, the minions huffed and shuffled their feet, sounding more like ticked off bulls than bears. Were there cattle shifters too?

Finally he ran out of delaying tactics, and the three of them walked down a series of hallways, Dee flanked by the men for the entire way. "What's with you guys, anyway?" he asked as they walked. "I've always kinda wondered what goes on in the heads of people like you. I doubt you consider yourselves evil. Are you true believers in Spurling's cult? What are you getting out of it? Just the money? Maybe you're natural followers and he just happens to be the leader you ended up with." Dee could certainly empathize with that.

The guy on his right gave Dee's shoulder a little shove. "Shut up, faggot."

Dee never picked fights, but today he didn't stop himself. It felt better than meekly going along with orders. "Ah, I see. You're insecure in your masculinity and this job makes you feel tough."

The man growled and looked as if he was going to do something more violent than shoving, but the other man barked, "Hey! Cut it out, Hunter."

Hunter did, in fact, cut it out, but he compensated by stomping more loudly as they walked. When they reached a set of tall double doors, Hunter's partner knocked before opening them and Hunter gave Dee a not-very-gentle push inside, causing him to stumble slightly.

He was in… a meeting room, an entirely unremarkable one. White walls with a couple pieces of bland abstract art and a large projection screen, industrial carpeting on the floor, and fluorescent lights overhead. A small stand in one corner held coffee supplies, while long tables were arranged into a rectangle in the center. About twenty people in suits sat around the rectangle. Most of them were white, middle-aged men, although a few were younger. Irina was there, standing beside Spurling. She wore a sleeveless red sheath dress and her hair was pulled back from her face in a tight bun. Her expression was grim, unlike Spurling, who grinned widely. The rest of the people stared at Dee, probably very much like he'd stared at the first alien he met.

"Thank you for joining us, Dee." Spurling managed to sound both threatening and patronizing. "These are my colleagues." He made a waving motion to indicate the assembly.

Looking closely, Dee thought he recognized a couple of them. CEOs of something, maybe. And they didn't look evil: no horns or fangs or anything like that. But then, he'd met people with horns or fangs who weren't evil at all, and books shouldn't be judged by their covers.

"Who's in charge?" Dee demanded.

A chuckle rippled around the room. "I told you," said Spurling. "It's not like that. We're a consortium."

That was unfortunate. Dee had the impression that it was easier to defeat an enemy with a single powerful leader; if you took out the head honcho, the whole thing would tend to collapse. He had no idea how you disabled an entire committee. Maybe Charles and Tenrael did—assuming that Dee could get them any useful intel. Which seemed unlikely under the present circumstances.

"A consortium trying to end the world."

"No, no, of course not. We simply want to improve things. You have to admit, the world has needed this for a very long time. And now we have the resources to act."

Dee couldn't tell whether Spurling truly believed this bullshit. He certainly seemed earnest, but then so did used car salesmen. Something interesting occurred to Dee: Spurling assumed Dee was stupid. Part of that was likely the superiority complex common in people like him, and he was possibly aware that Dee lacked even a high school diploma. Being underestimated might prove an advantage, especially if these people also underestimated Dee's powers. If only he could find a way to use that advantage.

"To act how?" he asked.

A sort of ripple went around the table, with everyone exchanging uneasy glances and shifting their postures. Spurling looked unhappy. "Son—"

"I'm not your son. And you're not much older than I am."

Spurling snorted. "I'm older than I look. Listen, you don't need to know the details. It's just what I told you before: a massive reorganization. A disruption. Things will be messy for a time, but the end results will be more than worth it. So much unpleasantness gone."

Everyone nodded, whereas Dee wondered what—or who—they considered "unpleasant." Maybe it was better not to know.

A man sitting to Dee's right cleared his throat loudly. He had a grandfatherly air, with snow-white hair and thick-rimmed glasses, but there was no warmth in his blue eyes. "This is wasting time. Either he's capable of doing what we want or he's no good to us. He doesn't need to know any of these things."

Dee might have responded, but Irina reacted for the first time, putting a hand on Spurling's shoulder and speaking. "Darling, if he has a better understanding of our goals, then—"

"Not now, Irina." Spurling shrugged away from her touch and a subtle expression flashed across her face. It was too quick for Dee to interpret, and he didn't really know her expressions well anyway, but he thought she might be angry.

"Show us what he can do," said a bald man wearing a button-up shirt over a gray tee.

"I'm not a new gadget," protested Dee, but nobody paid him attention. Instead, Spurling picked up a black remote control and poked at it, after which the room lights dimmed and a beam shone from an overhead projector that Dee hadn't previously noticed. A world map appeared on the wall screen.

"Are you familiar with these countries?" Spurling used a laser pointer to indicate two neighboring countries to the east of Italy.

"No." Dee had a poor grasp of geography.

"Doesn't matter. I wish for the northern one to attack the southern one. Immediately. Specifically, I want bombs dropped on the capital."

Dee tried not to shudder. "Why?"

"It doesn't *matter.*"

"But people will die."

Spurling made a sour face. "People always die. Nobody there is important. The countries have nothing to offer—no resorts, no interesting sites to visit, very little foreign investment. But they're both backed by the same European countries. Their conflict will destabilize things in that region, which is what we want."

Dee was aware that world powers played these kinds of games all the time. But it was jarring to hear someone speak about it so plainly, so matter-of-factly. As if it were nothing more than, say, paving over a garden to make a patio.

"That's asking a lot," Dee said, stalling. "Affecting an entire army thousands of miles away." Actually, he wasn't certain that this was beyond his abilities, but he had no intention of saying so.

"We don't need to affect an entire army—just the person in charge of it. The president. I'm going to wish that he orchestrates the attack right now. By the time anyone tries to stop him, it'll be too late." The screen changed to show a panoramic view of a small city with green mountains behind a scattering of high-rises. Most of the tall buildings looked a little run-down, but the surrounding houses were cute, with red tile roofs. A river wound lazily through the town, its riverbanks lined with parks. Cars, buses, and pedestrians crossed on several small bridges.

And then suddenly one of the high-rises turned into a pillar of fire and smoke, then another, then a swath of the little houses and two of the bridges. Dee realized he was watching the city being bombarded.

"AI simulation," explained the bald man proudly. "My company makes the software. Looks real, doesn't it?"

It did, sickeningly so. Some of the people in the room started cheering whenever a bomb hit its target. It was like they were watching someone play a video game. When the attack stopped after about five minutes, nothing was left of the city except fires and piles of rubble.

"See?" said Spurling. "Nice and quick. They'll retaliate, of course, and various other countries will step in, and things will get very interesting."

"People will die." Repeating it didn't help, but it felt necessary.

Spurling waved a dismissive hand while other people in the room huffed or rolled their eyes. "People *will* die," Spurling agreed. "Nobody important, though. Both of these countries are *takers*. They suck up our tax dollars and give nothing back. There are lots of countries like that, Dee, and lots of people in *this* country. At one time they might have been useful as laborers, but we don't need that any longer. Computers and machines will take care of that for us."

It didn't sound like hate. Didn't sound evil. If you removed all emotion, it was entirely logical.

"Move this along," said the grandfatherly man. He was looking at something on his phone.

Spurling nodded. "It's time, Dee. Show us what you got. Grant my wish so we can move our agenda forward expeditiously." He turned, clicked the remote, and a photo of a man appeared onscreen. He was middle-aged, white, and blocky, with impressively bushy eyebrows and a thin-lipped smile. His name was printed underneath the photo. "That's the president. He's in his country's capital right now. We can give you the geographic coordinates if you need them."

Dee didn't need them. Standing there in the stupid meeting room, he knew he could grant this wish. It was just a little nudge after all, and perhaps this president was already inclined toward such action. Maybe the guy stayed awake at night, imagining giving the orders and watching—no doubt from somewhere safe—as his weapons did what they were made to do.

The overhead lights brightened and Irina walked over, heels silent on the ugly carpet. She stopped when she was just a few feet away, and for the first time he noticed how thin she was. She was tiny, really. But he could see the corded muscles in her arms and the firmness in her jaw. With her gaze firmly locked on Dee's, she slid a ring off her finger and handed it to him on outstretched palm.

"That's an expensive charm," he remarked. Inane, but it was the first thing that came into his head.

"Plenty more where that came from."

"Does anyone ever grant *you* wishes?"

Very briefly, her mask slipped and her face almost crumpled. But she quickly regained her composure. "Only you, Deedee. That one time."

"And you granted my only wish too. My dog—Happy Meal. He was a good friend. The only one I ever had, until Achilles. I wish I was with Achilles now."

She answered quietly. "You can be, when this is all over. I'll make sure of it."

Yes, she probably could. Spurling didn't seem to care much about Bureau agents as long as they were no threat to his plans. Dee and

Achilles could remain untouched by the chaos, and no creatures would come along to disembowel Achilles or shoot him. Dee and Achilles would be comfortable. And Dee would wield true power instead of lurking on the edges of society and worrying about paying his rent or getting thrown in jail. All the bad things that would happen to strangers, those wouldn't be his fault. The world wasn't his responsibility. He hadn't asked for *any* of this.

Dee could picture it: he and Achilles in a nice house with lots of bookshelves and a big yard. Dee would learn how to garden. They could get a dog. They would spend hours together in their big bed and take lazy walks through the countryside. Achilles might be resistant at first, but he *had* wanted to quit the Bureau, after all. Dee and Irina could give him a little nudge or two as well.

And anyway, what was the use of refusing? Spurling and his gang were ultimately going to win. They had all the money, all the power. There was no point in taking a stand when you had nothing to gain from it.

Irina closed her hand around the ring as if reluctant to part with it. Despite her flippant dismissal of its value, she probably treasured it anyway. She had always liked shiny things.

Dee took it from her.

"Come *on*," said one of the men. "If I want drama, I'll watch Netflix." Several others mumbled their agreement.

Irina turned and walked back to her spot. Her stance was confident and businesslike. If she hadn't been standing behind the seated Spurling, she would have looked like a CEO. Except for her hair, which was in the process of escaping her bun as if it wanted nothing to do with present company.

Dee held the ring so tightly that it dug into his skin.

"I wish," said Spurling loudly, "for the president to immediately launch an attack on the capital, as we saw in the video. Is that specific enough for you, Dee?"

"Yes." Dee's own voice seemed to come from far away. From someone else. He would grant this wish and Achilles would understand, eventually. It was the only way that Dee could save him. They could have a life together.

And it would be as hollow and bitter as if it were the result of a love charm.

"It'd be better just to die," Dee said. To Irina, because nobody else would understand. To everyone else, he said, "I'd rather be in the black hole with the man I love than help you monsters."

A jolt went up his arm, his body felt so flattened that his heart and lungs didn't work. And the world went black.

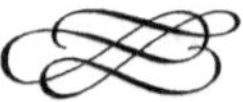

CHAPTER 39

It was Des's turn to sing again.

The group of them had been sitting together for what felt like centuries, since nobody could sleep, even if they tried. They'd all told stories from their lives. Any stories were allowed, as long as they were positive, hopeful, or funny. Abe had the biggest collection of tales since he'd been around the longest, and he was an excellent storyteller. But everyone had something to contribute. Even Achilles, who shared some anecdotes from his slightly misspent youth.

Quite a few of the stories had to do with love—romantic, familial, or platonic—because those worked especially well to stave feelings of doom and helplessness. Achilles surprised himself by remembering the times his sister had patiently helped him with homework or his parents had made a big effort to understand American customs and the English language so they could help him navigate childhood obstacles.

Periodically they'd decide to pause the stories and sing instead, but aside from Abe, Des was the only one with a decent voice. So he good-naturedly taught them songs from his childhood in Belfast. Some of them were raunchy, but that was fun too. Right now they were on the third round of a ballad about a drunk man who falls from a ladder and busts open his head, which didn't seem like it would be a cheery topic but was, nonetheless, because whiskey revives him at the end.

And then something heavy landed on Achilles with a thud, knocking him to the ground and pinning him in place.

It was a body… and gods, he *knew* that body. When Dee tried to scramble off him, Achilles held him tight, ignoring the commotion of everyone else around them.

Dee must have been stunned or confused, which was understandable, but he came to his senses almost immediately, cradling Achilles' face in his hands and bringing their foreheads together. "Achilles, Jesus, Achilles!"

Then they were both talking at once and everyone else was squawking and yelling and it was all chaotic. But Achilles didn't care because Dee was here, in his arms, right now.

Except then he wasn't, because Dee had wiggled free from his grasp and was frantically trying to pull Achilles upright. "Come on, come on," Dee chanted. "We gotta go. Gimme a charm."

"But we're—"

"Irina gave me a wish and sent me here but all the bad guys are gonna be royally pissed and I doubt it'll take 'em long to pull me out so come *on*!"

It took a few seconds for Achilles to process this, then he swore. "It's not just you and me, Dee. There's, uh…." He did the math in his head. "Ten. There's ten of us. I think that's all—we searched and haven't found anyone else—but that's a lot of people to move."

Dee paused and then let out a noisy breath. "I think I can do it. We don't have time to worry about it. Give me a charm, Achilles."

That was a little problematic since everyone was naked and there were no angels or demons with convenient feathers in their group. "Hair?" Achilles suggested.

"Too insubstantial."

Achilles was seriously considering biting off one of his own fingers when he heard a grunt, and then someone pressed something small, hard, and damp against his arm. "What's that?" he demanded, but he got it in his hand before anyone answered. "Did someone just knock out a *tooth?*"

"Veneer," answered Kurt. "It was loose anyway. I was meaning to see the dentist."

Dee grabbed the veneer away. "Hurry!"

"I wish all of us were safely out of here and…." Shit. Where should they land? "In my condo in LA." It seemed as good a choice as any. At least Achilles had some clothing there, and some cash.

After mumbling something very fast, Dee gave him back the veneer. "Hang on, everyone!" Achilles ordered. "This may be a bumpy ride." Then he made his wish.

* * *

SEVERAL PEOPLE PUKED, and most of them didn't make it to a toilet or a sink. Achilles could hardly blame them, although he was too busy to give his own nausea its due. As soon as he had his feet under him, he scooped Dee into his arms and started ordering people around.

"Mazur, get John comfortable on a couch. Abe, Kurt, and Des, raid the closet and dresser for clothing for everyone. Pandya, Lu, if you're finished barfing, clean it all up. Buhalis, see if there's anything edible in the kitchen."

The amazing thing was that everyone obeyed without a single quibble. As if Achilles was in charge, which had never before been his role. As if they trusted him to know what to do.

And at the moment, he did know what to do, because Dee was out for the count and Achilles needed to make sure he was okay. He set him down on the other couch, checked him over for obvious injuries, and breathed a sigh of relief when he didn't find any. Then he covered Dee with a blanket and sat on the floor beside him. "You okay?" He brushed hair away from Dee's face.

Dee's eyelids fluttered but didn't open, and he grunted softly.

"Is he hurt?" Abe, wearing a T-shirt and a pair of sweatpants that bunched around his ankles, handed Achilles a tee and pair of shorts.

"I think he's just exhausted. Doing his thing saps his energy." Achilles stood to get dressed.

"That was quite a thing he just did."

"He's fucking amazing."

Without opening his eyes, Dee smiled a little. That was wonderful to see.

Speaking of which, it was surreal to finally see everyone, all of them now arrayed in the living room wearing various items from Achilles' wardrobe. It had been years since he'd seen Kurt and Desmond, both of them now in their seventies. And John… well, it was painful to look at him. He was skeletal, his pale skin crossed with numerous angry-looking scars and his scalp bare except for a few wisps of transparent hair. He was sitting upright, though, propped by pillows, and his eyes were bright and clear.

Everything in the refrigerator had gone bad in Achilles' absence, but with some help, Buhalis managed to cobble together enough food from the freezer and cupboards to fill everyone's plates. They arranged themselves around the living room in chairs and on the floor, and Achilles reflected on the fact that this was, by far, the biggest gathering he'd ever hosted. In fact, it was the *only* gathering he'd ever hosted. His nice condo with the expensive furniture had been his alone. It was kind of nice to have guests, even under such bizarre and fraught circumstances.

Kurt was the first to state the obvious. "I'm incredibly grateful to be here, but you do all realize we can't stay, right?"

Of course not. It was far too obvious a place for them to hide out— and not really suitable for the next step in the plan. Which they wouldn't be able to attempt until Dee had recovered.

"I've been thinking about this." Achilles used a spoon to chase some rice around his plate. "And I know where we need to go."

"Where?" asked pretty much everyone all at once.

He sighed. "Bureau HQ. Assuming nobody's taken it over, that is." He waved hands to silence the questions. "It has plenty of space. There might be useful supplies there. And dammit, that's *our* building." In a way, it had been much more his home than this condo had been, and for longer.

"I agree," said Abe. "For the reasons you state. Also, some places are... charged. There's something special about them. I don't know if that location was always that way or if having HQ there made it that way—or maybe that schmuck Townsend did something to it. Anyway, it's good for what we have in mind."

The validation was nice, and nobody argued with the idea, so apparently they were set.

Mazur, who was very young, cleared her throat. "Um... how are we getting there?"

Shit. Nobody had a phone or a credit card. Achilles had left his car —which wouldn't fit all of them anyway—at HQ. It was too far to walk, especially for John and Dee. The two of them also wouldn't be able to manage public transport, even assuming there was a way to get to HQ by bus; Achilles had no clue whether there was. And Dee was in no condition to wish them all there.

Achilles started to laugh. He was aware there was an edge of hysteria to it, but the situation was so damned *idiotic*. They'd come so far, literally and figuratively, and now they were stalled by a few impassible miles of Los Angeles.

Abe put a gentle hand on Achilles' shoulder. "Are there shops nearby, boychik?"

"Um... yeah. There's a strip mall about a quarter mile north of here."

"And you have a little cash?"

Achilles had a couple thousand bucks, in fact, squirreled away in a safe, along with his passport and a few other important papers. He fetched the money and distributed some to each person. Even Dee, who was still asleep.

Abe and Lu set off. For lack of anything better to do, Achilles started cleaning up the kitchen and his colleagues joined in right away: emptying and scrubbing the fridge, washing and putting away dishes, wiping everything down. Some of them tackled the rest of the place, which had gotten dusty while he was gone. Maybe all of them knew the exercise was pointless—Achilles would probably never be able to return here—but it kept them busy, gave a sense of accomplishment, and settled their nerves.

They were just finishing up when Abe and Lu returned, both of them grinning broadly and clutching large plastic bags. They dumped the contents onto the coffee table.

"Cell phones?" asked Pandya.

"Yep," said Lu. "One for each of us. We found a phone store. It was a challenge at first since all we had was cash and they want credit cards. But Abe could sweet-talk candy from a baby. He worked it out."

Not the least bit modest about it, Abe gave a theatrical bow. "On our way back, I made my first call. Charles was very relieved to hear from us."

Achilles breathed a little easier knowing that the chief was still alive and well. "What does he want us to do?"

Abe gave him a steady look. "He believes in your plan. He will contact as many remaining agents as possible, and we'll meet at HQ."

The chief believed in him. So did everyone currently in the room, including Dee, who squeezed Achilles' hand. And if they could believe, then Achilles could damn well believe in himself.

"Let's do this," he said.

Without any need for discussion, Abe ordered a small fleet of Lyfts.

* * *

From the parking lot, HQ looked dark and a little sinister. Haunted, even. There wasn't any sign of life, which Achilles reminded himself was a good thing. He didn't know what they'd have done if it were occupied—especially if it were occupied by the enemy.

"Do you suppose they have this place under surveillance?" Mazur asked as they made their way en masse to the front door. Dee was shuffling along, slowly but on his own power. John, looking apprehensive, was supported by Kurt and Des.

"Maybe," Kurt replied. "But they'd have a hell of a time getting in. It's like a fortress."

That may have been true, but Abe got them through the big front doors with no problem. He was good with locks, and Charles had given him instructions.

Every sound they made echoed in the vast lobby, where the lights burned dimly over empty acres of white marble. Achilles felt an odd stab in the chest when he glanced at the vacant reception desk. He'd passed through here hundreds of times—thousands, maybe—and that desk had *always* been staffed by somebody, no matter what day or time. Sometimes it was a new recruit, and other times it was a more seasoned agent temporarily sidelined by an injury. He'd manned it himself a few times while recovering. Nobody liked working the desk, but although it was boring, it was also a good place to share gossip. Now, it sat abandoned.

John spoke quietly. "This… this is not where I was held." He looked around in confusion and maybe a little relief.

"HQ used to be downtown," Abe explained. "We moved here in the fifties."

"Does this place have cells too?"

"Yes," said Des. "And we've an entire prison in Nevada. We did, anyway. I was kept there for seventeen years."

John visibly squared his shoulders. "All right."

By this point, Dee had simply lain down on the hard floor, one arm pillowing his head. Achilles had already decided that the lobby was the best place to assemble, so he sent some people off to the gym in search of mats to soften the surfaces for Dee and John, and others to the armory to load up on whatever weapons they could find. A few agents did a quick recon of the entire building, just to make sure it was empty.

Just as everyone was reassembling, more people began to arrive. Tenrael and Ralph entered first, since they could fly. Achilles wished he'd been able to glimpse a demon and dragon swooping through the LA sky; that would have been a memorable sight indeed. Next came

Dash and Henry, who lived nearby and had apparently been hiding out for weeks. "More are on the way," Tenrael informed them. "Can we wait a bit longer?"

Achilles shrugged. "I hope so."

It had been late afternoon when HQ was reclaimed. Agents trickled in all evening and well into the night, some of them young, some with years of experience, and some retired. They were a variety of species. A few small groups ventured out for food, for additional clothing for the ten people who'd been in the black hole, and for cots and blankets. The lobby, for so long hushed and mostly vacant, swirled with activity, conversations, colors, and scents.

"It's like a party," said Achilles, who was sitting beside John and watching it all with wonder. Dee slept on despite the commotion.

John, although gaunt, had visibly filled out a little and was somewhat livelier. "All these people care. They're willing to risk their lives for what's right."

"You know, after talking to Abe, death doesn't bother me so much. I mean, I'd rather live, thanks very much, but…. I guess what's even more important is knowing I did everything I could to keep the balance from tipping too far."

Marek and Clay arrived shortly before dawn, fangs gleaming, and Jerry and Art showed up not long after. They both looked incongruously wild in the stark setting of the lobby, and Jerry scowled at the white walls. But they were eager to help and embraced Achilles like old friends.

Achilles got only a couple hours of fitful sleep in the morning but woke up feeling oddly refreshed. Maybe because he'd spent those hours spooning Dee, which was something he'd never expected to do again. Con and Isaac had arrived while he was asleep, and Owen and Keaton walked in the door just as Achilles finished breakfast. Terry and Edge were there too, and gods, Achilles hadn't seen them since he was brand-new to the Bureau. Terry remained handsome in his early seventies, like an aging movie star, and Edge was still fairly muscular and quietly intimidating. Kyle the nurse was there and gave Achilles a cheery wave. Diana Afolabi was deep in conversation with Con and Desmond. Even Agent Holmes had showed up, sitting in his wheelchair, looking terrifying.

"Quite a crowd," remarked Dee. He was sitting up now and had managed to eat a little, but he still had dark circles under his eyes.

Well, *a crowd* was relative. There were about forty of them now, and that was plenty to fill the lobby. It didn't make for a very big army, however. Not in comparison to what they were facing. And quite a few of the people in the room were well past their prime.

But Tenrael and Charles had lectured him about this—they'd told him that every person, every act counts. That sometimes one small thing may be just enough to tip the balance. History backed this up; Achilles could think of plenty of examples where the actions of a few turned the tide, for better or for worse.

Dee sighed heavily. "I'm sorry."

"For what?"

"It took so long to get you out of there. And I didn't really dig up much useful info."

Achilles blinked at him. "Dee. You pulled ten people out of a fucking interdimensional liminal space. *You* did this. Plus, now we at least know *something* about the enemy. Because of you." If Achilles had managed to believe in himself, Dee could damned well do the same.

Dee smiled a little. "Okay. I learned some stuff about djinns too. Irina and I are the last ones."

"Jesus, Dee. I'm sorry."

"It's weird to lose a heritage that I didn't even realize existed until a short time ago. I'm not sure how I feel about it."

"Well, if we survive, we can both get therapy. Maybe they'll give us a two-for-one discount."

"Yeah. We can start with my mommy issues. She did this, Achilles." He gestured around the room at large. "She gave me a wish so I could join you in the black hole. God knows what Spurling did to her, but *she* did this. And I don't know why."

Achilles, who'd been wondering how Dee got there, shook his head. "Maybe because she loves you."

"She's had a damned funny way of showing it."

"A lot of us do." Achilles thought about his own family for a moment before repeating himself. "A lot of us do. Hey, can you excuse me for a few?"

Dee yawned and lay back down. "No problem."

There was a corridor that led from the lobby to the cafeteria and atrium, its long walls lined with photos of agents who'd been killed in the line of duty. There was Santiago Bautista with a cocky smile, looking much younger than when he'd died. Achilles smiled back, then pulled out his phone and dialed a number from memory. He hoped it hadn't changed over the decades.

"Hello?" The woman's voice was achingly familiar.

Achilles swallowed, almost hung up, and swallowed again. "Lala?" he said. A return to a childhood nickname, crafted by a toddler who couldn't quite manage to say Atalanta. "It's Achilles."

There was a quick intake of breath, but she didn't hang up. When she spoke, her voice was even. "Are you dying? In prison? Broke?"

"None of the above." Not actively, anyway. "I just called because…. There's been sort of a lot going on. I've had time to think. And—you don't have to say anything back, you don't owe me anything, okay?—but I need to thank you for everything you did for me. And I need to tell you that I love you."

After a long pause, she spoke again. "I owe you an apology. I was looking for someone to blame, but you were just a kid. It wasn't your fault. I'm sorry. And I love you too."

He was crying now. The type of salty, bitter tears that stung like hell, but maybe that meant they were washing away some toxins. "Thank you."

"Can you…. You have two nephews and a niece. They'd like to meet their Uncle Achilles. Do you have kids?"

"Nope. Gay as a maypole, actually. But I have a… well, a partner." That was an apt term for how he felt about Dee. "His name is Dee."

"I'd like to meet him," she responded without hesitation.

"I'd like that too." Surprisingly, he meant it. "I'm sort of in the middle of a mess right now. Not my fault, but I'm trying to help clean it up. Can I call you once it's over?" Assuming, of course, that he was alive to do so.

"Please do, Achilles."

He ended the call, wiped his eyes dry, and went to rejoin Dee.

CHAPTER 40

*P*ulling ten people out of the black hole had felt like running a marathon while carrying a cement mixer on his shoulders. But Dee had accomplished it, and now Achilles and the others were at least temporarily safe. Dee had managed to get some rest and decent food, which helped revive him. As did the combined energy of all the people in the room. They might be frightened and apprehensive, but there was also an optimistic eagerness to the crowd. Everyone seemed excited to at least go down fighting.

Best of all, however, Achilles was there. He seemed to be sort of in charge of this circus, yet he spent every available moment doting on Dee. And his eyes, as he and Dee gazed at each other, were as bright and shiny as an anime character's. Dee had told him the whole story of what happened in Spurling's mansion—including Dee's temptation to start the damn war for his own selfish reasons—and Achilles still loved him. With that, Dee felt as if he could zap a hundred people out of the black hole. A thousand.

And that was good, because pretty soon he was going to be asked to do even more.

"You okay?" Achilles asked. He sat next to Dee on a mat, their backs propped against the wall, shoulders touching.

"Never been better."

"Dee...."

"Really." Dee leaned in against him. "Everyone here knows I'm a djinn, right?"

"Um, yeah. I mean, I've filled everyone in on what's going on, and you're central to that story."

"Right. But nobody's treating me like I'm a monster or a freak."

Achilles laughed. "You don't really stand out in this crowd." He gestured at the vampires napping in the corner, the dog shifter—who was currently a mastiff—panting beside his human partner, the house spirit with the pointed ears and bright clothing laughing with a small cluster of agents, the Sasquatch sitting next to his giant husband and whittling something from a chunk of wood, the demon deep in discussion with... whatever John was. Achilles definitely had a point.

"It's nice," Dee said. "Even if I didn't know I was a djinn, I *did* know that I was weird. I didn't belong anywhere, with anyone. But now...." He made a frustrated noise, unable to find the right words to express what he was feeling.

"You found your tribe. I felt that way too, back when Townsend first recruited me. I still didn't make close friends here, but that was on me. I pushed people away, I guess. Even so, I always felt like I belonged here." Achilles sighed heavily, no doubt mourning the loss of the Bureau. The makeshift band of warriors might be in HQ now, but things were definitely not back to normal.

Dee and Achilles were quiet for a while. Dee could have sworn that he felt strength and vitality flowing into him from the spot where Achilles was pressed against him. Achilles didn't seem to be drained, however. If anything, he had an excess of energy, wiggling his feet and tapping his fingers.

When there was a small commotion near the doors, Achilles leapt up to investigate. Dee couldn't see what was going on at first, but then Tenrael waded in and the crowd parted enough for Dee to see that Charles had arrived... and he'd brought Ish with him. Ish was magnificent: tall and broad, handsome. Wing feathers so white that they made the lobby's marble look drab and gray. He was naked, which shouldn't have been a big surprise since Tenrael also avoided wearing clothes. Shirts were pretty much out of the question anyway due to the wings. Dee didn't know the extent of Ish's psychological recovery, but he was certainly doing well physically.

While Achilles and Charles immediately fell into a discussion, Ish sailed over to Dee and knelt gracefully in front of him. "You have done well, my friend," he said and gave a warm smile.

Dee felt flustered, as if a beloved celebrity had complimented him. He even blushed. "I didn't…. Achilles, he—"

"Yes. Each of you is a good man. Together, you are great heroes. There is often immense power when individuals join."

Join. Dee considered that as he surveyed the room and saw all the couples. Not everyone was paired, by any means, but a lot of them were. Which made sense, because as Achilles had pointed out, it was hard for Bureau agents to form close relationships, so people tended to pair up with coworkers. But by now Dee had heard quite a few stories about the famous Chief Townsend, and it sounded as if he'd orchestrated a goodly portion of these matches. That might have been incidental, or a way to help keep his agents content. Or maybe he'd known that a day would come when the Bureau would need this kind of synergy.

"I'm going to do my best," Dee assured Ish.

"From the perspective of the world at large, the results are what matter. But for each person, the most important thing is the effort." With that entirely enigmatic comment, Ish stood and looked behind him, where Charles and Achilles were approaching.

"How much longer do you need to recover?" asked Charles without greeting or preamble.

Achilles glowered. "Hey, he's been through a *lot* lately, and—"

"It's okay," Dee interrupted. "I get it. Time is not on our side." He did a quick self-assessment. He was still tired, but he'd had a good day of rest. If he waited too long, it would be too late. "Give me a few more hours and I'll be ready."

"Are you sure?" Achilles asked.

Dee nodded.

Meanwhile, Charles was shifting his feet and looking uncomfortable. "My apologies. You've already contributed enormously, and I'm grateful. But the stakes are so high."

"I get it. No rest for the wicked." Dee smiled.

"All of us have been wicked," intoned Ish. "And all of us have the capacity to be good. It is unfortunate that wickedness is often the easier choice."

Also a little cryptic, Dee thought. But then he considered Irina, who'd done lots of rotten things out of self-protection but in the end had endangered herself to do what was right. Hell, Dee himself had taken his full name pretty seriously for a good chunk of his life. Maybe he'd never been downright evil, but he'd done a lot of things he regretted and not much that he was proud of.

Until recently.

According to Charles, Achilles, Abe, and several others, hope was a strong weapon. Deciding to do good after a history of doing bad—that was a form of hope, wasn't it? Dee thought so.

Achilles crouched so he could speak quietly to Dee. "Charles wants me to give a speech now. That's not really my thing. In fact, I'd rather face a bear shifter."

"So look at me while you're talking and imagine me in my underwear."

"I happen to know you're not wearing any."

That was true. In the shuffle to clothe everyone who'd been in the black hole, Dee had ended up with a T-shirt and sweatpants, both with Bureau insignias, and that was it. He hadn't especially minded.

"Even better," Dee said with a leer.

"Then I'll be too distracted." Achilles winked and stood upright again. "I guess I'm ready," he said to Charles.

Achilles looked unusually pale. It was funny that a person could go his entire life facing monsters, could willingly allow himself to be thrust into the hands of enemies… and yet was afraid of speaking to a crowd of his peers. But it made him more human in Dee's eyes, and more lovable.

Achilles stood straight against the wall near Dee and cleared his throat a few times. "Hey!" he called. And when that had little effect, he repeated much more loudly. "Hey! Listen up!"

Conversations quieted and stopped as everyone turned to look. He swallowed two more times before glancing at Dee—who waggled his eyebrows. Achilles straightened his shoulders. "The chief has asked me to give a quick debriefing about what we're working on here. I'm not going to lie; I don't know if this will work. But I hope it will. And you all know the stakes. Plus, every person in this room has put their life on the line before. Some of you have done it many times. And you've all chosen to be here today when you could have opted to be just about anywhere else. I think... I think if you're honest with yourself, you'll know we're taking the right path."

There were murmurings in the audience, and they sounded approving. Dee noticed that Ish and Tenrael had positioned themselves to flank the crowd. The two of them looked nothing alike, aside from their expressionless countenances and their unfurled, slowly fanning wings. Although according to some religions they were supposed to be ideological opposites, Dee saw similarities: ancient eyes, proud bearing, barely-concealed power. And both were demonstrating respect for Achilles.

"Here's the plan," Achilles continued. "As you all probably know, Abe can connect with spirits of the dead. He also tells me that when the spirit of a, um, righteous person possesses a living person, the possessed becomes very powerful. That was, um, how Chief Townsend came to be... what he was."

That caused a stir among the crowd, but Achilles held up his hands for silence. "So the idea is that Dee will grant my wish to have everyone here possessed by a good spirit. A... what are they called, Abe?"

"Ibbur," Abe called from the back.

"Right. And then we'll seek out the enemy and fight them. At least some of them are probably possessed too, by the way. By not-so-righteous men."

"Fight them how?" asked a tall woman with short, graying hair.

Achilles looked uncomfortable. "I'm not sure. But we'll be a whole gang of, of Townsends. I'm sure we'll figure something out."

This was a major gap in the plan, one that they'd been aware of. But without knowing exactly what their little army would be capable of or what actions the enemy would take, it was hard to be more specific.

But then someone else spoke up. "I have an idea. May I share it?" He was a handsome man in his forties.

Achilles looked slightly relieved. "Sure, Keaton. Go ahead."

"Thanks. So… I'm an empath, right? It turns out my talent is a two-way street. I can receive emotions from others, but if I try, I can also *send* them. When Owen and I were trapped by that Miller guy"—he shuddered—"we defeated him by pushing a bunch of positive emotions at him. We had an angel's help with that, I think." He smiled at Ish, who gave a slight bow back.

"That was just one guy," Keaton continued. "And I don't even know if he was all that big a player. But what I'm thinking is that all of you, with these ibburs inside you, you'd be like… like an enormous battery. I'd be like a jumper cable, directing the charge at the bad guys. But instead of electricity, the charge will be all the feelings that they loathe."

The room was silent as everyone considered what they'd heard. Dee thought that it was a lot of mumbo-jumbo and hocus-pocus. But so was just about everything he'd experienced since the Bureau came into his life. So was his entire existence, really. Achilles said that magic was simply science that nobody yet understood. Dee was willing to accept that. Especially since nobody seemed to have a reasonable alternative.

"I like it," said Achilles. "It… feels right. Can you direct your charge over distances? And when you don't know exactly who your targets are or where they are?"

Keaton winced. "I don't know. I haven't tried it. But… I doubt it."

Dee realized that he was standing, although he hadn't made the conscious choice to do so. He'd never done public speaking, but unlike Achilles, he didn't feel uncomfortable with it. "We have to bring them to us, then."

"How?" asked Keaton.

"Make a wish."

* * *

"IT'S NOT VERY EXCITING, is it?" Achilles said, looking around.

Dee shrugged. "I didn't think we came here for the décor."

The gathering in the lobby had broken up after everyone agreed to the plan and Dee had promised he'd be ready to facilitate the possessions soon. As people wandered off, many in pairs, Achilles had led Dee to his old office. It was dusty and unremarkable, with a desk and a couple of chairs, a small bookcase containing labeled binders and a couple of dozen volumes, and a well-worn loveseat that looked as if it came from Ikea. There were no windows, and the only adornment was a framed vintage poster for *War of the Worlds*.

Dee pointed at the poster. "You're a sci-fi fan?"

"Not especially. It was a gift from Orson not long after we met. Sort of a joke, since he was named after Orson Welles, who did the radio version, and the Bureau often deals with weird creatures, and…. It wasn't a very *funny* joke."

Dee thought it was interesting that Achilles had kept the poster even though they had broken up and Orson died. It was sweet, really —a small psychological slip from a man who had usually refused to admit how much he might care for someone else.

But again, décor wasn't the point.

Dee crashed into Achilles, hard, nearly sending them both sprawling onto the floor, and he kissed like he'd never kissed before. Achilles immediately got into the spirit of things and clutched him fiercely. Dee was ravenous, desperate, would have swallowed him whole if that had been possible—or would have *been* swallowed, because it was all the same anyway.

"You're hot," said Achilles, panting, his hands under Dee's shirt and spread against his bare back.

"Thanks."

"No, I mean physically *hot*, like you have a fever."

"I'm burning for you." Dee couldn't help it—he laughed. Then he used a thumb to smooth the lines of concern on Achilles' forehead. "Really, I'm fine. I swear I'm not sick. I just really need this right now. Need you."

Achilles looked only slightly relieved. "You're supposed to be resting."

"No, I'm supposed to be gathering energy. This will do me way more good than any amount of napping." Although he lacked scientific proof that this was true, Dee believed it wholeheartedly. This was a craving far more urgent than one for food or drugs.

He put his hands on Achilles' shoulders and looked him steadily in the eyes. "Do you want me?"

"More than I want oxygen."

"Then what I need you to do, Achilles my love, is tell me what I should do to you."

"But what—"

"Tell me what to do," Dee said firmly. A command seeking a command.

Achilles, eyes wide and cheeks flushed, let out a long breath. "Suck me off?"

The thrill that rushed through Dee's nerves nearly collapsed him, but he managed to keep on his feet. He grinned. "Say it like you mean it. Master."

"Jesus." Achilles' eyes briefly rolled back in his head and he shuddered. Then the corner of his mouth crooked. "Suck me off," he growled.

Oh, fuck. Dee actually fell to his knees now, and that was just as well because it was easier for him to unbutton Achilles' jeans and shove them past his hips, along with his underwear. Achilles was already hard, his cock heavy and warm when Dee took it in hand. Impulsively, Dee kissed the very tip. Achilles' answering moan was so deep that Dee felt it in his bones.

And yes, Achilles was right—Dee *was* hot. Coals smoldered in his core and his skin felt as tender and sensitive as if he had a bad sunburn, yet it wasn't painful. Or if it was, he welcomed this pain. He wasn't sure which was the case.

He had the sudden mental image of his body as a hot air balloon, a roaring flame at the center, lifting him upward into a stormy sky. In order to keep from floating away, he needed an anchor. Something to, quite literally, ground him.

He solved that problem by deep-throating Achilles' dick.

This wasn't something he'd done before, or something he would have imagined himself capable of. He'd been sort of working up to it lately and had been nowhere near accomplishing it. But yep, Achilles filled his mouth and throat. Salty, solid. A connection not just to Achilles himself but to the world at large, a satisfying reminder of all that was good.

"Dee…." It was barely more than a whisper and certainly wasn't an official wish. No magic charms were involved. But it worked anyway, because Dee moved his head slightly, scraped oh-so-lightly with his teeth, and did his damnedest to make Achilles fall apart.

Although Dee remained fully dressed, his own cock untouched, his entire body buzzed with pleasure. Every tiny sound that Achilles made, the sensation of Achilles digging fingers into Dee's shoulders, Achilles' pulse drumming against his tongue… these were as delightful as any amount of groping or fucking had ever been. *Dee* was making his beloved react this way, and it was Dee's name that his beloved moaned.

"D-Dee, I'm going… to…."

Dee hummed his approval.

And when Achilles came with a roar, Dee came too, both of them riding the aftershocks until it was all too much and they collapsed in a messy heap on the office floor.

"Oh," Achilles said after a while. It was the sound of a person who'd just made a discovery.

Since Dee wasn't yet capable of speech, he grunted in reply. When he had the breath and operational brain cells for it, he'd inform Achilles that he felt fully recharged, more powerful than he'd ever been. He could make wishes that moved mountains. He could definitely call forth friendly spirits. He could—

Someone pounded on the door.

"Achilles? You in there? It's Ralph."

Achilles was already on his feet, awkwardly scrambling to pull his clothing back up. "Hang on, hang on."

Dee stood too and tugged down his T-shirt, hoping it covered any evidence of their romp. He'd need to clean up before facing the crowd. He watched as Achilles rushed over and flung open the door.

Ralph looked at them, smirked, and then shook his head. "I did a surveillance flight with Keaton. They're almost here."

"Who?" Achilles demanded.

"A couple carloads of trouble."

Achilles went pale and turned to face Dee. "Well, I guess we won't have to wish them here after all."

CHAPTER 41

As Achilles, Dee, and Ralph hurried down to the lobby, Achilles knew he should be angry at himself for getting distracted with Dee. He should have been the one to suggest some kind of surveillance, and he shouldn't have disappeared while everything was so unsettled.

But in fact he wasn't angry. Not when it could very well have been the last chance he and Dee had together. And definitely not when Dee was bouncing at his side like Tigger, his aura so vibrant that he practically left a rainbow trail behind him down the long hallway. Achilles had never seen him so bright and energetic. The blowjob may or may not have been magic, but there was no way that Achilles could make himself regret it.

"You literally flew around LA? With a guy on your back?" Dee asked Ralph.

Ralph, who looked amused despite their impending doom, nodded. "Literally."

"But don't people notice?"

"You'd be surprised how few people look up. We were pretty high, so anyone who saw us likely assumed I was a large bird."

"Oh." Dee leapt forward to press the elevator button. "And how could this Keaton guy tell that bad guys were coming this way?"

"He's an empath—a strong one. He's familiar with the emotional signature of these people because he encountered one before."

"He *destroyed* one," Achilles pointed out. "He and Owen."

The elevator doors opened and they piled in. "Right," Dee said. "He was the guy who spoke up during your speech. The jumper cable."

Soon they were in the lobby, filled with the roar of conversation. People stood in small clusters or milled around. Ish and Tenrael, wings spread, flanked the front doors like strange and threatening statuary.

"Are you ready?" Charles asked Dee immediately. "I know you haven't had much time to rest."

Dee clapped his hands briskly. "I'm good. Let's do this."

Ralph leaned close to Achilles and whispered something that sounded a lot like *magic dick*. Achilles pointedly ignored him.

It occurred to him then that the general mood in the room was… eagerness. A tinge of anxiety, but no more than that. They were like a team ready to play in the national championship: keyed up, optimistic, and ready to go. He hoped that carried through after everyone was subjected to the ibbur possession.

There was a bit of shuffling as people took their positions. Abe, Dee, and Achilles stood near a wall facing the crowd. Charles was nearby, but he was clearly willing to let Achilles run the show. Keaton stood close to Tenrael and Ish, looking resolute.

Achilles spoke loudly into the sudden silence. "Gods, I'm proud to be one of you." Then he pulled something from his pocket. He'd retrieved the item from his desk drawer while Dee was admiring the *War of the Worlds* poster. "Here's your charm," he said to Dee, holding it out.

"Your Bureau badge?" Dee asked, eyes wide.

"One of them. The other… I don't know what happened to it. Ashley Dunn probably took it."

"It's going to disintegrate when you make your wish."

Achilles smiled. "I'm hoping it'll add a little oomph to the whole thing."

Returning the smile, Dee wrapped his hand around the badge, closed his eyes, and whispered the wish that they'd previously practiced.

He was quite a sight. His hair, which had seemingly grown longer in the past couple of days, stood out from his head in a wild halo. His lips were unusually red and full, possibly a side effect of their session in the office. He stood tall and straight, and although he was wearing a boring—and probably not very clean—Bureau exercise outfit, he might as well have been wearing flowing silk robes and a dazzling crown. He was clothed in power, and he was the most beautiful thing that Achilles had ever seen.

"Here." As Dee returned the badge, a spark leapt between them. Achilles' cock immediately hardened, despite its recent workout, and he didn't give a shit whether everyone noticed. Let them see what Dee did to him.

Achilles took a few breaths. This time, he wasn't nervous about public speaking. He simply wanted to make sure he did this right.

"I wish… that ibburs will come right now and possess everyone in this room who welcomes them."

That was it. For several seconds, absolutely nothing happened. Before Achilles had time to fear that they'd failed, however, Abe called out something in Hebrew. A prayer, Achilles thought. And something happened to the atmosphere in the lobby. The large room felt… full. It was briefly hard to breathe, and then fluctuated very fast between frigid cold and stifling heat and back again. All of the marble on the walls and floor faded, looking like gray curtains with the light shining through, but remained solid to the touch. Achilles heard a cacophony of sounds: crying, laughter, conversation in dozens of languages, birdsong, waves crashing, bullets whizzing, animals roaring, engines revving, sirens blaring. The reek of death made him gag but was quickly replaced by the scent of a spring meadow and… his mother's cooking?

Dee collapsed to the floor and lay on his side, eyes open and chest moving evenly.

Abe spoke again, voice broken. First in Yiddish and then English. "Oh, my darling Thomas."

A few feet away, John fell to his knees. He looked much younger and healthier, and his face glowed with joy. "Welcome back, Harry."

Others called out names as well, but Achilles didn't catch them because something tickled in his brain and made his nerves tingle. He felt as if he were wearing too-tight clothes, as if he were a little tipsy, as if every scar on his body had suddenly reopened and then healed even more quickly. And oh gods, he was so *strong*!

A familiar voice spoke inside his head. "This is quite a party you're throwing, Spanos."

"Bautista?" Achilles whispered.

"Santiago. First names, seeing as we're sharing a body." Santiago chuckled with Achilles' throat and mouth.

"I am so sorry. The bear… and you… and I—"

"That shifter killed me. Not you. And you need to stop shouldering blame for things that weren't your fault. You're not the center of the universe. Lots of shit happens that's nothing to do with you. Taking responsibility for all that is a form of hubris, Achilles."

Oh. That was true, wasn't it? Admitting it was humbling, but it also lightened Achilles' soul.

"Okay," said Santiago. "Your body's a pretty good machine. Let me in the driver's seat."

At the door, Keaton shouted, "They're here!"

Achilles glanced once more at Dee, who hadn't moved. "It's all yours, Santiago. Hit the gas."

CHAPTER 42

*D*ee had experienced a lot of weird lately, but this topped it all. As soon as Abe finished his prayer, or whatever it was, he started glowing in a way that was impossible to describe. He wasn't like a lightbulb or anything like that; in fact, maybe *glow* wasn't the right term for it. It was a sort of buzz, although Dee couldn't hear or feel it. Maybe it involved a sense he'd never used before and that had no name.

In any case, Abe glowed, then dozens of sparks appeared in the lobby. They zoomed around for a few seconds, as if searching for something, before each one disappeared into a particular person. Immediately, each person was... expanded? It was as if they had gained an extra dimension. Dee could see a shadowy figure overlaying each one of them.

Oddly, none of this frightened him. It was beautiful, in a way. Especially when each person's face alit with wonder and, in some cases, joy. Dee actually felt slightly envious of them, although everyone had agreed that it was best if he remain unpossessed—in part because he was already drained and in part because nobody knew how possession would affect a djinn. Assuming it was even possible.

Tenrael, Ish, and Henry also remained fully themselves, although

Ralph, Jerry, and the other not-quite-humans in the room welcomed the ibburs.

Charles, however, was even more remarkable, because he had not one shadow, but two. One of them was rounder and balder than Charles and, even from several yards away, smelled of cigarette smoke. The other was slender. Dee couldn't discern the shadows' facial features, but he had the definite impression that the slender shadow was grinning.

Achilles seemed to be in a conversation with himself. Or, more likely, with the shorter shadow that had attached to him. Dee, who couldn't muster enough energy to move a muscle, strained to hear what Achilles was saying. Something about a bear. Ah, his ibbur must be the agent who'd been killed when Achilles was so badly mauled.

Dee wondered whether the ibburs chose hosts who were specifically connected to them in some way. It would make sense if that were so. And, Dee hoped, it might make the union stronger.

Then Keaton shouted and Dee had no more time to wonder.

The dual front doors burst open violently, wrenched from their hinges. Several men stampeded inside and then began committing the most ordinary act of violence imaginable: they opened fire on the Bureau agents with some very large guns. The noise was deafening. Agents shouted, blood spurted crimson against white marble, and Dee tried desperately but uselessly to crawl away.

He couldn't cry out, not even when several agents fell to the floor. Not even when some of the fallen were people he knew and had started forming friendships with: John. Kurt. Dash. Isaac.

No! It couldn't end so easily. So *stupidly*.

But before grief could begin to set in, two things happened. First, a dragon, a demon, and a very large dog set on the shooters, stopping the carnage while creating new carnage of their own. The blood that flowed now did not belong to Bureau agents.

And at the same time, the agents who had fallen rose to their feet. Although their clothing was bloody, they didn't move as if they were injured. Together with the other agents, they formed a tight semicircle, shoulder to shoulder, their backs to Dee and their fronts toward the door. Achilles was among them. When he shot a quick look over his shoulder at Dee, he was grinning wildly. Dee tried to smile back.

Within moments, the shooters were nothing but gory corpses. Dee didn't rejoice in their deaths—they might have been ordinary people simply trying to pay the bills—but he wasn't sorry about it either.

The room was quiet now aside from heavy breathing, the air thick with anticipation. Dee managed to move his legs a little, then considered an attempt to sit up but discarded the idea. He was marginally less vulnerable while horizontal on the floor.

Charles spoke—only it didn't sound like him at all. "Keaton, son, are you ready?"

Keaton sounded shaky when he answered. "I can't find… can't find a target. There's nothing out there but sunshine."

"They're out there, boy," said Charles.

Abe moaned loudly, cursed in Yiddish, and then spoke in strangled English. "It's trying… to get in me."

Charles ran over and grabbed his shoulders. In a new voice, this one with an English accent, he spoke again. "Tommy? Tommy, protect him."

"I'm trying," responded Abe—also in an English accent.

Then Abe spoke again, in his own voice. "Kill me! Kill me before it gets in."

"No!" shouted several people at once.

"Kill me! Please!" Abe collapsed to his knees, holding his head in his hands as if to keep it from exploding. "You can't let this happen." He made a keening sound, a terrifying growl, a string of words in a tangle of languages. "Catch the bullet, catch the bullet, let me catch the bullet."

Then his English-accented shadow spoke again, voice tight. "Do it, Birdie."

And Charles pulled a handgun from his pocket and shot Abe in the heart.

Dee cried out. Surely there must have been another solution. But already Abe's body lay crumpled on the blood-streaked floor. He didn't get up again. He was a small man, short and wiry, and in death he seemed diminished. An empty shell.

To Dee's considerable surprise—and perhaps everyone else's—Tenrael knelt beside him and uttered a brief prayer in Hebrew. Still on his knees, he looked up at Charles, whose expression was stricken. "Thank you, Master, for sparing Birdie the burden of this act."

"May his memory be a blessing," Charles said. In his own voice.

"I don't understand," Dee whispered. But nobody heard.

Three men entered through the doorway, apparently unarmed. One of them was Spurling, and Dee recognized the other two from the conference room, both in their forties, white, and dressed as if they'd stepped off a golf course. All three of them appeared annoyed but not especially worried.

Spurling chuckled. "This is what the mighty Bureau has come to? A handful of has-beens in workout clothes?"

"We never claimed to be mighty," said Charles. No, Dee realized. That had to be Chief Townsend.

"A waste of taxpayer dollars. Coddling monsters. Colluding with them even." Spurling sneered in the direction of the dragon, who looked very much like he wanted to bite Spurling's head off. "And now you're trespassing on federal property. Authorities are on the way to take you into custody."

"He's lying," Keaton said. "They're scared and—"

Keaton collapsed, writhing and screaming. When Owen ran to his side, he collapsed too. Dash and a couple of other agents pulled out handguns and fired at Spurling and his companions, but the only result was that the three of them rocked back slightly when struck. There was no blood.

"Guns are useless," Townsend rumbled to his agents. At which point several of them—Ralph and the dog included, leapt forward, no doubt intending to repeat their previous mayhem. But all it took were careless little gestures by the three men, and those agents joined Keaton and Owen in shrieking agony. Nonaffected people had to rush to get out of the thrashing dragon's way.

"Stop it!" bellowed Charles in his own voice. "None of this is necessary."

One of Spurling's pals huffed a laugh. "No, but it's fun to watch." He made another motion and fully half of the agents were in agony. As were Tenrael and Ish. And it wasn't stopping—their pain went on and on, and anyone who moved to help was immediately on the floor as well.

Dee put his hands over his ears, blocking the terrible sounds that echoed off the hard surfaces. This small gesture signaled that he'd regained enough energy to move a little. Sitting up, he scooted backward until he was flush against a wall. He looked to see what Charles was doing, but the chief simply stood there, expression grim. Dee couldn't even see Achilles anymore. He'd never felt so terrified and helpless. Hopeless.

He knew that hope was the best weapon—he'd had that hammered into his head repeatedly—but he couldn't muster it. And he didn't see the point in trying, seeing as Keaton, their jumper cable, was either unconscious or dead.

Jesus, what was the point of it all anyway? His own people, whom he'd barely known, were now functionally extinct. The only person he'd loved was fighting a losing battle. Spurling and his buddies would win, and with the exception of a few elite assholes, *Homo sapiens* would soon go the way of the dinosaurs. And shit, maybe the rest of the world would be better off for it. Humans certainly had made a mess of things. Maybe it was best if their time was ended. Maybe Dee should—

Dee gasped. The trio near the front door weren't just felling agents with pain. They were also doing exactly what Dee's side had planned: blasting the enemy with emotions. They were spewing despair like a crop duster dumping poisons, and there was nothing he could do about it. If he drew attention to himself by speaking out, he was likely to end up tortured or worse.

But he couldn't just *sit* here, dammit.

What if he could muster enough energy for a wish? He wasn't at all sure he was capable, and even if he were, he couldn't think clearly enough to devise an appropriate one. What *he* wished was that the screaming would stop, the bad guys would disappear, and everyone would be safe. That was, of course, far beyond the realm of possibility.

He gathered his will and, using the wall against his back for support, slowly rose to his feet. Everything looked worse from this angle. Abe dead near the center of the room; what was left of the original intruders near the door. Blood smearing the white floor like morbid abstract art. Agents unconscious, or thrashing on the floor, or frozen in place. Spurling and his companions looking on with expressions of smug satisfaction.

Achilles stood very still, hands fisted at his sides, face turned away from Dee. At first Dee was slightly hurt by this, until he noted the stiffness of Achilles' posture and realized he was deliberately trying to avoid drawing attention to Dee.

It didn't work. Spurling cocked his head and caught Dee's eyes. "Well, too bad. You could have had everything."

"Irina?" Dee asked through gritted teeth. He saw Achilles turn to look and wanted to say something to him, but held his tongue.

Spurling huffed a laugh. "We never needed her. Or you, for that matter. You might have eased a few things along, but...." He shrugged. "No big deal."

Dee took a page from Charles's book. Not because he expected it to do any good but because he had to make the effort. "You can still turn back from this. You could do so much good if you tried. You could be heroes. You could love and be loved."

A flash of emotion showed on one man's face, but Spurling and the other man sneered. "Love is for weaklings," said Spurling. Then he made a gesture that felled every agent and sent Dee to his knees, blind with pain.

When Dee could register his surroundings again, Spurling and pals were gone, and everyone was shakily rising to their feet. Achilles came stumbling over at once. "Are you hurt? What did he—"

"I'm okay." Dee took a few breaths. "But they're not done with us, are they?"

Achilles mutely shook his head.

As if the question itself had summoned bad news, someone shouted, "We're locked in!"

The doors had been somehow replaced on their hinges, and no amount of force or stabbing at the keypad would open them.

"Back doors!" Charles roared. "Get out!"

It wasn't a stampede—the agents were too well-trained for that. The ones who were in better shape helped the ones who could barely walk, Achilles put an arm around Dee's waist to support him, and everyone moved quickly toward the hallway that led to the café.

And then the explosions began.

For a brief moment, Dee's addled brain assumed they were experiencing an earthquake. But reality broke through a split second later, and he realized that something was hitting the building with tremendous force, making it shake, causing chunks of the ceiling to fall. The electricity cut out, plunging them into complete darkness, and somewhere in front of them, the walls collapsed with an ear-splitting rumble.

Dee choked on air thick with dust and he clutched at Achilles. Agents shouted, and Dee couldn't tell whether they were cries of pain, surprise, or anger. The ground shook so violently that he fell, pulling Achilles down with him.

Then he smelled the oily chemical reek of synthetic objects burning.

"We're trapped!" someone yelled.

"They're bombing us!"

Several people shouted, "Fire!" just before alarms began to shriek.

Heart pounding, lungs straining, Dee knew they were all about to die.

He took the only option remaining, holding Achilles tight and speaking into his ear. "I love you. I don't regret anything. I love you."

"Gods, I love you," Achilles replied hoarsely. Instead of breathing, they kissed ferociously.

Dee didn't want to die, but knowing that he'd tried to help, knowing he was loved—those things gave him a sense of peace.

And a final bit of hope rose within him like a champagne bubble. He franticly tore at his shirt. "Make a wish. Wish for an escape."

"But you—"

"Wish!"

Achilles' throat sounded shredded, but he whispered, "I wish we could all get out of this place."

The familiar tingle ran down Dee's spine, exhilarating even amid the devastation, even as the building burned and collapsed around them. If anyone had been able to see him, they would have been appalled at his ghoulish, manic grin. He thrust a piece of fabric into Achilles' hand and repeated: "Wish." He added, for good measure, "Master."

It sounded as if Achilles laughed before he made his wish.

There was another *boom!*, louder than all the rest. Dee felt it in his bones and waited for everything to fall on them.

Instead, an entire wall collapsed outward, blinding him with sudden light.

"Evacuate!" yelled several people at once.

Dee was smiling as he lost consciousness.

CHAPTER 43

The parking lot of the Sherman Oaks Trader Joe's was chaotic. Bureau agents covered in dust and blood—a couple of them naked—lay on the pavement or moved about, tending to the injured as best they could. Customers and employees stood outside, mostly gaping, although a few had pitched in to help. Sirens wailed from all directions, helicopters buzzed overhead, and a few blocks away, the shell of Bureau HQ smoldered, sending black smoke into the sky.

Charles, Tenrael, and a few others were doing their best to keep everyone calm and organized. Some of the more intact agents had been ordered to keep onlookers at bay, while others commandeered first aid supplies from the store and from bystanders' cars. Charles was now deep in conversation with a cluster of police officers and firefighters.

Achilles knew perfectly well that he should be helping. But all he could do was sit with Dee's head in his lap, waiting to make sure that each breath was followed by another. He was dimly aware of being bloody and bruised, that he was still coughing up soot and dust, that his muscles ached from carrying Dee for several blocks. However, Dee's breathing was all that mattered.

In, out.

In, out.

A hand gently touched Achilles' shoulder, and he looked up to see Henry, whose usual bright and diverse clothing was muted with a layer of white-and-gray dust. "Do either of you need first aid?" he asked gently.

"No. I think he's just… drained."

"And you?" Henry looked skeptical about Achilles' condition.

"Fine. Henry, do you know…. How many did we lose?"

Henry's expression turned grave. "Mazur. Lewis." He glanced across the parking lot. "Cruz is… not good. But his ibbur is trying hard, I think."

Ibbur. Gods, in all the confusion and terror, Achilles had forgotten about that. "Santiago?" he ventured, very quietly.

Been here the whole time, dude.

That made sense. The final zap from Spurling had been stronger than any Achilles had felt before, but he'd recovered fairly quickly. "I'm sorry I dragged you through this mess. You gave your life already—and once should be enough."

I'm here willingly. Just like everyone else.

Henry nodded as if he'd heard Santiago. Maybe he had; Achilles wasn't sure exactly what talents the house spirit possessed. With another gentle shoulder tap, Henry hurried away to help someone else.

Achilles was left with Dee, Santiago, and a lot of regrets. "I fucked up. We had them right there in front of us, and—"

We all fucked up. We thought it would be easy and we were wrong. Besides, I thought you were going to cut out the hubris crap.

Right. Achilles sighed and smoothed hair back from Dee's forehead. He wished he had a damn cloth to wipe the debris from Dee's face. But he'd already used up all his wishes. He did something dumb instead: he hummed a song. He didn't know the name of it—if it even had one—and if it had words, he'd never learned them. But his mother used to hum that tune while she worked, and sometimes his father would join in. He hadn't thought about it in years, but it soothed him now, and he hoped it soothed Dee as well. Achilles noticed that Dee's breaths perfectly matched the song's rhythm.

In, out.

In, out.

We're not perfect, but we're badass, man. Look what we've been through. Some of you are still kicking, and the rest of us, well, we're here too.

"Maybe we're all just phenomenally stubborn."

I'm good with that.

In, out.

In, out.

You know what, though? Those assholes who attacked us, they probably think everyone's dead now. I bet they figure that when they destroyed HQ, they destroyed us too.

"Maybe. But if you think I'm going to spend the rest of my life in hiding, I won't."

Good.

Achilles started to scratch his beard, realized it made bits of debris fall onto Dee, and stopped. He was tired and was tempted to lie down next to Dee, but the pavement was hard, and sleeping wouldn't improve the situation they were all in. Besides, the neighborhood sounded like a war zone. From what he could glean from bits of conversations, the enemy had hit HQ with a drone attack, and they'd damaged the surrounding neighborhood too. Emergency personnel were still assessing civilian casualties, but someone within the federal government had already informed the media that this was a terrorist attack committed by people who were in the country illegally.

In, out.

In, out.

"Okay, Santiago. Their wrong assumption about our demise gives us a potential advantage. How do we use that?"

Beats me. I never was a strategist.

"Me either. I'm just hired muscle."

Naw. Muscle's a dime a dozen. Townsend recruited you because you had something important to add. Just like the rest of us. Every damn one of us makes a contribution somehow.

Achilles considered this. "Maybe he was wrong about me. Maybe he was wrong about a lot of things. He's not helping a whole lot right now, is he?" He waved toward Charles, who was still talking to first responders—a task that could undoubtedly be managed without being possessed by Townsend.

He was right about your man Dee, right?

"Well, yeah. Dee's incredible. Jesus, even after he'd granted huge wishes, he managed to blow a hole in the wall so we could escape."

With your help. You made the wish.

"Yeah, but—"

"You empower me." Dee didn't open his eyes until after he spoke, and when he did, he stared right at Achilles.

"You need to rest," Achilles scolded, although he was secretly rejoicing that Dee seemed to be recovering.

"Don't need rest. Need *you*." Dee reached up, his hand shaky, and grabbed Achilles' arm. "My master gives me strength."

Think about it, dude. You guys screw, he's superman. Super-djinn.

Achilles scoffed. "I don't have a magic penis."

Worked when you kissed too. Or when you simply touched him. You guys got synergy.

Dee smiled. "Refill my tank, master. We can do more."

Hearing those words from Dee's mouth made Achilles *almost* believe. He wanted to believe. He wanted to be Dee's support in every way possible.

He looked up and noticed how many agents were offering help of various kinds to their partners. Maybe they all had synergy of some sort. Keaton, for example, who'd endured more torture from Spurling than anyone else, was walking hand-in-hand with Owen, and together they were checking on the more severely injured. Keaton's empathic gift was probably useful when rendering first aid.

Wait. Empathy. That had been the key to the original plan, but Keaton had quickly been put out of commission. He seemed functional now—but Spurling and his buddies were likely far away, well out of Keaton's range.

Unless....

Yes! You're onto something, dude.

"Dee, if I gave you a jumpstart, do you think you'd have another wish in you?"

"Are you going to fuck me right here in the parking lot?" Dee's eyes sparkled with humor.

"Um, maybe not." Especially with Santiago inhabiting him. He didn't want a threesome.

I'm not even into dudes. Santiago seemed amused too.

Achilles bent at the waist and kissed Dee—upside-down, Spider-Man style—before easing out from beneath him. He slipped off his filthy shirt to pillow Dee's head. "Hang on. Be right back." And then he ran.

First he found Keaton, who'd just finished some kind of consultation with Isaac regarding Con's injuries. It looked as if Con would have new scars to add to his extensive collection, but he was awake and alert.

"Keaton, I think I need you. Can you guys go wait near Dee?"

"You're excited about something," Keaton said, head cocked slightly. "Hopeful. All right, we'll meet you there."

The next stop was Charles, more challenging due to the surrounding cops and firefighters. For once, Tenrael wasn't nearby; he and Ish were lurking behind a minivan, maybe hoping nobody would take much notice of them. The last thing Charles needed was to try to explain an angel and a demon to the LAPD.

Achilles marched up to Charles, hoping he looked at least a little official and authoritative. "Chief? Need you for a few minutes."

Charles smiled—an expression Achilles had rarely seen on his face—and spoke in a voice that wasn't his, although it was familiar. "Is that so, son?" He nodded briskly at the nearest cop. "I have something to attend to. As you can see, my men and women have things under control here. I recommend you direct your resources elsewhere. You're needed by others."

The cop was an older man who had clearly Seen Some Shit during his tenure. But he took a half step backward. "Just don't take off, Mr. Grimes. We still got a lot of questions for you."

"Of course." Charles pivoted and headed toward Dee.

"Do you know what I have in mind?" Achilles demanded, hurrying to keep up. "Did you know the whole time? 'Cause it would have been nice if you'd shared that info."

When Charles replied, he sounded young. And British. "We were confident you'd think of something, but we didn't know details. Your thoughts and actions are your own. Free will and all that rot."

Achilles might have shared his opinion of this, but Santiago shushed him, and anyway by then they'd reached Dee, Keaton, and Owen. Dee was sitting up, and although he looked awful, he looked considerably less awful than he had fifteen minutes before.

Achilles immediately sat next to him, arm around his back. "Let's not waste time. I'm going to do my best to give Dee an energy boost. Then I'm going to wish that Keaton's reverse empathy is temporarily magnified. Chief, you're going to get the whole gang radiating as much hope, joy, love… you know the drill… as much of that as they can. Then Keaton, you're going to blast Spurling and the rest of those fuckers with all your might."

Keaton blinked. "I've never done that when the, um, target wasn't present. I don't even know where these people are."

"That's where Dee's wish is going to help. What if you could target them from a distance? Like… heat-sensing missiles."

"Um…." More blinking.

Owen nudged him. "You can do it, Kay. I know you can."

Maybe Owen shared a magical connection with his partner, or maybe it was just a confidence boost from a loved one—which was magical in its own way, really. In any case, Keaton shrugged and nodded. "Worth a try."

Achilles did his part next, kissing Dee long and hard. The kiss tasted of ashes and plaster and blood, but that was of no concern. Dee was warm and alive. He was in Achilles' arms, kissing him back. And that was a glorious thing. Achilles forgot that they had an audience, and even forgot that the kiss was supposed to be accomplishing something besides making him desperately, achingly hard. He might very well have laid Dee down and screwed him after all, Trader Joe's parking lot be damned, but Charles made a loud throat-clearing noise.

"We should get on with it," Charles said in his own voice. "Give me a few minutes to get orders out."

He trotted away, leaving the four of them—six if you counted the ibburs—in a somewhat awkward silence. Owen broke it first. "You two got the angel out of that place. Thank you."

"You found him," Achilles pointed out.

"He saved Keaton and me. When we were really stuck, he gave us a way out."

"I get it!" Dee looked considerably more animated than before the kiss. "It's more than synergy. Doing what we can to help others, that's part of the point, isn't it? It helps tip the balance."

"Big time," Achilles agreed.

They waited. There were still sirens and helicopters around and over them. HQ continued to burn. The world still seethed with hatred, fear, greed, and other poisons. But the fight wasn't over.

Charles came back at a full run, flanked by Tenrael and Ish, and all three of them looking like that ancient image of the devil and angel on someone's shoulders. Achilles glanced around and saw that every agent in the parking lot was looking their way. Even the injured ones. And damned if they weren't smiling and giving thumbs ups.

"Do it," Dee said, and added more softly, "Master."

Achilles looked around for something to use as a charm. A rosemary bush grew at the nearby edge of the parking lot. It was covered in tiny purple flowers, and when he broke off a sprig, the scent reminded him of the roasted lamb his mother used to make on special occasions. It had been his birthday meal every year.

Smiling, he handed the herb to Dee, whose face flushed, pupils dilated, and breathing became quick and shallow as he worked. He was grinning when he handed it back.

Deep breath. "I wish," Achilles said. His voice broke and he had to start again. "I wish that, for as long as needed, Keaton can extend his reverse empathy to Spurling and all his compatriots, wherever they may be."

The rosemary disintegrated and Dee wilted against him, trickles of blood coming from his nose and ears. Achilles wanted to sob and scream, but now was not the time for that. Grief could come later.

Owen stood behind Keaton, steadying his shoulders, and Keaton closed his eyes.

"Now!" Charles shouted, three voices combined into one.

Holding Dee tight, Achilles thought about how remarkable Dee was and how much Achilles loved him. He thought about everything he hoped they'd do together: A comfortable little home to share. Hours spent cooking meals, reading, watching TV, socializing with friends, making love. Vacations. Maybe even couples therapy.

He laughed at the last thought, which made the good feeling in his gut intensify.

He remembered that his sister was willing to reconnect with him, that she had kids she wanted him to meet.

He thought about the friendship bonds he'd recently strengthened with several people, and how much he'd like to work on those.

He celebrated how brave his colleagues were, and how wonderfully varied they were in species and abilities, and how grateful he was to allies such as the coyotes and aliens.

He concentrated hard on how brave Dee was, how strong, how worthy of love.

Santiago joined in too. He had memories of riotously festive family gatherings, and he recalled the face of every being—human or otherwise—that he'd helped during his career. He also dwelled on the beauty of the rivers where he used to kayak, the satisfaction in his own strength when he'd exercised, the music he used to blast on his car radio.

Music! Achilles replayed the song his parents hummed and every other tune that he'd listened to, in sad times and in happy ones. Orson used to sing "Oops, I Did It Again," mostly because Achilles pretended to hate that song, and that was a happy memory too.

"A hero," Dee slurred, eyes closed, slumped heavily against Achilles. The bleeding continued. "A genuine Greek hero, minus the stupid heel. And he's mine."

The final words were so faint that Achilles barely heard them. He whispered into Dee's ear: "I'm yours. You're mine. I love you."

Something… shifted.

It wasn't a huge change. It was like when the urge to sneeze goes away, when your clogged ears pop, when the grade you were dreading turns out to be a B, when the recipe you thought you'd messed up tastes delicious. It was the rain stopping just as you had to go outside. The lost key turning up beside the couch. The new outfit fitting just right. The cute person across the room smiling back at you. The gift you chose making the recipient laugh with delight. The dog at the park bounding over to make friends with you. The drab plant outside your door suddenly bursting into glorious bloom one morning. The kind compliment from a stranger. The shared joke. The embrace. The certain knowledge that if you fell, someone would catch you.

These were small things that didn't seem like much when taken by themselves. But added together, they amounted to something big. Something *good*. These were the things that shifted the balance.

A rustle passed through the agents in the parking lot, through the bystanders and the remaining first responders—like a breeze through treetops on a stifling hot day—and in its wake, it left smiles and more relaxed postures. Some people started to weep, but with relief rather than sadness. Some embraced.

In Achilles' arms, Dee was unconscious, blood tracking scarlet through the dust on his face and clothing. His hair formed a wild, curly cloud. His breaths came rarely, barely stirring his chest. His usual warmth was gone, leaving his skin cool to the touch.

"Dee." Achilles' throat felt thick and his eyes stung with tears. But Keaton was still concentrating, and Achilles couldn't abandon the effort now. Every effort counted.

So Achilles held Dee a little tighter and hummed his parents' song and thought about how lucky he was to have had Dee, even if for such a short time. Dee had enriched Achilles' existence beyond measure, and if Achilles survived, every day of his life would be a tribute to Dee. "Thank you for making me a hero," he whispered.

Death isn't the end of someone, Santiago said. *Look at me. The dead live on in the memories of the living and in the deeds they've accomplished.*

Achilles felt the truth of this and it gave him comfort.

"He's stronger than I imagined," said a new voice. Achilles gasped when he looked up and saw Spurling walking toward him.

Achilles would have leapt to his feet and attacked, but that would have meant letting go of Dee, which he absolutely wouldn't do. Besides, there was something off about Spurling. His gait was awkward, as if he were struggling to make every step. And if Achilles wasn't mistaken, Spurling's eyes held compassion.

"Don't fucking touch him!" Achilles growled.

Spurling's smile wasn't cruel or mocking. "You love him."

"Of course I do, you—" Wait. That didn't sound like Spurling. The voice was higher pitched, like a woman's, and held a trace of an accent.

"Garrick stayed nearby," said not-Spurling. "He wished to see the building entirely destroyed. But when your friend attacked Garrick"— she gestured toward Keaton—"I was able to step in. I'm not alone in here, but I am in control for a few moments."

"Are you… Irina?"

"I can't stay. I no longer belong on this plane, and I can't undo the harm I've caused my son. I regret being a terrible mother. I love him, though and perhaps I can grant one final wish for his sake." She tore a button off Spurling's expensive jacket and waited.

This was too good to be true. But wasn't now the very best time for hope? Achilles looked at Dee, whose breaths were now so shallow that Achilles might be imagining them. He nodded at Irina. "I wish he wouldn't die." A sob escaped him; he couldn't help it.

Irina was crying too. She grasped the button, closed her eyes, and murmured in a Slavic-sounding language. When she opened her eyes and held out the button, Achilles hesitated. What if it was a trick?

Trust her, Santiago advised.

So Achilles did. He took the button and repeated his wish. The button turned to powder, indistinguishable from the debris already on his hands. The universe paused.

Dee took a deep, shuddery breath and opened his eyes. They were bloodshot but aware.

"I love you, Damnation," said Irina. She sounded far away. Spurling's body shuddered violently and fell to its knees.

"What are you doing?" Spurling roared—in his own voice. Achilles wasn't the least sad to hear the pain and rage and confusion. This was a man who hadn't envisioned the possibility of losing.

"Power and wealth and hate die when you do," said Achilles. "Love and generosity survive."

Spurling shrieked inhumanly and shuddered repeatedly. Something started to peel away from him, and although it was invisible, Achilles could sense it. Could smell its rotten-meat stench. It separated completely from Spurling with a sickening *splorch*, hung for a moment like the ghost of a shadow, and then… ceased to exist. When Spurling screamed again, his throat sounded torn. Blood gushed from his nose, ears, eyes, and mouth, more black than red and foul-smelling. He shuddered one more time, then disintegrated into fine dust that settled on the blacktop and disappeared.

"Achilles?" Dee was clutching him tightly. "What…?"

Before he could finish the question, Keaton exhaled loudly and Owen helped him to sit down.

Santiago spoke. *Looks like the party's over, dude.*

"Did we—"

It's not a win. It never is. But we tipped the balance. You can feel it, can't you?

Yes. Achilles could. "Thank you for—"

All part of the job. And now I've earned my retirement, don't you think?

"Are… are you going to be okay?"

Something's calling me. Not sure what it is. But… yeah. It feels like a call I want to answer. It feels really good. You two take care now.

And that quickly, Santiago was gone, leaving nothing inside Achilles except a tiny scar—one he was proud to carry.

All around him, people said good-bye to their ibburs. "I'll join you soon, Harry," said John. "Just a few more books to read first."

Charles was smiling. "Peace at last, Birdie? You've served well past your time. Thomas and Abe will be glad for the reunion." He shook his head a little. "Townsend, you old bastard. You've earned your rest too. Thank you."

Achilles relaxed into the warmth of the sunshine and then jolted, suddenly remembering the vampires. Their ibburs had protected them until now, but.... Oh. There they were, in the parking lot, looking pleased. Dee's magic must have truly been long-term. Achilles waved and they waved back.

Somebody had given blankets to Ralph and Edge, who'd resumed attending to the injured, although nobody seemed seriously hurt any longer. Even Cruz was sitting up on his own. Tenrael had his arms around Charles, and Ish had his arms around both of them, the trio looking like a very strange Renaissance-era statue—probably an allegorical one. Kurt and Desmond, Art and Jerry, Isaac and Con, Terry and Dash, and so many others. They were still here. Alive. Heroes.

And Dee was in Achilles' arms, filthy and beautiful and vibrant.

"Master," Dee said, grinning. "I wish you'd kiss me."

Achilles granted his wish.

EPILOGUE

The sound of ocean waves carried to Charles and Tenrael's front porch from the beach just a few blocks away. Charles could smell the sea salt as well as a hint of coffee and frying bacon from a nearby café. He enjoyed the scent of bacon, even though eating meat made him violently ill. He sat with a slice of cherry pie, a glass of fresh-squeezed lemonade, and the biography of a woman who'd spied for the Union during the Civil War. Tenrael and Ish were inside the house, where Ish had been working his way through Mel Brooks' movies. The last that Charles had seen, Ish had been laughing through *History of the World: Part I.* Tenrael, who was a night person, was probably still asleep, and Charles might very well climb back into bed with him after finishing the pie.

Charles had just about everything he'd ever wanted. He was even smiling.

Until a black Jeep parked at the curb in front of his house and he saw who was inside.

Not for the first time in his long life, Charles wished he could tolerate booze. He sighed, set down his dish on the little table beside his rocking chair, and waited for Achilles and Dee to join him on the porch.

They had a dog with them, a scruffy yellowish beast that wagged its tail, sniffed Charles's leg, and then sprawled contentedly on the weathered boards.

Both men looked good. Achilles had apparently opted to keep the beard, his hair was carefully styled, and he wore a dark suit and white shirt. He resembled one of those handsome real estate agents who put their smiling photo on their For Sale signs. Dee, on the other hand, reminded Charles of a musician who was successful enough to live comfortably but didn't spend his free time jet-setting or taking drugs. He wore jeans and a plain black tee, and his curly hair had grown long enough to tie into a disorderly ponytail.

"Nice place," Achilles said by way of greeting. "In this neighborhood, I bet you could get over three million for it." Now he sounded like a real estate agent too.

Charles suppressed a chuckle. "I bought it for four thousand dollars in 1929. I'm not planning to sell."

Achilles and Dee nodded, and the three of them fell silent. Charles noticed that they wore matching wedding bands. Sometimes he still marveled at the freedoms gay people enjoyed nowadays, although he was also acutely aware of how fragile those freedoms were and how much progress still needed to be made for all those who remained disempowered.

"Do you want to come inside?" Charles finally asked. "Ish would like to see you."

"How's he doing?" Dee looked concerned.

Charles shrugged. "Sometimes he's entirely lucid and brilliant. Sometimes he's in his own world. Mostly he's somewhere in between." Honestly, Charles didn't know how much of this was due to Ish's long, terrible captivity, and how much was his nature. He was the only angel that Charles had ever met.

Achilles leaned back against the porch railing, arms loosely crossed, and Dee stood beside him. They could have taken the other two chairs—the porch held three now—but then they wouldn't be facing Charles.

"The Supreme Court ruled that it was illegal to dissolve the Bureau," said Achilles.

"I'm aware." It was one of several favorable rulings that had occurred since HQ was destroyed.

"Those of us who want our jobs back can have them. And they'll likely be recruiting some new agents too." Achilles glanced at Dee, who didn't appear surprised by this but was clearly a little bemused. Charles wasn't as talented as Townsend had been at identifying promising recruits, but Charles was sure that Dee would make a very fine agent. Like everyone else, he was flawed. But he was also a good, brave, talented person.

Achilles waited a moment, and when Charles didn't answer, continued. "They're trying to decide where to build the new HQ. Probably somewhere more centrally located within the Western Division. I hear they're planning a park for the old site. There will be a memorial there for the agents and local residents who died that day."

"Abe would be amused, I think," Charles remarked. Abe's talent for communing with spirits had always given him an unusual take on death; he viewed it as a transition rather than an end. Even when his beloved Thomas had passed away, Abe had confided that his own sadness was a selfish one born of loneliness rather than grieving on Thomas's behalf. He'd been comfortable knowing that Thomas had simply moved on.

"Hey, I have a question about Abe," said Dee. "It's been bugging me, and Achilles doesn't know the answer. I saw a lot of agents get shot up by Spurling and his friends, but none of them died. The ibburs did a quick healing, right?"

Charles shrugged. "Something like that."

"But when you shot Abe, he died, even though he had an ibbur in him. From what I hear, Townsend—also possessed at the time—was originally killed by gunshot too. How come?"

This was a reasonable question, although Charles shuddered slightly at the memory of killing Abe, who had been in the Bureau as long as Charles and was a friend. But the killing had been necessary. Charles knew that then and was equally convinced of it now. It had certainly been what Abe wanted. In fact, Abe had been eager for some time to rejoin Thomas.

"The difference, Dee, was that neither Abe nor Townsend wanted to survive. Abe had to sacrifice himself to avoid being possessed by a dybbuk. Townsend… well, he knew something was coming, and I guess he decided he'd be more helpful on the other side. He's the one who shepherded all the ibburs to us when you granted that wish." And he was damned smug about it too, lecturing Charles even as chaos reigned. But Charles would spare everyone else knowledge about that. Townsend deserved his due as a hero too.

Dee appeared satisfied with this explanation. He shifted his feet nervously, however, and sighed. "It's not over, is it? The fight."

"It's never over. If you want to get philosophical, I suspect that it's not even a fight—it's a push-pull rhythm, like a heartbeat. As long as it remains in balance, life continues."

He'd thought about this a lot and had discussed it at length with Tenrael. While this notion wasn't exactly comforting, it wasn't entirely awful either. It meant that life had a point. And it meant that every single effort, no matter how small, mattered. Every time someone did something to keep the balance from tipping the wrong way, the heart gave another beat.

Charles took a sip of lemonade and leaned forward. He needed to say this next part out loud. "I used to think of myself as a monster. And people have used that term for shifters like Edge, for fantastic creatures like Ralph and Jerry, for vampires like Marek and Clay, for—"

"For djinns," Dee said.

"Yes. But they're wrong. The real monsters are those who try to tip the balance the other way, and who persist in those efforts without remorse or redemption. Do you see?"

"Yes," said Dee and Achilles in unison.

"So we eternally fight the monsters rather than becoming them, and in a way, that's beautiful. Each of us can make that decision, no matter our species or our past or even our current circumstances."

Charles realized he was lecturing. Maybe Townsend had rubbed off on him. He sat back in his chair and waited, because he knew they hadn't yet reached the real reason for this visit.

"I got a call from Washington, DC," Achilles said.

Ah. Now they'd gotten there. Charles raised his eyebrows.

Achilles was frowning. "They want me to be the new chief. *Me.* That's ridiculous. You're the chief."

"Not by choice, and not any longer."

"But I *told* you, they're reconstituting the Bureau, and I'm sure they'd give you back your old job, and then—"

"I told them you should be chief."

Achilles gaped. Dee didn't look surprised, which was interesting. But Achilles was a deer caught in headlights.

"Why the fuck would you tell them *that?*" he demanded.

"Because I'm done. We both know I did a piss-poor job of dealing with the most recent crisis. No, don't argue—it's true. People died. We *all* nearly died, and then the war would have been lost. No more heartbeat. The only reason that didn't happen was because the two of you kept things going. Yes, you had a lot of assistance. But you led.

"And the other thing," Charles continued before Achilles could protest, "is that I'm old. Not so long ago, you came to me with the intention of resigning. Well, imagine how I feel. I've worked for or with the Bureau for nearly a century. I've seen so many people I cared about hurt or killed. I've—" Damn it, he was going to cry. He *never* cried. "I want to enjoy time with Tenrael. I want to help my father heal and get to know him. I want to sit on my porch, listen to the ocean, and eat pie."

Dee pulled a plastic packet of Kleenex from his jeans pocket and handed it over. Charles wiped his eyes and blew his nose, thankful that neither of them was making a fuss about his show of emotion.

"I'll still help if I'm needed," Charles conceded. "Consulting work. But only when necessary."

"I get it," Achilles said quietly. "But me as chief?"

"All anyone will ask of you is to be the best hero you can be." Charles chuckled wryly. "Which is a huge expectation. But it's one you can fulfill."

Achilles stood silently for a moment, and then an expression of acceptance and determination settled onto his face. "In *The Iliad*, my namesake rejoined the war because he was furious. It was ugly. If I do this, it's not because I'm angry." He clasped Dee's hand. "It's because I love."

Charles glanced at the front door and saw Tenrael standing there, magnificent. Smiling at him. "Love can be an excellent motive," Charles said.

He stood and brushed crumbs from his legs. "Come inside, have some pie, and visit Ish. The Bureau can manage a bit longer without us."

Tenrael stepped aside and Charles paused to kiss him, hard. Then the new chief and Dee and the dog followed him inside, where it smelled of sweet warm cherries. Ish's laughter filled the living room, and the bookshelves overflowed.

Home, Charles thought. *Family*. Things worth fighting for.

"Thanks, Townsend, you old bastard," he whispered.

Then he headed toward his sunlit kitchen, ready to slice more pie.

Dear Readers,

Thank you for joining me for thirteen volumes of *The Bureau*.

This series started with a bit of a fever-dream: What if the love child of Ray Bradbury and Dashiell Hammett wrote gay romance? That was the question that sparked *Corruption*, the first—and shortest—story in the collection. In case you wondered, that story is a bit over 11,000 words long. *Concluded* clocks in at about 107,000.

These stories have allowed me to indulge my passion for noirish heroes, many with conflicted pasts, and repeatedly address the question *What is a monster?* I've also been able to romp through a variety of locations, mostly in the Western United States, and visit every decade since the 1920s.

You may have noticed that this last installment is more political than usual. That was unavoidable for me as a worried human being. But also I sincerely wish (see what I did there?) that my readers can carry from this book a message of hope and empowerment. I truly believe that every action by every person makes a difference.

I have to admit that I've fallen in love with the characters in *The Bureau*. Even Townsend! I'm going to miss them. Perhaps in the future I'll revisit them with some short tales. I feel as if *Concluded* really does conclude the primary story, but as Achilles likes to point out, the fight never ends.

I'm grateful to my editor, Karen Witzke; my proofreader, Allison Behrens; the wonderful narrator for the audiobooks, Joel Leslie; and the cover artist for this series, Reese Dante. And I'm especially grateful to you for joining me on this journey.

Kim

July 2025

THE BUREAU OF TRANS-SPECIES AFFAIRS

For many years the United States government has been aware that *Homo sapiens* is not the only sentient species inhabiting the country. Some other species were native to the continent, while others immigrated along with humans. Early on, these nonhuman species (NHS) were largely ignored when they lived peacefully within human communities. At other times they were deemed a threat and local efforts were made to eradicate them. The federal government was not involved in these early efforts.

During the Civil War, both the Union and Confederate armies recruited members of the NHS, with varying degrees of success.

By the early 20th century, some local law enforcement agencies expressed frustration with their inability to deal effectively with the special needs of NHS. Localized incidents of mass violence occurred in several locations, most notably the Omaha Zombie Epidemic of 1908, the Manchester (New Hampshire) Melusine Drownings of 1911, and the Eugene (Oregon) Sasquatch Riots of 1915.

In response to these incidents, as well as a heightened desire for increased federal control, President Wilson created a new federal agency in 1919 called the Bureau of Trans-Species Affairs. The mission of this agency was to communicate with NHS, to control them, to investigate reported dangerous actions committed by them, and to bring them to justice or eliminate them when necessary. Since then, the Bureau has been quietly active throughout the United States. Its jurisdiction has expanded to include humans who engage in magical or paranormal activities.

Over the decades, a great many dramas have unfolded among the people who work for the Bureau. The **Bureau stories** are a collection of these tales. Each involves different protagonists and is set in a different era, yet all focus on the adventures and struggles of the Bureau's agents. These novellas can be read in any order.

*****The Bureau of Trans-Species Affairs: Strength, Intelligence, Honor*****

More about the books in this series.

- **Book One: Corruption**
- **Book Two: Clay White**
- **Book Three: Creature**
- **Volume One (Compilation of Books One through Three)**

- Book Four: Chained
- Book Five: Conviction
- Volume Two (Compilation of Books Four and Five)
- Book Six: Conned
- Book Seven: Caroled
- Book Eight: Camouflaged
- Volume Three (Compilation of Books Seven and Eight)
- Book Nine: Caught
- Book Ten: Chambered
- Volume Four (Compilation of Books Nine and Ten)
- Book Eleven: Consumed
- Book Twelve: Connected
- Volume Five (Compilation of Books Eleven and Twelve)
- Book Thirteen: Concluded

ABOUT THE AUTHOR

Kim Fielding is very pleased every time someone calls her eclectic. Winner of the BookLife Prize for Fiction, a Lambda Award finalist and a Foreword INDIE finalist, she has migrated back and forth across the western two-thirds of the United States and, after a long exile, has recently returned to Portland, Oregon. She's a university professor who dreams of being able to travel and write full time. She also dreams of having two daughters who fully appreciate her, a husband who isn't obsessed with football, and a house that cleans itself. Some dreams are more easily obtained than others.

Kim can be found on her website: http://kfieldingwrites.com/
  Facebook: https://www.facebook.com/KFieldingWrites
  and Bluesky: @KFieldingWrites
  Her e-mail is kim@kfieldingwrites.com

ALSO BY KIM FIELDING

Series

The Bureau

Greynox to the Sea

Love Can't

Ennek

Bones

Stars from Peril

Novels

Office of the Lost

Rook's Time

Crow's Fate

The Taste of Desert Green

Potential Energy

The Muffin Man

Teddy Spenser Isn't Looking for Love

Hallelujah (with F.E. Feeley Jr.)

Blyd and Pearce

A Full Plate

The Little Library

Ante Up

Running Blind (with Venona Keyes)

Staged

Rattlesnake

Astounding!

Motel. Pool.

The Tin Box

Venetian Masks

Brute

Novellas

Shelf-Made Man

Man of His Dreams

Bread Crumbs

Regifted

Bite Me: An Elucidation in Three Acts

Farkas

Ash Believes the Impossible

A Very Genre Christmas

Gravemound

The Solstice Kings

Dei Ex Machina

The Golem of Mala Lubovnya

Refugees

The Dance

Transformation

Summerfield's Angel

The Tale of August Hayling

Phoenix

Grown-Up

The Pillar

The Border

Housekeeping

Night Shift

Speechless

Guarded

The Downs

Short Stories and Collections

Dog Days of December

Firestones

Dreidels and Do-Overs

Get Lit

Christmas Present

Act One and Other Stories

Exit through the Gift Shop

Dear Ruth

Grateful

The Sacrifice and Other Stories

Saint Martin's Day

The Festivus Miracle

Joys R Us

Alaska

A Great Miracle Happened There

Violet's Present

Standby

Anyplace Else